fever

fever

maya banks

BERKLEY BOOKS, NEW YORK

THE BERKLEY PUBLISHING GROUP
Published by the Penguin Group
Penguin Group (USA) Inc.
375 Hudson Street, New York, New York 10014, USA

USA / Canada / UK / Ireland / Australia / New Zealand / India / South Africa / China

Penguin Books Ltd., Registered Offices: 80 Strand, London WC2R 0RL, England
For more information about the Penguin Group, visit penguin.com.

This book is an original publication of The Berkley Publishing Group.

FEVER

BERKLEY® is a registered trademark of Penguin Group (USA) Inc.
The "B" design is a trademark of Penguin Group (USA) Inc.

ISBN 978-1-62490-365-6

PRINTED IN THE UNITED STATES OF AMERICA

Cover photo by Boris Mrdja/Shutterstock.
Cover design by Rita Frangie.
Interior text design by Kristin del Rosario.

For really terrific friends who always have my back.
You know who you are. Love you!

chapter one

Jace Crestwell tapped Gabe Hamilton on the shoulder and when Gabe turned, Jace grinned. "You've hogged my sister long enough. It's my turn to dance with her."

Gabe didn't look happy with the interruption. He and Mia had been solidly glued to one another for the past hour, but he grudgingly took a step back and Mia smiled radiantly as Jace took Gabe's place.

The entire ballroom of the Bentley Hotel was decorated for Christmas, a nod to the fact that above all else, Mia loved Christmas, and it was also a well-known fact that Gabe would do damn near anything to make his new fiancée happy.

And, well, Gabe moved fast when he wanted something, if nothing else. He'd started planning the engagement party the moment he got his ring on Mia's finger. Almost as if he were afraid she'd change her mind unless he got the ball rolling immediately.

It was pretty funny for Jace to see his friend in knots over a woman. The fact that the woman in question was Jace's sister was a little weird, but Mia was happy and that was all he could ask for.

"Are you enjoying yourself, baby girl?" Jace asked as he turned her around on the dance floor.

Her entire face lit up. "It's fantastic, Jace. The whole thing. It's positively magical. I can't believe Gabe pulled this off so fast. It's just . . . *perfect*."

Jace smiled back at her. "I'm glad you're happy. Gabe will be good to you or I'll kick his ass. I already made that clear."

Her eyes narrowed. "If he isn't good to me, it's not you he has to worry about. *I'll* be the one kicking his ass."

Jace threw back his head and laughed. "That I have no doubt about. You made him work for it. I gotta admire that."

Mia's face became somber and Jace frowned, wondering what could have possibly made her so serious on a night she should be over the moon.

"I know you gave up a lot for me," she said in a quiet voice. "I always wondered if the reason you hadn't married and had children of your own was because of me."

He stared at her like she'd lost her mind.

"Maybe now you can stop worrying about me so much, and you know . . ."

"No, I don't know," he said. Then he shook his head. "You're a nut, Mia. First of all, just because you're getting married doesn't mean I'm going to stop worrying about you and looking out for you. That's just a fact, so get over it. Second, don't you think if I'd gotten married before now, especially when you were younger, that it would have made things *easier*? For both you and me? You would have had a mother figure instead of being stuck with an overbearing, overprotective brother as your sole source of support."

She stopped mid-dance and threw her arms around him, hugging him fiercely.

"I don't regret a single thing about the way you raised me, Jace. Not a thing. You did a wonderful job and I'll always be so grateful for all the sacrifices you made for me."

He hugged her back, still shaking his head. Nut. Total nut. She was aglow with happiness over her impending marriage to Gabe, and now she wanted everyone she cared about wrapped up in that same glow. God help him. He and Ash should probably be ducking and running.

"It was no sacrifice, Mia. I don't have a single regret either. Has it ever occurred to you that I didn't *want* to get married and have kids?"

She pulled back with a frown and then her gaze skirted sideways to where Ash was standing across the room with Gabe. "Yes, I suppose it did."

Jace barely suppressed a sigh. It was obvious Mia had a very good idea of his and Ash's sexual proclivities when it came to having threesomes with the same woman. It wasn't exactly something a brother wanted his sister to know about his sex life, but there it was. He wouldn't apologize for his lifestyle, but neither was he going to get into a conversation about it with his baby sister.

"Play hard and live free," he said by way of explanation.

Mia frowned and cocked her head upward.

Jace chuckled. "It's our motto. The three of us, Gabe, me and Ash. Only you changed the game for Gabe. Doesn't mean Ash and I are eager to follow his lead."

She rolled her eyes. "For God's sake. You make Gabe sound like a pussy."

Jace cleared his throat. "If the shoe fits . . ."

Mia pounded him on the shoulder. "I'm so going to tell him you said that!"

Jace laughed again. "The man would probably admit to being a complete pussy when it comes to *you*. And that's not a bad thing. I want him to treat you right."

They were interrupted when Ash stepped in, sweeping Mia into his arms.

"My turn," Ash proclaimed. "Gabe's only going to wait so long before he reclaims her, so I'm getting my dance in now while his parents have him occupied."

Jace leaned forward and kissed Mia on the forehead. "This is your night, baby girl. I want you to remember it forever. Have fun."

Her smile lit up the entire room. "Thank you, Jace. Love you."

He touched her cheek and then moved back as Ash swept her away.

Jace retreated to the far side of the room and stood back, observing the goings-on at the party. It was small—what Gabe and Mia wanted—a night to celebrate their love.

It sounded corny as hell, but then one only had to look at the two to know they were complete goners. He still wasn't entirely certain how he felt about his best friend hooking up with his little sister. There were fourteen years separating them and he knew damn well what Gabe's sexual demands were.

He cringed, remembering the scene he'd walked into when he'd gone to Gabe's apartment unannounced several weeks earlier. He needed bleach for his eyes because there were just some things a brother never, *ever* needed to see regarding his baby sister.

He still had concerns over whether Mia really knew what the hell she was getting herself into, but Gabe was a complete mush pile when it came to her. Hell, the man had humbled himself in front of half of New York City to get her back, so Jace guessed Mia would be able to handle whatever Gabe dished out.

Jace was just going to not think about it.

He sighed as his gaze wandered over the crowd and the festive environment. Mia had been a huge part of his life ever since their parents had been killed in a car accident. She had been a late-in-life "oops" baby, but she'd been adored by him and their parents. When they'd died, it had been a life-altering event for both him and his sister.

At a time when he'd been in college and only focused on beer, girls and having a good time with Gabe and Ash, he'd been forced to take responsibility for six-year-old Mia. Gabe and Ash had both been a huge source of support for him and perhaps in a lot of ways Mia had cemented their friendship. So he supposed it was only fitting that he'd be giving her into the care of his best friend now that she was an adult and making her own life.

It would be an adjustment for him, now that Mia wasn't solely his responsibility. Not that he planned to go anywhere, but things were different now. She was in a serious relationship and she wouldn't be turning to him with her problems. It should be a relief, but instead sadness settled into his chest at the idea that his baby sister no longer needed him as she once had.

His gaze settled on a young woman picking up glasses and plates from the tables. It was the second time his eyes had settled on her that night though she hadn't been out much, just periodically to do cleanup. She wasn't one of the servers. He hadn't seen her circling with trays of hors d'oeuvres or champagne. She was dressed in black pants, a white shirt and an apron.

He studied her a long moment before realizing what it was that had interested him. She looked completely out of place. And he wasn't entirely certain what gave him that impression. The longer he stared at her, the more he thought she looked like she should be an attendee at the party. Not cleaning up after the participants.

Her hair was upswept into a messy bun like Mia wore sometimes, secured with a clip, and the result was a sexy mass of mussed hair that begged a man's hand to tug at it and set it free. Midnight black, unruly curls, some of which had escaped the clip and tumbled down her neck.

She was slight, not as curvy as he usually liked his women. Narrow hips and small breasted but enough curves straining at the white button-up shirt to be tempting. The rest of her was small. Dainty. Almost fragile.

When she turned, presenting him with a view of her face, he sucked in his breath. Her bone structure was small. Delicately rendered. High, prominent cheekbones, almost as if she were underweight, and a small chin. But her eyes. Jesus, her eyes. They were enormous in her otherwise small face. A brilliant shade of blue. Shock blue, like looking at ice. They were startling against the jet black of her hair.

She was mesmerizing.

Then she hurried away, her arms straining at the weight of the tray that held all the dishes she'd cleared from the tables. His gaze followed her across the room until she disappeared through the door for the kitchen staff.

"Not your usual fare," Ash murmured beside him.

Jace broke from his reverie and turned to see that Ash had already finished his dance with Mia. A brief look toward the dance floor told him Gabe had reclaimed Mia and that the two were once more solidly glued together. Mia's eyes were alight with joy and laughter, and some of his earlier tension eased. She was in good hands. And she was happy.

"What the hell are you talking about?" Jace said, an edge to his voice.

"The chick bussing the tables. Saw you checking her out. Hell, you were practically undressing her with your eyes."

Jace frowned and remained silent.

Ash shrugged. "I'm game. She's hot."

"No."

The denial came out more emphatic than Jace would have liked. He wasn't even sure where the emphasis came from or why he was suddenly tense.

Ash laughed. "Loosen up. It's been awhile. I'll go work my charm."

"Do *not* approach her, Ash," Jace growled.

But Ash had already sauntered away in the direction of the kitchen, leaving Jace standing there, fingers in tight fists at his sides. How the fuck was he supposed to explain to his best friend, a friend he regularly shared women with, that he didn't want Ash within a mile of this one?

chapter two

Bethany Willis rubbed her palms down her worn pant legs and briefly closed her eyes, swaying as she stood in front of the basin containing all the empties she'd collected from the ballroom.

She was tired. So damn tired. And hungry. The best part of this gig—besides the fact it was cash paying—was the food. She was allowed to take leftovers, and judging by the amount of food bustling in and out of this place, there was going to be plenty.

Rich people always did things in excess. There was no way the number of people invited to this party justified the amount of food and booze being fronted. She mentally shrugged. At least she'd get a decent meal, even if the stuff was too fancy for her palate.

There'd be enough for Jack too.

A wave of sadness engulfed her and just as quickly, guilt. She had no business feeling this way because Jack had come back around. He did that. Disappeared for days and then reappeared, usually when he needed a place to crash, a friendly face. Food. Money . . . Especially money.

Her chest squeezed because she knew what he did with the money he asked for even as he hated to do so. He never looked her in the eye. Instead he dropped his gaze and he'd say, "Bethy . . . there's this thing. I need . . ." And it was all he'd say. She gave him money because she couldn't do anything else. But she hated the way he said

"Bethy." Hated that nickname when it had once been one she adored because it had been given to her by someone who cared for her.

Jack. The only person in the world who'd ever tried to shield her from anything. The only person who'd ever given a damn about her.

Her brother. Not by blood but in every way else it counted. He was hers just like she was his. How was she supposed to ever turn her back on him?

She couldn't. She wouldn't.

There was a sound at the side door, the one that opened to the alley where the trash was taken out. She glanced up to see Jack leaning against the frame, his head tilted back so he could glance down the alleyway. That was Jack. Always one eye on escape. He never went into any situation unwary and without his escape route planned.

"Bethy," he said in a quiet voice.

She flinched, knowing why he'd come. She didn't say anything and instead reached into her pants pocket for the wadded-up bills she'd stuffed there. Half up front. Half when she went off duty for the night. Jack would get this half. The other half would have to feed her until she found another gig, and she didn't know when that would be.

Hurrying to where he stood, she pressed the bills into his hand and watched uncomfortably as his gaze skated sideways, not making eye contact with her as he shoved the money into the ripped, torn jeans. His stance was uncomfortable. She knew he hated this. She hated it too.

"Thank you," he whispered. "You okay? You got somewhere to sleep tonight?"

She didn't, but she wasn't going to tell him that. So she lied instead. "Yeah."

Some of his tension eased and he nodded. "Good. I'm working on it, Bethy. I'll have a place for both of us soon."

She shook her head in denial, knowing it was what he always said, and also knowing it wasn't going to happen.

He leaned forward and kissed her forehead. For a long moment, she closed her eyes and imagined different circumstances. But that was pointless. It was what it was and wishing for it to be different was like pissing in the wind.

"I'll be checking on you," he said.

She nodded. And then, as he started to melt back into the shadows of the alley, she looked up and said, "Be careful, Jack. Please?"

His smile was just as shadowy as the night. "Always, babe."

She watched him go as the knot in her throat grew bigger. Damn it. Rage built but she knew it was also a useless emotion. Her fingers curled and uncurled at her sides and the itch invaded. The need, the craving. She fought it, but it was a hard battle. A victory that wasn't completely solidified. She hadn't thought about the pills in a long while, but tonight the need was there, ensconced in hunger and emotional pain.

The need for oblivion. Just that short window of time when everything felt better and more manageable. When things looked up, even if for a few short hours.

She couldn't go back to that. She'd fought too hard to make it out and she'd lost everything in the process. Some might say that would be even more reason to allow herself that slow slide back into the inky past. But she had to be strong. She wasn't that person any longer.

"Your boyfriend?"

The dry question startled her and she whirled around, her heart racing as she took in the man standing across the kitchen staring at her.

He was one of the richies. A guest at the party. More than just a guest, as Bethany had seen him close to the couple celebrating their engagement. And God, but the man was gorgeous. Smooth. Polished. Like he'd stepped right out of a magazine solely devoted to everything beautiful and wealthy. A world she damn well didn't belong in.

He shoved his hands into those expensive slacks and continued to stare at her, his pose indolent and arrogant. His green eyes flicked over her as if judging her, almost as if he were considering whether to deem her worthy. Of what? His notice? It was a ridiculous thought.

He had blond hair. And she'd never really been attracted to blond men, but his hair wasn't simply blond. It had at least four different shades, ranging from muddy to wheat and all shades in between. He was so gorgeous that it hurt to look at him.

"You going to answer me?" he asked mildly.

Mutely, she shook her head and, to her surprise, he laughed.

"Is that no you're not going to answer me, or no he's not your boyfriend?"

"He's not my boyfriend," she whispered.

"Thank fuck for that," he muttered.

She blinked in complete surprise and then her eyes narrowed as he advanced toward her. Quickly she moved to the side so she wouldn't be pinned against the door. She couldn't leave, so running wasn't an option. She needed the other half of her pay too badly and she wanted that food.

But just as quickly he closed in on her again, moving into her space until her pulse leapt erratically and she began to eye the alley door, suddenly uncaring whether she'd get paid or not.

"What's your name?"

She glanced up at him. "Uhm, does it matter?"

He paused a moment, cocked his head to the side and then said, "Yeah. It matters."

"Why?" she whispered.

"Because we're not in the habit of fucking women we don't know the name of," he said bluntly.

Whoa. There was so much wrong with that statement she didn't even know where to begin. She put her hand up in automatic defense before he could get any closer.

"We?" she demanded. "*We?* What are you talking about? Who the hell is *we?* And I'm not fucking anyone. You. We. They. No way."

"Jace wants you."

"Who the fuck is Jace?"

"And I've decided I want you."

She barely suppressed her snarl of rage. Barely. She grit her teeth and then went on the attack.

"I am not putting up with sexual harassment on the job. I'm filing a complaint and then I'm out of here."

To her further surprise, he merely grinned and then reached out to touch her cheek.

"Cool your jets, sweetheart. I'm not harassing. I'm propositioning. Big difference."

"Maybe in your book," she pointed out.

He shrugged like he didn't particularly care if she agreed.

"Who the hell is Jace?" she repeated. "And who are you? You don't proposition a woman without giving your name. And you have problems not knowing a woman's name before going to bed with her? What is wrong with you? You didn't even introduce yourself."

He laughed again and it was a warm hum that felt so good she wanted to hang on to it forever. It was a carefree sound and she bitterly resented it, was so jealous she wanted to burn with envy. This was a man who had no problems. Had no cares—except who he wanted to go to bed with next.

"My name is Ash. Jace is my best friend."

"I'm Bethany," she said reluctantly. Then her eyes narrowed. "And you both 'want' me?"

He nodded. "Yeah. Not so unusual. We share women. A lot. Threesomes. You ever had one? Because if not, I guarantee we'll make it an experience you won't forget."

Her nostrils flared. "Yeah. I have. Nothing special."

Something flickered in his eyes. She could tell she'd surprised him but oh well. He should expect to have it handed back to him when he made outrageous propositions like this.

"Then maybe you're fucking the wrong men."

Her eyes went wide at that because what could she possibly say in response? There was no doubt she'd made a habit of fucking the wrong men. No earth-shattering discovery there.

"Ash."

The sound was explosive in the confined area of the kitchen and Bethany jerked her head up to see another man standing in the doorway, his brooding, dark gaze scorching the flesh right off Ash's bones. Ash didn't seem overly bothered that this guy was obviously pissed.

Bethany was.

This guy was the one she'd caught watching her when she'd ventured out to bus the tables. Twice. She'd felt his gaze on her. Burning a path over her skin until she'd shivered with the intensity. Where Ash was lighter, carefree, that whole package of *wealthy and I know it* and *I don't gotta do nothing except what I wanna*, this man was . . . He was Ash's polar opposite.

Intense wasn't the right word. It didn't even come close to describing him. He looked like a complete badass, and she knew badasses. She had plenty of experience with men on the street and from the streets, and she had the sudden thought that she'd rather take her chances with the devil she knew rather than this man staring holes through her.

Dark eyes, dark hair. Really great hair. It was mussed and unruly and longish. A lock fell over his forehead and she imagined him pushing it impatiently back without care over whether it messed it up more. It hung down his collar, giving him an untamed, wild look that probably made women want to try to tame him. Tanned skin. Not the fake tan some of the metrosexual pretty boys went for. There was a ruggedness to him even as he screamed wealth and polish like Ash did. It was just a different kind of polish.

Where Ash wore his wealth like a skin, like he'd always known it, this other guy looked like he'd accumulated his wealth later in life and wasn't yet as comfortable in it as Ash was.

It was a ridiculous assessment, but there it was. There was something dangerous about this other man. Something that made her stand up and take notice.

"Jace," Ash returned mildly. "Meet Bethany."

Oh shit. Shit. Shit. Shit.

This was the threesome guy? Ash's best friend? A man involved in the outrageous proposition Ash had just given her?

Jace's lips tightened and he stalked forward. Bethany instinctively backed away.

"You're scaring her," Ash said, a reprimand in his tone.

To Bethany's surprise, Jace pulled up short, but he was still glaring holes in Ash. At least it wasn't her he was glaring at.

"I told you not to do this," Jace said in a quiet, angry voice.

"Yeah, well, I didn't listen."

Bethany was utterly confused. But then Jace turned to her and there was something in his gaze that caught her breath.

Interest.

Not just a look like a man gave a woman when he wanted to fuck her. It was something different and she couldn't put her finger on it. But then, he'd watched her all night. She knew that because she'd watched him too.

"I'm sorry," Jace began.

"Does this offer come with dinner?" she blurted.

She was instantly mortified, but she also knew in that one moment when he looked at her, that she didn't want him to walk away. Not tonight. Tonight, she wanted one night in the sun. Where it was warm and bad things didn't happen. She wanted one night to forget her life, Jack and all the problems that came with both.

This man could give her that. She was absolutely positive on that count. And if he came with Ash, she'd just have to take that too.

She did not want to walk out of this hotel into the cold and back to what awaited her.

"What?"

Jace stared at her like she'd grown two heads. His brows drew together and his gaze became even more piercing, like he was peeling her from the inside out.

She gestured toward Ash. "He said you two wanted a threesome. I'm asking if the offer comes with dinner."

"Well, yeah," Ash said, his tone suggesting he was insulted.

"Okay then," she said before she could change her mind.

She knew it was stupid. She knew it was one of the most stupid things she'd ever done, but she wasn't going back.

"I have to finish here first," she said while Jace just stood there, silent and brooding, his gaze never leaving her even once. Not to look at Ash. Not to look away. Fixed on her.

"No you don't," Ash said. "You can cut out at any time."

She shook her head. "I get the second half of my pay when I'm done. I have to finish."

"Party's about to break up. Gabe's not going to remain out on a fucking dance floor when what he really wants is Mia at home in his bed," Ash said. "I'll cover your second half."

Bethany went cold and she took a step back, ice forming over her face. Then she shook her head. "I changed my mind."

"What the fuck?" Ash demanded.

And still Jace stood there. Silent and forbidding, watching her the entire time. It was unnerving and suddenly that alley door was looking better all the time.

"I'm not for sale," she said in a low voice. "I get that I asked for dinner. I shouldn't have. You were offering sex. But I won't be paid for it."

Pain crept over her. Distant memories, not ebbing. Choices. Consequences. It all drifted together until it was a murky, impenetrable darkness surrounding her. One day. Just one day in the sun. But the sun wasn't for her. It never had been.

A low, muttered curse tore from Jace's lips. The first sound he'd made in forever. Then that mouth tightened. He was pissed.

His gaze skated sideways at Ash and it was then she realized he was pissed at Ash. *Really* pissed.

"I told you not to do this," Jace ground out. "Fuck it, man. You should have listened to me."

This was getting worse. Evidently Ash wanted some action. Jace did not. Ash wanted to approach her. Jace did not. Could this get any more humiliating?

"I've got to get back to work," she said, hastily backing away until her escape route to the door leading back into the ballroom was secure.

And just as quickly, Jace was there, sliding over, a barrier to her freedom. He was so close she could smell him, could feel his heat wrapping around her and it felt so damn good that she wanted to do something really stupid and lean into him. Just so she could feel it brush over her skin.

Then his fingers slid underneath her chin, a touch so gentle she couldn't help but respond, lifting with him so that her gaze met his.

"You finish work. We'll wait. Then we'll have dinner. Anything in particular you like? And do you want to go out or eat in the hotel room?"

The questions were softly worded. They sounded intimate. He never looked at Ash once. His stare was solidly fixed on her and she was too mesmerized to look away. And she promptly forgot that she'd changed her mind about sleeping with them.

Jerking herself from the intensity of the moment, she glanced down, taking in her clothing. There was no going home and changing. No home. No clothes. Certainly nothing she could wear to any place these two would set foot in.

She cleared her throat. "Hotel is fine, and I don't care. If it's hot and tastes good, I'll eat it. Nothing too fancy. In fact, what I really want is a burger. And fries."

She'd kill for both right now.

"And orange juice," she finished in a rush.

Amusement glimmered on Ash's lips but Jace was still utterly serious.

"Hamburger. Fries. Orange juice. I think I can handle that," Jace said. Then he checked his watch. "People will be cleared out in fifteen. How much time you need to finish?"

She blinked. "Uh, not everyone will clear out in fifteen minutes. I mean even if the guests of honor leave, people always hang out afterward. Especially when there's food and drink."

He cut her off before she could say more.

"Fifteen minutes, Bethany. They'll be gone."

It was a promise. It wasn't speculation on his part.

"How much time you need?" he asked impatiently.

"Thirty minutes maybe?" she guessed.

He touched her again, his fingers gliding over her cheek and up to her temple, where he toyed with loose tendrils that had fallen from her clip.

"Then we'll see you in thirty minutes."

chapter three

Twenty-five minutes was how much time it took for her to realize she was out of her mind. Twenty-five minutes to know she'd made a huge mistake.

Bethany washed her hands and then checked her pocket again to feel the folded bills. The kitchen had died down and most of the staff had left except for those remaining behind on clean-up duty. That wasn't her gig, thankfully. Her job was done.

She hesitated as she glanced between the door leading to the alley and the door that led back to Ash and Jace.

Jace hadn't lied. The ballroom had cleared in fifteen minutes. She wasn't sure how he'd managed to pull that one off, but then he seemed the type of man who always got what he wanted.

Now all that was between her and a night of hot sex and good food was that door.

The door to the alley swung open as one of the guys hauled a sack of garbage out to the trash bin. A rush of cold air blew in, penetrating Bethany to the bone. She shivered as chill bumps raced across her arms.

That was her other option. Cold. Loneliness. Another night of uncertainty.

Put that way, door number two seemed like the only logical choice.

She pushed off the edge of the counter she was leaning against and walked toward the exit. As she reached it, she took in a deep breath and let herself out.

Jace stood there waiting, hands in his pockets, leaning one shoulder against the wall. His gaze found her and penetrated as swiftly as the cold air had a moment earlier. Only this time, instead of a bone-deep chill, heat spread like wildfire through her veins.

"You ready?"

Even before she responded, he moved, pushing off the wall and then he was next to her, his hand sliding around her nape, his thumb brushing over the soft skin right at her hairline.

Damn but the man's touch was lethal.

"Ash is in the room taking care of dinner."

She glanced up at Jace, for the first time directly meeting his gaze. "So we're staying here?"

A smile twitched the corners of his mouth. "I own the hotel. Seems as good a place as any to stay for the night."

He owned the hotel. Okay, not that she didn't know he and Ash were stratospherically out of her league, but hearing those words, *I own the hotel*, just reinforced that she should have chosen the cold over temporary warmth.

"Obviously I didn't prepare for this," she murmured as they headed toward the elevators. "I don't have any clothes or . . . stuff."

She wanted to laugh because the entire conversation was absurd. Even if she'd known, she wouldn't have been prepared because she didn't have stuff. She had nothing except the hope of the next day being better than the last.

Again, Jace's mouth twitched and his eyes gleamed as he ushered her into the waiting elevator.

"You won't need clothes. Or . . . stuff."

Her hands trembled and her knees shook. This was her last chance to back out. He leaned forward to punch the button to the top floor. The door was still open. It would be easy to walk out, say she'd changed her mind and slip into the cold night, embracing what was *real*.

Jace suddenly looked at her, his gaze seeking, almost as if she'd broadcast her thoughts in real time. He stared at her a long moment, his finger pressed against the button to the floor. When she made no move, he straightened and leaned against the far wall, still studying her as the doors closed.

"You're nervous," he said, still staring at her.

She gave him a *duh* look and he smiled again. He had a killer smile. It wasn't easy and charming like Ash's. Smiling seemed to come natural to Ash, like it was in his makeup to be this easygoing, flirtatious guy who women fell all over themselves for. Bethany didn't get the impression that Jace was much of a smiler. He seemed way more serious than Ash. And if she was honest, that brooding, badass persona hit every single one of her buttons. Because this was a man she'd feel safe with for the night. He was a man a woman felt very secure around.

"Nothing to be nervous about," he murmured as the elevator stopped.

As she started to step off, he put his arm out to stop her and then he pulled her into his arms. She landed against his chest and his head was angled so their mouths were close. So close she could feel the harsh exhalation of his breath.

"Bethany, there's nothing to be nervous about," he said again, that mouth hovering so temptingly over hers.

He trailed a finger down her cheek to the corner of her mouth just as the elevator started to squawk because the doors had been left open for so long. He ignored it, focused on her, watching and absorbing like he could reach into her thoughts. Or like he wanted to, at least.

"I'm okay," she whispered.

And then he smiled. Really smiled. Not one of those twitch movements where it looked like he was about to smile or that he was fighting it. A full-on, teeth-flashing smile. And man, did he have beautiful teeth. Perfectly straight. Ultrawhite. Million-dollar smile. But then, everything about him was aces . . . right down to his shoes.

So far out of her league. So far it wasn't even funny.

Visions of *Pretty Woman* danced in her head. *Cinderella*. A one-night fairy tale. Only she knew better than to ever dream of happy endings. Fairy tales were nice to read. They were nice to think about. But they weren't remotely realistic. Fairy tales didn't happen to girls like Bethany.

So she'd take her one night and tomorrow she'd go back to doing what she did best. Living one day at a time, taking it as it came. Surviving.

He gestured for her to proceed from the elevator, and as soon as she stepped out, he fell into step beside her, his arm wrapping securely around her waist. It felt good. Too good. It was too easy to get all wrapped up in the fantasy. This man didn't give a damn about her. He wanted to get laid. She wanted warmth and food and a means of forgetting her shitty existence. That was an arrangement she could deal with.

A moment later, he opened the door to a sprawling suite. She hesitated just inside the door as she saw Ash setting out plates of food onto the polished dining table. There were three places set and it was obvious she was in between them. Her glass of orange juice was sitting by a plate with a burger and fries and on either side were plates with steaks.

The smell wafted to her and her stomach immediately clenched. She was starving and she'd never smelled anything so good in her life.

Ash turned and gave her that lazy smile, his eyes glowing with charm.

"You ready to eat?" Ash asked.

Oh yeah. She was ready to eat. It was all she could do to calmly nod and not throw herself at the table and start tearing into that burger.

Jace put his hand to her back and guided her toward the table. Clenching her fingers to disguise the shaking, she took her seat and then pushed up to the table and the delectable plate sitting before her. Still, she picked up the glass in a casual manner, like she wasn't starving and could hardly wait to dig into her food. She sipped at the juice but put it back when it hit her empty stomach hard.

Maybe food first was a better option.

Burger, fries and even orange juice was a luxury—one she was going to enjoy every second of.

As Jace and Ash took their seats on either side of her, she nabbed a fry, dragged it through the little container of ketchup sitting next to her plate and then slipped it into her mouth.

"You sure you don't want some steak?" Ash asked, nodding downward at his plate.

As she stared at the succulent piece of beef on his plate, her mouth watered. And the smell. God that delicious smell was killing her.

"Uhm," she began.

Without another word, Ash cut a section of his steak and then forked it onto her plate. It was a little pinker than she liked, but what did she care? It didn't even matter to her what it tasted like. It was food.

"Thanks," she murmured.

She was aware of Jace's gaze the entire time she ate and so she very carefully restrained herself, making sure she took her time and didn't seem too eager. She chewed each bite carefully. Sipped at her juice and was grateful when she finished that Ash produced more.

She wanted to eat all of it, but her stomach rebelled. She had gone too long without enough and she was used to surviving on far less. Her stomach refused to take another bite when she was barely half done with the burger and only a few bites into the steak.

"You aren't eating much," Jace observed when she pushed her plate back.

"I snacked on party food earlier," she lied. "It was really great, though. Thank you."

He studied her a long moment and she fidgeted uncomfortably. He didn't look as though he believed her, but he didn't push the issue. And why should he care if she ate or not? She was here because they wanted sex. They wanted to scratch an itch, though why with *her*, she'd never comprehend. She highly doubted they had any problem getting any woman they wanted in bed, which meant they could be as choosy as they damn well wanted to be.

"Few things you should know," Ash spoke up.

Her gaze drifted to his and he'd lost that playful, flirty look. His eyes were serious. Brimming with hotness that took her breath away. In that moment he looked just like Jace did. A hell of a lot more brooding and . . . badass. Which was kind of weird considering the word *badass* would have never come up in one of her descriptions of Ash.

"We call the shots in the bedroom. What we say goes. We'll take care of you. We'll see to your needs. We'll make damn sure it's good for you. But we're in control. If you have a problem with that, you need to say so now before we get into this."

A heady thrill rolled right through her body. Was he kidding? She fought her overpowering response to his statement and forced herself to be smart about this. Yeah, being taken care of for the night was not a turn-off. Giving up power and control for one night where she didn't have to think, didn't have to do, didn't have to do anything but feel? Not a deterrent.

But she needed to know exactly what this kind of a deal entailed and how deep their kink ran.

"I think that depends on what you want," she said in a low voice. "I'm not into anything that even comes close to playing with my life."

Jace's brow furrowed and he shot Ash a quelling look. "You've scared the shit out of her now, man. I told you to chill and let me handle this."

"She deserves to know what she's getting into," Ash said calmly. "I didn't lie to her and I won't mislead her."

"Appreciate that," Bethany said dryly.

Jace reached for her hand, curling his fingers around hers. It was . . . sweet. And strangely not in keeping with his badass look and those brooding stares he'd sent her way. This was a guy she would have expected Ash's speech to come from. For him to lay down the law to her and tell her it was his way or the highway.

"We won't hurt you, Bethany. What Ash means is that we like control. We like . . . submission. Not saying tonight has to be all about that. Just shooting you straight."

"I get it," she said softly.

"And?" Jace prompted.

"And what?"

"You good with that? Can you handle it?"

She took a deep breath and nodded. "I'm good with it."

"Thank fuck," Ash muttered. "Now if we're done with all the talking, can we get to the naked part?"

"Ash."

Jace said his friend's name like a warning. Then he turned back to Bethany, his hand still snugly circled around hers.

"Go into the bedroom. You can use the bathroom to get comfortable, do whatever you need to do. Undress and wait for us on the bed."

The soft words whispered over her skin, making her entire body hum with arousal. The man was positively lethal.

Wordlessly, she found herself obeying his soft command and rising from her chair. Her hand slipped from his as she backed away and then she turned, tearing her gaze from his as she walked toward the bedroom.

chapter four

She was sitting in the middle of the bed, naked, the sheets in a whirl around her, bunched as she pulled them to cover her nudity. Jace was the first to enter, his gaze immediately finding her. Ash followed behind, his fingers already going to the buttons on his shirt.

Even as Ash was undressing, making no bones of what he wanted, her gaze was riveted on Jace. Locked to him in a silent reverie that was unbreakable. His nostrils flared and his jaw flexed and clenched. There was a near-naked gorgeous man in the room and all she could do was stare at the fully clothed one, waiting and wanting so badly she hurt.

"Let go of the sheet," he said in a soft voice. "I want to see you."

It was soft, but no less of a command, one that sent a shiver over her skin. Carefully, she let the sheet slide from nervous fingers. It glided down her body to gather at her waist, baring her breasts to his piercing stare.

"Up on your knees," he said. "Push the sheets aside. I want to see all of you."

If she were smart, she'd fear this man. This situation. It had been an impulsive decision borne of desolation and a need for a temporary reprieve from her reality. No one knew she was here, at the mercy of these two men. No one cared. No one would worry if she simply disappeared. Except Jack. And how would he know? She hadn't told him anything other than she had a place to stay tonight, and at the time it had been a lie.

"Second thoughts?"

She glanced up to see Jace studying her intently, his expression indecipherable. Her gaze skated sideways to where Ash stood, naked, gorgeous, his erection jutting forward. When she peeked back at Jace, he frowned as though he didn't like her looking away from him.

Her mouth dry, she licked her lips and then she shook her head. "No."

It was another lie. She'd had plenty of second and third thoughts but she kept coming back to the fact that tonight she wanted the oblivion found in a different kind of drug. She wanted to be warm. To know a moment's peace. Was it too much to ask?

Jace started toward the bed as she levered up to her knees, allowing the sheets to fall completely from her body. When he reached the edge, he reached for her and then hauled her into his arms, his mouth descending in a fiery rush over hers.

She closed her eyes and surrendered, melting into his strong arms. The air crackled around them. Their desire was a living, breathing entity that swelled to enormous proportions.

His tongue pushed in, soft and velvet, warm over hers. Soul-deep comfort. His hands skimmed down her arms, gripping her tighter and then pulling her even closer as the heated sounds of their kisses rose and filled her ears.

And then Ash was there, momentarily pulling her attention from the moment. His hands slid over her bare back and the bed dipped as he moved in behind her. She tensed against Jace and then Ash's warm mouth pressed to the curve of her neck and she relaxed. He was going slow, not overwhelming her. He seemed content to allow Jace to take the lead.

Jace pulled away, and her mouth tingled from his rough possession. He stared down at her, his dark eyes scorching over her skin. Her breath caught and held. She stared back, her chest tight with anticipation.

Ash's hands skimmed over her shoulders, his mouth at her neck, but she only had eyes for Jace as she waited for the moment he staked his claim. She wanted his hands on her body. His mouth on her skin. Him inside her, covering her. He was a man who would always make a woman in his care feel safe, and she was a woman who wanted to feel safe.

As Ash's hands slid down her arms and then more firmly back up to grasp her shoulders once more, Jace began to unfasten the buttons of his shirt. Ash pulled her back against his chest, cradling her against his body as Jace slipped out of his clothing.

Awareness simmered low in her belly as Ash's heat surrounded her. His palms slid up her belly to cup her breasts. He lifted and weighed the slight swells in his hands and then he brushed his thumbs over her nipples, causing them to go instantly and achingly erect.

She sucked in her breath when Jace's pants hit the floor and he stood in front of her in only a pair of black boxer briefs. They were tight, encasing muscular thighs and very clearly outlining the rigid length of his erection.

The man was beautiful in a scary, oh-my-God way she'd never experienced. Light and dark. Ash and Jace. Two completely different personalities.

Jace was intensely brooding, his gaze devouring her as he reached for the waistband of his briefs. She forgot to breathe. Forgot Ash's sensual assault on her breasts. Jace's cock surged from his underwear and strained upward, thick and pulsing.

Jace stepped forward, leaned down and roughly hauled her from Ash's grasp and into his arms. She landed against him, his skin a shock against hers. Her knees barely brushed the mattress as he held her for his kiss. His arms wrapped securely around her, one hand splayed possessively over her ass and the other between her shoulder blades.

Her breasts were crushed against the hard wall of his chest, and she promptly forgot all about Ash's hands, which had so gently caressed and teased her nipples. Her entire body was on fire. This was . . . insane. It transcended simple lust or need. She knew nothing about this man and yet she knew she needed him like she'd never needed anything in the past.

"Her pussy is mine."

Bethany blinked as she heard the low growl tear from Jace's throat. His words were bald in the silence and then Ash's chuckle skittered through her ears.

"Not like you to be so selfish, man," Ash said, amusement still evident in his voice. "But I can deal. Her mouth is sweet and I bet her ass is even sweeter."

Jace shifted and power coiled tautly through his arms. She almost expected him to toss her down and fuck her brains out, but his touch was exquisitely gentle as he lowered her to the bed. There was a reverence in his hold that mystified her.

Her back met the mattress and then his hands slid over her body, caressing and touching as if he couldn't help himself. His palms glided over her breasts and then to her belly and finally to her hips. He positioned her so her ass was right at the edge of the bed and her legs dangled over.

To her utter shock, he knelt on the carpeted floor between her thighs. Her breath hiccupped and tore violently from her throat as he lowered his mouth.

Oh God.

"Going to taste that sweet pussy," he breathed out.

When his tongue touched her clit, her entire body spasmed. Using his fingers to spread her farther, he licked her again and she shuddered as pleasure rolled through her body.

Ash feathered a hand over her jaw, turning her toward him. Her lips met the tip of his cock, and she hesitated.

"Open up, sweetheart," Ash said.

Though it was prettily rendered, it was not a request. There was nothing remotely cajoling in his voice. It was a command and one she didn't think to refuse. Her lips parted and he fit his cock to her mouth, easing inward as he put one hand to her head to hold her in place.

"That's it. Suck it," Ash said as he pushed farther in.

His quiet groan hovered and his fingers tightened against her scalp. She closed her eyes, allowing Ash to dictate the pace. It was fine because she lacked the concentration to be in control. Jace was destroying her with his mouth. His wicked, beautiful mouth and tongue.

Jace wasn't at all tentative. He stroked his tongue over her clit and then down to her entrance and pushed inward, sucking and licking like she was a delicious treat. Ash leaned up and over her, angling himself into a more dominant position, so she had no choice but to take his cock as deep as he wanted her to take it.

And then Jace's mouth left her for the briefest moment. "Don't hurt her, Ash."

Ash immediately stilled. Tension she could feel rolled off his body. He stiffened and withdrew and she could see him turn in Jace's direction, his expression one of fury.

"When have I ever hurt a woman, Jace?"

There was a lot in his voice. Pissed off, surly alpha male rising to the surface. Gone was his playful, flirty demeanor and in its place was something altogether different.

"Jesus, what the fuck, man? Really? You'd say that kind of shit? What the hell are you thinking?"

Bethany tried to sit up, suddenly wanting to not be between these two men. But Jace put a gentle but firm hand on her belly and held her down. He didn't even look at her, but kept his hand there, a silent order for her to stay put.

"It was just a warning," Jace said in a quiet voice. "I don't want to overwhelm her."

Ash was silent as the two men stared hard at each other. Ash's lips curled and then he seemed to read something in Jace's gaze that made him back down. Ash's eyes went blank and then he lowered his mouth to Bethany's, kissing her in a manner clearly meant to comfort and reassure.

"I won't hurt you," he whispered against her mouth.

"I know," she whispered back. And she did. Because Jace wouldn't let him.

"Hands and knees," Jace said, interrupting the brief tenderness between her and Ash.

She glanced down to see the intensity in Jace's gaze and she shivered all over again.

Even as she went to turn, Jace was there, his hands against her skin as he helped her to her hands and knees. As soon as she was in position, Jace pressed a kiss to the small of her back.

"Have to get a condom, baby."

And then he left her and cool air brushed over her skin, eliciting a wake of chill bumps.

Ash delved his fingers into her hair, brushing the strands back in repeated, gentle motions as he positioned himself in front of her. Up on his knees, he angled his cock to slide it back into her mouth. He kept one hand in her hair and with the other, he caressed her cheek and jaw, petting and coaxing her as he inched his way past her lips.

His scent filled her nostrils as his taste filled her mouth.

And then Jace was back, his hands covering and caressing her ass. He kissed the small of her back again and then let his tongue slide up her spine. She shivered to her toes and closed her eyes as Ash thrust deeper into her mouth.

She wanted Jace inside her. Needed it. Wanted him filling her over and over, pushing away the darkness, warming her from the inside out.

Finally, Jace cupped one hand over her ass and, with his other hand, guided his cock to her entrance. He rubbed the condom-covered tip from the mouth of her pussy down over her clit and then up again to glide through her wetness. He was testing, ensuring she was ready. She fidgeted and then gasped out a *please* around Ash's cock.

Jace went still. So still that for a moment she thought she'd done wrong. And then he pushed inward. His hand tightened on her ass and she realized what his restraint was costing him. He seemed so afraid of hurting her. Did she seem so fragile to him? What had he seen in her eyes that would make him all but insult his best friend and make him treat her so reverently?

"Beautiful," Ash murmured as he stroked inside her mouth again.

"Beautiful," Jace echoed.

Jace pushed in to maximum depth, his balls straining against her mound. Then he held himself there, his hands sliding over her back, eliciting strong shivers from her very core. She closed her eyes, loving the sensation of being filled, so full she stretched around his erection. Each movement through hypersensitive tissues made her twitch and quiver.

He withdrew and then rocked forward again, slow and sensual, utterly controlled. She didn't want control. She wanted him to lose it. To bury himself hard and fierce. She wanted to get lost, immerse herself so deeply in the experience that she thought of nothing else but the breathtaking pleasure she knew they would give her.

She pushed back against Jace, her mouth sliding over Ash's rigid penis, his taste rough, masculine on her tongue.

Jace smacked his hand over her ass, startling her, but the sensation wrenched a groan from her mouth, vibrating over Ash's cock.

"Patience, baby," Jace murmured. "Want to make this good. You're so fucking sweet. Don't want it to be over too quickly."

"Fucking hell," Ash moaned when her tongue swirled around the mushroom head of his cock. "Not going to last this way. Her mouth is like silk."

She smiled, suddenly confident in her ability to make them as crazy as they were making her.

"Sweetheart, you keep working that mouth around my dick the way you are, I'm going to come all over that tongue, and like Jace said, definitely don't want this over with too quickly. Want to fuck that mouth for as long as possible."

Jace's hands tightened on her ass. His entire body went tense but she knew it wasn't from impending release. He seemed . . . agitated. Every time Ash spoke, Jace went rigid. Almost like he wanted to forget the other man was present. How weird was that? It was obvious from the way Ash had spoken that this was not an unusual practice for them. She briefly wondered if they swung both ways, but they'd kept a careful distance from each other. There'd been nothing to hint that they were remotely attracted to each other. Now her? They were definitely attracted—at least physically—to her.

Jace resumed his careful thrusts, his cock growing larger with every push. He seemed near to exploding and she wondered if she would even be able to accommodate him if he got any bigger. But the sensation of so much cock stuffed into her pussy was amazing.

He withdrew, dragging the head of his cock to the mouth of her pussy then pulled out even more until the tip barely rimmed her opening. Then he shoved in, quick, hard, hot.

She gasped and her entire body spasmed. She shook uncontrollably, her hands suddenly weak and unable to support her. Her arms folded and Ash caught her, going down to a sitting position so her mouth was still solidly around his erection. He caressed her hair, one hand on her chin, the other stroking through her tresses. It was . . . nice. They seemed so caring, which was stupid of her to even think.

They didn't give a shit about her. She was just pussy to them. A piece of ass.

"Didn't say you couldn't come, sweetheart," Ash said gruffly. "Just that Jace and I want to last a little longer. You'll come again. I guarantee that. Don't hold back. I want that mouth working around my dick while you come and Jace wants that pussy to grip him like a fist."

"Ash . . . Shut up," Jace growled.

Ash went silent, but her body coiled, seemingly released by Ash's husky words. Her orgasm rose, like flame to dry wood, crackling and blazing out of control. She couldn't stay still. Ash's hand tightened at her chin when she threatened to let his cock fall from her mouth. He pushed in deeper, seeking depth as she pushed back frantically against Jace.

"Please," she gasped out around Ash's cock. "Harder, Jace. I need it harder. *Please.*"

"Fucking hell, Jace. Give it to her," Ash said in a strained voice.

Jace's big hands spread out over her back, stroking reverently before sliding down to cup her ass in a deliciously possessive grip. He began to thrust hard. Rapid. Stroking deep, the friction so utterly delicious that the room began to spin around her.

She closed her eyes and sucked Ash deeper, her mouth tightening. Her entire body shook with the force of Jace's possession. The pressure was exquisitely unbearable. The rush began low in her belly, coming from the very heart of her, tightening viciously, coiling, snapping like a whip, spreading like wildfire.

"Goddamn!" Ash groaned. "Fuck it all, I'm going to come."

Just as her own orgasm flashed, a spark that quickly became a full-on explosion, the first jet of hot semen hit the back of her throat. She cried out but the sound was quickly muffled when Ash thrust upward, her lips brushing against the wiry hairs at his groin.

She writhed uncontrollably and she heard Jace's muttered curse. His hands tightened on her ass until she knew she'd wear marks from his fingers. Faster, wetter, the slick sounds of his cock diving through her pussy loud in the silence.

She swallowed the hot liquid spurting from Ash's cock and some spilled over her lips. Then he carefully lifted her head and eased himself from her mouth. He gently laid her head down so her cheek rested against the mattress and he continued to stroke her hair, his fingers soft and caressing against her head, while Jace continued his relentless assault on her senses.

Jace powered into her, picking up speed, his hips slamming against her ass. She closed her eyes and lay there, limp, utterly sated, delighting in the aftershocks of her orgasm as Jace continued to thrust.

And then he went rigid against her ass, burying himself deep and holding himself while his body jerked and spasmed. His body came down over hers, blanketing her back with his warmth. He pressed a tender kiss to her shoulder. It was . . . nice. So very gentle. *Loving.*

"Did not intend for that to happen so fast," Jace murmured against her skin. "But fuck, baby, you're so goddamn sweet."

His words hit her, warming her more than their touch, her orgasm. Settling into her heart, spreading feelings she'd be better off not examining. Sex was not a new experience for her. Meaningless sex was definitely something she'd become adept at in her days of mindless coping and searching for answers she had no place searching for. But this . . .

She had to put an end to this stupid thought process. This meant nothing. No different from the other strings of meaningless, mind-numbing sex. For her to think any differently was just opening herself up to pain and misery.

Ash lowered his head, his lips feathering across her cheek. "I'll get you something to drink. Want more OJ?"

"Yeah," she said in a dreamy voice, still reveling in the feel of Jace inside her, his heat surrounding her and his hard body cupped so protectively over hers.

Ash moved away from the bed and when he was gone, Jace kissed her shoulder again. Then to her dismay, he lifted himself up and eased out of her. A whimper of protest she did not mean to escape fluttered past her lips.

"Have to dispose of the condom, baby," he whispered. "I'll be right back."

She was instantly cold the minute his warmth left her. Cold on the inside. She slid down to her belly, sprawled over the bed, unsure of what was supposed to happen next. Did she get up and leave? Did they expect her to sleep over? In the past, she'd known the score. This was totally out of her scope of experience. Besides, she had nowhere to go from here. Just back into the cold. She didn't want this night to end. Sadness gripped her. She should have never agreed to this. While it had been a temporary reprieve and a welcome change from the loneliness that was her life, she knew it would just suck all the more when she was forced to leave.

Jace crawled back on the bed and she lifted her head, fearful of what she'd see. She opened her mouth to ask if she should leave, but he pulled her into his arms, cradling her against his side.

Okay, so maybe he didn't want her to leave yet. That worked for her.

She snuggled into his body, his natural heat a luxury she refused to deny herself.

A moment later, Ash returned, crawling up on the other side of her. Jace's hold immediately tightened on her, his arms a barrier to Ash touching her in any way.

"Got your OJ," Ash said.

Jace carefully lifted her into a sitting position, but he came with her, his arm remaining solidly around her. It was a little bizarre to be sitting between two naked men while she drank orange juice, but it felt decadent.

She sipped gratefully at the juice, her mouth dry and a little sore from accommodating Ash's size. Other parts of her would be sore as well. It had been a long time for her. But it was a sensation she would hold close to her, a memory of one night away from the reality of her life.

"Should I go now?" she asked awkwardly as she handed the glass back to Ash.

Ash's lips tightened and Jace's arm became like a steel band around her waist.

"Fuck no," Jace bit out. "We're not even close to being done. You're staying over. Too damn cold to be out tonight and it's late. Don't want you going anywhere at this hour."

She tried very hard to control her sigh of relief, but her body sagged against Jace's and he kissed the top of her head.

"Give us a minute to recover and we'll go again," Ash said.

Desire gleamed in his green eyes. He studied her a moment as Jace's hand slid up to her breast, cupping the small mound, his thumb lightly brushing over her nipple. She'd just had the most awesome orgasm of her life and already her body wanted more.

"You said you've had a threesome before," Ash said casually. "You think you can take Jace in your pussy and me in your ass? You ever done that before?"

Her cheeks went crimson, the heat scorching over her face. She shook her head, too embarrassed to vocalize her response. The image his question evoked burned hot in her mind. The idea of taking both men in that way at the same time gave her a heady buzz of desire.

"Want to try it?" Ash asked with a grin.

"You don't have to," Jace murmured next to her ear.

"If you've had a threesome, how did it go down if you weren't taking on two men at the same time?" Ash asked curiously.

Her cheeks still burned and she couldn't even meet his gaze. For someone as experienced with sex as she was, she felt like a stupid virgin.

"Like before," she said in a low voice. "Like we just did."

"Ah," Ash said. "One fucked your mouth while one fucked your pussy."

She nodded.

"Ever had anal sex then?"

"Ash," Jace growled a warning. "For fuck's sake. Lay off. You're embarrassing her."

Ash shrugged. "Not much to be embarrassed about. We're sitting here butt naked and we just fucked her."

That was true enough.

"Yes, I've had anal sex," she said.

"Did you like it?" Ash asked.

"Not really, no," she admitted.

"Then we won't do it," Jace said firmly.

His jaw was tight and his gaze was fixed on Ash as if daring him to pursue the matter.

She cleared her throat nervously. "I'd like to try. I mean, the guy I was with wasn't exactly . . . good. You know, nothing like you two."

Ash chuckled.

"Don't, baby," Jace said in a quiet tone. "You don't have to do anything because you think it's what we want."

"You'd make it good," she whispered.

"Hell yeah," Ash said, his lips twisting as if she'd insulted him. "Not going to hurt you, sweetheart. We'll take it nice and slow and if you don't like it, we'll stop. It's hot as hell, though."

Yeah, she could absolutely see that much. What woman wouldn't want men like Ash and Jace initiating her in a situation like this?

"You hungry?" Jace asked. "You didn't eat much. Want to eat something else before we go again?"

He pushed back a strand of her hair, tucking it behind her ear as he spoke. She glanced up at him, taking in his beautiful chocolate brown eyes.

"I could eat something," she murmured. And it was true. She was suddenly famished and the idea of finishing her leftover burger appealed.

"I'll order up more room service," Ash said, moving to the phone on the nightstand.

"You don't have to do that," she protested. "I left half my burger."

"We'll get you something fresh and hot," Jace said, leaning down to kiss the corner of her mouth.

"You want another burger or something else?" Ash asked, holding the phone to his ear.

"Any kind of sandwich," she said, not wanting to be picky. "And hot chocolate, if it's not too much trouble."

Ash smiled. "No trouble at all."

chapter five

Jace watched Bethany as she sat cross-legged on the bed eating the club sandwich they'd ordered from room service. She seemed to savor every single bite, eating with a reverence he didn't often see. She didn't hurry, but there was an urgency to her movements he couldn't quite figure out.

And she sipped at the hot chocolate, her face going dreamy with every sip. He wished they'd gotten more than one cup.

They hadn't wanted her to get dressed—Jace wanted her here in his bed, right where he could see her, feel her and touch her when he wanted. Ash had dressed when he'd gone to meet the room service attendant.

It would be so easy to tell Ash to leave so Jace could enjoy the rest of the night alone with Bethany. He liked the idea of it being just the two of them, here and naked, enjoying each other and sliding into making love as often as they wanted.

"That was really good," she said when she drained the last of the hot chocolate. "Thank you."

"Welcome," Jace said in a low voice.

Ash cleared away the plates, taking the dishes back into the living room. When he returned, he immediately stripped out of his clothing, and Bethany sucked in her breath at the air of expectancy that had invaded with Ash's return.

Jace watched her closely, looking for any sign that she was hesitant about what was going to happen next. If she looked even the least bit reluctant, he was going to pull the plug on the whole damn thing, and he didn't care if it pissed Ash off or not. This whole evening was ten kinds of fucked up. He didn't want his best friend here, sharing his woman.

His woman.

Jace had already laid claim and yet he was about to let Ash fuck her. Again. Twisted didn't even begin to describe this.

"Up on your knees and use your mouth on Jace, sweetheart. Don't want to rush into this. I'll take it slow and easy, get you worked up so we don't hurt you."

Her eyes widened and Jace's senses went on alert. The hell he was going to let Ash run this show. They'd do this Jace's way, even if it wasn't what he wanted to begin with.

Jace shook his head, stopping Ash as he headed for the bed.

Then he simply turned to Bethany, kissing her sweet mouth, stroking his tongue inside. She tasted of the chocolate she'd just drank. Warm and delicious. Her breaths escaped in little gasps, bursting into his mouth. He wanted more. So much more.

"Going to work you up," he said echoing Ash's statement. "But going to do it my way. Want you hot and wet. And the way I'm going to make sure that happens is to lick you until you're about ready to come."

She shivered delicately, her entire body quivering with his words. She was so damn responsive and he liked to think she was that way just with him. He hadn't imagined her being focused more on him. Maybe it was wishful thinking, but he was not wrong about this. Ash was there, yeah, but the connection between Jace and Bethany had been intense. No mistake there.

"Lie down and spread your legs for me," Jace said, inserting an edge of command in his voice. She'd responded well to his authoritative voice earlier, and she did the same this time, her eyes darkening, her face going soft with submissiveness.

Forgetting about Ash—Jace didn't even know where he was at the moment—he traveled down Bethany's body, kissing and sucking at her neck, then her breasts, tracing a lazy trail down her flat belly to the soft curls between her thighs.

He inhaled, savoring her musky scent of arousal. She was already wet and glistening as he parted her plush folds. Pink and perfect, tiny and as delicately rendered as the rest of her. It was like opening petals to a flower and finding dew inside. He blew gently over her clit and watched as it puckered and strained upward.

Then he swiped his tongue over the taut bud, enjoying the instant jerk of her body. He lapped gently, taking care not to be too rough with her most sensitive parts. He explored every inch of her velvety heat, sliding downward to circle her opening with his tongue and then nuzzling it with his lips.

She twitched uncontrollably beneath him, arching upward to seek more of his mouth. He glanced up, wanting to know it was him she was responding to and was satisfied to see that Ash was only now taking position at her breasts. Ash hadn't touched her yet. Her reaction belonged solely to Jace.

He returned his attention to her pussy, sliding his tongue inside her, fucking her with rapid, short strokes. She went wet on his tongue, the sweet rush filling his mouth. He could do this all night. He loved the taste of her. Loved the feel of her on his tongue. Soft. Silky. Like nothing he'd ever imagined.

He knew she was inching toward release. Her body grew more taut and her breathing sped up. He glanced up again to see Ash's mouth close around one erect nipple and for a moment he watched. He may not like Ash being with this woman, but the sight of his friend sucking Bethany's nipples was erotic as hell. It was a rush that never got old, watching another man pleasure the woman Jace was fucking.

"Do you like what he's doing, Bethany?" Jace asked, his tone husky and gruff with desire. No, he didn't want Ash here, but for the moment he could lose himself in the sheer eroticism of watching her react to having two men make love to her. "Do our mouths feel good on you, baby?"

"Y-yes," she hissed out. "It feels so good, Jace. Nothing has ever felt better."

Satisfaction gripped him. She may have had threesomes—kinky sex—whatever the hell she'd been into before, but those men had never given her the kind of pleasure he would. He'd make damn sure of that.

He rubbed his thumb over her clit and then placed an open-mouthed kiss to her entrance, shoving his tongue roughly inside, giving her a little more edge. He wanted her close. He wanted her senseless before they took her at the same time. Hurting her was not on the agenda. He liked pain. Ash liked pain. Liked inflicting pain. With the right woman. Not that Bethany wasn't that woman. There was a whole lot Jace ached to do with her and to her. But not tonight. Tonight was all about simple pleasure. Not the kind that accompanied the sharp, heady pain when inflicted in just the right manner.

There'd be plenty of time for that later. And there was definitely going to be a later. This wasn't a one-night thing for him. He'd have Bethany back in his bed. Tomorrow night, in fact. But it would be with him and him alone. No Ash. No one else. Just him and Bethany, exploring the many, *many* ways he wanted to fuck her.

He sucked one last time at her clit and then rose up on his knees, his hands holding her knees to steady her shaking.

"Here's how we're going to do this, baby. Ash is going to play with your ass a little while. Ease you into this. You're going to use your mouth on me while he plays. He'll get inside you, make sure you can take him that way. Once we're certain you're with us, then you'll get on top of me and I'll get inside your pussy. Then Ash will get inside your ass. You still up for this?"

Ash drew away so Jace could see her face. Her eyes were glazed with passion. Hazy, a little drugged, but burning with need.

She licked her lips and then nodded.

"The words, baby. I want the words. I have to be sure you're with me on this."

"Yes," she murmured in a husky voice. "I'm with you."

"Thank fuck," Ash muttered. "Can't wait to get inside that sweet ass. I'll be gentle, Bethany. You're going to enjoy it this time."

Her mouth wobbled into a crooked, drunk grin. "I already know I will."

Jace crawled up the bed and then helped Bethany to her knees. "Get between my legs, baby. Ass in the air for Ash."

She positioned herself between his legs, and he stared down at her dark head so close to his dick. He was about to come all over her face and she hadn't even wrapped her luscious mouth around him yet. It was going to take every ounce of his control to make this last until he got inside her.

Ash went into the bathroom and returned with lubricant before crawling up behind her ass. Jace's gaze met Ash's over Bethany's body and he sent his friend a silent warning. Ash rolled his eyes and heaved a sigh before he began squeezing out the gel onto his fingers.

The moment Ash's fingers touched Bethany, she went still. Her head lifted so she was looking at Jace and he could see the fire burning in her eyes. Her fingers curled around his dick and it immediately jumped, growing even harder at her touch.

"Suck it," he murmured. "Slow and deep."

The moment her mouth closed around the head, her tongue sliding like rough velvet over the sensitive underside, he closed his eyes and reached down to thrust his hands in her hair.

Then she went still again, her mouth tightening briefly around him. He glanced up to see Ash positioning himself, guiding his cock between her ass cheeks.

"Is it too much, baby? If you need him to stop, tell me."

She shook her head, her tongue licking over his dick. She closed her eyes and took him deeper, lavishing sweet affection all the way to his balls. Fuck, but she had a wickedly talented mouth.

Then she gasped. Her head came up in alarm, her eyes flashing wide. A look at Ash told him that he was inside her. Jace palmed her face, caressing her cheeks with his thumbs. "Look at me, baby. Focus on me and breathe deep. That's it. Don't fight it. Let it happen. He'll go slow. Let yourself feel how good it is and then think of what it'll feel like when we're both inside you."

Her eyes darkened and she inhaled deeply. Then they closed and she let out a sigh. Ash didn't look any different, his head thrown back, his hands palming her ass as he pushed forward those last remaining inches.

"God," she choked out. "You're both so big!"

Ash chuckled. "Glad we please you, sweetheart."

Ash's movements were slow and gentle, two things he typically was not. But Jace appreciated that Ash had dialed it down a notch with Bethany. Ash might have looked the more easygoing of the two, but when it came to sex, Ash liked it hard, rough and to be in total command. They always chose women who didn't mind that, because neither man was easy. And yet tonight, Jace found himself going against his every instinct. He wanted to be gentle and caring, ease Bethany into the experience. And he'd demanded that Ash do the same.

With any other woman, Ash would already be balls deep in her ass and fucking her down and dirty.

"How you feeling?" Jace asked Bethany. "Think you're ready to take me and him at the same time?"

Her eyes flew open and she swallowed around his cock, driving him damn near insane.

"Jesus, baby, you keep milking my dick like that, I'll never make it long enough to get inside you again."

She smiled and sucked his cock, allowing it to slide nearly from her mouth. Then she swirled her tongue around, teasing the head.

"I'm ready," she said in a breathy, excited voice. "I want you both."

Ash immediately withdrew, impatience flaring in his eyes. He wanted back inside her every bit as much as Jace wanted to get inside her.

"Come here," Jace commanded, reaching for her.

She crawled up his body, straddling his hips. He reached down to grasp his dick, fisting the base as she rose up on her knees to let him position himself.

"Take it nice and slow, baby. Don't want to hurt you."

She planted her hands on his belly, her touch like fire on his skin. Then she slowly came down over him and he watched every expression flash across her face and into her eyes as she slid down, enveloping him in her silken heat.

Her eyes became half-lidded, the blue becoming smoky as she gradually worked her way down. She paused a moment, her gaze becoming wider as she worked to take the last two inches of him.

She glanced down, checking the progress herself and then, as if determined to take him the rest of the way, she looked back up, her determination glinting fiercely. She leaned forward, adjusting the angle, and then he was home with one firm push.

He was bathed in her fire, liquid pleasure surrounding him, soaking him, pulling and clutching at him like a greedy mouth.

He moved his hand and then grasped her hips, his fingers curling into her plump backside. Then, unable to remain still, he lifted his hands, gliding along her sides until he reached her breasts. He cupped and caressed, plucking at the nipples until they were puckered and rigidly erect.

"Is it too much?" he asked hoarsely.

"Fuck, hope not," Ash said in an equally hoarse voice.

Jace's gaze drifted over Bethany's shoulder to see Ash on his knees, his features strained. Ash's eyes glittered with heat and lust and then he reached forward, planting his hand in the middle of Bethany's back. Bethany flinched, reacting to Ash's touch. Jace's response was immediate. He pulled her closer to him, not wanting Ash's hands on her. Which was laughable, considering Ash would put a much more intimate part of himself firmly inside Bethany's body in a matter of seconds.

Still, Jace met Ash's gaze, silently warning him to take care. He didn't care if it pissed his friend off. Bethany was too important. She wasn't one of their typical flings or a one-night stand. He planned for her to be around a hell of a lot longer and she'd damn sure be in his bed. The last thing he wanted was for them to scare her off and have her swear off any further contact with Jace.

"Need you to relax for me, love," Ash said, his hands finding Bethany's back again. His palms skated over her shoulders, squeezing in a reassuring manner.

"I'll be easy and take it as slow as you need me to. Going to be a hell of a lot tighter with Jace already inside you. Your body won't want me in there."

Bethany held her breath, evident in how still her body went and the fact that her chest wasn't moving. There was no fear in her gaze, but Jace could see uncertainty, as if she doubted whether Ash would be able to push in as he had before.

Jace rubbed his hands up and down her body, over her breasts, soothing and petting, trying to relax her further. He nodded to Ash and then pulled Bethany further toward him so the angle would be better for Ash's penetration.

Ash rubbed lubricant over the condom stretched around his cock and then he gently fingered Bethany, applying the gel inside and out, stretching her with his fingers.

"Okay, love, I'm coming in. Push back against me if you can and don't fight it. Don't want it to hurt more than it has to. And once I'm in, it'll feel good. I promise."

Her eyes widened and she let out a small whimper when Ash began to press in. Jace could immediately feel an increase in pressure as Ash sought entrance. He groaned as Bethany's pussy clamped around his cock. Bethany's lips thinned and she closed her eyes, strain evident in her forehead.

"You okay?" Jace whispered.

Her eyes opened and she breathed out, "Yes. Fine. Don't stop."

"Hell no," Ash said. "Not stopping now. Take a deep breath, sweetheart. Going to push in all at once. I'm almost there. Better to get it done with."

Even before she could suck in a breath, Jace felt the jolt of her body opening for Ash's invasion. Felt the exquisite tightness of her pussy contracting around him. The pressure was unbelievable, her pussy suddenly the tightest fist. He didn't know how the hell he was going to move, but he figured he'd let Ash do most of the thrusting.

"Christ, she's tight," Ash breathed out. "I knew this ass would be sweet, but this is unbelievable." Ash came to a stop, fully embedded. He leaned over her back, nuzzling against her neck, giving her time to adjust to the sensation of having two cocks buried in her at once.

"What do I do?" Bethany whispered. "I mean, what am I supposed to do? I feel like I can't even move, that if I do, I'll come apart."

Jace cupped her cheek and rubbed his thumb in a soothing manner over her cheekbone. "You don't have to do a single thing, baby. We'll do all the work. I just want you to relax and enjoy the ride."

"Okay," she breathed. "I can do that."

Ash eased back, causing her pussy to ripple over Jace's cock. He clenched his jaw, inhaling through his nose as he fought off his release. Then Ash pushed forward, gentle and slow. Bethany moaned and leaned farther into Jace, her breasts nearly touching his chest.

Jace dropped his hands to her waist, curled his fingers underneath her ass and lifted slightly, arching up as he lifted. Soon, he and Ash found a rhythm they were well used to and they took turns, thrusting and retreating.

"Never imagined this," she said in a strained voice. "It was never this good before."

Ash chuckled. "Told you, sweetheart. You've been fucking the wrong men."

She stiffened momentarily and Jace wanted to kick Ash's ass for bringing up what was evidently a tender subject for her. But then, what woman wanted to be reminded of the other men she'd slept with while she was fucking someone else? For that matter, the very last thing *Jace* wanted was to be reminded of the other men who'd possessed Bethany first.

Jace lifted his head and took her mouth, kissing her deeply, mimicking his dick planting itself deep in her pussy. He curled his hand around her nape, tangling in her hair as he anchored her against his mouth, deepening his possession. He wanted to be as deep inside her in as many ways possible. Mouth, tongue, dick. He wanted inside her and not just physically.

Her mouth moved up and down over his as Ash put more force into his thrusts. She gasped every time Ash bottomed out, the soft sigh escaping into Jace's mouth. He swallowed them up, sucking in the air she breathed.

His balls ached, his dick was engorged and rigid, ready to dive deep and explode. He fought it, wanting her with him, wanting to ensure she received pleasure before he took his.

Ash's hands slid around between her and Jace, cupping and molding her breasts. He tweaked at the nipples and her kiss became more urgent against Jace's mouth. She wiggled and bucked, as much as she was able, stuffed full of two huge dicks. Jace knew she was close because she'd gone unbelievably wet, enabling him to thrust more easily.

"It hurts," she moaned. "But God, it feels so good."

"Hell yes, it does," Ash agreed.

Jace refused to leave her mouth long enough to say anything. He reclaimed it the minute she went silent and arched upward, planting himself to the balls.

"Jace," she whispered, his name swallowed up.

But Jace had heard it and a surge of triumph scorched through his veins, sending him spiraling over the edge. She hadn't called Ash's name in the heat of passion. She'd called his.

"Going to come," he gritted out. "With me, baby. Let go now."

Her hands that had been firmly pressed to his chest suddenly left his skin and then dove into his hair, tightly fisting the strands. She returned his kiss, nearly savage as she took his mouth every bit as hard as he'd taken hers.

Breathless, frantic, hot. Their tongues rolled and clashed, their lips arching and molding against each other.

Her cry was sharp, echoing across the room. Her head flew back, her breasts arched forward. She closed her eyes and let out another cry as she went liquid around him, her release catapulting Jace to his own.

He followed her, his own cry mixing with hers. He vaguely heard Ash's growl and then the entire bed shook as Ash pounded into her ass, forcing her forward onto Jace's chest.

Jace caught her, wrapping his arms tightly around her, holding her as Ash drove into her over and over. She nuzzled into his neck and hung on to him as if she feared falling. And then Ash went still, his face showing agonizing strain. He leaned over, his chest pressed against Bethany's back, and the three lay there, quiet, shaking, still quivering in the aftermath of explosive orgasms.

Holy fuck but Jace felt turned inside out. He'd come so hard, it had felt as though every ounce of liquid in his body had been ejaculated into that condom. He'd never resented a condom so much in his life. He wanted to come inside Bethany. Feel her squeezing every drop of semen from his cock.

He reached up for a lock of hair, toying idly with it as he attempted to regain control of his shattered senses. He wasn't sure what the fuck had gone on here exactly. All he knew was that Bethany was a complete game changer.

She lay over his chest, sandwiched between the two men. Her

eyes were closed and her chest heaved as she struggled for breath. Ash uttered a groan and then finally levered up, pressed a kiss to Bethany's shoulder and then he slipped from her ass, alleviating the intense pressure around Jace's cock, which was still buried in Bethany's pussy.

She moaned softly and Jace immediately wrapped his arms around her, covering the bare expanse of her back now that Ash was gone.

"I'm wasted," Ash said. "Long day, long evening. I'm going to leave you two to it and crash in the other bedroom."

Jace nodded, relieved. Ash never did stay after. He never slept with the women. He fucked them and then left them to Jace. Not that Jace typically indulged in cuddle time either, but he at least shared a bed with their partners afterward.

But he made no move to separate himself from Bethany. He liked the feel of her surrounding him. He was still hard even after the mind-numbing orgasm, and he also knew he should pull out soon before the condom leaked or broke under the strain, but he couldn't bring himself to do it. Not yet. He wanted a few more moments of her in his arms, her limp, warm body cuddled sweetly into his.

She stirred against him and he stroked her hair, kissing her forehead as she fluttered around him. God, but she was making him even harder.

"Need to take care of the condom," he said.

When she would have lifted herself off him, he wrapped his arms around her and rolled so she was beneath him. Then he eased from her pussy, regretting every inch he lost of her.

Her eyes were a mixture of sleepy and confused, almost as if she couldn't quite process what had just taken place. That made two of them. He had no idea what the hell had happened. He could safely say he'd never felt so . . . *possessive* . . . over a woman, much less one he'd only met a few hours ago and one he knew nothing about.

It was a situation he'd remedy immediately.

His nature was to control. To come in, take over. It was what he wanted now. It was his first instinct. To lay down the law, inform Bethany that she was his and that he'd take care of her now.

There were several problems with that and they buzzed heavily in his mind as he rose from the bed, tore off the condom and disposed of it. Not bothering with his underwear, he crawled back onto the bed and pulled Bethany into his arms before reaching down to pull the covers over both of them.

He didn't want to scare the hell out of her and he had a very good idea that she wasn't like other women. She was different. Somehow more fragile. The last thing he wanted was to push her too hard and scare her away.

The other problem was . . . Ash. What the hell to do about his best friend? A friend he shared everything with and had never had a problem sharing a woman with.

Never again would he share Bethany with Ash.

He closed his eyes, inhaling her sweet scent as he surrounded her with him, with his touch. Hell, who was he fooling? It wasn't that he was surrounding her with him. No, he was surrounding himself with . . . *her*.

He sighed, knowing that this wasn't going to be easy. It was likely going to be messy as hell. He'd talk with Ash in the morning. Let his friend know how he felt and go from there. He had no idea how Ash would respond. It wasn't as if this had ever come up between them. They were always so in tune with each other. Jace had never had to worry that he would tire of a woman before Ash or vice versa. Or that he'd want a woman Ash wouldn't. They were in sync. Their bond went deeper than simple friendship.

Only now, things had changed in a huge way. Ash was his friend. His brother. As close to him as Mia. And yet for the first time, Jace sought to cut him out of the picture. He wanted no part of Ash when it came to Bethany. And that was fucked up. He knew it was fucked up. But it didn't change a damn thing.

He just hoped to hell that Ash would understand. He had to.

He glanced down at Bethany, knowing he'd been quiet. He'd said nothing to her since Ash had left, other than he had to take care of the condom. Not exactly romantic.

Fuck it all. He was worried about being romantic?

He shouldn't have worried. Bethany was sound asleep, her eyelashes resting gently on her cheeks. He sucked in his breath at how beautiful—and vulnerable—she looked. He was instantly assailed by a fierce surge of protectiveness that defied explanation.

Whatever this was between them, it wasn't going away. It was here, tangible and solid. Now he just had to figure out how to play this out, because when morning came, he was not letting her go.

chapter six

Jace came awake with none of the sharpness he usually possessed. He was a habitual early riser. He didn't even own an alarm clock. He woke every morning at the same time no matter whether it was a workday or not.

This morning, however, he roused reluctantly, his body loose and sated, contentment slogging through his veins. He reached automatically for Bethany, wanting the feel of her skin beneath his fingers.

Finding only an empty spot, he frowned and came more fully awake, rising up on his elbow to stare at the very vacant space next to him. The only evidence she'd been there was the indented pillow, though she'd spent the majority of the night with her head nestled on his shoulder, her body curled into his side.

How the hell had Bethany gotten out of bed without him knowing it? He shook his head and threw his legs over the edge of the mattress. He pushed upward, stretching as he went in search of her.

He ambled into the living room of the suite, rubbing his hand over his nape and up into his hair. It was completely silent. And empty.

His gaze went to the closed door of the second bedroom just across the living room and he was struck by the thought that it was very possible Bethany was inside that room. In bed with Ash. He clenched his fists and inhaled sharply. He strode across the distance and hesitated once he reached the door, his hand hovering over the handle.

The very last thing he wanted to see was Bethany in Ash's arms.

Rage sizzled hot in his blood. He sucked in several breaths in an attempt to get control. His hand tightened around the handle to the door until his knuckles were white.

He gave the handle a sharp twist and pushed inward, his eyes immediately seeking the bed. His gaze narrowed and his brows came together when he saw Ash sprawled on the bed. Alone. No sign of Bethany anywhere.

Ash stirred and his eyes opened. His head lifted, and he scowled when he saw Jace.

"Is the hotel on fire?"

Jace didn't answer and Ash's head flopped back onto the pillow.

"No? Then go the fuck back to bed and leave me the hell alone," Ash grumbled. "It's too goddamn early."

"I was looking for Bethany," Jace said quietly.

Ash's head came back up, his gaze sharp. "I left her with you, man."

"She's not there. She's not anywhere in the suite."

Ash pushed himself up to his elbows, the sheets tangling at his waist. "She bail?"

Jace's lips tightened. "I don't know. Maybe she just went down for something."

Ash lifted an eyebrow as if to say he thought Jace was a dumbass. Jace blew out his breath and turned around to walk back out of Ash's room.

"Hang on a sec, man, and I'll help you look," Ash called.

"I got it."

Jace's gaze swept the room again, looking for anything. A clue. Something that told him she'd be back. When he got back to the bedroom where he and Bethany had slept, he noted this time that none of her clothing was where it had been tossed the night before. There was nothing that suggested she'd been here at all.

"Jace, she left a note."

Ash's voice drifted to Jace and Jace strode back out of the bedroom to see Ash standing in the living room in front of the coffee table holding one of the stationery note cards with the hotel logo. Ash held it out as Jace walked over and reached for it.

Flipping it open, he frowned as he read the feminine cursive that flowed across the surface.

Thank you for a wonderful night and for dinner. You made it special. I'll never forget it or you.

—Bethany

"Son of a bitch," Jace muttered.

He turned away from Ash and then savagely threw the note across the room. It hit the wall and fluttered downward. She'd left! Without saying a word. Without waking him up. She'd slipped from his bed and walked away. He didn't even know her fucking last name. Or where she lived. Or how to find her.

He'd thought he had time to find out all of those things. He'd planned to learn as much as possible about her over breakfast. He'd had it all worked out. Breakfast in bed. Spoil her ridiculously. Make love again, preferably after Ash left. And then let her know in no uncertain terms that they *would* be seeing each other again.

"What's the problem, man?" Ash asked quietly.

Jace spun back around. "She's *gone*. That's the problem."

Ash's lips tightened and he sent an inquisitive look in Jace's direction. "What, exactly, were you wanting from this? Another night? Two? Then what? It's not like we ever do long-term. I realize this may not have gone the way you wanted, but you have to appreciate the irony of her being the one to walk away. That's usually what we do. She made it a hell of a lot easier on us."

Jace's teeth ground together, his nostrils flaring as red-hot anger whipped up his spine. It took every ounce of control not to lash out at his best friend. He exhaled forcefully and then lifted his gaze to meet Ash's.

"Yeah. Easier."

He couldn't keep the disgust from his tone. Didn't even care. He turned and stalked back into the bedroom to get dressed. He yanked on his pants and shirt, not bothering to shower or shave. He had no idea how long ago Bethany had left and he wanted to make sure he questioned the staff in the lobby and the doorman.

His mind was already working through his options when he walked back through on his way to the door.

"Jace?" Ash called.

Jace paused and turned to see Ash still standing in the living room, a troubled expression on his face.

"What's going on, man? You've acted differently with her from the moment you saw her at the party. We've fucked a lot of women together but last night you didn't act like you were down with what we were doing at all."

"I wasn't," Jace said quietly.

"Then why did you do it?"

Jace stared at him a long moment. "Because it's what I had to do to have her."

Without waiting for a response, Jace turned and left the room. He got on the elevator and stabbed the button for the lobby and simmered with impatience as he waited for the doors to close.

Yeah, Ash was going to think he'd lost his fucking mind. Maybe he had. He certainly couldn't explain this . . . He didn't even know what to call *it*. Obsession?

He knew it wasn't simple lust. He'd experienced that plenty of times. Lust was uninvolved. Lust was about sex and sating a need. Physical release with no emotional involvement.

And yet how could he possibly think he had an emotional connection to Bethany when he knew nothing about her?

He stepped off the elevator with purpose. She may have run, but he was damn well going to haul her back.

Half an hour later, he was ready to put his fist through a wall. After questioning every single employee who may have seen her, he'd gotten exactly nowhere. The doorman reported seeing her walk out of the hotel just after dawn. She hadn't asked for a cab, hadn't hailed one herself. She'd simply walked away.

Without a fucking coat.

It was half raining, half snowing and it was goddamn cold. And she'd walked out without a coat.

What frustrated him even more was that he wanted to track down the catering service and demand information on Bethany, but it was Sunday, which meant that until Monday, he was screwed.

chapter seven

Jace got out of his car after telling his driver to circle and wait and then pulled up the collar of his coat to prevent the drizzle from sliding down his neck. He hurried toward the women's shelter that was sandwiched between an older Catholic church and a soup kitchen on the fringes of the Hell's Kitchen neighborhood.

It would be getting dark soon, a fact that aggravated him, not because of the approaching evening, but because it had taken him all day to gather the information he wanted. And it had taken until now to track her down.

The only information the catering service had on file was her full name and this address. Had Bethany listed another employer as her contact information? He could have called the shelter to get information, but the moment he'd gotten the barest hint of where she might be, he'd left his office and had come straight here.

He ducked inside the door and shook off the rain. An older woman looked up from where she sat at a desk a short distance from the door, alarm in her eyes. He supposed it wasn't an ordinary occurrence for a man to burst into a women's shelter, and if his employees were anything to go by, he'd been brooding and moody the entire day so he was sure he didn't look very friendly.

"Can I help you?" she asked as she hurried forward.

His gaze swept the interior, taking in the smallness, the sparseness of the room—and it was merely a room. Cots filled most of the space. There was a sitting area toward the back, with a dilapidated couch and a few odd chairs situated around a television.

There were maybe ten women in view and he was struck by how subdued they were. They ranged in age from very young to quite old and they all had a tired, hopeless look to their eyes that made his gut seize.

Was this what his Bethany did? Did she volunteer her time here and then work odd jobs when she could for extra money? He felt a surge of pride. He remembered her reaction to the notion that they were somehow paying her for sex. And she hadn't stuck around when it had to be obvious to her that he and Ash had money. Ash had been right about one thing. It was usually them ending things with women. Never once had they had a woman walk away from them with no expectation for what she could gain monetarily.

Even with his coat on, the inside of the shelter felt chilly to him. His gaze narrowed when he saw that most of the occupants wore more than one layer of clothing. Even the older woman standing in front of him had a jacket and gloves on.

"Why the hell don't you have the heat on?" he demanded.

The woman looked startled. And then she laughed. He blinked, not expecting that kind of response.

"You'll have to take that up with the city," she said, anger vibrating in her voice. "They've cut so much funding that we can't afford to fix the heat. It went out last week. All we have are a few portable heating units, and we use those at night so the women can at least sleep warm."

Jace cursed under his breath.

"Was there something I can help you with, Mr. . . . ?"

He extended his hand. "Crestwell. My name is Jace Crestwell, and yes, there is something you can help me with. I'm looking for someone who works here. Her name is Bethany Willis."

The woman took his hand but frowned. "I'm Kate Stover. It's nice to meet you, Mr. Crestwell. But we don't have anyone named Bethany who works here."

His brows drew together. "She put this as her contact address on an employment document."

Ms. Stover pursed her lips a moment and then she sighed. "Many of the women use this address," she said quietly. "It helps when trying to obtain employment. Some businesses aren't too keen on hiring a homeless woman."

Jace stared at her, not fully comprehending what it was she was suggesting. No. It couldn't be. But if it was . . . Ms. Stover was eyeing him with suspicion, and her lips had gone tight, as if she already regretted what little information she'd given.

He cleared his throat and made his best effort to appear nonthreatening and as if he hadn't just been blown away by the possibility forming in his mind.

"Ms. Stover, I'm very interested in hiring Bethany. It's a very wellpaying job and it would certainly improve her circumstances. If you're concerned that I'm a jealous lover, crazy ex or current husband, I can assure you I am none of those. I can provide my business name and a number of references and you may call my partners in business as well as my receptionist to verify my identity and my intentions."

As he spoke, he shoved his business card at her and watched her eyes widen in surprise. She stared up at him, studying him a long moment. Uncertainty was evident as she grappled with whether to trust him. He held his breath, waiting. Until finally she appeared to relax and her gaze softened as she returned his card.

"You said her name is Bethany. Can you describe her to me?"

Jace cleared his throat, barely able to speak past the knot growing there. "Petite. Very thin. Young. Maybe mid-twenties? Black hair. Hangs past her shoulders. She was wearing it up in a clip. And she has very vivid blue eyes. Unforgettable."

At that, the woman's eyes brightened with recognition and then her face softened. "Yes, I know Bethany. She was here Saturday morning to see if we had a bed for the night. It was regrettable, but I had to turn her away." Sorrow was heavy in the older woman's face. She lifted her hand to smooth the silver strands of her hair away from her face. "It's the thing I hate most about volunteering here, when I have to turn women away because we have no room for them. A job would most certainly be welcome in her circumstances, I'm sure. She spoke about using this address to give prospective employers, but they were odd jobs. A permanent job would be wonderful."

Jace's mouth dropped open in shock. This wasn't what he'd expected at all. He wanted to refute that Bethany was homeless, even as his nagging suspicion had swelled the moment he'd begun speaking to Ms. Stover, but then he thought back to Saturday night. The shabbiness of her clothing. The tired look in her eyes. The way she'd asked if dinner was part of the proposition. Sweet mother of God. He felt sick to his bones. Had she accepted Ash's offer because it was the only way she had a place to sleep that night? Had she felt she had no other choice?

"Have you seen her since then?" Jace asked tightly.

Ms. Stover shook her head regretfully. "No. But she comes through every so often. She's stayed here before."

"Do you know anything about her? Anything at all that would help me find her?" Jace said urgently. Then he tempered his eagerness and adopted a calmer tone. "I'd prefer to hire her but I can't keep the job open forever. It's imperative I locate her at once."

He was going to hell for lying to an elderly woman, especially one who ran a shelter for women who were no doubt abused by bastards who'd lie just as he was lying. But no way was he ever going to hurt Bethany. If he could find her, he'd make damn certain she didn't spend another night on the streets. The idea of her being there now made him want to put his fist through the wall, and that definitely wouldn't go over well in a women's shelter.

"I'm sorry, but no. She's very quiet when she's here. Keeps to herself. I did give her the name of a few other shelters but I'm sure she's familiar with them all."

"I want those names," Jace said flatly. "How long?"

Her eyebrows went up in question.

"How long has she been coming here?"

"I've only been working here a year, but in that time she's come in maybe a half dozen times."

Jace's chest tightened until it was difficult for him to breathe. Bethany—his Bethany—was homeless. She'd been in his arms, safe, for one night, and with all his wealth, the ability to provide the very thing she needed the most, he had let her slip away. Back into the cold and uncertainty.

God, even now, she was somewhere on the streets. Without a coat. Cold. Hungry. No protection.

"Do me a favor please, Ms. Stover."

He shoved his card back into her hand, closing her fingers around it.

"If you see her again, you call me immediately. Day or night. My cell number is on here. Call me the minute you see her and don't let her out of your sight until I get here. Can you do that for me?"

Ms. Stover frowned, and she looked at him oddly. He was quick to excuse his urgency before she became suspicious again and blew his story all to hell.

The hell of it was, he absolutely did sound like some deranged, obsessed, abusive boyfriend bent on hunting down his runaway lover. Jesus. If Ash could see and hear him, he'd have Gabe down here and they'd both physically subdue and haul his ass out of here. Then they'd likely hire him a fucking shrink.

"I'm sympathetic to her plight, Ms. Stover. She's a qualified candidate, and now that I know her circumstances are what they are, it's even more important that she be the one to receive my offer. I could hire someone else, but she needs the job. Can you contact me please?"

He was proud of his even tone. He'd even managed to convince himself he hadn't lost his fucking mind.

Ms. Stover relaxed and then smiled, tucking the card into her pocket. "I'll call you if I see her."

"Thank you," Jace said.

Then he gazed around the room at the women huddled on the cots and in the chairs and on the couch. And he tried to control the anger that rushed through his veins.

"You'll get your heat, Ms. Stover."

Her eyes widened.

Even as he turned to walk back out to his car, he pulled his cell from his pocket and began to make calls.

chapter eight

Bethany shook violently as she stumbled across an intersection. It took all her concentration to remain upright. One foot in front of the other. If she fell now, she'd be run over. New York drivers weren't exactly pedestrian friendly.

She picked up her head, her breath blowing out in a fog and she saw the church just one block down. She was nearly there. A whispered prayer fell from her lips. *Please, God. Let them have room today.*

Some of the numbness had worn off. Some of the shock had crumbled and reality pushed in. She turned her palms up, seeing the scrapes and the blood. Her pants were torn at her knees and at her hip and there were identical scrapes there, blood slick on her skin. It cemented the denim to her legs, which was freezing on her.

Tears pricked her eyelids. How could Jack have done it? Her vision blurred and she sucked in her breath, determined to make it the last block to the shelter. Even if they could only offer her refuge for an hour, a place to warm up, clean her scrapes and rest her bruised body, it would be enough.

She had no money. She had nothing at all. The cash she'd so carefully hoarded was gone. Jack owed some very nasty people and they'd come to collect. From *her*. While she'd lain, stunned, on the icy ground, they'd yanked the bills from her pocket. One had kicked her in the side and then they'd left her with a sharp reminder that Jack owed them a *lot* more and she had a week to come up with it.

She bit her lips as more tears threatened. She was exhausted. She was sick to her soul. She was hurting and so cold and hungry that she just wanted to curl up and die.

Relief made her weak when she reached the door of the shelter. For a moment, she was afraid to walk in because if she was turned away she wasn't sure she had the strength to walk back out again.

Closing her eyes and sucking in a deep breath, she put her hand out and pushed open the door.

She was immediately hit by a warm blast of air that felt so good that she went weak and nearly wilted on the spot. It hadn't been this warm the last time she'd come. The heat hadn't been working.

Inside, she could hear the sounds of the other women. They sounded almost . . . *happy*. And shelters weren't generally happy places. Tantalizing aromas wafted through her nostrils. She inhaled and her stomach growled. Whatever they were eating smelled wonderful.

She took a hesitant step, allowing the door to close behind her. The warmth was so welcome that for the longest time she couldn't move as feeling started to return to her hands and feet. It was welcome and very unwelcome all at the same time because with that feeling came pain.

"Bethany, is that you, dear?"

Bethany's head popped up, her brow furrowing. She hadn't ever given her name here, had she? She searched her memory but couldn't place whether she'd ever told the volunteer anything.

But she nodded, not wanting to do anything to lessen her chances of being able to stay.

"What on earth happened?"

The volunteer gasped when she approached Bethany and Bethany winced at the woman's expression.

"I'm okay," Bethany said in a low voice. "I just fell. I was hoping . . ." Her throat threatened to close in on her. "I was hoping there was room for me tonight." Even as she finished, she braced herself for rejection, unable to bear the thought.

"Of course there is, child. Come and sit down. I'll get you a cup of hot cocoa and you can eat as soon as you warm up."

Relief was staggering. It swept through her body, nearly toppling her where she stood. Bethany saw warmth and kindness in the woman's eyes and she relaxed as euphoria set in. They had room for her tonight! She would have a warm place to sleep. And food! It was enough to make her want to weep.

She trudged after the volunteer and frowned as she took in the occupants. There seemed to be more women today than there had been the last time Bethany had come seeking shelter. And there hadn't been room for her then. Had they expanded? Gotten more beds?

"I'm Kate," the woman said just as she stopped by a chair pulled off to the side of the others. "Have a seat right here. I'll get your cocoa and then we'll work on getting you something to eat. You'll need to have those cuts looked at."

"Thank you, Kate," Bethany said huskily. "I really appreciate this."

Kate urged her down and then patted her on the hand. "I'll be right back. Everything is going to be all right, honey."

Perplexed by the strange promise, Bethany sank into the chair and promptly sagged, all her strength gone. Her hands shook and she curled them into her thin shirt, trying to warm them faster. The cuts stung but they weren't serious.

Her gaze found Kate as she bustled around the kitchenette preparing the cocoa. She was on her cell phone and it was obvious that whatever she was talking about was urgent. After a moment, she shoved the phone back into her pocket and took a cup from the microwave. After stirring, she brought the steaming mug over to where Bethany sat, and gently placed it in her hands.

"Here you are, dear. Sip it. It's hot. Everything is going to be all right now. I don't want you to worry."

It was the second time she'd offered the blind assurance to Bethany but Bethany was too tired to dig any deeper. If she weren't so hungry and cold she'd just curl up in one of the cots and sleep for the next twenty-four hours. Or whenever they kicked her out again.

Jace sat in his office staring broodingly at the pile of documents in front of him. It had been two fucking weeks since Bethany had slipped away and he was no closer to finding her now than he had been that first morning. It was not for lack of trying on his part.

Work was suffering. Most of the employees avoided him. Even Gabe and Ash had been keeping their distance. Thankfully, Mia was so wrapped up in her wedding plans that she seemed oblivious to Jace's preoccupation and surliness.

Christmas was a mere week away and he couldn't stand the thought of Bethany cold and alone, no bed, no food. *Nothing.*

He curled his hand into a fist and was tempted to punch a hole in his desk.

His door opened and he was about to snarl out a dismissal to whoever intruded on his privacy when he saw Ash walk in. Something in his friend's expression stopped his retort.

Ash was . . . well, he was typical Ash. Irreverent. Didn't give a fuck. Was rarely serious. Today, though, he looked . . . serious. Like he had something on his mind.

"Fuck, is your family harassing you about Christmas?" Jace growled.

There was really only one thing that ever got under Ash's skin. His family. Ash spent most of his time—and holidays—with Jace and Mia. They'd taken Mia to the Caribbean at Thanksgiving just a few weeks ago to help nurse her broken heart when Gabe had pushed her away—thank God that rejection had been short-lived—but it was true that Ash spent far more time with Gabe, Jace and Mia than he ever had with his own family.

"There's something you should see," Ash said in a quiet, serious tone that wasn't typical for him.

Alarm skittered up Jace's spine and circled his neck in a chokehold.

"Is something up with Gabe and Mia?" he demanded. He'd kill the bastard if he broke Mia's heart again.

Ash flopped a folder down on Jace's desk. "You'll probably be pissed at me over this, but I'm your friend and this is what friends do. You'd do the same damn thing for me."

Jace's eyes narrowed. "What the fuck are you talking about, Ash?"

"While you've spent the last two weeks looking for Bethany Willis, I've been looking for information *about* her. You need to let this go, man. Walk away now. She's bad news."

Heat washed through his veins as he stared back at Ash. "I'm going to pretend you didn't just say that I should forget about a homeless woman we fucked. A woman we clearly took advantage of, whether we knew it at the time or not. A woman who has no shelter, no food, no *damn coat* to keep her warm."

Ash held up his hand. "Just read the goddamn report, Jace."

"Why don't *you* just tell me why you think she's bad news," Jace said acidly.

Ash sighed. "She has a prior for drug possession. She hasn't held a steady job. Ever. She was in foster care most of her life. Graduated high school but never went on to college."

Jace's jaw ticked and he stared down at the folder on his desk. Then he lifted his gaze back to Ash, who stood there staring at him. "And you don't think those are very good reasons to help her now?"

"If you were only helping her, no," Ash said. "But you and I both know you aren't just helping her. You're fucking *obsessed* with her, Jace. I've never seen you like this. You need to snap the fuck out of it.

We fucked her, yeah. We've fucked a lot of women. Not sure why this one stands out from the rest."

Jace surged upward, ready to take Ash's head off when his cell phone rang. He yanked it up, checking the incoming number, but it wasn't familiar and wasn't tagged in his contacts. Normally he'd ignore it, but he hadn't ignored a single call since he'd been searching for Bethany.

"Jace Crestwell," he said shortly, still glaring at Ash.

"Mr. Crestwell, this is Kate Stover from St. Anthony's Women's Shelter."

Jace's pulse accelerated and he dropped into his chair, shutting Ash out. "Yes, Ms. Stover, how are you?"

"She's here," Kate said bluntly. "She just came in. She's . . . hurt."

His stomach bottomed out and fear was thick in his throat. "What? What happened?"

"I don't know. As I said, she only just arrived. I have her sitting down and I'm making her a cup of hot chocolate now. She doesn't look good, Mr. Crestwell. She's clearly frightened and exhausted and, as I said, she's injured."

"Sit on her if you have to," Jace growled. "I don't care what you have to do. Do *not* let her leave before I get there."

He shoved the phone into his pocket and surged out of his chair. As he passed Ash, his friend's hand shot out to grab Jace's arm.

"What the fuck, man? What's going on?"

Jace jerked his arm from Ash's grasp. "I'm going to get Bethany. She's hurt."

Ash swore and shook his head. "This is a bad idea."

Jace left his office and entered the hallway. He could hear Ash hurrying up behind him as he reached the elevator.

"I'll go with you," Ash said in a grim voice.

Jace stepped onto the elevator and when Ash would have followed, Jace put his arm out to block his friend. With his other hand, he punched the button for the bottom floor and then pushed Ash back.

"Stay out of this, Ash," Jace warned in a soft tone. "It doesn't concern you."

Ash's nostrils flared and his eyes blazed a moment. Jace knew it was a shitty thing to say, but then Ash had been pretty shitty himself.

"Yeah, you're right. You don't concern me at all," Ash said, heavy sarcasm laced in his voice.

He pushed back from the elevator allowing it to close, his lips tight as Jace disappeared from view.

chapter nine

Jace ordered his driver to the shelter and told him to step on it. He couldn't be certain that Bethany would stick around, and he wasn't about to take any chances. Not when she'd already disappeared on him once.

Kate had said Bethany was injured and his mind was filled with images, none that were good. They hadn't gotten into specifics. Jace had been too impatient to get to her. How the hell had she gotten hurt?

A woman alone on the streets . . . There were 1,001 ways for her to get hurt and every one of them made Jace's gut clench.

When his car pulled up in front of the shelter, he directed his driver to wait. Hopefully he wouldn't be long, but he was prepared for anything.

He strode toward the entrance, the wind biting through his coat. When he opened the door, his gaze immediately swept the room, searching out Bethany. Then, finally, he saw her. In the back. Off to one side, away from the others. She was sitting in a chair, pale and looking lost. Still, he drank in the sight of her, relieved beyond words that she was here. He could see that her pants were torn at the knees and on one side. He could also see the bloodstains on her clothing and the raw scrapes on her elbows. What the ever-loving hell?

Before he could start over, Kate stepped in front of him, her face creased with worry.

"Will you be taking her with you, Mr. Crestwell?"

"Oh yes," he said quietly. "She's coming with me. I'll take care of her. I promise."

Kate's expression eased. "Good. I worry about her. About all of them."

He started to step forward, eager to get to her and to see how badly she was hurt, but Kate stopped him once more.

"I want to thank you," she said in a soft voice. "For everything. The heat. The food. The generous donation. Look around you, Mr. Crestwell. All these women have a warm place to sleep and food to eat because of you."

Jace grimaced, uncomfortable with her gratitude. He nodded briefly and then headed for Bethany. Her eyes were closed. She looked asleep sitting up. He took the opportunity to study her more closely and he swore at what he saw.

She looked even thinner if possible. There were shadows under her eyes. She was pale.

And she was hurting.

He knelt quietly in front of her. As soon as she sensed his presence, her eyes flew open and she flinched away, panic firing in her eyes.

"It's all right, Bethany," he murmured.

Her eyes widened and he was gratified to see that her fear disappeared, but it was quickly replaced by confusion.

"Jace?"

His name came out a cautious whisper, almost as if she didn't believe it was him kneeling in front of her. Then she straightened and she turned her hands inward, hiding the scrapes and the blood.

"What are you doing here?" she asked in a trembling voice.

His expression hardened and he stood. Her gaze followed him up and without saying anything, he simply reached down and plucked her slight weight from the chair.

She landed softly against his chest and he cradled her possessively, determined that nothing else would hurt her. Then she stiffened and her mouth fell open with a gasp.

"What are you doing?" she hissed.

He strode toward the door, his grip tightening when she began to struggle.

"Taking you away from here," he bit out.

She began to protest in earnest and Jace caught Kate's worried stare. He nodded to reassure the older woman and then he tightened his hold on her further.

"Enough," he ground out. "Don't fight me. You're worrying Kate. I'm not going to hurt you. I promised her I'd take care of you. Don't make a scene. Do you want to frighten all the women?"

She bit her lip and went limp. Slowly she shook her head. "No," she whispered. "But you can't just carry me out of here, Jace."

"Watch me."

He shouldered his way out of the door and the burst of cold air made her instantly shiver. He swore under his breath, pissed that she wasn't better protected from the cold. Her clothing was no barrier to inclement weather at all.

"You're scaring me."

Her voice was small and he could feel her trembling in his arms, whether from the cold or from true fear he wasn't sure.

"I won't hurt you and you goddamn well know that."

Her gaze was haunted as she stared up at him. He paused at the curb as his car approached, ignoring the stares from passersby.

"How do I know that?"

His lips tightened. "If you don't already know it, you soon will."

The car stopped and his driver hurried out to open the back door. Jace leaned in to settle Bethany on the seat and then he slid in beside her. She sighed the moment she made contact with the heated seats.

A moment later, the car pulled into traffic and silence settled over the backseat.

"Where are we going?" she asked, the tremble still evident in her voice.

He reached for her hands, turning them both palm up so he could inspect the scrapes.

"What happened, Bethany?"

She went so still against him that he had to look to make sure she was breathing. There was such darkness in her eyes—*hopelessness*—that it took his breath away. And he knew, without a doubt, that he'd done the right thing. No matter what demons she battled, what her present or past circumstances had been. He'd done the right thing by tracking her down and taking her away.

Bethany tugged her hands away from Jace and turned her face to the window. What on earth was he doing? How had he found her? *Why* had he found her?

Seeing him in the shelter had been a huge shock. One that had rendered her incapable of the simplest thought process. She barely offered a token protest when he'd hauled her away and stuffed her into the back of his car. Wasn't this kidnapping?

"Bethany, look at me."

Though his tone was gentle, there was no mistaking the command in his voice. It was one she couldn't help but obey. She turned her chin and peeked up at him from beneath her lashes and her breath caught in her throat.

He was such a beautiful man. So dark and brooding. Power emanated from him. Anyone would be a fool not to sense his strength. It was plain for all to see. He wore authority like he'd been born to it.

Though she'd sworn he was a man who'd always make a woman feel safe, at this very moment she was a nervous wreck. The look in his eyes suggested she wasn't safe at all, though she wasn't sure what it was she wasn't safe from.

He wouldn't harm her. Of that she was sure. But there were many other hurts than just physical.

"Don't be afraid of me."

Her lips twisted. "That isn't something you can just dictate. Telling someone not to be afraid of you doesn't make it so!"

His gaze hardened. "Have I given you any indication that I'm going to hurt you?"

"You just carried me out of the shelter against my will! What you did was kidnapping! Why were you even there, Jace? How and why did you find me? I don't understand." Her words came out much higher than she intended. There was a shrillness to her voice that spoke of her panic.

He put his fingers to her cheek, pressing in just enough that she felt his touch and was powerless to turn away.

"You need me," he said simply.

Her mouth gaped open and she stared back at him in astonishment. She had no idea what to say to that. What could she say?

Then he leaned forward and put his lips to her forehead in the gentlest of kisses. She closed her eyes, savoring the sweetness of the gesture. This man was trouble with a capital *T. She* was in trouble. In a big, big way.

Tonight you're coming back to my place," he said as he sat back in the seat. He spoke with a calmness she sure as hell didn't feel. "Tomorrow I'm taking you to my sister's apartment. She's not using it anymore. It's furnished, so you won't have need of anything."

Her mouth fell open again at the certainty to his voice. It wasn't a question. He wasn't asking her anything. He spoke as if it was already decided. As if she had absolutely no say in her destiny.

"This is insane," she whispered. "You can't just rearrange my life like this. I can't stay in your sister's apartment."

He lifted one eyebrow and leveled his steady gaze at her in a manner that made her feel stupid.

"You have somewhere else to stay?"

She flushed. "You know I don't."

"Then I fail to see why this is an issue. Mia isn't using the apartment. She's living with Gabe until they marry. Her roommate has moved in with her boyfriend. It's empty and it's paid for. You'll stay there, at least for now."

Her brow crinkled at the addition of "for now."

He smiled as if realizing the source of her confusion.

"Eventually you'll move in with me but I accept that you need time to adjust to our . . . situation."

"You *are* crazy," she muttered. "I've been kidnapped by an insane person."

Jace scowled as they pulled to a stop in front of an ultramodern high-rise across from Central Park. A steady rain was now falling. He reached across to take her hand, pulling her toward the door as he climbed out.

"Hurry so you don't get wet," he said even as he rushed toward the entrance.

She was forced to run to keep up with him and by the time they got inside, she was out of breath. She grimaced as the denim stuck to her knees ripped away, aggravating the scrapes all over again.

Jace saw her expression and he swore as he stared down at her torn jeans. Taking her arm, he directed her toward the elevator and ushered her inside. Despite his effort to get them inside before they got wet, her clothes clung damply to her and she shivered.

The elevator opened into an elegant foyer with marble floors and a huge, crystal chandelier suspended from the ceiling. He nudged her forward and she stepped hesitantly into his apartment.

"We need to get you out of those clothes and I need to tend to your injuries," he said grimly.

His statement made her hug herself tighter as if she could keep her clothes on with her action. Yes, he'd seen her naked, but the idea of being naked in front of him again made her feel extremely vulnerable.

She'd called him crazy, but she was more insane than he was because she was allowing this. It could be said he'd given her little choice, but she hadn't fought *that* hard.

"We need to talk, Jace," she stammered out. "This is nuts. I can't be here with you. I don't even know why you were at that shelter or how you knew I'd be there!"

He put a finger to her lips and his expression brooked no argument. "There'll be plenty of time to discuss our situation after you've had a hot shower and I've looked at those scrapes. You're right. We have a hell of a lot to discuss, and believe me, we'll get there. But my first priority is ensuring that you're taken care of."

She glanced down at her bedraggled appearance and decided that a hot shower would definitely be welcome. Whatever his explanation was, she'd deal with it a lot better when she was warm and dry.

"Okay," she murmured.

His mouth twitched suspiciously. "There. That wasn't so hard now, was it?"

She frowned. "What?"

"Giving me control. I'll warn you now, Bethany. I'm very used to getting my way."

What the . . . ? She hadn't said anything about giving him control!

She opened her mouth to tell him just that but he lowered his lips to hers and kissed her, thoroughly shutting her up in the process.

chapter ten

Bethany sat on the bathroom counter as Jace meticulously examined every scrape and cut on her body. And he was thorough. She was completely naked and he hadn't left a single inch of her skin unexamined.

His lips were set into a fine line but he remained silent while he tended her wounds. She was still cold. Cold on the inside. Bone deep. She wasn't sure she'd ever feel warm again.

After she'd spent several minutes shivering, Jace cursed—something he did commonly around her—and lifted her down from the counter.

"I'll start the shower. You need to warm up. After you get out, I'll bandage the scrapes. I don't think you need stitches in any of the cuts but I'll apply antibiotic ointment so they don't get infected. While you're in the shower, I'll fix us some dinner."

He didn't wait for her agreement. That was pretty laughable since he hadn't asked her for her opinion once. He leaned in, turned on the shower and then came back to where she was standing without a stitch of clothing on. And to think she hadn't thought her day could get any more bizarre.

He slid one hand up her bare arm to her shoulder, squeezed reassuringly and then left the bathroom. She sagged against the counter and then turned to survey her reflection in the mirror. She looked like death warmed over. Tired. Haggard. Worried. Scared.

There were a million words that swirled in her mind.

She closed her eyes and swayed precariously until she gripped the edge of the counter to steady herself. For tonight, at least, she was safe. Even if she had no idea what had possessed Jace, she was fiercely relieved that he'd brought her here. Where no one could possibly find her. Where even Jack wouldn't know where she was.

A reprieve. However short it was, she welcomed it.

Knowing she was wasting hot water, she stepped into the shower and groaned as the heat cascaded over her aching body. It was sheer bliss. The most wonderful thing she'd ever felt.

She tossed her head upward, letting the spray wash over her face and down her neck. Her scrapes stung as the hot water abraded them, but she was careful to clean all the cuts in her skin.

She remained in the shower until her body grew heavy and sluggish from being exposed to the intense heat for so long. After rinsing her hair one last time, she reluctantly turned off the water and stepped out.

Warm air washed over her, surprising her. She glanced upward to see that Jace had evidently turned on the bathroom heater and it was nice and cozy after her half-hour shower. He had decadent towels. Huge and fluffy, so soft that she felt surrounded by a cloud. She could almost wrap it twice around her body.

It was sinfully wasteful, but she used two towels, one for her body and the other to wrap in her hair. It was a frivolous luxury that gave her a giddy thrill to indulge in.

She blinked in surprise when she realized that there was a change of clothes lying on the counter that hadn't been there before. And a thick robe hanging on the back of the door. There was also a pair of slippers. The man had thought of everything.

Her gaze tracked to the clothes again and she frowned. Like he kept women's clothing just lying around his apartment?

She picked up the pair of jeans and the T-shirt and quickly saw that both were too big. Not by much, and truthfully, a year or so ago they would have fit. She hadn't been as thin then. Not as lean. More fleshed out. She'd had more of an actual shape.

Now she was reduced to boobs and not much else. No hips. Not much of an ass. Angular features due to weight loss. Life on the streets was hard. It aged a person before their time.

After taking the time to dry herself completely, she pulled on the pair of panties stuck between the jeans and the T-shirt, embarrassed that she was borrowing some other woman's underwear. There wasn't a bra, and she supposed it didn't really matter anyway. She only had two and both were almost falling apart. The one she'd taken off—or rather Jace had taken off—was dirty and torn. It wasn't salvageable.

It wasn't as if he hadn't already gotten up close and personal with her boobs. Seeing her without a bra wouldn't be a shock.

She tugged the T-shirt over her head and it hung loosely over her hips. It didn't even stretch tight over her breasts, which meant whoever the shirt belonged to was more endowed than she was.

After pulling on the jeans, she took the towel off her head and dragged her fingers through her hair in an attempt to rectify the bedraggled wet-cat look. She was only moderately successful and she wasn't about to rummage through Jace's drawers to borrow a brush.

She blew out a deep breath, squared her shoulders and then turned to the door. She hesitated, her hand gripping the knob. Total chicken. The idea of facing Jace terrified her. Not because she thought he'd hurt her but because she knew she didn't stand a chance against him.

Worse, she wasn't certain she wanted to stand up to him. It was far easier to allow him to take charge. Being taken care of was such a foreign concept that it tempted her. It dangled before her like the proverbial carrot before the donkey.

She jumped when the door vibrated against her hand.

"Bethany? Are you finished?"

Swallowing, she opened the door to see Jace standing a few feet away. He glanced down her body and frowned.

"I need you to take those jeans back off. I was supposed to bandage you up before you got dressed."

"I forgot," she said in a low voice. "I assumed since you left the clothing there that you intended for me to get dressed."

"Not a big deal. Come into the living room. We'll do it there."

He reached out his hand to cup her elbow and then he guided her out of the bathroom, back through his bedroom and then into the sprawling living room.

He had a truly spectacular view of the city with panoramic windows.

"Slip out of your jeans," he said. "Then get comfortable on the couch. Dinner is just about ready. By the time I get you all fixed up, we can eat."

Knowing it was useless to argue, she unfastened the pants and let them fall down her legs.

"I know they're too big," Jace said as she kicked them away. He reached for her hand and pulled her down to sit next to him. "We'll go tomorrow and get what you need. The very first thing you're getting is a damn coat. It's freezing out there and you've been running all over this damn city without proper clothing. That shit stops now."

There was steel in his tone and yet some of the deeply entrenched cold began to dissipate at the edge of concern in his voice. He spoke like a man who genuinely cared about her well-being.

She mentally shook herself because that kind of fantasy was dangerous territory. She'd learned the hard way that she could rely on absolutely no one but herself to take care of her. And even she had let herself down. Just like all the others.

He leaned toward the coffee table, where a small first-aid kit rested. There was a long moment of silence while he applied ointment to each and every scrape and then affixed gauze and tape on the large ones and put large Band-Aids on the smaller cuts.

Before she realized his intent, he pushed her back on the couch and lifted her T-shirt.

"I don't have any cuts there!" she cried when his hand skimmed over her belly.

His expression was murderous as he lifted his gaze to hers. "No, but you have bruises. What the fuck happened out there, Bethany? Who did this to you?"

He sounded so pissed that she flinched from the anger in his voice. It was instinctive to withdraw. Self-preservation.

A low hiss escaped his tight lips. "Goddamn it, Bethany, I'm not going to hurt you. I will never hurt you. But I want to know what son of a bitch *did*."

"Y-you s-sound so a-angry."

"Hell yes. I'm furious! But not at you, baby." His voice softened as he called her *baby*, and something inside her went soft as well. "I'm pissed at the bastard who put his hands on you. And you're going to tell me exactly how this happened."

She went pale and her eyes widened.

Then, when she hadn't thought he could do anything else to surprise her, he leaned over her and lowered his head to her ribs. He pressed a kiss to each and every bruise, his mouth so tender she barely felt the pressure.

Dear God, how was she ever going to resist this man?

"Do you need something for pain?" he asked.

"I'm okay," she whispered. "Just hungry."

He immediately lifted his head, his mouth tightening once more. "How long has it been since you ate? And don't lie to me."

She swallowed hard, but she didn't lie. "Three days."

"Son of a bitch!"

His jaw bulged and he turned away as if collecting himself before he faced her again. When he did return his gaze, there was fire in his eyes and he still looked as if he'd explode at any second.

"You have to give me a minute," he muttered.

He visibly inhaled and exhaled through his nose before finally rising from the couch. He put his hand down, palm up, waiting for her to take it and get up too. When she let him help her stand, he reached down to snag her jeans. Then he guided her hand to his arm and told her to hang on while she put her feet through the pants legs.

After he fastened the fly, he took her hand and guided her into the kitchen. The entire apartment was an open concept with one room flowing into the next. The dining room, or rather dining area, was in front of the kitchen and off the living room to the side. There was an island-bar combination, which enabled whoever was cooking to see into the dining room as well as the living room.

He lifted her onto the high-backed bar stool and then walked around to the stove top, where three different skillets were simmering. She watched with interest while he drained pasta and then tossed it into the skillet with the sauce. He gave it an expert twist, and added seasoning before serving two plates. Lastly, he speared a chicken breast, which had been sautéing in the last pan and sliced it into thin pieces before arranging it over the pasta.

"Voilà," he pronounced as he handed it over the bar to her.

"I'm impressed," she said sincerely. "It looks and smells wonderful. I wouldn't have thought you cooked."

He lifted an eyebrow. "Why not?"

She felt heat bloom in her cheeks. "I don't see a lot of wealthy, eligible bachelors cooking for themselves."

He laughed. "I raised my younger sister and at the time we couldn't afford to eat out or pay someone else to do the cooking. I was just a poor college student trying to survive."

"Where were your parents?"

His eyes flickered. "They were killed in a car accident when Mia was six years old."

Bethany frowned in concentration. "You must be quite a bit older than her then if you were already in college."

"Fourteen years," he confirmed. "She was an 'oops' baby, born when my mother was in her forties. She had me quite young and they thought they were through."

"It's pretty cool that you raised your sister," she said quietly.

He shrugged. "Not much else to do. I wasn't going to abandon her. I'm the only family she has."

He walked around, holding his own plate and then sat beside her on the next stool. He glanced over to see she hadn't even taken a bite and he frowned. "Eat, Bethany."

She dug her fork into the succulent-looking pasta and inhaled as she raised the bite to her lips. It smelled divine.

When it hit her tongue, she closed her eyes and sighed.

"Good?"

"Delicious," she said.

He suddenly got up and she saw him go around and get two glasses that were out on the counter. He placed a glass of orange juice in front of her and she went soft. He'd remembered that she'd asked for orange juice last time.

She savored every bite, every sip until she was beyond full. Pushing the plate away, she gave a contented sigh. "Thank you, Jace. That was wonderful."

He stared at her for a long, silent moment. "I like the way you say my name."

Her brows furrowed. What was she supposed to say to that?

Knowing they had a lot to talk about—she absolutely had to tell him that she wasn't moving into his sister's apartment!—she wrapped her fingers nervously around each other and peeked up at Jace.

"Jace?" she said softly. "We need to talk."

He nodded, his lips pressed firmly together. "Bet your ass we do. Let's go back into the living room. I have questions I *still* don't have answers to."

She blinked and then drew her brows together. Before she could tell him that she was the one planning to do the talking, he urged her up from her chair and put a firm hand on her back to guide her into the living room.

After parking her on the couch, he turned on the fireplace. She sighed as the flames licked upward. It gave the room such a homey feel, and then she shook her head at the absurdity of that thought. What would she know about a home? Home was what you made it, and she and Jack had made home out of some pretty barren places.

Bleakly, she thought back to the places, or rather nooks, they'd made home over the years. In a few cases, she'd been fortunate to land a job for an extended period and they'd actually gotten to live in a shabby efficiency motel. It hadn't been much, but she'd been delighted to have a permanent residence and not one they had to move in and out of based on occupancy.

"What are you shaking your head about?" Jace asked with a frown.

She looked up to see that he'd slid onto the couch beside her. He was close—within touching distance—and his heat and scent wrapped around her, warming her from the inside out.

Without thinking of the consequences, she was instinctively honest.

"I thought the fire made the room seem so homey, and then I realized how ridiculous the thought was since I know nothing about what makes a home."

She heard the sadness in her voice before she realized it was there. Instantly she bit her lip, knowing she shouldn't have said anything at all.

Jace looked as though someone had punched him in the face. Then he bit out another swear. It was long and vicious and it sent a chill skittering up her spine.

She flinched when he reached out to touch her cheek and then he dropped his hand down to her waist, where the shirt covered the bruises. He found the spot that ached the most, however, and cupped his palm over it.

"Who did this to you, Bethany? What the fuck happened out there? And don't lie to me. I want the whole bloody truth."

She sucked in her breath, her eyes wide. She couldn't tell him.

How could she? He'd toss her out so fast her head would spin. But wasn't that what she wanted? To be able to go? He couldn't very well keep her. But even as she thought it, she had doubts. He seemed so . . . determined.

Jace was staring hard at her, silent and expectant. He wasn't going to let her out of this.

"I can't tell you that," she said in a choked voice. "Please don't ask me, Jace."

His lips thinned even further and anger glittered in his eyes.

"Let's get a few things straight, okay? I already know a lot about you. You're homeless. You have a prior drug possession charge. You haven't eaten in three days. You have no money. No place to sleep and someone out there put their *fucking hands on you*."

All the blood drained out of her face. Her stomach knotted viciously and shame crawled over her shoulders and seized her by the throat. She gave him a stricken look, her humiliation so keen that she wanted to cry.

Jace moved his hand from her abdomen up to cup her cheek. He brushed his thumb tenderly over her cheekbone, his gaze softening as he took in her horror.

"Bethany," he said in a quiet voice. "I knew all this before I came for you. Doesn't that tell you anything?"

"I don't know," she whispered, unable to look at him any longer.

She dropped her gaze, closing her eyes. She felt so . . . unworthy, and she hated that feeling. Hated it with a passion. She'd spent a lifetime feeling unworthy, unlovable. Not good enough.

"Look at me," he said firmly.

When she hesitated, he lifted her chin with his hand until her face was directed toward him. But her eyes were still shut.

"Open your eyes, baby."

When she did, her vision was obscured by the sheen of tears that threatened.

"Don't cry," he said huskily. "What it says is that it doesn't matter to me. I knew that about you, and I still went to the shelter. I've been looking for you for two goddamn weeks. I've scoured every fucking shelter I could find, hoping like hell to find you in one of them. And when I didn't come up with you anywhere, it made me livid because I knew you were out there on the goddamn streets, cold, hungry and alone. Where I couldn't protect you. Where I couldn't make sure you had enough to eat. Where you didn't even have a fucking coat to keep you warm."

Despite his command for her not to cry, a tear slipped down her cheek and collided with his hand. He leaned forward and pressed a kiss to her face and then he kissed his way upward, removing the damp trail.

"Now, tell me who did this to you," he said, anger vibrating in his voice. "I want to know everything. I'm going to take care of you, Bethany, but I have to know what I'm getting into here."

She shook her head adamantly. "You can't. Jace, I can't move into your sister's apartment. You can't just sweep in and take over. Life doesn't work that way. It never has."

Impatience glittered in those dark eyes. "Life works however the hell you *make* it work. And the hell I can't take over. Not to hurt your feelings, baby, but you haven't done such a great job taking care of yourself. I'm going to change all that."

"But why?" she burst out. "I don't get it. I was a one-night stand for you and Ash. I can't do that again. You were my relapse. I can't go back down that road. I won't. I've worked too hard to get to this place."

She was shaking by the end of her outburst. And deeply shamed that she'd just blurted all that out. Wasn't it bad enough that he knew about her arrest? Now he'd think she was a whore on top of being a drug addict.

"What place?" Jace demanded. "A place where you have no home? Nothing to eat?"

"To a place where I could gain back my self-respect," she said quietly.

She edged backward on the couch, ready to bolt toward the door. Jace seemed to know exactly what she was contemplating. He moved fast, before she could even blink. He was right up next to her again, arm wrapped around her waist. Trapped. She wasn't going anywhere.

"Start talking. Everything, Bethany. Tell me what you mean by 'relapse.' And then you're going to stop avoiding the question I've asked you four times already. I want to know who the fuck put their hands on you," he said menacingly.

Not knowing what else to do, she leaned into his chest, burying her head on his shoulder. He seemed surprised but then he wrapped both arms solidly around her, surrounding her with his strength and warmth. He rubbed a hand up and down her back and he pressed kisses to her hair.

And he waited. He sat there with her firmly in his embrace, and he remained quiet, almost as if he could see her struggling to work up the courage to tell him what he wanted to know.

There was no way he'd want her after she told him everything. No way in hell. One part of her was relieved. It solved the issue of him taking over and butting into her life. But a huge part of her was devastated.

Jace was pure temptation. He did and said all the right things. Things that went straight to her heart, and worse, they inspired the one thing that she'd given up long ago. Hope.

"It's a really long story," she said against his shirt.

"I'm not going anywhere, baby. We have all night. I'm here. I'm listening."

God, he was too good to be true. She closed her eyes and inhaled sharply, sucking in the smell of him. And then finally she drew away.

"Why don't you let me get a blanket. We'll get comfortable on the couch and sit in front of the fire. You talk and I'll listen. Deal?"

She took a deep breath and then took the plunge. "Deal."

chapter eleven

Jace pulled her into his arms and she snuggled against his side, curving her body into the hollow of his shoulder. He arranged the blanket around them and tucked the ends securely over her body. When he was done, he kissed the top of her head and she knew it was time.

Time to lay bare her soul. To tell him all her shameful secrets. The things that haunted her sleep to this day. He simmered with impatience—had been all evening—and yet he'd displayed remarkable restraint. He was likely ready to strangle her, but this wasn't easy for her and perhaps he knew it.

"For as long as I can remember, it's always been Jack and me," she said quietly.

Jace tensed against her. "Who the fuck is Jack?"

"My brother," she said truthfully. It wasn't a lie because he was her brother. It didn't matter that they didn't share a parent. Jack was her guardian angel. And now she was his.

His grip around her loosened the tiniest bit and he went back to smoothing his palm up and down her arm.

"Nobody wanted us when we were young, and so we were in and out of foster homes. Sometimes we got split up. Other times we were together. Mostly in group homes of some sort. As we got older, we rebelled, especially if we were going to be placed apart. We got into trouble. A lot."

Jace kissed her temple and left his lips there a long moment, offering her silent support.

She pondered a moment the best way to get the nuts and bolts of her past out without spending a lot of time on details. The story wasn't pretty. It definitely wasn't all hearts and flowers. The very last thing she wanted was for Jace to feel sorry for her. But he needed to know enough to understand what he was getting into. Just like he wanted. She knew he wouldn't want her after finding out the mess she was. But at least she had one more night where she could pretend that things were very different for her.

Sadness gripped her and she knew it showed in her expression. Jace brushed his knuckles down her cheek and she could see his frown from the corner of her eye.

"Tell me, Bethany. It won't make a damn bit of difference."

But she knew it would. It always did. It always would.

She sucked in a deep breath and plunged forward. Better to have done with it quickly. Like ripping off a bandage instead of peeling it slowly. "When I was eighteen, I was in a bad car accident. I was in the hospital for months. Broke both legs. It really sucked. I had to basically learn to walk again. Lots of therapy. The pain was overwhelming. I got hooked on painkillers. In the beginning, my using them was absolutely a legitimate medical necessity. When I took them, everything was better. No pain. They made me confident, able to face the world. They made everything seem not so bad and hopeless. I began to need them, not for physical pain, but for emotional well-being. When I tried to go off them, it was horrible."

A low growl escaped Jace's throat and she blinked back tears. Of course he'd disapprove. He was probably disgusted with her weakness. Jace didn't strike her as a person who ever needed anything or anyone. He was strong. She wasn't. She never had been.

"That was what the drug possession charge was for," she mumbled. "I was no longer able to get the prescription from my doctor and the pain and psychological effects were so horrible. I just couldn't cope. So I did something stupid and I bought them . . . illegally. What's bad is that I didn't even use them. I got caught in a sweep. Didn't have a prescription. Got arrested for having a schedule-three controlled substance. I got off with a slap on the wrist, but it was a hard lesson to learn. Even though I got off pretty light, it fucked up a lot for me. It's hard to get a job when you have that arrest on your record. No one wants to hire an addict."

Jace squeezed her to him and she felt him tremble against her. Anger? She couldn't look at him. Couldn't bear to see the censure in his eyes. She'd beat herself up enough over the years. She wasn't going to let someone else do it for her.

"You said Ash and I were a relapse. You said that night that you'd had a threesome before. Where does that fit in?" Jace asked quietly.

More shame crawled over her shoulders until they slumped downward and her lips drooped in dejection.

"Baby," Jace said in an aching voice. "Everything. You tell me *everything*, we'll never talk about it again unless you want to. But you need to get that shit out. It's like poison. And until you realize that it doesn't change a goddamn thing for me, it'll eat at you. You'll always worry. So we get it out, put it to rest and then we move forward. Okay?"

She nodded, a roar in her ears. She couldn't possibly believe what he was saying. He didn't know everything. He was trying to be noble, but he wouldn't feel that way when she finished.

"When I was trying to get off the meds, I went through a really bad time when I tried a lot of bad things to cope with withdrawal and the psychological dependence on the drugs. I used sex as a balm, only it never worked. It only made me feel worse about myself. I had several partners during that time," she said painfully. "Threesomes. One on one. It didn't really matter to me. I was just looking for something to ease the pain. Just needed a way to escape for a little while. I wanted to be . . . wanted. *Loved*."

Jace hugged her even tighter to him, holding her against his chest so she couldn't even move.

"I wasn't so stupid that I didn't use condoms. The guys were probably worried they'd catch something from me. I had a reputation, Jace," she whispered. "It wasn't a good one."

She nearly choked on the words. Hated admitting that. Hated putting it out there that way. But she wasn't going to lie. Jace deserved to know everything. He was a good guy. Too good to be true. He didn't deserve to be saddled with someone like her.

"What the fuck is going on in your head right now?" Jace demanded, his voice cutting through her morose thoughts.

"You deserve better."

Jace swore viciously. "You're honest. Blunt. Normally I'd like that. Hell, I'd love it. I appreciate honesty and someone who speaks the truth without regard to consequences. But goddamn it, Bethany. *I deserve better*? What the ever-loving fuck is that about? What about what *you* deserve? Have you ever given thought to that?"

She didn't have an answer to that question.

Jace shook his head and squeezed her harder. "I don't care how long it takes, baby. You're going to see you like I see you. You're going to get it through your head that you deserve better. And I'm going to make damn sure you get it."

She swallowed and breathed back the tears. How could he see her as anything? He didn't know her.

"What else?" Jace asked. "Give it all to me. Get me to where you are right now."

"There's not much else to tell," she mumbled. "After the drug possession charge and the string of meaningless sex partners, things just disintegrated. It was my fault. I could have done better. I could have been more responsible. But I wasn't and I paid the price. No one would hire me and I didn't have the money to go to school and make a better life by getting an education. The accident took so many months out of my life. And I was tired and beaten down. I couldn't even think beyond the next day, much less look ahead a few years to see what life could be like down the road."

"Jesus," Jace muttered. "How old are you now?"

Her brows scrunched together. "Your investigation didn't tell you that?"

"I said I knew a lot. I didn't say I knew everything," he said dryly. "I hit the important points. Your age doesn't mean jack shit to me, unless you tell me you're still a minor."

The attempt at a joke heartened her, injecting just a tiny bit of lightness into her chest.

"I'm twenty-three," she said, wincing even as she said it. Way too old not to have her shit together. Way too old to be homeless, uneducated and jobless.

"Still a babe," he murmured.

She glanced sharply at him. "How old are you?"

"Thirty-eight."

Her eyes widened. There was fifteen years' difference between them. Fifteen!

"And Ash?" she choked out.

"Same." Suddenly his voice was clipped and he didn't look happy that she'd mentioned Ash.

"Wow," she mumbled. "I would have never guessed you were thirty-eight. You're fifteen years older than I am."

"So?"

She blinked at the blunt assessment. She glanced up to see challenge in his eyes.

"Does it bother you?" he asked, though his tone suggested he didn't really care if it bothered her. He looked determined and resolute.

"Doesn't it bother *you*?" she asked hesitantly. "Surely there are more sophisticated women you could have. Educated. Older. *Better.*"

His jaw bulged as he clenched it. "Now you're just pissing me off."

She sighed unhappily.

"You didn't answer my question. Does it bother you?" he persisted.

What could she say? If she were truthful it would only seal her fate even tighter. If she said it did bother her, he might not even care. Or it would make her look like a superficial bitch.

"Bethany?"

"No," she blurted. "It doesn't bother me. The age difference, I mean. But it doesn't mean that we can do this or that you should have anything to do with me. I'm so wrong for you, Jace. You have to see that. We live in completely different worlds. So different that I can't even fathom the differences. I'll never come close to your life."

"There's only *one* world," Jace said, anger tightening his voice. "We live in the *same* goddamn world, Bethany. More important, you're there. I see you. I want you. You're here in front of me. If that doesn't put you solidly in my fucking world, then I don't know what does."

Her pulse accelerated until she was lightheaded and working to squeeze air into her lungs.

"Now that we've gotten all that out of the way, you're *finally* going to tell me who the fuck put their hands on you and *why*."

He sounded super pissed off again, only this time she knew he was in no way angry with her. He was furious, yes. No doubt there. There was a blackness and rage in his eyes that made her shiver.

She bit her lips and looked away, her stomach bottoming out. He'd never understand. So far, she'd left out a lot of her relationship with Jack, revealing only that he was her brother and that they were close. Jace would never ever understand. Not in a million years. He wouldn't care what Jack had done for her or that she owed him so damn much that she'd do anything—anything at all—to repay that debt. Even go to hell and back.

"Bethany."

Her name came out in a warning growl. He was losing his

patience, and so far he'd displayed a remarkable amount of said patience. She was lucky he hadn't throttled her by now. She got from him that he wasn't used to being denied anything. He was a man who got what he wanted. People didn't tell him no. Not if they valued their skin.

She let out a forlorn-sounding sigh.

"What are you into?" he asked softly.

Her eyes flew open and she whirled to meet his gaze, her own earnest and imploring. "I'm not into *anything*."

Her response was so vehement that it was obvious he accepted it as truth. He relaxed only the slightest bit, but there was still fire in his eyes.

"Tell me, Bethany. Don't make me ask again."

The authority in his voice made her pulse react. Power emanated from him. Her heart thudded painfully against her chest wall and she licked her lips repeatedly as she worked up the courage to tell him the last of it.

"Jack owes money," she whispered.

Jace's gaze narrowed instantly. "Say that again?"

She cleared her throat. "Jack owes money. They want it. He can't repay it. They threatened me. Said I had a week to come up with it."

She rushed on, not allowing Jace to respond. She was afraid of his response and so she recklessly surged forward, talking fast. She was probably incomprehensible, but at the moment she didn't care.

"I can't come up with that kind of money in a month, much less a week! Jobs are hard to find right now. Everyone picks up odd jobs during the holidays. And I don't look the part to do the better stuff. They took all the cash I had. It was all I had to eat with. To survive on until the next job comes through. I don't know what to do, Jace. I'm terrified for Jack."

Jace's mouth gaped open and he stared incredulously at her. "You're scared for Jack."

She nodded.

"You're scared for Jack," he said again, with more emphasis.

Again she nodded.

"God-fucking-damn. Those bastards came at *you*. They *hurt* you. They fucking *threatened* you! And you're scared for *Jack*."

"Yes," she whispered.

He exploded in a litany of eyebrow-scorching curses that had her wincing. He turned, letting her loose as he sat forward on the couch, his hands clenched together between his thighs.

"Son of a bitch," he snapped. "Did it ever occur to you to be scared for yourself?"

She swallowed and nodded. "After today, yeah."

He turned swiftly back to her. His eyes sparked with anger.

"What I want to know is how they even knew about you," he said in a soft, furious voice.

It was a question Bethany had asked herself. Repeatedly. Ever since they'd shoved her to the ground, stolen her money and kicked her in the ribs. Why had they come after her? How did they even know of her existence?

Jack wouldn't . . . She shook her head, because she was being stupid. How else would they have known? How would they have known how to find her? Jack had to have told someone. And that broke her heart.

Tears pricked her eyelids and they stung. It was like having acid in her eyes.

"Tell me what happened, Bethany," Jace said in a more gentle tone. He was holding her again. She was against his chest, cradled in his arms. His lips pressed to her hair and his tone was soothing and infinitely tender.

She closed her eyes as her warm tears collided with Jace's shirt.

"They knew how to find me," she choked out. "I don't know how." Liar. She knew. It was the first lie she'd offered Jace, but somehow admitting the truth made it irrevocably so. And she couldn't deal with that right now. Denial was kinder.

"They shoved me to the ground. It's how I got the scrapes and cuts. They told me I had a week to get the money Jack owed them. Then they stole the cash I had out of my pocket. They left and said they'd look me up in a week and that there was nowhere I could hide from them. They told me they'd find me. No matter what."

"Fucking bastards," Jace spat. "Goddamn chickenshit sons of bitches. Preying on a defenseless woman instead of the prick who borrowed the money in the first place. And Jack *let* them."

She stirred, ready to defend Jack, but Jace tightened his hold on her. A warning to remain silent.

"Don't even go there, baby." His tone was ice. So forceful that she instantly obeyed. "Don't dare defend him when what he did was indefensible."

She sagged against him, closing her eyes once more. She turned her face into his chest, clutching at him with both hands.

"How much does he owe?" Jace demanded.

Bethany pulled away only enough that her words wouldn't be distorted. "F-f-five thousand dollars." It may as well be a million. Five thousand dollars was as impossible as ten million dollars.

"I thought I could try peddling," she said, nearly choking on the words. "I've seen others do it and they make decent money. I only have a week though, so I'd need to work hard. So maybe you understand now why I can't move into your sister's apartment."

"Oh *fuck* no."

Jace exploded, his body suddenly pulsing with tension. He sat straight up, carrying her with him. He pulled her away so she stared him in the eye and he was angry. Very, very angry. His face reddened and his lips were white from pressing together so fiercely.

"You're done. Finished. You aren't setting foot back on the streets again. You've lost your ever-loving mind if you think I'm going to let you walk back out there with those fuckheads gunning for you."

The blood drained from her face. "They'll hurt Jack. I can't let that happen, Jace."

"You leave Jack to me," he bit out.

She shook her head, hysteria rising. This situation was fast getting out of control and she had to stop it now. She bolted upward before Jace could haul her back down and she took hasty steps backward so he didn't reach for her.

"I have to go," she blurted. "Thank you. For everything."

And then she turned and ran, praying the elevator would open immediately.

chapter twelve

Jace lunged for Bethany, but she just slipped from his grasp and made a mad, erratic dash toward the elevator. Damn female didn't even have shoes on. Where the fuck did she think she was going?

The elevator door opened immediately and he surged ahead, arm outstretched to prevent the doors from closing. He missed by two inches.

He wanted to beat his head against the fucking wall. Instead he picked up the phone and called down.

"This is Jace Crestwell," he said calmly. "There is a woman coming down the elevator. She has no shoes on. Under no circumstances are you to allow her to leave this building. I'll be down as soon as the elevator reaches my floor again."

"Yes, sir," came the crisp answer.

Satisfied that Bethany wouldn't escape, he punched the call button for the elevator and stewed while he waited for it to come back up. And as he waited, he processed everything Bethany had had to say.

He was facing an uphill battle. Bethany didn't think she was worthy of him. Which was laughable. He was no goddamn saint. He and Ash had fucked their way through half of Manhattan and for no other reason than they wanted to.

How the hell could he judge Bethany for using sex as a coping mechanism when he'd essentially done the same thing? And Bethany had certainly had a harder life than Jace. She at least had an excuse. Jace couldn't say the same.

The elevator doors opened and Jace hurried on, jabbing the button for the lobby with his thumb.

The situation with Jack was trickier but not insurmountable. All he had to do was keep Bethany out of it and make damn sure she was safe. Over his dead body would she rush in to save fucking Jack. She hadn't said it, hadn't admitted it, but he'd seen the knowledge in her eyes. The crushing sadness that accompanied the realization that she'd been betrayed by someone she loved and trusted.

Jack had thrown her to the wolves. The asshole had used her as a guarantee for money he never intended to pay back. Jace was besieged by the urge to go hunt the fucker down and exact some old-school justice.

When the elevator finally arrived on the first floor, Jace hurried out, looking left and right for sign of Bethany. To his relief, she was sitting in the corner of the lobby, the doorman and the security guard flanking her.

A smile quirked his lips when he saw that she was holding a Styrofoam cup of coffee and that the doorman had engaged her in light conversation. As if seeing a barefoot woman fleeing a building in winter was an everyday occurrence.

Her gaze flickered over him when she saw him approach and fear brewed in the brilliant blue depths. He felt sucker-punched. She was *afraid* of him.

"Bethany," he said in a calm voice. "Let's go back up now and leave these two gentlemen to their work." Then to the two men he said, "Thank you both for seeing to my Bethany. I wouldn't want her out in the cold dressed as she is."

"No, of course not, sir," the doorman said briskly. Then he smiled warmly at Bethany. "It was nice to meet you, Miss Willis. I hope to see you again soon. If you ever have need of anything, do not hesitate to ask."

"Thank you, Roger," she said with a smile.

Jace lifted one eyebrow. He'd lived here for some time and he'd never had the occasion to know the doorman's name. He was ashamed of that fact now, given that she'd learned Roger's name in less than five minutes.

The security guard gave Jace a short nod and then smiled in Bethany's direction before returning to his post. Bethany sighed and rose, thrusting the cup toward Roger.

"Thank you," she said again. "It was foolish of me. Thank you for stopping me and for being so kind."

Jace tucked Bethany's hand in his and pulled her toward the elevator. He didn't say anything to her on the trip back up. Just held her closely, melded to his side. He liked the feel of her against him. Soft and pliant. A perfect complement to his much harder body.

But then he frowned as he realized she was pliant because she was . . . defeated.

Oh *hell* no. She wasn't going back into his apartment as some whipped puppy.

As the elevator doors slid open, he tugged her against his chest and tipped her chin up so she was forced to look at him.

"You come into this apartment, you do it with your chin up and your shoulders back," he said. "You don't come in here beaten down or scared. This is your place. Your sanctuary. This is the one place, above all others, where you are absolutely safe from the outside world. From judgment and harm. Got it?"

She stared at him a long moment, her eyes somber and thoughtful. But what hurt him the most was that for a brief moment, hope flickered in her gaze and just as quickly shut down. Like hope was such a foreign concept that she wouldn't allow herself to have it.

Then finally she nodded and whispered, "Got it."

He kissed her forehead, feeling her tremble against him. "No, you don't get it, baby. But you will. I promise you that."

He tugged her into his apartment and let the elevator doors close behind them. She looked exhausted. Physically and emotionally. It was relatively early by his standards, but at the moment he couldn't think of anything more he'd like to do than to take her to bed and let her sleep in his arms. He wanted her to feel protected. Safe. Most important, cherished. Like she mattered.

She didn't have any experience in any of those. That much was evident in the painful retelling of her childhood and her adult years. He couldn't change her past, but he could sure as hell change the present and alter the course of her future.

"Let's go to bed. You're wiped," Jace said.

Her gaze skittered nervously up to his. Her eyes were wide in her face, giving her a haunted look. She really was too thin but her beauty . . . it shone like a beacon. There was something arresting about her eyes and her face. He couldn't explain why he'd been so inexorably drawn to her that very first night he'd seen her across the room at Mia's party. But he'd known even then that she was his.

"Baby, I'm not going to jump you," Jace murmured.

He took her hands and rubbed his thumbs up the backs, working in soothing circles.

She swallowed and then nodded. "I'm tired."

"You're wiped," he repeated.

Still holding her hand, he pulled her toward his bedroom and once there, he closed the door behind them. Then he turned and grasped the hem of her shirt and began tugging it over her head.

She clamped down an arm, her eyes flaring with alarm.

He waited a moment, staring intently into her eyes. "Baby, in that bed, there is nothing between us. No clothing, barriers, nothing. I said I wasn't going to jump you, and that's true. I won't lie to you. But you aren't wearing those clothes to bed. Besides the fact they don't fit you worth a damn, anytime you sleep in my bed, you're naked."

"I'll get cold," she said with a frown.

He smiled at the quick excuse and her attempt to keep that barrier between them. She'd learn soon enough that he'd allow none between them.

"I'll keep you warm."

She bit her lip in consternation and then sighed, lowering her arm in a gesture of surrender.

"Remember," he said softly. "You don't come here beaten down and defeated. You hold your head up. You submitting to me doesn't mean you're anything less. I'm a demanding bastard. No doubt about that. But the very last thing I want is for you to be some mindless puppet."

Confusion clouded her beautiful blue eyes. "I guess I don't understand. Any of this. I'm confused, Jace. This is so . . . *overwhelming.*"

He kissed her nose and then slowly worked her shirt upward. "We have all the time in the world. I want you to trust me. As long as you can do that, everything will work out just fine. I'll take care of you and I'll never do anything to overwhelm you."

"But I just said I'm overwhelmed!" she protested.

He grinned and tugged the shirt the rest of the way, baring her breasts—and the bruises—to his gaze.

"I just want you naked. Overwhelming would be if I was going to fuck you tonight. That'll come tomorrow. Tonight is for you to adjust to being here."

Her mouth fell open. "And you don't consider that overwhelming?"

"Nope."

"Evidently you and I have different opinions on what constitutes being overwhelming," she muttered.

"Now that I like," he said with satisfaction.

She lifted an eyebrow as he went to work on the fly of her jeans.

"You being sassy. You've got fire, Bethany. You haven't lost that. You're fucking perfect for me."

"You're crazy," she muttered again. "Or maybe I'm crazy."

"As long as we're crazy together, I'm good with it."

She threw up her hands as he worked the jeans down her legs. "You honestly do always get your way, don't you?"

He smiled again and helped her step from her jeans. "I already told you that. Nothing worth having is ever easy, baby. And you don't get things without fighting for them." He leaned down and brushed his mouth across the bruise at her ribs. "Be warned. I'm fighting for you and I have no intention of losing."

As he lifted his head, he saw hope flash again in her eyes and this time it stayed there. She stared up at him in awe, her entire body trembling. He could see that it was finally sinking in. That this was real and that he was deadly serious.

"Lose the underwear," he said.

This time she didn't offer any argument. There was only brief hesitation as she slipped her thumbs into the waistband of the silky scrap of material. A moment later, the panties fluttered to the floor and she toed them away.

"Get into bed and wait for me there," he said in a soft but firm voice. "I'm going to shower and then join you. Get comfortable. And Bethany?"

She lifted her gaze to meet his in response to the address.

"Don't try to go anywhere. I've locked the elevator and even if you managed to get to the lobby, they won't let you leave here without me."

"Am I a prisoner then?" she asked huskily.

He smiled. "Never that. But I'll do what I have to in order to ensure your safety. Even if it means making sure you can't leave while I'm in the shower. Now get into bed so you don't get cold. I'll adjust the heat."

Leaving her standing there, he strode into the bathroom and

turned on the shower. He purposely gave her the time to get into bed on her own and a few minutes to get over her nerves before he joined her.

Bethany was going to take a lot of patience—a lot more than he was used to giving a woman. Before, if the woman wasn't fully on board, he cut ties quickly. He knew what he wanted and he didn't have any desire to hook up with a woman who didn't give him exactly what he demanded.

She was also going to require a firm hand, and that he didn't mind at all. He relished the thought of taking care of her. She'd learn quickly what he expected, and he'd enjoy every minute of lavishing his care and protection on her. In time so would she.

There were things he needed to take care of. He mentally went over his list as he quickly showered. Security was of utmost priority. He couldn't have her unprotected when those bastards had no compunction about coming after her for this money Jack owed them.

And she needed outfitting from the feet up. There was the issue of Mia's apartment, though Jace knew she'd spend little to no time there. He was tempted just to move her right into his apartment, but he didn't want to completely overwhelm her from the start.

She needed the semblance of independence before he brought her fully under his control. Even if he controlled all aspects of that independence. It was a little warped—okay, a lot warped—but he wanted her to regain her confidence. Have at least the perception of making her own choices even if she did it in a completely safe environment.

She'd have her own place. They'd date. He'd shower her with affection. They'd spend time together. Eventually, when she was more secure in her role in his life, he'd move her into his apartment. From there? That was as far as he'd gotten. And he knew that until the day she was living in his space he wouldn't rest easy.

Until then, he had to ensure that her problems disappeared. He frowned as he stepped from the shower to towel off. Jack was a big problem. She obviously had a lot of loyalty to him and he was bad news. He couldn't allow Jack to interfere in her life and put her in danger. Which meant Jace was going to have to step in. Something Bethany likely wouldn't appreciate.

Not bothering to dress, he wrapped the towel around his hips and walked back into the bedroom.

His gaze softened and a smile curved his lips when he saw that she was already sound asleep. Her head was on his pillow, or rather, in the middle of the mound of pillows and she was snuggled tightly under the covers. They were pulled to her chin and her lashes rested delicately on her cheeks.

Everything about this image was right. She belonged in his bed. Never had he felt such a keen sense of satisfaction over a woman being in his bed. This was right. *She* was right.

He let the towel drop and then he carefully pulled the covers far enough back that he could slide in. She stirred only slightly, uttering a sleepy sound that brushed pleasingly over his ears. He gathered her close, curling his arms protectively around her, and then he arranged her head so it rested on his shoulder.

He hooked his leg over hers so that she was solidly molded to his body. Then and only then did he relax and fall into sleep with her.

chapter thirteen

Bethany awoke to a hard male body wrapped solidly around hers. For a moment she panicked as she sought to gain her bearings. She was disoriented and couldn't immediately place her surroundings. Then, as her eyelids fluttered open, she saw Jace's eyes on her, watching her come awake, and the previous day came back to her in a flash.

She stared wordlessly at him, overwhelmed by the fact that he'd essentially taken over her life. And how much her life had changed in less than twenty-four hours. She couldn't even grasp it all. It seemed unreal. And yet . . . welcome.

Even as she knew she should resist, a big part of her was relieved. She'd been alone and fending for herself, eking out a spartan existence for so long, and to have this man sweep in with promises to care for and protect her was dizzying. And so very tempting.

Her life wasn't much. But it was what she was used to. How was she supposed to make the adjustment from her world to his?

Yes, he'd been adamant that they lived in the same world, but she knew better. They may occupy the same universe, but his life was so different than hers that she couldn't even comprehend it. He had wealth and power. His life was well ordered and he had exacting standards. What on earth did he want with her? *Why* did he want her? It made no sense to her. It defied all logic.

"What the hell are you thinking?" he murmured.

"That I have no idea why you're so determined to involve yourself with my problems," she whispered back. "I don't understand why a man like you would want someone like me. It's crazy, Jace. I can't fathom it. None of it. It's like a bizarre spin on the Cinderella story— only for girls like me, there aren't happily-ever-afters."

"I'm starting to regret every time I ask you what you're thinking," he grumbled. "You're too damn honest. I was thinking more along the lines of you thinking how gorgeous I am. Or maybe that you woke up fantasizing about me fucking you while you're still half asleep. That other shit you've been thinking is just fucked up, and I swear if it takes me forever, I'm going to get that crap out of your head."

She laughed, relaxing against the pillow. His eyes gleamed when she laughed and his hold tightened around her.

"God, you have a beautiful laugh," he said hoarsely. "And your smile. Jesus, it knocks the breath out of me."

Her entire body reacted to the look on his face.

"You can't talk to me like that," she breathed. "Nobody says things like that to a woman he just met. It's insane."

"I just did. And I plan to keep saying them until you believe every word."

She shook her head, trying to drive away the muddled confusion swirling in her mind. Any moment now, she'd awaken in the shelter and all of this would have been a dream.

"You're real," she whispered.

He rolled, shifting his body above hers so he looked down into her eyes. His body settled, covering hers as the sheets twisted around his hips. He maneuvered until her thighs were spread and she could feel his heavy erection right between her legs.

"I'm real, baby. This is real. *We* are real. The sooner you accept that, the sooner we can move forward and you can be happy. I want you to be happy. I want you to be content. Warm. For you not to have to worry about your next meal. Most of all, I want you to know without a doubt that I've got your back. And your front. And your sides. I've got all of you and I'm not letting go."

"How can you want me after all I told you last night?" she whispered.

He leaned down to kiss her, his body pushing more firmly into hers. He reached with one hand, sliding under his pillow, and retrieved a condom. She watched in shock as he lifted up his body after tearing away the wrapper with his teeth and sheathed himself with the latex. It all happened so quickly, so expertly, that all she could do was gasp when he slid fully into her.

Then he paused, still staring down at her, his eyes oddly tender. "All I know is that when I looked across the room that night at the party and saw you, everything changed for me. There was instant recognition. No, I didn't know anything about you at that point, but what I did know was that you were going to be mine. As for that bullshit about me not wanting you after you told me about your past, well, it's just that. Bullshit. We all make mistakes, baby. Nobody is perfect. I'm not. You're not. It would be boring as shit if we were."

Tears pricked her eyelids and he kissed the corner of her eye before any could spill over the edge.

"Don't cry, Bethany. Not here in our bed. Not with me inside you. I want you to shut out everything else except me and you and the way I make you feel. Forget everything but *this*."

He pulled back and then eased forward, pushing gently until he was all the way back in again.

His voice changed, becoming more serious, but his gaze never left her. "I'm not saying this is going to be easy. I'll make mistakes. You'll make mistakes—mostly about trying to draw attention to the differences between us. I realize it'll take time for you to get over this mindset that you're somehow not good enough for me. It pisses me off but I get that you can't change a lifetime of seeing yourself the way you do overnight. But I'm going to work on it and I'm going to wear you down, so just be forewarned. I'm a persistent bastard and I never walk away from something I want, whether in business or my personal life."

She reached up, wrapping her arms around his neck, and pulled him down to meet her kiss. He seemed surprised by the sudden gesture and he let her take control of the kiss.

"Shut up and kiss me," she whispered against his mouth.

He smiled, his lips curving against hers. "Now that I can do, baby."

They went silent as their tongues tangled and clashed, twisting and rolling until she was breathless and panting. He groaned low in his throat and pushed his arms underneath her so he could gather her closer against his body.

His hips arched fluidly, his cock sliding in and out of her body until she was dizzy with pleasure. And he was so close. There wasn't a part of her that he wasn't touching in some way. His body was pressed against her and she could feel every twitch, every time his muscles coiled and bunched with the effort of his movements.

It hit her as he tore his mouth from hers and pressed a line of kisses down her jaw to her neck that this was nothing like the meaningless sex she'd experienced. There was nothing dirty or emotionally bereft about this.

It wasn't even like the threesome she'd had with Jace and Ash.

For the first time in her life, she was making love.

And it sounded absurd. It sounded trite and cheesy and a whole host of other words that escaped her. It made her sound like a silly twit who couldn't separate feelings from sex.

But the simple truth was, the only feelings she'd experienced previously were of shame, self-loathing, embarrassment, hopelessness . . .

She didn't know how to process the bombardment of emotion Jace evoked. She was overwhelmed and not in the way she'd said the day before. He surrounded her, touched her, filled her. Filled places that had long been left hollow and aching. He reached into the very heart of her and spread warmth and contentment.

She hugged him to her, not wanting even the barest of inches to separate them. She clung to him as he rocked into her, deeper, harder, penetrating to her very soul.

Overwhelming? Definitely. Everything about Jace rocked the foundations of her existence. He'd upended her life in a matter of hours and yet she didn't feel panic. Maybe she should. She was back in his bed—after only hours of being back with him—and yet it didn't feel wrong. It didn't feel cheap. And wasn't that what was important?

She closed her eyes, still clinging fiercely to him. She was utterly wrecked by the enormity of what was happening even if she didn't fully comprehend it.

"Baby."

Jace's tender voice pulled her from her scattered thoughts.

"Look at me, baby."

She opened her eyes to see him staring intently down at her. There was concern in his expression and a look of tenderness that matched his tone.

"Are you all right?"

She nodded, not trusting herself to voice her response.

"You sure?"

Again she nodded and hugged him tighter. "Kiss me."

"You never have to ask for that."

He kissed her. Fierce. Possessive. She shivered and arched her body, only wanting to be closer to him.

"How close are you?" he whispered.

"Almost there," she whispered back.

"Tell me what you need to get there."

"You," she said. "Just you."

His eyes flashed and his jaw clenched. Then he was kissing her again. Harder. Hot. Until she was breathing his air and he was breathing hers.

They were locked together so tightly that she didn't even know

how he managed to keep thrusting. Her release built low and deep—
so deep that it felt like she was being turned inside out.

It was scary and huge, overwhelming in the best possible way.
This she didn't fear. Not this time. It felt so very right. That should
have scared her too. It was then she realized that no matter how ridiculous it sounded, she trusted him. She trusted him to take care
of her. No matter that she didn't really know him. That they'd only
been together twice and only for a matter of hours. She knew he
wouldn't do anything to hurt her. She just knew it.

"I trust you," she whispered.

She had to give him this. Knew how important it was. He wanted
her trust and at the same time he acknowledged that it would take
time. But she wanted to give this to him now because he was giving
her so much and this was all she had to give him. Nothing else. There
was nothing she could give him that he didn't already have. Except
herself. It wasn't enough but it was what he wanted—what he said he
wanted—and it was the only thing she had to give.

"Ah, baby," he groaned. "You undo me."

He began to move faster, harder. It was as if her words sent him
right over the edge. His control was gone and she reveled in the ferocity of his possession.

She went slick around him and he moved easier, pushing into her
until she gasped at his depth.

And then she began to unravel. Everything she'd held so tightly
within for so long began to loosen.

It was too much. He'd said she undid him, but in truth she was
the one coming completely undone.

She squeezed him tight, never wanting to let go. She wanted to
live in this moment where nothing could touch her, where nothing
else mattered. It was so easy to forget her life, her circumstances.
Because in his arms she was strong. She was worthy.

Gasping his name, she closed her eyes against the sudden surge
of tears, but even then she felt them slide hotly down her cheeks.

Never had she been so devastated by an orgasm, and it seemed such a tawdry word, completely incapable of describing what was happening.

The world blurred around her. All she could feel was him. Inside her. His mouth on her skin. His cock buried deep. Two halves of a whole.

She floated downward, her body weightless, her mind completely adrift. She wasn't even sure she was conscious.

And then she became aware of Jace's weight covering her. He was limp and his chest heaved with exertion, but he felt so good, so solid on top of her. She never wanted him to move.

She pressed her lips to the hollow indention at his collarbone and savored this connection. Savored the feeling of being wanted. Of being cherished and cared for on an emotional level.

He shifted and she started to protest but then she caught sight of his expression and she stopped. He levered up enough that he brought his hand to her face and she realized that her cheeks were wet with her tears.

"Hey," he said gently. "What's this?"

She was embarrassed over her reaction. How could she explain the enormity of this feeling? She tried to look away, but he wouldn't let her. He lowered his head and kissed away the damp trails and then lifted his head to stare into her eyes once more.

"Bethany?"

There was concern in his voice, which made her feel all the more foolish.

"I'm okay," she choked out.

"Are you?"

"I've never been more okay," she said softly.

He seemed to understand then. He smiled and kissed her again.

"Let me get rid of the condom and then we need to talk," he said.

Alarmed, she let him roll off her and waited as he discarded the condom. Then he was back on the bed, reaching for her to tuck her into his side.

He stroked through her hair, silent as he held her against him.

"I don't want anything between us," he finally said.

Not fully understanding what he meant, she stayed quiet as she waited.

"We need to get you an appointment so we can have tests and then we need to put you on birth control. I don't want to wear condoms. I want no barrier between us. I'll, of course, continue to use them until it's safe, but you're mine and I want unfettered access to you. All of you. Are you okay with that?"

Even though she knew—he'd certainly made himself clear—hearing that he had every intention of them having sex on a regular basis threw her for a loop. It all sounded so . . . permanent, and she knew a relationship between them could be anything but.

"Baby? Talk to me. You're too damn quiet. Are you freaked out? Am I moving too fast?"

She nearly laughed. Now he was worried about moving too fast? She didn't even know he had any concept of moving too fast.

"I don't have a problem with birth control. But Jace, we have to talk."

He kissed her, effectively silencing her.

"We don't need to talk about anything other than getting you what you need. What we need," he amended. "It's a fact that you're going to be in my bed. Eventually my apartment. I'm trying to give you space to work this out. I don't want to overwhelm you but you need to know that I'm serious about this. And I'm going to fight any statement from you that begins with you not being with me."

"Wow," she breathed.

"Anything else you need to say?" he asked, amusement coloring his voice.

"I guess not," she murmured.

"Good. Then let's have breakfast and then I'll take you shopping."

"But Jace, what about work? You can't just take off shopping with me on a whim."

"There are perks to being the boss," he said smugly. "One of them being that I can take a few hours off. It's not like I'm going to get fired."

"Well, okay then."

He patted her on the ass and then rolled out of bed, leaving her lying there on her side.

"I'm going to shower right quick and then you can have the bathroom while I start on breakfast. Sound good?"

She nodded, unable to keep the smile from curving her mouth.

He smiled back, his eyes lighting up. "You need to do that more often and if I have my way, you will."

Her brow furrowed in puzzlement. "Do what?"

"Smile."

chapter fourteen

Shopping with Jace was an exhausting, thrilling, completely *baffling* experience. He swept through the department stores and countless boutiques like a man on a mission and he was exacting in his requirements. It occurred to her that he had a lot of experience in shopping for a woman and she didn't like the jealousy that seized her. Until Jace wryly commented that he'd made countless shopping trips with his younger sister over the years.

When it became obvious that Bethany wouldn't choose any of the dreadfully expensive items that Jace was convinced she needed, he forewent asking her altogether and took charge. He bulldozed his way through the stores, pointing out what he wanted in her sizes and had the saleslady collect them.

After outfitting her in all the necessities, from underwear—which was horribly awkward—to bras—equally awkward—to jeans, shirts and dresses she had no clue why she'd ever need, he then purchased sweaters, two coats—one short and one long—and three pairs of fur-lined boots.

"I don't want your feet getting cold," he told her.

She was appalled and at the same time her heart melted at the care he took in picking out every single purchase.

By the end of the five-hour marathon, Bethany's head was spinning and Jace's driver had to help carry all the purchases to the car.

There was a veritable mountain of bags and boxes in the trunk and they still had to stuff many of them in the front seat.

Bethany sagged into the seat, bewildered by the way the day had shaped up. Yes, he'd said he was taking her shopping. She figured he'd buy a coat—since he was so pissed that she didn't own one—and maybe a few items. She'd never expected an entire wardrobe and enough clothes to wear every day for a month without duplication! She didn't even want to know what all this had cost. She'd refused to look at the price tags after she'd made the mistake of peeking at the first one. She'd nearly fainted and Jace had frowned and promptly directed her gaze elsewhere.

Jace reached over for her hand and squeezed. "Everything okay?"

She nodded. "I've never done that before. I mean obviously, but not even on a smaller scale. Most of my shopping—if you can call it that—has been at thrift shops and Goodwill stores."

He scowled. "Those days are over, Bethany. I want you to forget them."

She sighed. Over until he moved on, got over his . . . She wasn't even sure what to call his seeming attraction to her. Whatever it was wouldn't last forever and going back to her life would be even harder afterward. Before it had been all she knew but now? Jace was giving her a taste of how different things could be.

They pulled up in front of a sleek, modern-looking building on the Upper West Side and Jace got out, extending his hand to help her from the car. After instructing his driver to see that the bags were brought up, he directed Bethany toward the entrance.

Once inside, he introduced her to the doorman. Evidently Jace had already notified him that she'd be staying in the apartment because it was more a case of formality than introducing a new situation.

Then Jace gave her a tour of the facilities and the amenities offered by the building. She couldn't imagine taking advantage of any of them. Having an actual apartment was a luxury she couldn't even wrap her mind around. To have all of the extra perks blew her mind.

She was relieved when they finally got on the elevator and rode up to the apartment. Her nerves were shot. She was frazzled by all the shopping and she desperately wanted a quiet place to decompress.

Jace unlocked the door and then held it open for her. "Let's go see your apartment, baby."

Her apartment. She still couldn't comprehend being given an entire apartment. It was insane. Jace was insane. But then she'd already covered that ground.

When she walked in, her breath caught and she stopped dead in the middle of the floor. And she stared. Tears welled and a sob crept out of her throat.

Jace wrapped an arm around her and squeezed. "Baby."

He dragged out the word in an aching voice that made her heart turn over in a fluttery cartwheel.

"It's beautiful, Jace," she whispered.

"Yeah?"

"It's perfect."

He smiled and kissed her on the nose. "And you haven't seen it all yet."

"I've seen enough to know it's perfect."

And it was. The living room and kitchen blended together in one large room with an open concept she loved. But the color scheme was what made it absolutely perfect. Done in earth tones, the room—the entire apartment—had a homey, cozy feel that was the epitome of everything she'd ever wanted in a place to live.

And the kitchen was state-of-the-art stainless steel appliances. A chef's stove. And it looked to be fully stocked with cookware and cutlery. Her hands itched to get into that kitchen and cook.

"Come on," he said. "I'll show you the rest and by then your bags should be up."

They did a brief tour of the bedrooms and the bathrooms and

when they came back there was a growing pile of bags being deposited inside the door. A moment later, a tall, very muscular man strode through the door followed by a slightly shorter and stockier man. They both looked like guys out of a bodybuilding magazine. Beefed-up arms. They just *looked* like badasses.

The man in the lead had shades that he flipped up and Bethany instinctively pushed in closer to Jace's side, seeking his protection. These men reminded her too much of her run-in with the guys who'd wanted money from Jack.

"They won't hurt you," Jace murmured.

He slipped his arm around her and squeezed her against him. Instantly she felt . . . better. More secure. It didn't matter that the men were twice Jace's size. Veritable mountains and they looked . . . questionable at best. She was next to Jace and he wouldn't allow anyone to hurt her.

At Jace's words, the front man pulled up short and frowned. He held up his hand to halt the other guy and they both stood a short distance away, careful to maintain the space between them and where she stood.

"Mr. Crestwell," the front man said. "I'm Kaden Ginsberg and this is Trevor Dixon."

Jace extended his arm, stepping forward to shake each of their hands. "Thank you both for coming."

He turned and motioned Bethany forward. Hesitantly, she stepped in Jace's direction and eyed the two newcomers with caution.

Jace held out his hand for Bethany to take and she slipped her fingers into his. He laced them together and tugged her forward so she was once again at his side.

"This is your security team."

She couldn't formulate a response. Security team? Why on earth did she have a security team? She cast a bewildered look in Jace's direction.

"Why?"

The one word came out cracked and hoarse.

His lips pressed together in a gesture of impatience. Then he turned to Kaden and Trevor. "Let's sit in the living room. We have a lot to talk about. I want your absolute assurance that Bethany will be safe in your care when I can't be with her."

Kaden nodded. "Of course."

Jace put a hand to Bethany's back and urged her toward the couch. He sat down next to her, linking his fingers with hers. They were so close that their thighs touched. She leaned in closer as she cautiously eyed Kaden and Trevor. They sat across from the couch in two chairs that looked far too small for their bulky frames.

"You look like professional wrestlers," she blurted. Then she felt like a complete moron and she dropped her gaze to stare at her and Jace's linked hands.

Kaden chuckled, forcing her to look back up. He had a really good laugh. Not at all mean sounding. It was soft and vibrated over her ears. It was . . . nice.

"It helps in my line of work, ma'am."

"Oh yeah," she muttered.

Jace squeezed her hand and then directed his attention toward her security team. She felt ridiculous calling them that. The whole thing seemed so utterly bizarre that she couldn't wrap her head around it.

He glanced back at Bethany, his eyes serious. "Kaden and Trevor will accompany you everywhere when I'm not with you. They'll shadow your every move—and I do mean every move. When you're here, they'll be here. If you go out, they go with you."

Her eyes widened. "But why? I don't get it. Jace, this is crazy. I'm nobody. Nobody cares about me. I have nothing, so no one has any investment in me. There's nothing to gain by kidnapping me or God knows what else you're thinking."

Jace sighed. "Do you forget that a day ago those bastards had you on the ground? That they kicked you and threatened you? They gave you a week to respond. What do you think's going to happen when that week comes and goes, Bethany? Think they're just going to forget about you because they suddenly can't find you where you usually hang? I'm going to make sure they don't get anywhere near you and part of doing that means Kaden and Trevor here are going to stick to you when I can't be with you. Which means that you go nowhere without them. You understand?"

"You really think they'll find me here?" she whispered.

"Let's just say I'm not taking any chances."

Kaden cleared his throat. "Ma'am," he said politely. "Men like that don't give up easily. They have a point to prove. If they don't make those points, they lose street cred. If it's perceived they wimped out on collecting a debt, it means more people will decide not to pay up. They operate on fear and intimidation. If people cease to fear them, then they are rendered ineffective and they go out of business. They aren't going to let that happen, so yes, they will make the effort to come after you. Trevor and I are going to make sure they don't succeed."

Her mouth formed a silent O and she stared wide-eyed at Jace.

"You understand now?" Jace asked quietly.

She nodded but she was still reeling from all the sudden changes in her life.

Jace's driver brought in a small bag and handed it to Jace. It wasn't one she recognized, though there'd been so many that she lost track of them hours ago.

Jace pulled out a box, opening it to reveal a brand-new cell phone. He popped the battery in, powered it up and then fiddled with it for several long minutes. Then he pulled out his cell and punched buttons before finally tossing the phone toward Kaden.

"Program your numbers into her phone. I want her to have you on speed dial in case anything ever goes wrong."

Bethany's eyebrows drew together as Kaden and then Trevor rapidly punched buttons before returning the phone to Jace. Then Jace handed her the phone.

"I programmed my number in. It's number one on speed dial. Kaden is number two and Trevor is number three. My office number is four and my apartment is number five. Carry this phone on you at all times, and if you don't want me freaking out thinking you're in an alley dead somewhere, then you better damn well answer when I call. Got it?"

Numbly, she nodded. Holy shit but her head was spinning in circles. She could barely breathe and her head was starting to ache horribly. Fairy tales didn't happen for girls like her and yet she'd walked right into the middle of one. But this one wasn't destined for a happily-ever-after. That only happened in fiction. She was too well acquainted with the way things worked in real life. Real life sucked. But it was real. It was unapologetic. It made no excuses. It just was.

Jace leaned over and kissed her forehead. "I've got to run into the office. I have a meeting I can't miss, but I won't be gone long. Kaden and Trevor will stay with you until I get back. Groceries will be delivered soon as well. Make sure one of them answers the door and you stay out of sight until they give you the all-clear. And whatever you do, listen to whatever they tell you. Their job is to keep you safe. Make it as easy for them as possible by cooperating. Okay?"

"Okay," she murmured.

"If you need anything, call me. I'll have my cell on me even during my meeting."

She nodded mechanically.

He kissed her again. "We'll go out for dinner. Wear one of your new outfits and be sure to bring your damn coat. It's supposed to snow tonight. Then we'll spend the night here so you can get acquainted with your new apartment."

She marveled at how arrogantly he assumed he would be staying with her. She also marveled at the fact that she didn't correct him.

Didn't offer argument. And she marveled at the relief that surged through her blood when she knew she wouldn't be alone.

Lost. Already she was lost in him. So completely immersed that she wasn't sure she'd ever find her way out again. When he decided to walk away, it would break her in a way nothing else ever had. Her life. Her addiction. Her fuck-ups.

He had power over her that she'd never imagined another entity having. And that scared her more than the thought of drugs, sex or the men who'd threatened her.

chapter fifteen

Jace strode into the building that housed the HCM offices and rode the elevator up. If he didn't have this damn meeting, he would have ditched work altogether today. He didn't like leaving Bethany on her own so soon after he got her back.

No, she technically wasn't on her own, but he still didn't like leaving her to fend for herself.

When he walked into Gabe's office a few minutes later, he saw that Ash was already there—as was Gabe—and the way Gabe looked at him, that flash of concern in his eyes, he knew that Ash had been running his mouth.

Jace's mouth set into a firm line and he plopped into the chair in front of Gabe's desk.

"Let's get this over with," Jace said tersely.

Ash didn't meet his gaze and instead stared straight ahead at Gabe. That was fine with Jace. He didn't have time for the intervention both of his friends were likely plotting.

Gabe frowned but didn't offer argument. Jace was five minutes late—not typical for him at all. Ash and Gabe were probably convinced he'd lost his goddamn mind.

Maybe for the first time he'd found it. He and Ash had been fucking the same women for years. How messed up was that? Gabe didn't blink an eye over that practice. But he was going to pass judgment because Jace had finally found a woman he had no intention of sharing?

And Gabe had no damn room to talk anyway. He'd lost his freaking mind over Mia. Jace's sister, for Christ's sake. Jace hadn't ripped Gabe's head off, though he absolutely should have. The bastard had been pathetic enough without Jace heaping more punishment.

Jace blinked when he realized they were already well into the meeting and he had no clue what had been discussed so far. When there was a prolonged silence, Jace figured out quickly that they were all waiting for his input. Damn it.

Ash sent him a look of disgust and then plowed ahead with the information Jace should have provided. Ash handled it like a pro, his charming, polished mannerisms easily winning over the group of investors on the other end of the line.

Jace gave a sigh of relief when it was finally over. Ash packed up his shit and walked out of Gabe's office, never once speaking to Jace. Real mature. Jace shook his head and prepared his own exit. He was already thinking ahead to where he wanted to take Bethany for dinner. He'd call her on his way out and give her a heads-up so she could get ready.

"Jace, a minute, if you don't mind."

Gabe's quiet tone filtered through Jace's thoughts. He frowned when he saw Gabe's expression.

Fuck.

He wasn't down for a come-to-Jesus moment with Gabe. Why the hell couldn't his friends just back the fuck off?

Even as he thought it, he acknowledged that he wouldn't do the same if the positions were reversed. He'd gotten into Gabe's face plenty during his time with Mia. But goddamn it, Mia was Jace's sister. He had a vested interest in Gabe's treatment of her. Bethany had absolutely no connection to Gabe or Ash. Well, not unless you counted the fact that she'd fucked Ash, but Jace was trying his best to forget that fact.

The image of his best friend with a woman Jace considered his was burned into his mind. He may never get rid of the sight of Ash's mouth and hands on her skin.

"Make it quick," Jace growled.

He stood, refusing to sit, because sitting gave leeway for this to become an extended thing. Jace had better things to do. Like take his woman to dinner and then take her home and fuck her.

"What the hell is going on with you, man?" Gabe asked softly.

Jace made a sound of impatience. "Nothing is going on with me."

"That's not what Ash says."

"Ash needs to keep his fucking mouth shut."

Gabe's frown deepened. "What's going on with you and Ash? This isn't like you. Ash is as tight-lipped as you are, but it's obvious you're pissed at each other. He said you're all sorts of fucked up over a woman. Anything you want to talk about?"

"Bethany is not up for discussion," Jace said in a frigid tone. "Besides, if there's anything you want to know, I'm sure Ash's background check will provide fodder for gossip between you two."

Gabe's expression turned from concern to pissed off in two seconds flat. "What the fuck is up your ass, Jace? I'm not gossiping about anyone. I don't know fuck about some goddamn background check. I don't even know who the hell Bethany is and I'm damn sure not gossiping about her with Ash. Ash hasn't said fuck-all either, for that matter."

Jace knew he was being a dick. He knew he was a flaming hypocrite. He'd never let his friends get away with the shit he was pulling. But he was still pissed at Ash for trying to warn him off Bethany. And if he were completely honest, he was still pissed that Ash had fucked her. Maybe he'd never forgive Ash for that even though Jace had gone along with it. Even with his instincts screaming like a motherfucker, he'd allowed it to happen. He'd hated every goddamn minute of it, but he'd still let it happen. Maybe he hated himself most of all.

"Bethany is someone I care about," Jace said, forcing himself to speak calmly. "That's all you need to know. She needs help—my help—and there's no way in fuck I'm turning my back on her."

"Do you need my help?" Gabe asked.

And there it was. The unconditional friendship that had existed since they were in college. Always there, at each other's backs. They'd taken some knocks, no doubt. Gabe's relationship with Mia had been the most recent threat. But not even the fact that Gabe was fucking Jace's baby sister and that he'd broken her heart in the process had been able to destroy the bonds of friendship that existed between them.

Gabe had made things right with Mia. He'd made them right with Jace.

Jace sighed and then his hands relaxed, his fingers uncurling from the tight fists they'd formed.

"No, man, but I appreciate it," he said in a low voice. "I'm not crazy. I'm not obsessed." Okay, maybe he was, but it sounded a hell of a lot creepier than it was in reality. "This is something I have to—*need* to—do. Bethany's different. She's *special*. And I don't even completely understand why or how. But I saw her and things changed. Everything changed. And I have to go with it now or spend the rest of my life regretting it."

"I get that," Gabe said slowly. "Believe me, I get that."

"Yeah, I guess you do. Mia," Jace said by way of saying he understood.

"Yeah. Mia."

"Then you get why I just need some space and time to deal with this my own way."

Gabe nodded. "I get it. Ash would too, if you just explained. He's pissed, Jace. Not because of Bethany. Not because you've seemingly gone off your hinges. He's pissed because he's worried about you and you've shut him out. You more than anyone know he'd do anything in the goddamn world for you."

Jace briefly closed his eyes as guilt sludged through his veins. "Yeah, I know."

Fuck it all. He hated it when Gabe was right. Smug, superior bastard. Even now he had that knowing glint in his eyes.

"I gotta get out of here. I left Bethany at the apartment. She's taking Mia's old place."

Gabe lifted an eyebrow in clear confusion. "Surprised you didn't lock her up in your place. Ash said things were pretty . . . intense."

"How the fuck would he know?" Jace muttered. "I wanted to give her some space. Some time to adjust before I just take over. And you know that's what will happen. Me taking over. It's inevitable and I want her secure and confident in herself—in me—before this turns into something else entirely."

Gabe nodded. Yeah, he'd understand better than anyone. Except Ash. The need and desire for control was a trait all three shared. Not just in certain aspects. In everything. In and out of bed. But yeah, *especially* in bed.

Bethany had seen nothing of the way things would be with him and she was already so fragile, so damn unsure of herself and her place in the world, that Jace was extremely reluctant to move things too fast. If he scared her shitless and she ran, he'd never forgive himself.

"Work this out with Ash," Gabe said quietly. "You know it'll eat at you both until you do. And before you bitch because I'm getting too personal, this affects the business too. We can't afford fuck-ups because you and Ash are at fucking odds. And if you won't think of me, the business and your own self and the fact that you'll feel like a complete asshole for throwing away a nearly lifelong friendship, think what it will do to Mia. She loves you both. Think what it'll do for Bethany if she ever finds out she drove a wedge between friends and business partners."

"Jesus, you're a manipulative bastard," Jace said in disgust.

Gabe's mouth quirked up at one corner. "Mia has said that about me a time or two."

Jace shook his head. Then he changed the subject because he was tired of having his personal life dissected by his best friend.

"Decided on a wedding date yet?"

"Fuck me," Gabe muttered.

Jace's eyebrow went up and he laughed. Then he laughed harder. "Wish you could see yourself, man. You look like you swallowed a lemon. What the hell is my sister doing to you?"

Gabe ran a hand through his hair. "Look. I just want to get married. I want my ring on her finger, her last name to be mine, her signature on a marriage certificate. Everything else is inconsequential. I'd do whatever she wanted, whether it was holding the mother of all weddings, the likes of which this city has never seen, or eloping to Vegas."

Jace winced. "Uh, if I get any kind of vote, can we not go with 'the likes of which this city has never seen'? That sounds all kinds of fucked up."

"Tell me about it," Gabe muttered.

"So what's the problem? Sounds like you're being uncharacteristically accommodating."

Gabe ignored the ribbing. His expression was utterly serious when he responded. "I love her. I'd do whatever the hell it took for her to be mine. This wedding is for *her*. I've been there, done that, didn't want to do it again at all until her. The problem is, she hasn't decided what she wants. And until she does, the wedding is on hold. I don't know the date because there is no fucking date. Part of me wants to lay down the law and tell her we're getting married at New Year's but the other part of me wants this to be special for her because it's the *only* goddamn wedding she's ever going to have."

Jace smiled. It was funny as hell to see his friend in knots over a woman. Especially since the woman in question was Jace's baby sister. Some of the tension in his chest eased. This was his family. Gabe. Ash. Mia. Always had been. It had been the four of them for nearly twenty years. And family looked out for family. Hell, he got ten kinds of pissed every time Ash's family gave him shit. He'd damn near taken Gabe's head off for hurting Mia. And then he'd felt sorry for the bastard and hated to see him hurting when Mia refused to accept his groveling.

"You're family, man," Jace whispered. "Never going to forget that."

Gabe blinked, but his jaw tightened. "Always. We'll become brothers by marriage, but we were brothers long before that. Just thank God I never viewed Mia as a little sister—or at least that shit stopped when she hit adulthood."

Jace burst out laughing and held his hands up. "Okay, okay, can we not have this conversation? She *is* my sister and I do not want to hear how you see her. It's disgusting enough having to watch you two together."

Gabe grinned and then he grew somber once more. "Go make this right, Jace. Ash is hurting. His family is giving him shit. You know it's that time of the year. They don't give a shit about him ten months out of the year and then they want to pretend at Thanksgiving and Christmas. And now this with you . . . I know we're all three friends. I don't ever question it. But I also know that you two are closer. Always have been. Whatever happened between you hit him hard. He hasn't been himself. He's all brooding and silent. Now you, I expect that from. Total brooding, moody bastard on a good day."

Jace flipped him the finger.

"But Ash? That's not like him. He's irreverent as shit and has a fuck-it-all attitude. Fix this. I worry about both of you and if it's all the same to you, right now I don't want to worry about either of you. All I want to worry about is getting my ring on Mia's finger and moving forward with the babies she wants."

Jace groaned. "Christ, man, really? You had to go there?"

Gabe smirked. "Hey, I didn't give you details."

"Thank fuck," Jace muttered. Then he sighed. "And yeah. Ash. I'm on it."

He started for the door but when he got there he paused and turned around.

"Thanks, man," he said sincerely. "I know I've probably never said this. At first I was too pissed off to ever give you this. But I'm glad Mia has you. She'll never find a better man. I know you'll take care of her."

For a long moment Gabe was silent. His jaw ticked like he was trying to keep his reaction in check. Then he simply nodded. "Appreciate that, man. You'll never know how much."

Jace smiled faintly. "Oh, I think I do."

Again he started to go and then Gabe's call halted him as he got into the hall.

"Jace?"

"Yeah?"

"When am I going to meet her?"

Jace gripped Gabe's doorknob and breathed deeply. Then he met Gabe's gaze and said, "When it's time, you will. Absolutely. Right now there's a lot we have to work out."

Gabe nodded. "Good luck."

"Thanks, man," Jace murmured.

Then he turned and went in search of Ash.

chapter sixteen

Jace leaned against the doorway of Ash's office and waited for his friend to get off the phone. Ash was turned away—he had no idea Jace was standing there or that he'd opened the closed office door. Which meant that the phone call was absorbing all of Ash's concentration because he hadn't so much as acknowledged Jace's presence.

"I don't really give a fuck what you and Dad want," Ash said acidly.

Jace grimaced. Gabe was right. Ash's family was fucking with him again. Persistent assholes. Jace had never known of a more shallow, self-absorbed lot than Ash's family. Jace was mystified how Ash had come from a pit of vipers and not been shaped or influenced by them. God knew the rest of his siblings hadn't fared as well.

Gabe and Jace both used to tease Ash about being adopted. It was the only logical conclusion. Ash was so different than his parents and his siblings. Where they were calculating, selfish malcontents, Ash was laid back, had a good heart and was loyal to his bones. His family? Would stab you in the back before you ever got all the way turned around. Hell, they'd stab you in front. They didn't give a shit. They'd leave their shoe prints all over you on their way past.

"Your manipulation won't work. There is no way in hell I'd spend Christmas with my *beloved* family. I'd rather have my fingernails plucked out with pliers," Ash bit out.

Jace sighed. Same old shit. Every fucking year. He was convinced they only wanted Ash around so they'd have someone new to torment. When Ash had been younger, he'd made the attempt to keep peace, to be a good son and brother. He'd attended the family gatherings—such as they were.

The first two years, he'd gone alone. Gabe and Jace had immediately noticed a difference. Ash had brooded for weeks after and it had taken a long time for him to get back to himself. After the second year of that shit, Jace and Gabe put two and two together and the next year, they'd insisted on going with him. After that experience, they both had vowed never to allow Ash anywhere near his family without a solid support network.

It may seem ridiculous, but Ash's family was fucking *poison*.

After a few years of either Jace or Gabe or both accompanying him and witnessing firsthand the dysfunction that was the McIntyre family, Ash had told his family to fuck off and he hadn't gone back. Not for lack of trying on their part. Jace knew that Ash was deeply shamed by his friends seeing his family and instead of letting them continue to see his family in action, he'd simply pulled the plug. Which suited Jace just fine. Ash was a better person when he wasn't around the cesspool. He was happier.

"We're done with this conversation. Don't call back. I won't take your call next time," Ash warned.

He hung up the office phone and then swiveled in his chair. He did a double take when he saw Jace standing in the doorway and then he frowned.

"What are you doing here? Would have thought you had shit to do."

Jace sighed again and sauntered farther into the office. He slouched in one of the chairs along the wall and put his hands behind his back, leaning so he could pull Ash into his gaze.

"Look, man, I was an asshole. You know it. I know it. I also know you just got finished talking to your bitch of a mother and now you're in a shitty mood so you'll bite at me. I deserve it, so I'm okay with it. What I'm not okay with is this space between us."

Ash's lips tightened. "You put it there, man."

"Yeah, I get that too. I'm trying to apologize here, Ash. Don't be a hard ass. Let me do it."

Ash leaned back and drawled in a familiar tone that sent relief through Jace's chest, "The mighty, arrogant, demanding bastard Jace Crestwell humbling himself to make an apology? Do go on. This I gotta see."

"Fuck you," Jace muttered. But he was already grinning.

Family.

Just as he'd observed in Gabe's office. Just as he knew—had always known. This was his family. And it was a family he wanted Bethany to have too.

"Now that's an unusual apology," Ash said. "Fuck you . . . I'm sorry . . . They sound *almost* the same."

Jace laughed. "God, you are such a dickhead."

Just as quickly, he sobered and met Ash's gaze.

"I'm sorry, man. I was a dick. I overreacted. I know you were trying to help. Trying to look out for me. I appreciate it. More than you know. But I'm good. I promise. You may think I'm crazy. That I've lost all perspective. But I've got this. I'm solid."

"What do you have?" Ash asked curiously. "You have to see this from *my* perspective, man. We have a threesome with a woman. Not unusual. Woman disappears next morning. Not unusual. The only atypical part of this equation is that she walked away instead of us issuing her the walking papers. So when you go apeshit over the fact she left, I'm thinking, okay, he's pissed because he wasn't the one cutting her loose this time. And I get it. Maybe you weren't done with her. You're a control freak like me. You like to make the rules. She broke them when she walked out. What I did not expect was for you to turn the city upside down looking for her."

Jace sighed. Yeah, when Ash described it, things sounded bad.

"If you could have seen yourself these last two weeks, Jace. You looked like shit. You were absentminded. The very last thing on your mind was work. Mia came in to see you twice and you blew her off both times."

Jace's brows came together. "Bullshit. She didn't come in to see me."

Ash sighed. "You don't even remember her coming in? Or do you just not remember being a dick to her?"

"Christ. She really came to see me?"

Ash nodded. "You bit her fucking head off, which prompted Gabe to want to bash your skull in. I told him to back off, that you were having a bad day."

"Shit."

"So there you are, barely existing in those two weeks. Acting like some insane, obsessed person. So I do some checking. Then you find her and go off half-cocked. Then I don't see you again until a few minutes ago and you act like nothing happened. All of this after you told me to stay out of it and that it didn't concern me."

Jace blew out his breath and rubbed his hand over the top of his head. "Okay, you've made your point. I was a dick. That was out of line and we both know it."

Ash made a rude noise. "I don't give a fuck that you were a dick. You think this is about my feelings being hurt? I'm worried about *you*, Jace. Worried about how wrapped up in this woman you are. I'm worried that she's all wrong for you and you can't see it because she's got her fingers wrapped around your balls."

Jace breathed through the instant surge of anger that hit him. Ash was his friend. He was worried. Jace was going to be rational about this if it killed him.

"She needs me," Jace said, fully aware of how lame it sounded. But fuck, he couldn't even explain it himself. How the hell was he supposed to explain it to Ash?

Ash studied him a long moment and then his lips parted with a sigh. "This is going to piss you off, but it needs to be said. I could back off, let you do your thing, but we both know if the situations were reversed and this was me acting the way you've been acting that you'd be in my face and you wouldn't back off. So hell if I'm going to do it. You're my brother. More of a brother than my own. You and Gabe both. We busted his balls over Mia. He deserved it. Now I'm going to bust yours over Bethany. Because someone has to."

Jace's fingers clenched and he was tempted to walk out. But Ash's words seared through his anger, effectively taking the wind out of his sails. They *were* brothers. In every sense of the word. And yeah, he wasn't so pissed off that he didn't realize he'd absolutely be busting Ash's balls if his friend had pulled a stunt like this.

"Just say it then," Jace said in resignation.

"You took care of Mia for a lot of years," Ash said in a quiet tone. "Always looked out for her. Hell, you were father *and* brother to her. She needed you. Now suddenly she doesn't. Not in the way she did before. She's no longer your responsibility. She has Gabe and her focus is going to be primarily on him."

"What are you getting at?"

Ash blew out a long breath. "Don't you find it ironic that within days of Mia becoming engaged to Gabe that your head is turned by a woman in need? And I don't dispute she needs help, Jace. I'm not an asshole. Her situation is ten kinds of fucked up. But the fact is, you're a provider. A caretaker. And Bethany is your Kryptonite. She's down on her luck. She's pretty. And you like the idea that she needs you. Have you considered that maybe you need a break from being a sole provider and that maybe you should live a little without becoming weighted down by another person in need?"

"What the fuck is all of that?" Jace demanded. "Are you even listening to yourself? Mia wasn't some kind of goddamn weight. She's my sister. I'm her only family. I have never once resented having to take care of her."

Ash held up his hand. "You know damn well that's not what I'm saying. Pull your head out of your ass. Mia belongs to all of us. I never suggested for one minute that she was some kind of unpleasant burden. I was there while she grew up. I have almost as much invested in her happiness as you do, okay? That's not my point. Mia was never my point. My point is that you're at loose ends now that Mia has Gabe and she no longer needs you in the same way she did before. And you latched on to Bethany, who is like Mia only ten times more in need. You saw a woman in need and that appealed to the provider in you. Not saying it isn't noble. Not saying you're a dick for wanting to help her. What I am suggesting is that you're in too deep and that you need to take a step back and gain some perspective. You can help her without becoming so fucking emotionally invested. What do you really know about her? You're acting like you're goddamn soul mates and you know fuck all about her."

"I'm going to ask you to shut up now before you really piss me off," Jace bit out.

"So I'm wrong?"

Hell yes he was wrong. Wasn't he?

Shit.

All that psychological crap Ash spouted spun around in Jace's mind. And it *was* crap.

When all else failed, honesty was always the best way to go. It wasn't as if he and Ash weren't always straight with one another. The idea of trying to dissect whatever this was—this *obsession* with Bethany, as Ash had labeled it—made him twitchy.

Jace dragged a hand through his hair and was tempted to pull it out in frustration. "Look, Ash. I won't bullshit you by saying I have all the answers, okay? But if you're trying to say that I have some kind of savior complex when it comes to Bethany, you're wrong. I was interested in her from the moment I saw her at Mia's party and I damn sure didn't know all the crap about her that I know now. I didn't know she was homeless or that her situation was so crappy. I just knew I wanted her. And that didn't change when I found out all this other stuff. All it did was make me more determined that I was going to be a part of her life."

Ash's expression grew pensive but he remained silent as Jace struggled with how to explain his reaction to Bethany.

"How fucking shallow would it be of me to back away from her once I found out that her situation isn't the best in the world? Like she's suddenly not good enough for me? That shouldn't matter, right? If I was interested in getting close to her before then, that shouldn't change just because she doesn't measure up to my financial status or because she doesn't have a place to sleep."

"Christ," Ash muttered. "Now I feel about three inches tall."

Jace stifled the smile that twitched the corner of his mouth. It would be okay. Ash was nothing if not a huge softie. Especially when it came to women. Ash may not have acted like it, but Jace knew that at the core of this all was Ash's deep concern for him. He got that. He appreciated it. But Ash had to understand that this wasn't some fucking charity case.

"I'm guessing I won't be invited to another threesome," Ash said dryly.

Jace scowled and Ash held up his hands.

"I get it. She's yours."

"This isn't a joke," Jace said darkly. "I'd like to forget that three-some ever happened. And when you see Bethany—and you *will* see her—I really don't want this to be a topic of conversation. It's going to be awkward as hell. I don't want her to be embarrassed. I don't want to give her any reason at all to back away. I'm already having one hell of a time making her see things my way. And I really want to forget the fact that you've seen her naked. That you've had your dick in places that, from now on, are mine and mine alone."

Ash shook his head, his expression priceless. "Holy fuck, man. You're serious. I mean, really serious. I never thought in a million years that you'd fall so fucking hard for a woman in so short a time. How long did it take? Five minutes? Hell, I should have seen it that night, but how could I have? You've never acted that way over a woman. You were growly and possessive from the start but I ignored it."

Ash leaned forward, his arms planted on the desk. "I know I asked this but now I really have to ask. If you felt this way about her, then why the hell didn't you just tell me? That night should have never happened. For God's sake, *why* did you let me fuck her?"

Jace closed his eyes briefly and when he reopened them Ash was staring a hole through him. There was genuine confusion in his friend's eyes. And regret. As though he feared that night was forever going to be a bone of contention between them. Jace didn't want it to be. Maybe he was being naïve. It was fact that Bethany and Ash would cross paths again. If she was going to be a part of Jace's life—and she absolutely was—then she and Ash would see each other a lot. He wasn't about to turn his back on a friendship that was as deep as any blood tie. But what if it made things forever awkward?

Ash could deal. Of that Jace was positive. But the unknown in the equation was Bethany. How would she react to Ash? Did she have feelings for him? Did she still desire him? It was obvious she had been turned on by both men when they'd had sex with her. Would Jace have to always worry that Bethany would be looking in Ash's direction or that she'd even pursue him? .

It was enough to drive him crazy and it was stupid to dwell so hard on that. He wasn't being fair to Bethany. It was obvious she was freaked out by that night and the fact she'd had a threesome with him and Ash. He couldn't assume the worst about her and be suspicious before he ever gave her a chance. Their relationship would be doomed by jealousy and mistrust before it ever had a chance to get off the ground.

"Jace?" Ash asked in a quiet voice. "Why'd you let it happen, man? I don't get it. You have to know I would have understood. I would have been surprised as hell, but I would have absolutely backed off. I'd never let a woman come between us."

But Jace had. Hell, he'd put Bethany between them because he'd been desperate and he'd seen her waver. He'd been so afraid of having her walk away that he'd hastily agreed to something he was vehemently against.

It hadn't been fair to Bethany and it sure as hell hadn't been fair to Ash.

"I fucked up," Jace said in just as quiet a voice. "It was completely my fault. I thought at the time it was what I *had* to do. Before I could step in and put an end to it, she agreed. And once she agreed, I didn't feel like I could say never mind, we're not having a threesome, but oh by the way, I still want to take you home and fuck you. And then she seemed to have second thoughts and I panicked because I didn't want her to walk away. It was all so goddamn fucked up and it got out of control before I could fix it. And I regret every single minute."

Something flickered in Ash's eyes and he went silent. He settled back in his chair and looked away.

"Is this going to change things?" Ash finally said. "Between you and me? You sound like Bethany's going to be around a long time. What does that mean for us because of that night?"

Unease crawled over Jace's skin. If only he could go back to that night, he'd never say a goddamn thing to Ash. He'd have never brought Bethany to his attention. And he damn sure would have never fucked her with Ash.

And now Ash was voicing the same concerns that Jace had himself. This was huge. He could not let his relationship with Bethany ruin his relationships with the people who meant the most to him. But neither could he let her go. He had to make this work, which meant handling the entire situation as delicately as possible.

"All it changes is that you're not sleeping with her again," Jace said with more confidence than he felt. He hoped to hell he wasn't deluding himself. "I'm sure the first couple of times that we're all together will be awkward. But it'll only stay awkward if we make it that way. You're both in my life, man. I'm not choosing between you.

I hope to fuck I never have to. All we can do is make sure it doesn't become an issue. But I need your help. Your . . . support."

Relief simmered in Ash's eyes. "You going to name your first kid after me?"

"Jesus. Now who's moving fast? Pump the brakes, Ash. I'm not marrying her."

"Yet," Ash muttered.

"There's a hell of a lot we have to work out," Jace said in a grim voice.

"Anything I can help with? You asked for my support, but man, you gotta know you have that. You've always had it. That's not going to change."

Jace hesitated for only a moment, relief buzzing through his blood like potent alcohol. Then he related the entire chain of events involving Bethany from start to end. When he finished, Ash's face was contorted into a fierce scowl.

"Motherfuckers," he swore. "They beat up a helpless woman because her asshole brother borrowed money he had no way of paying back? And the little bastard hung her out to dry? Jesus, my family may be batshit crazy but they've never sicced a bunch of street thugs on me."

Jace snorted. "Not yet, anyway."

A glimmer of amusement lighted Ash's eyes. "True. Give them time."

There was a lengthy pause. Silent understanding.

"I don't like you getting involved. I know some people. I can get them on it. Make sure the assholes get their money and a message not to fuck with Bethany again," Ash said. "That is, if that's the way you want it to go down. I assume you want that debt paid."

"You know people?" Jace said incredulously. "What the hell, man? What kind of people do you know who would handle a situation like this? And yeah, whatever it takes. I want the debt to go away. Not because I give a fuck about her asshole brother but because

I want Bethany safe and I want her removed from any possible situation that threatens her."

Ash shrugged. "Never know when you might need these kinds of people. They owe me a favor anyway. I gave them good stock tips. And I comped their stay in one of our hotels."

"I'm not even going to ask . . ."

"Better that way," Ash said cheerfully. "Not people you'd invite to Thanksgiving dinner anyway."

"I'm getting that," Jace muttered.

Ash's expression became more serious. "How much money are we talking here?"

"Five thousand."

"That's all?"

Jace sighed. "It's a fortune to Bethany. As she said, it may as well be a million. She was going to fucking *peddle* to raise the cash."

It still scared the hell out of him to think what could have happened if Kate hadn't called him the day Bethany wandered into the shelter. Or what would have happened if Bethany hadn't gone back. That she could even now be on the streets and vulnerable to God knew what . . .

"Fuck," Ash bit out. "Jesus Christ. *Peddling?*"

"Yeah, that pretty much sums up my reaction."

"She needs a fucking leash," Ash muttered.

"Figuratively, she's going to have one," Jace said calmly. "She's not going anywhere without the men I hired to protect her and when she's not with them, she'll be with me. Hopefully once you arrange for her debt to be paid that threat goes away. But I still have to address the issue of Jack."

"Well, and it doesn't appear that she's sold on the idea of you two as a couple yet," Ash said dryly.

"She will be."

Ash lifted an eyebrow. "You sound confident."

"I won't entertain the alternative."

"And that is?"

"Her not being a part of my life."

There was a pregnant pause and Ash shifted uncomfortably. "Look man, I'm way overstepping my boundaries here."

"As if that's stopped you before," Jace said dryly.

Ash chuckled. "True. Not a fan of boundaries, particularly where my family is concerned."

Again that word. *Family*. And yeah, Ash, Gabe and Mia were his family. He'd said that Mia was the only family he had and that wasn't true. Gabe and Ash . . . They'd been there. Always been there. Stepping in when his parents had died. Steady, unwavering loyalty the likes of which Jace had never imagined.

Maybe he'd taken it for granted over the years. It had been a huge mistake. Other people didn't have this. Unconditional support. He was lucky.

"How is this going to work?" Ash asked. "You and Bethany. I know you, man. You and I, we're alike. Hell, so is Gabe. Cut from the same cloth. We like control. Dominance. Not the pretend kind. We can play it light, but that's all it is. Playing. At the end of the day, you and I both know that any serious relationship is going to be about ultimate control."

Jace nodded. He didn't even attempt to deny it.

"So how is this going to play out with Bethany? Is she ready for that from you? Is she prepared? Does she even have a fucking clue how it's going to be? Because with another woman, she gets freaked out, she doesn't go far. Back to her apartment. You know where to pick up. You call her or go see her. Work it out. That isn't the case with Bethany. She freaks, she runs, you may never see her again."

"Fuck, don't you think I know that?"

It came out more explosively than he intended but it was a testament to the uncertainty he felt when it came to this woman. How fucking helpless he was and how Ash had managed to voice his biggest fear.

If he didn't play this just right. If he came on too hard. If he did anything to scare Bethany, she could bolt. Back into the night. Back onto the streets, where those assholes—and a million others—waited. Where he couldn't protect her. Couldn't take care of her. Where he'd be absolutely fucking helpless to save her from the dangers of being alone and vulnerable.

"So what are you going to do?" Ash asked quietly. "How you going to play this?"

"I don't know," Jace said in resignation. "Fuck if I know. I know what I want. I just have to hope like hell that I play it right. And I have to hope it's what she wants and can accept from me."

chapter seventeen

Bethany submerged in the huge sunken tub and blew gently at the suds foaming close to her mouth. She felt positively decadent. Like someone from a movie. She'd piled her hair on top of her head in a messy arrangement that she thought looked rather sexy. Pinned-up tendrils floating down. Suds climbing from the water and candles lit around the perimeter. It was perfectly cliché, but she didn't care. It gave her a whimsical delight and she'd learned a long time ago to enjoy simple pleasures, however they came.

The hot water surrounded her, comforting and making her loose and limber. Jace's sister obviously had a love for candles. Girly candles that smelled wonderful. And they were pretty. Fancy candles that were likely expensive. Not the cheap kind you got at a dollar store.

And the bubble bath. She'd been positively gleeful when she'd found it in one of the bathroom drawers. It too was expensive. A name brand she recognized. At first she'd hesitated to use it, but the temptation had been too great and she'd delightedly dumped it into her bath as it was drawing.

She cupped a handful of the suds and then blew them across the water, laughing as they scattered and drifted like leaves in autumn.

"You're so fucking beautiful, you make my chest hurt."

She gasped and automatically sunk lower in the water, her gaze jerking to the doorway where Jace leaned, his eyes on her. His hands were shoved in his pockets and his lazy gaze drifted up and down the bathtub.

"When did you get here?" she squeaked. "I didn't expect you for another hour, at least."

He grinned and pushed off the doorframe to saunter across the bathroom until he stood next to the tub, looking down at her.

"Are you saying you wouldn't have been in the tub soaking if you'd known I was going to be here this soon?"

"N-no," she stammered.

"Pity," he murmured. "I could get used to finding you this way."

He sat on the edge of the tub and reached out to touch her cheek, rubbing his fingers over the curve and then down to her jaw.

"Everything go okay here?"

She nodded, still unsettled by his presence in the bathroom. She was in a vulnerable position and it made her uneasy.

"Kaden and Trevor give you any issues? Are you comfortable with them?"

She shook her head and then nodded, answering both questions before sinking lower in the tub. So maybe she wasn't completely comfortable with having two hulks in her living room, but they hadn't been a bother and they'd tried hard to be as obscure as possible. Or as obscure as two mountains could be anyway. And she didn't want to come across as ungrateful. That Jace was going to such lengths to make her feel safe overwhelmed her. People just didn't do things like Jace did. Nothing in her experience with the human race had ever led her to believe that white knights like Jace existed.

Jace chuckled. "Baby, if you go any lower, you're going to drown."

He dropped his hand down, delving into the water. She sucked in her breath when he curved his fingers underneath her breast and then thumbed over her nipple. It responded immediately, puckering as a delicious thrill coiled in her belly, spreading lower to the juncture of her thighs.

Her clit pulsed and ached. All the man had to do was touch her and she was a wreck. Her breaths hiccupped erratically from her mouth and the warm water suddenly seemed unbearably hot.

"Is there room enough in there for two?" he murmured.

Her eyes widened and she stared up at him, unsure of whether she'd heard him correctly. Guys like Jace didn't crawl into girly baths complete with suds and candles. Did they? And did she want him to?

Because guys also did not crawl into a tub with a woman unless they expected a lot more than a bath.

It was a loaded question.

She licked her suddenly dry lips and eyed him nervously.

"Was it that hard of a question?"

Flushing, she shook her head and then shocked herself by saying, "You can come in."

She was acting positively wanton. But she felt . . . bolder around him. Which was laughable because he still sent butterflies winging into her belly with one look. He definitely made her nervous—and she was still grappling with what his expectations were. This entire situation just seemed . . . insane, for lack of a better word. But somehow he managed to make her feel confident, and that was saying a lot because *confident* was never a word she would have used to describe herself before.

Cautious, yes. Wary? Definitely. She'd learned to weigh every situation, every person. Always look at underlying intent, because no one did anything without wanting something in return, and so far? The only thing she'd been able to figure out he wanted was . . . her. She certainly had nothing else to offer.

His gaze was gentle and he stroked his thumb over her nipple again. "But do you *want* me to?"

"Y-yes," she said huskily. More confident this time. Yes, it was a word she was coming to terms with. She liked it. Liked the sensation of being sure of herself.

Satisfaction gleamed in his eyes. He rose from the edge of the bathtub and stripped out of his clothing, tossing it toward the counter. She couldn't help but stare at his naked physique. He was so damn beautiful. She soaked him in, memorizing every detail.

The tight coil of muscles that marked his arms, his legs, his chest . . . The dark smattering of hair that lined an enticing path from his chest down his midline to his groin. And the lazy, kind of messy wash of dark hair that fell over his forehead and flipped out at his ears to fall inches below his neck. Her fingers itched to dive into the silky locks, twine them around her hands, just as she'd done the night he and Ash had sex with her.

It was strange that she remembered every aspect of him from that night in stark detail and yet Ash kind of blurred in her memory. It was Jace's mouth, his hands, his cock, the feel of his body over hers, hard and demanding, that played over and over in her mind.

And now he advanced on her, bristling with an air of dominance. Lust and authority swirled in those delicious brown eyes, the color so dark that it was hard to separate his pupils from the irises. Yet, there was tenderness in his gaze, almost as if he tried to hide the demanding look that was second nature to him.

"Do you work out?" she blurted.

He halted at the edge of the tub, his hand gripping the side. He glanced up at her and then grinned. "Like what you see, baby?"

"You're beautiful."

For a moment he looked almost embarrassed. It was absolutely cute to see a thirty-eight-year-old man who was so poised and confident falter for just a moment. She'd done that to him. Yeah, confidence was kind of nice for once.

"You're the beautiful one, Bethany. So damn beautiful that I can't get enough of staring at you. I stood there in the doorway watching you forever. I could look at you all day and never get tired of it."

Heat shot into her cheeks and she ducked self-consciously.

"So do you work out?"

"Yeah. There's a gym in my apartment building and at work. I try to hit it every day but that's not always possible."

"You have a great body," she said shyly.

"You're good for my ego."

She smiled as he threw his leg over the side and into the water. A moment later, he turned so he was facing her and he slid into the water, his feet gliding up the outside of her thighs until they rested just at her waist. He reached down, lifted her feet so they weren't lodged in his crotch and rested them atop his thighs.

"That's better," he said.

"Everything go okay at work?" she said, reaching for a neutral topic.

He smiled at that and let out a chuckle. Her brow furrowed in confusion. "What's so funny?"

"You sound positively domestic. Asking your man how his day at work went."

The heat left her cheeks. She was sure she paled and then she dropped her gaze, embarrassed by her presumption. Just as quickly, her earlier confidence fled, leaving a giant gaping hole as uncertainty took firm hold.

"Hey," he said softly. "What the fuck, baby?"

He leaned forward, causing the water to swirl and ripple around her. It sloshed up her neck but suddenly her chin was lifted as he nudged upward with his fingers. She reluctantly met his gaze.

"Bethany, I liked it. Do you have any idea how much I looked forward to coming back to you? That I hated every fucking minute of my time away from you? I counted the minutes until the goddamn conference call was over. Hell, I didn't want to leave you to begin with."

Warmth reentered her face and she smiled, bigger this time. Confidence crept back in, easing the flutter of insecurity that had threatened to take root.

He reached for her, pulling her toward him. Clumsily, she got to her knees, water sluicing down her body. It lapped precariously close to the edge as she straddled him.

She was just a bit higher than him, enough that her breasts just cleared the surface of the bubbles and were directly in front of his face. He didn't look as though he minded at all.

He wrapped both arms around her, easily encompassing her waist and then she was pressed firmly to his chest, their wet bodies colliding.

He slid his cheek over the swell of her breast and when he got to the nipple, he sucked it gently between his teeth, giving it an experimental tug. When she moaned, he sucked harder, finding a rhythm that was destined to drive her insane.

She wiggled in his arms, against his body. She was slick but he held her tightly, not allowing any space between them.

Never lifting his mouth from her breast, he moved one of his hands down to the juncture of her legs, where she cradled his cock against her pussy. The other arm remained firmly around her, anchoring her so she couldn't move.

His fingers brushed across super-sensitive skin, flicking ever so lightly over her clit as he went seeking lower, finding her entrance before toying with it. Circling, teasing, inserting barely the tip of his finger inside before retreating.

She palmed his shoulders and then curled her fingers into the muscles in his back. Her nails dug into his skin, but he didn't protest. He kept sucking at her breast, moving to the other to give it equal attention.

A deep sigh escaped her. Pleasure was liquid silver in her veins, spreading to every part of her body. Never had she imagined being pleasured in a tub full of suds and hot water. It felt sinful and so very naughty. Deliciously so.

Fairy tale. Definitely a fantasy. Some bizarre alternate reality because things like this did not happen in Bethany Willis's life. They never had. Never would. But it was nice to live the dream just for a while. As long as it lasted.

In this dream, she was wanted. She was desirable. She and Jace were equals. There wasn't an overwhelming disparity in their lives, their statuses. She fit into his world. She *belonged.*

The last made her chest ache even as Jace slid two fingers deep inside her, causing completely different parts of her body to ache. His gaze lifted to hers, his eyes piercing and so intense as he worked deeper into her. He thumbed her clit again before spreading the two fingers, stretching her.

Belong.

She wanted to belong to him. Wanted to believe in something more than one more night on the streets and the hope that she'd still be alive come morning.

Damn him for making her dream, even for a moment. This wasn't real. He wasn't real. She had no idea what game he played, but she couldn't let him make her believe. He would break her heart. He would break *her.*

His fingers slipped deeper and she cried out when he pressed into a point so sensitive that she nearly came on the spot. She shuddered wildly in his arms and gripped his shoulders tighter. When she realized her nails were likely breaking the skin, she yanked her hands away.

"Sorry," she said in a stricken voice.

His arm left her waist long enough for his hand to grip one of hers. He lifted it back to his shoulder, clamped it down and then he did the same with the other.

"I like it," he said huskily. "Mark me, baby. Dig those nails deep. I love the way they get sharper when you experience pleasure."

She closed her eyes and threw back her head when he slipped deep with his fingers again, caressing the slick walls of her pussy. He found her G-spot again and exerted just the right amount of pressure.

Her thighs spasmed and she went weak, but he held her close, supporting her as she leaned her forehead against his.

"Wonder how fast I can get you off," he murmured. "You're so fucking responsive. So hypersensitive. Every time I touch you, you do this sexy little shiver that makes me crazy. Your nipples pucker and become so hard that all I want to do is spend the night sucking them."

She gave a full-body shiver at the husky, naughty words murmured so close to her mouth. He smiled. Smug and beautiful. So damn cocky but so damn gorgeous that it made her weak.

"Yeah, baby. Just like that."

His thumb stroked her clit, adding the perfect amount of pressure as his fingers continued to glide through her wetness. His teeth grazed her nipple, toying, teasing, and then he sucked hard, tugging strongly.

"Jace," she whispered.

It was all she could manage to say. His name. Her anchor.

Her hands left his shoulders and went to his hair, diving into the unruly strands. She loved the messy, dark look he wore. He had beautiful hair. She curled her fingers into the silky mass and gripped so tightly she could swear she'd pull him bald.

She rose up from the suds, water cascading down her body as she rode his fingers.

"That's it. Ride my hand, baby. Come for me."

She fidgeted and ground downward, wanting, needing more. She cupped the back of his head, holding him against her breast as he sucked and nipped at her nipple. Each time he bit into the puckered crest, a liquid bolt of pleasure seared through her veins like fire.

"My baby likes that," he said, lust and approval thick in his voice.

Oh yeah. She liked it all right.

Her release rose sharply. So fast it left her breathless and straining, her entire body so tight it was painful. She bucked upward and then back down, her body frantically seeking ultimate satisfaction.

She felt pulled in a dozen different directions. His mouth, his hands, his body. He was everywhere all at once. She was drowning in pleasure. Awash in pure sinful sensations.

His thumb pressed over her clit and then did a tight roll. He kept rubbing in a taut, circular motion. Her breath hiccupped and then she held it, a cry escaping.

"That's it," he said in a gentle voice. But his next words contradicted that gentleness. Gruff. Authoritative. Demanding obedience. "Come for me, Bethany. Let go *now*."

She was helpless to hold on. His words washed over her, snapping that rigid tension building and coiling low in her belly. It ricocheted through her body with enough force to completely shake her. She spasmed against him and slid down his body, her head falling to his shoulder.

He caught her, holding her so she didn't fall farther into the water. She buried her face in his neck, sucking in deep breaths as her chest heaved against his. She bucked and writhed as his fingers did their magic. Never had she had such an explosive orgasm from a man's hand. Everything about Jace unhinged her. She had no control around him.

For the longest moment, he held her, rubbing his hand up and down her back as she breathed into his neck. Weak, shaking, completely wrung out. She was wrecked. So limp she didn't have a prayer of holding herself up.

He dipped his head down to kiss and nibble at her shoulder, sending chill bumps racing down her back.

"I need to get you out and dried off. You're getting cold."

"'Kay," she mumbled.

He eased her off and back, water lapping up her arms as he settled her across from him. Then he rose and she let out a sound of appreciation as she saw his rigid erection straining upward. Engorged and tight. She licked her lips, unaware she'd done so until she caught Jace's expression as he stared down at her.

"For God's sake, baby," he said hoarsely.

She blinked and gazed up at him innocently. "What?"

He growled low in his throat. "Tease."

She smiled as he got out of the tub and reached for one of the towels folded on the counter.

Even though he'd gone in to work, he'd taken the time to ensure she was taken care of. There'd been a steady parade of delivery people through her apartment bearing food, toiletries, household supplies, linens. Things she wouldn't have even thought of. But Jace had.

She shook her head. The man was freaking perfect. Did he have any faults? Well, besides his bossiness, his take-charge attitude, the fact that he'd basically kidnapped her and he wouldn't take no for an answer.

The more she thought on those supposed faults, the more she thought they weren't faults at all.

Jace wrapped a towel around his waist and then reached down for her hand. He held another towel in his other hand and when he pulled her to her feet and helped her step from the tub, he enveloped her in its warmth.

He quickly dried her and then arranged the towel around her so she'd be warm before leading her into the bedroom.

"You in the mood for anything in particular tonight?" he asked.

There was a small overnight bag by the bed and he reached down, pulling out underwear and a change of clothes. She saw he had jeans and a T-shirt. Definitely casual. She mentally went over the contents of her new wardrobe. She had a blingy pair of jeans and a gorgeous turtleneck with a cardigan and scarf that would be casual but still looked nice. And boots. She had a beautiful pair of fur-lined boots that would look awesome with the jeans.

"Finger foods," she said before thinking better of it. Then she flushed. Jace hardly looked the type who went for cheap finger foods. He was more a caviar kind of guy. Expensive steaks, expensive cuts of meat she couldn't even pronounce and dishes with sauces she also couldn't pronounce.

But he went on like he didn't notice her gaffe. "There's a place not too far from here. Ash and I took Mia not so long ago. It's a pub that serves terrific appetizer-type foods. The nachos are good. They have burgers, wings, all the usual suspects."

Her mouth watered. "That sounds utterly perfect. Can we go?"

He smiled and pulled her into his arms. "You get dressed and I'll take you."

chapter eighteen

Jace sat in his office, completely distracted by his thoughts. There was a pile of notes from Eleanor, the receptionist, of calls he had to return. E-mails to respond to. Financials to study. He had a videoconference in forty-five minutes, but his concentration was shot.

He hated that he'd put Bethany up in a separate apartment. At the time, it had seemed like the right thing to do. He hadn't wanted to overwhelm her. He knew he had to move slow—or at least slower—or risk frightening her away. Because he knew the minute she moved into his apartment, into his space, into his bed, it was all over.

So here he was, having installed her into Mia's old apartment knowing damn well he wasn't going to spend any time apart from her—only what he had to in order to get his work done and fulfill his obligations. But if having her own apartment gave her a semblance of power and at least the guise of having a choice, then he could deal. Because he knew she had neither power nor choice. She was his. Belonged to him. That didn't change because she had the appearance of independence.

He was biding his time, waiting for the right opening to make his move. And then she was completely and utterly his. And he'd be damned if they spent any time apart.

The last week had been a hell of sorts. He was living out of an overnight bag, spending his nights in Mia's old apartment because it was where Bethany was. He had a routine of sorts, where he left her in the mornings with Kaden and Trevor and then dismissed them when he arrived in the afternoons. But at least she was safe and watched over. Until he had her firmly ensconced in his own apartment, he wouldn't rest easy.

A soft knock sounded at his door and he looked up to see his sister standing hesitantly in the doorway, her gaze wary. She was likely studying his mood, and if Ash was right, she had reason to after Jace bit her head off the last two times she'd come to see him.

"Hey, baby girl," he said, allowing the affection he felt for her to shine through.

She relaxed, relief crossing her pretty features, and walked into his office.

"Thank God you're in a better mood," she said.

He chuckled but then quickly sobered as he rose and went around his desk to pull her into a crushing hug.

"Ash told me what a dick I was to you. Sorry, sweetheart. It probably doesn't make you feel any better that I don't even remember you coming in to see me. Ash swears it happened and he also swears I was a complete asshole and that Gabe wanted to rearrange my face for upsetting you. I deserved it."

Mia's brow crinkled with concern as Jace pulled away and motioned for her to sit down.

"Is everything all right, Jace? You haven't been yourself. And you haven't said anything about Christmas, which is why I came to see you. Gabe and I want you and Ash to spend it with us. Gabe's parents are going to come over but for the most part it's just going to be us. Like old times," she added softly.

He hadn't given Christmas much thought. All his thoughts had been occupied by Bethany. He glanced down at his desk calendar and realized it was just a few short days away.

His first Christmas with Bethany. Bethany, who had nothing.

Who likely had never had a tree, presents, had never been surrounded by family and good friends. Instead, Christmas had been just another day on the streets. Cold, hungry. A time to feel even more lonely than usual.

Hell, he hadn't put up a tree in his apartment. Hadn't made certain she had one for her apartment. Hadn't taken her Christmas shopping. Hadn't taken her down to Rockefeller Center, as he had with Mia so many times in the past, to see the tree.

He blew out his breath and lifted his gaze to his sister, who sat staring at him, concern darkening her rich brown eyes. Eyes that were a mirror of his.

"I met a woman," he began.

Mia's eyebrows shot up and she leaned forward in her chair. "Whoa, wait. You met a woman? As in this isn't someone you and Ash hooked up together with?"

Jace winced. "For God's sake, Mia. I'm not discussing my sex life with you. What the hell do you know about Ash, anyway?"

She rolled her eyes. "Oh please. It's not exactly a secret that neither of you have gone solo in a long time."

Jace cringed. Well hell. The very last thing he wanted his baby sister to know about was his and Ash's propensity for threesomes.

"So this woman. I take it Ash isn't involved?"

Jace sighed. "He's not now."

Mia's lips formed an *O*. "So he was then. Awkward!"

"Well, it could be. At least at first. Look, Mia, she's different."

Mia nodded knowingly, a wide smile curving her lips. "Oh my. My big brother has finally fallen. This is worth the price of admission."

Jace shook his head. "Just listen, please?"

As if sensing the importance, she dropped the teasing air and her expression became more serious.

"What's going on, Jace? Is everything okay?"

Jace ran a hand through his hair and leaned back in his chair. "As

I said, she's different, Mia. Way different than you and me. Gabe or Ash. Bethany is—was—homeless."

Sympathy immediately darkened Mia's eyes. If nothing else, his younger sister had a heart as big as the world.

"How did you meet her then?" Mia asked.

"She was working your engagement party. Of course, I didn't know all of that then. To make a long story short, Ash and I hooked up with her even though I knew I wanted her to myself from the very start."

"That's pretty screwed up," Mia muttered.

"Tell me about it. Anyway, she bailed the next morning and I spent two weeks turning the city upside down looking for her. The shelter called me when she came in looking for a place to sleep, and she'd been roughed up by assholes her brother owes money to."

Mia's expression was stricken. "Oh no! Jace, is she okay?"

He nodded. "Just scraped up. That was a week ago. She's fine now."

Her brow furrowed. "Why haven't I met her? Why hasn't anyone met her?"

"I plan for you to," he said quietly. "I want her to spend Christmas with us. I don't want her to be alone and I damn sure don't want to tell her that I'm going to spend Christmas with my family and have her feel like she's nothing to me by not inviting her too."

"Of course not. Of course we'd love to have her," Mia said in a rush. "I'm looking forward to it. Is she staying with you? Surely you didn't let her go back to the streets."

Jace scowled. "Hell no. I've put her up—temporarily—in your old apartment."

Her eyebrow rose. "Temporarily?"

"Very temporarily," Jace muttered. "Just until I move her in with me."

Mia's mouth formed the same O of surprise it had earlier. "You're serious about her."

"Do you think I'd be bringing her to Christmas if I wasn't? When have I ever risked what you and me and Gabe and Ash have by bringing in an outsider? You're my family, Mia. All of you. No way I'd let just anyone enter that inner circle."

"Then I really can't wait to meet her," Mia said softly. Then her expression grew thoughtful. "Does she have any friends? It doesn't sound like she has anyone at all. How old is she?"

Jace shook his head. "She's your age. She's had a hard life. Never had a chance, really. But she's smart. She's sweet. She lights up the entire room. I can't explain it, Mia."

Mia's smile broadened. "Oh, Jace, I'm so happy for you! And it definitely sounds as though she could benefit from some girl time. Is it all right if I swing by the apartment sometime? She could go out with me and my girls."

Jace hesitated, hating what he had to say next. But Ash knew and it was likely by default Gabe knew. Mia would have to know so she didn't do anything to put her foot in her mouth later.

"I'm not sure that's a good idea," he said slowly. "Bethany has had some . . . issues . . . in the past with addiction. May not be a good idea to throw alcohol at her and I know you and your girls tie one on when you go out."

"She can drink water with me," Mia said firmly. "Not like I have a good tolerance for alcohol anyway. The important thing is that she get out with girls her own age and make friends. Unless you have a problem with it?"

Jace found himself shaking his head. "No. No problem. I appreciate this, Mia. You're an angel. I'm sure Bethany will appreciate it. But a warning. She's quiet and she's definitely shy. It would be easy to overwhelm her and I know your friends can be a little pushy."

Mia shot him a glare. "They're the best kind of friends and they won't be mean to Bethany. I wouldn't let them, even if they were the type to do it."

Jace smiled at her ferocious defense. And she didn't even know Bethany yet.

"I have every faith you'll take good care of her. But, Mia, there's something else you need to know and Gabe will be made aware too."

She groaned. "You have to get Gabe involved?"

"When it comes to your safety, yeah, I do."

Her brow furrowed up and her nose scrunched into an adorable line.

"I've assigned bodyguards to Bethany. As I told you already, some assholes who want money from her brother roughed her up. I'm not taking any chances until that situation is resolved. Which means if you're going out with Bethany then those bodyguards go too and they look out for you and your girls. We clear?"

She rolled her eyes but nodded.

"I'd like to see the poor fool who tries to take me and my girls on," Mia muttered.

Jace chuckled because she likely had a point. But still, he wasn't taking any chances.

Mia rose and then came around his desk to wrap her arms around his neck. She hugged tightly. "So you and Bethany will come for Christmas?"

He kissed her cheek. "Yes, baby girl. You can count on it."

As Mia headed for the door, she nearly collided with Ash on his way in. Ash put his hands out, grasped her shoulders and then laughed.

"Whoa there, sweetheart."

"Hey, Ash," she said in a cheerful voice.

Ash dropped an affectionate kiss on top of her head. "I need to see Jace about something. I'll see you around later, okay?"

She held up her hands. "I know when I'm being dismissed. Guess I'll go see if Gabe has time for me."

Ash snorted. "As if he wouldn't. Ever."

She grinned, waggled her fingers and then disappeared down the hallway.

Ash turned back to Jace and then closed the door. Jace lifted his eyebrows in question as Ash made his way to the chair Mia had vacated. He tossed another folder onto Jace's desk before sitting down. Jace was really starting to hate those damn folders. They never contained anything good.

"Bethany's brother's debt is taken care of," Ash said with no preamble. "Good news is the assholes who roughed her up weren't interested in anything but getting their money back. Plus sizeable interest, of course."

"Of course," Jace said acidly.

"Bethany should be good now."

Jace nodded. "Thanks, man."

"But there's something else you should know. Not sure what it means, but I figure you need all the information you can get."

Jace's shoulders sloped downward and he leaned back in his chair. "What now?"

"Bethany's brother? Jack Kingston. Not her brother at all. No blood whatsoever. But they're tight. Been on the streets together ever since they left their last foster home. Well, they weren't even in the same foster home. I should say since Bethany left her last foster home, since Jack's older and he'd been out of the system for a while. Apparently he busted her out or at least came for her and she ran away. They've been together ever since."

Jace frowned. "So what are you suggesting?"

Ash held up his hands. "I'm not suggesting anything, man. I'm giving you the facts so that you have them all at your disposal. Bethany calls him her brother. Thought you should know he's not. Now as to what that means, I have no idea. But you should be aware of the fact that she could be running a pretty slick scam. She milks you for what she can and Jack's debts are paid."

It pissed him off but he would have to be stupid not to at least consider what Ash was saying.

"Thanks," Jace murmured.

"Sorry, man. Know it sucks. May not even be true, but you have to be aware of the possibilities."

Jace nodded. "Yeah. I know."

Jace's cell rang and he glanced down to see Kaden's number flashing on the LCD. He held up a finger to Ash and then yanked the phone to his ear.

"Yeah?"

He listened a moment, his blood going cold. Anger surged in close behind as Kaden related his report.

"Stay on it," Jace barked. "You find her. I'm on my way."

He put the phone down and glanced up at Ash, who was listening in confusion.

"Bethany ditched her security and disappeared."

"Oh shit," Ash murmured. "What are you going to do?"

"If she's going to walk away, she's damn well going to say it to my face," Jace bit out. "She owes me that damn much."

chapter nineteen

Bethany pulled her coat tighter around her and walked through Madison Square Park—she'd lost count of the city parks she'd searched—hoping this was where she'd find Jack. She'd searched all their usual haunts but had come up empty. She'd even checked the shelters she and Jack frequented, hoping that maybe he had a warm place to stay for the night.

She hadn't intended to be this long. Jace would be angry. No, he'd be *furious*. She'd snuck away from her security detail, Jace's faithful watchdogs, because really, what could she have said? That she planned to go searching the not-so-great parts of the city for her brother because she was worried?

They'd have pulled the plug on that idea so fast her head would have spun.

"Bethy, what are you doing here?"

Jack's voice cracked over her like a whip and she spun around, relieved to see him standing in the lengthening shadows wrought by evening's fall.

"Jack, thank God," she breathed. "I was so worried."

She went to him, intending to hug him, but he pulled back, putting his hands to her shoulders. His gaze scraped up and down the length of her body, his eyes shrewd.

"You're looking good," he said quietly.

He didn't ask where she'd been. Didn't ask anything at all. He just stared at her and told her she looked good like they were old acquaintances who'd bumped into each other on the street.

She hastily dug into her pocket for the piece of paper she'd written her address on. Then she shoved the folded paper at him.

"I have a place, Jack. It's a nice place. On the Upper West Side. You could come. Have a place to stay. You'd be safe there."

He stared at the paper for a long moment before finally taking it and shoving it into his pocket without looking at it.

"Heard you got hurt," he said, pain creeping into his voice. "You have to know I never intended that to happen, Bethy."

She stiffened as anger she didn't feel she had a right to possess edged over her.

"How did they even know about me, Jack? Why would they come to me for money you owed them? Why did you borrow it? How on earth did you plan to pay it back?"

He shook his head, sorrow and fatigue weighting his shoulders until they drooped. His expression was grim. Hopeless and as gray as the twilight surrounding them.

"I'm sorry," he said simply. "I endangered you, Bethy. It's best you aren't around me now. Whatever you've gotten yourself into now . . . it's good. You should stay away from me. I'll only bring you down."

She shook her head adamantly and she leaned forward to grab him into a hug. For several long seconds, she held him and his arms remained stiffly at his sides before finally he enfolded her in his embrace and hugged her back just as fiercely.

"It's always been me and you," she said, her voice muffled against his tattered jacket. "I'm not leaving you, Jack. You'd never have left me."

He pulled away and touched her cheek. "Listen to me, Bethy. It's not safe for you out here. It's never been safe. The best thing you can do for me is to go back to your apartment on the Upper West Side. Live your life. Embrace the good. Don't do anything to mess it up. And be happy."

Tears filled her eyes. "How can I be happy when you're out here?

Am I supposed to be happy knowing I have a safe place to stay, food to eat and a bed to sleep in when I know you're out here on the streets?"

He grinned crookedly. "I'll be fine. I've always got an angle working."

"You're not fine," she insisted.

He sighed. "Maybe I'll come look you up."

She latched on to that, hope taking hold. "Do that, Jack. Promise me. It doesn't have to be this way. I've met someone. He's . . . He's good to me. Things can change now."

Jack smiled. "I'm happy for you, Bethy. Really. But how well do you think your man is going to take to another man sniffing around his woman?"

"If he can't accept you, then I don't want to be with him," Bethany hissed out.

Jack touched her cheek again, his breath puffing out in a visible cloud. It had begun to snow again, the flakes spiraling between them, landing wetly on his shoulders and seeping through the thin, worn material. Cold had settled in, gripping the city in its relentless grasp. She couldn't bear the thought of Jack being out here, at the mercy of the elements and those who would do him harm.

"Please, Jack. Come back with me," she begged. "You can't hide from them forever."

One corner of Jack's mouth lifted. "Problem is solved. They have their money. In their business, it's not personal. They aren't going to come after me as long as they have their money."

Confusion wrinkled her brow and she began to shake as the cold permeated even the thick coat Jace had bought her. Her knees trembled and her breath stuttered over numb lips.

"Go back to your man, Bethy," Jack said gently. "You're cold. He'll be worried. You shouldn't be out here."

"Neither should you!"

"I'll be fine. I always have been."

She searched his gaze, looking for any indication that his eyes were dulled by drugs or alcohol. But they were bright. Tired and lines of fatigue etched his brow, making him look older than his twenty-five years. He didn't look like a young man. He looked like one with the weight of the world on his shoulders. A man much older than his age, a man who'd seen and experienced more in his young life than men twice his age.

"Do this for me, Bethy. Be happy. Be safe. I'll look you up sometime. We'll catch up. It's time for you to get on with your life. I've held you back far too long."

Her mouth dropped open in shock. "No!" she whispered. "Jack, you saved me. You've never held me back. It's me who's held you back. You've always taken care of me, always looked out for me."

He shook his head and gently turned her back toward the street. "If you believe that, you're a fool. It's always been you taking care of me, Bethy. You picking up the pieces. You making sure we eat, have a place to sleep. I've done you no favors."

Tears pricked her eyelids and froze on her cheeks. This sounded too much like good-bye, like he was sending her away forever.

"Come on. I'll get a cab for you. You got money?"

She nodded numbly. Jace had given her cash and she felt hugely guilty about using it to escape the men he'd hired to protect her. But now, if she was going back, she had to hurry. He'd be frantic, and she'd have to face him with what she'd done.

Jack walked her to the street and she was blinded by the glare of headlights, blurry through her tears. He waved at an oncoming taxi and it slowed, pulling to the curb.

"It'll make me happy to think of you in a cushy apartment having a good meal and staying warm."

She threw herself into his arms and hugged him fiercely. Hot tears rolled down her cheeks as he hugged her back.

"I'll miss you, Jack," she choked out.

And she realized it was true. Even as she knew his shortcomings.

Even as she knew all they'd endured and the fact that she'd struggled to ensure they had food and that he had money for the demons that drove him. Guilt crowded into her mind, heavy and suffocating. How much had she contributed to his addiction?

All she knew was that she couldn't tell him no. Not after all he'd done for her, all he'd *suffered* for her. A part of her had known that if she hadn't come through, he would have turned to other, more dangerous methods to get what he needed and she hadn't wanted that. And yet somehow it hadn't mattered. He had borrowed money. Money he hadn't been able to repay.

She frowned as she started to duck into the cab. "Jack?"

"Yeah."

"You said the money was taken care of. How did you pay them back?"

Fear paralyzed her. What had he done?

He shrugged and started to swing the door shut. "I don't know. When I went to see them about an extension, they said the debt was paid. I'm not going to argue with them. I just want you safe and away from here."

She sat numbly as he shut the door and then he stepped back, disappearing into the darkness. Her throat closed in and she nearly flung open the door and ran after him because she feared this would be the last time she saw him.

The cab started forward, preventing her from doing just that. She stared back as long as she could before they merged into traffic.

She bowed her head and clutched her arms tightly around herself in an effort to alleviate the swelling grief.

The city passed in a blur of traffic lights, Christmas decorations, honking horns and stop-and-go traffic. She wasn't aware they'd arrived until the cab driver gave her a gentle prompt.

"Ma'am? We're here."

She yanked herself from the melancholy surrounding her and sat forward, digging hastily into her pocket for the fare.

"Thank you," she murmured before opening the door and stepping into the cold.

She hurried toward the apartment entrance only to be met by the doorman, who looked hugely relieved.

"Miss Willis, thank God."

She didn't register him saying anything else but her brow puckered in confusion at the idea that he would be relieved. He ushered her toward the elevator and as the doors closed, he already had a cell phone to his ear.

She dragged herself into her apartment—her apartment. She felt like a fraud. Seeing Jack tonight brought home the fact that she didn't belong here. She didn't fit into this world. She certainly hadn't earned this. She didn't even have a job.

How long could it possibly last? Until Jace got over his current infatuation? She still wasn't sure what it was he saw in her or why he'd bother. Not when there were only too many women more than willing to take her place.

If there was one thing she'd learned in the past week when she and Jace went out, it was that there was no shortage of female interest. And the women were understandably shocked that Jace would be with someone like Bethany. Not that they knew anything of her circumstances, but it was very clear that she wasn't even close to his socioeconomic status. For all practical purposes, Jace was slumming.

She winced even as she sagged onto the couch, not even bothering to take off her coat. She was still cold, even within the warmth of her apartment. Cold on the inside, the kind simple heat didn't thaw.

She laid her head back against the cushion and closed her eyes. She should call Jace. He'd probably been trying to reach her. But in a really stupid moment, she'd forgotten her cell phone here at the apartment. She'd been so intent on sneaking away from Kaden and Trevor that she'd left it here on the counter.

Flinching ahead of time at the dressing-down she'd receive, she pushed up from the couch to go in search of her phone. She needed to at least text Jace to let him know she was okay.

More guilt surged over her. Now, back at the apartment, realization settled in at just how irresponsible and selfish she'd been. Jace had been nothing but kind to her. And she hadn't even taken her phone so he would know she was all right. Maybe it had been subconscious to leave the phone because Jace would have started blowing it up the minute Kaden reported her absence, and she would have felt even guiltier about ignoring his calls.

She found the phone, just where she'd left it, on the bar in the kitchen. She flinched when she saw the sheer volume of missed calls and texts. From Jace. From Kaden. From Trevor.

She pushed it away, not even wanting to look at them, but she still had to let Jace know she was okay.

With a sigh, she reached for it again just as the door burst open and Kaden and Trevor surged into her apartment. Startled, she dropped the phone and took a hasty step back before she fully registered who it was.

"Thank God," Kaden muttered. "Are you all right? Did anyone hurt you?"

She mutely shook her head, her eyes wide at the look in Kaden's and Trevor's eyes. Then without another word, Kaden yanked up his phone.

"Mr. Crestwell. Yeah, I got her. She's back at her apartment. Looks okay. I haven't had a chance to question her. I knew you'd want to know. Okay. I'll see you shortly."

Kaden closed the phone and then turned his furious stare in Bethany's direction. Trevor stood just behind him, arms crossed over his chest, a scowl firmly planted on his face.

Kaden advanced, stalking toward her until her kitchen felt small and suffocating.

"Do you mind telling me what the ever-loving fuck you thought you were doing today?" he seethed.

"I—"

He yanked up his hand, evidently not finished.

"Trevor and I were frantic. Mr. Crestwell was losing his mind. He hired us to protect you. He hired us to ensure your safety. Do you mind telling me how the hell we're supposed to do that when you pull a stunt like you did today?"

"I'm sorry," she whispered.

Tears burned her eyelids but she blinked furiously, determined not to break down in front of these men.

"You're sorry." He blew out a long breath. "You could have been raped, killed, horribly injured. Take your pick. And you're *sorry*. Jesus."

The blood drained from her face. She started to explain that she'd been perfectly safe when the door banged open again and Jace strode in, his features set in stone. He looked cold. Unmovable.

He spared only a quick glance in her direction before turning his attention to Kaden and Trevor.

"Thank you. You both can go now. I'll take it from here."

"And do we report in tomorrow morning?" Kaden asked.

Jace hesitated a long moment. "I'll let you know."

Bethany couldn't breathe around the panic knotting her throat. This was it. Jace was going to toss her out. They were over. He was pissed. It was just as well. The longer she existed in this fantasyland, the worse it was going to be in the end. Better to end it now before she forgot what her life was really like.

Kaden and Trevor left the apartment after both directed meaningful glances in her direction. They both said the same thing. Stupid. Foolish.

Her mouth wobbled and she clamped her lips together. She wasn't going to make a fool of herself. She'd face this with as much dignity as she could possibly gather.

She carefully put the phone back on the bar and then walked toward the bedroom, Jace's gaze following her every step.

"I'll just get my stuff," she said quietly. "I'll be out in a few minutes."

She went into the bedroom, fighting against the surge of tears that bathed her face. And then she realized she had nothing to pack. No things to collect. This was all Jace's. Stuff he'd bought her. Even if she took them with her, she'd have no place to put them.

Then a firm hand closed over her shoulder. He turned her sharply to face him and then looked taken aback when he saw her tears.

"Mind telling me what the *fuck* this is about?" Jace demanded.

"I know you're angry," she said in a low voice. "I'll be out in just a few minutes. I'd appreciate a cab, but if not I can walk."

His jaw clenched and bulged and a look of utter fury entered his eyes.

"You think I'm kicking you out?" he asked in an incredulous tone.

She flinched. "Aren't you?"

He swore. "Goddamn it, Bethany. You and I are going to have a long talk. This has been a fucking day from hell and I'll be goddamned if I'm going to end it with you walking out on me."

She blinked in surprise. "You don't want me to go?"

"Does it *look* like I want you to go?"

Her mouth went dry. "But you're so angry. A-a-and you didn't ask Kaden and Trevor to come back tomorrow."

"Would it do me any fucking good?" he snapped. "You aren't exactly complying with their protection."

She flushed and looked away. "I'm sorry."

"Fuck it all, Bethany, I thought you'd left *me* today. What was I supposed to think? You took off. No note, no phone call. You wouldn't answer your phone or my texts. I was in a fucking panic because I couldn't find you anywhere."

"No!" she said in a stricken voice. "I wasn't leaving you! I just had something I needed to do. I came back."

He nodded. "Yes. You did. And that's the only reason why I'm not completely losing my mind here. But that doesn't excuse the fact that you took off to God knows where without the men I hired to protect you. I made it abundantly clear that you weren't to go *anywhere* without them. What about that did you *not* understand?"

His grip tightened on her arms and he hauled her against his chest. She stared up at him wide-eyed, her tears forgotten. He looked furious, absolutely. But not for the reason she thought. He thought she'd left him?

She reached up to touch his face, seeing for the first time the fear that accompanied his anger.

"I wasn't leaving," she whispered.

"Thank fuck for that," he muttered. "But Bethany? You and I have a hell of a lot to go over. I've tried to play this as delicately as possible but fuck it. Not doing that anymore. It's time we do this my way."

chapter twenty

Jace had to let go of her and take a step back, putting distance between them. His breaths hurt, squeezing from a chest so tight it felt as though it was in the grip of a vise.

He had to get his shit together.

First things first. Before they could work out the evolution of their relationship—hell, he'd been patient for a week. Yeah, it wasn't much time, but for him? It may as well have been a fucking year. He'd never waited this amount of time for something he wanted. But before he could lay down the terms of their relationship, they had to address the reason she'd taken off, *without protection*, without telling anyone *shit*.

That made him insane. For the space of a few hours she'd been beyond his control. Beyond his ability to provide for her, to protect her. He still couldn't dwell on those hours without losing his tenuous grip on his sanity.

Maybe Ash was right. Maybe he was utterly obsessed. But *obsession* seemed such a mild term for his thoughts and feelings where Bethany was concerned.

Where did it come from? Was this how Gabe felt about Mia? Why he'd lost any and all control when it came to her and why he'd been determined that no one would come between them?

Jace didn't have an explanation. Some things just were and such was this *obsession* with Bethany. He wasn't going to fight it. Hell, he couldn't. He was utterly powerless when it came to her, and he lost all reason. All ability to make rational decisions.

Jesus, if this is what love and emotion did to a man, he wasn't at all sure he wanted it. But he wanted Bethany. With every breath. With every conscious thought. He wanted her and he wasn't letting her go without one hell of a fight.

"Are you all right?" he asked when he had a better handle on himself.

He stared at her, checking for any sign that she was hurt or shaken. But all he saw was uncertainty as she carefully watched him with large, wounded eyes. Christ. She'd thought he was kicking her out when he was the one who thought she'd walked out on him.

"I'm fine," she said in a low voice. "Jace, I'm sorry. I know what I did was stupid."

"Stupid? Yeah. That about covers it. Jesus, Bethany. Do you have any idea what could have happened? I know you've lived on those streets and it's only by the grace of God you haven't already become a statistic in a city full of sad statistics. Why did you do it? Where the fuck did you go? What did you think you were doing?"

She sank onto the couch as if her legs would no longer hold her up. Her hands trembled and she pulled off her coat, laying it in a neat arrangement beside her. He couldn't sit yet. He hadn't calmed enough. So he paced back and forth in front of her, waiting.

"I had to find Jack," she said quietly.

"Jack."

The one word was explosive in the living room. Fucking Jack. She'd risked her life because she had to find Jack. A man who'd thrown her to the wolves. Who hadn't given a shit about her when he'd borrowed money he hadn't a hope of repaying and then left her with the fallout.

"You had to find Jack," he repeated.

"I was worried," she said, near pleading. "He's all I have, Jace. And with those men . . ."

Jace huffed in a huge breath. "Exactly, Bethany. Those men are exactly why you shouldn't have gone off on your own. Did it ever occur to you to talk to me about it? To talk to Kaden and Trevor, who are hired to protect you? Do you think I hired them for the hell of it? Do you think I make it a practice to hire a professional security firm to follow people I don't care about around?"

She dropped her gaze and he continued on, needing to get this out, needing to rid himself of his anger and the images of her lying on a sidewalk bleeding.

"And he's not all you have. You have *me*."

Her gaze jerked back up, her eyes stricken. "I didn't mean it that way, Jace. *Please* believe me. I know I sound so ungrateful. I didn't mean to make you feel like you weren't important. I just meant he's the only *family* I have. For so long, it's been just me and him."

"He's not your brother," Jace said tightly, addressing the other issue that had bothered him ever since Ash had given him that piece of information.

Fuck, Ash's warning played over and over in his head. Was she playing him? Was he the victim of some scheme hatched by two down-on-their-luck lovers to take him for a ride? Staring at her, he didn't see it. But then, maybe she was one hell of a good actress. There was no guilt in her expression as he revealed that he knew Jack Kingston wasn't her brother. Or maybe he was only seeing what he wanted to see.

There was only sadness.

"Am I being played, Bethany?" he asked in a dangerously low tone. "Is this a scheme you and Jack have going? Did you give him the money I left for you?"

All the blood drained from her face. It was so stark, the look of utter horror, the absolute revulsion that spread across her features. In that moment he knew he'd been terribly wrong to even suggest such a thing, even if he'd never really bought it to begin with. It had come out, a product of his fear and anger and frustration. He'd felt the need to bite at her, to make her feel, just for a moment, what *he* was feeling. He regretted it with everything he had as he watched her falter, her pale face looking like he'd just pulled the rug right out from underneath her.

She rose unsteadily, her knees buckling. She almost went down and he lunged for her but she yanked back, the color completely leached from her face. Her expression scared him. More than her disappearance. More than the idea of her playing him. Her eyes were haunted and betrayed, so wounded he wondered if she'd ever recover.

Haltingly, she walked toward the kitchen, her gait that of a much older woman. Her shoulders were hunched in a defeated posture and her chin was lowered. Her arms wrapped protectively around herself as if defending herself from a gut punch.

He watched with a growing sense of dread as she riffled through one of the kitchen drawers. A moment later, she pulled out a familiar envelope. The bank envelope he'd gotten when he made the withdrawal. Inside was several thousand dollars in cash, mostly in twenties. It had been stuffed full, and it was still stuffed full.

She carried it back over to where he stood but she wouldn't meet his gaze. She held it out to him, her hand shaking so badly that he caught her hand in his to stop the trembling. When she tried to pull back, he tightened his grip and held on, fearing that if he let her go he'd never get her back.

"I used a hundred dollars," she whispered. "I'm sorry. I took a cab downtown. I thought it would be quicker. I didn't want to be gone long because I knew you'd worry. So I took a cab there and back. I tipped. Maybe I shouldn't have. But I know what it's like to need money and taxi drivers don't always get good tips."

She was babbling and it hurt him to hear the pain in her voice that was caused by his misjudgment.

"Baby," he whispered.

He pulled her to him and she was rigid against his body.

"Baby," he said again. "Tell me why you went. Tell me why you couldn't discuss this with me."

Even as he spoke, he walked backward, pulling her with him. He dropped onto the couch and tugged until she perched on his lap. He wrapped both arms around her so she couldn't flee, and judging by her expression, he still had a long way to go before she willingly stayed.

"I had to tell him to be careful," she whispered. "I didn't want those men to hurt him and I knew he couldn't pay them back. And I had to tell him about . . . us. He'd worry when he didn't see me. I basically disappeared and I didn't want him to think I was dead or that I'd just moved on and left him."

Jace knew the matter had been taken care of but Bethany didn't. And now he was curious—genuinely curious—why she'd left the cash he'd given her here. There was enough in that envelope to have paid Jack's debt and yet she'd left it behind.

"There was enough cash in that envelope to pay Jack's debt," Jace said quietly.

Her voice was barely a whisper. "Yes, I know."

"Why didn't you take it to him?"

She tensed against him but when he said nothing else, her shoulders slumped and she looked at him, disappointment burning in her eyes.

"I'd never do that," she said softly. "It wasn't my money. I wouldn't take it from you to pay Jack's debt. Jack got himself into that situation. If *I* had the money, I'd give it. No reservations. What's mine is his. But that money wasn't mine. I'd never take advantage of you that way. You've been so good to me, Jace. I don't want to repay that kindness with deceit, even if what I did today is just that."

Jace sighed. "Jack's debt is paid off. The men are no longer interested in you or Jack. They have their money and that's all they cared about. That's why I told Kaden and Trevor that I wasn't sure I'd need them tomorrow. Not because I'm kicking you out."

Her gaze became troubled and her lips turned down into an unhappy frown.

"What did you do, Jace?" she whispered.

"I took care of the matter."

She shook her head. "No. It wasn't your problem. I don't want you involved."

Tears were shiny in her eyes and his heart squeezed as she fought them.

"You are most definitely my concern," he said gruffly. "I did it because those sons of bitches came after you for the money. That I won't allow. I'll do anything in this world to keep you out of harm's way. There's absolutely nothing you can say to change my mind on that score, so save your breath."

He slid his fingers along her jaw and then feathered the tip of one over her full lips.

"Now that we have that out of the way, there's more we need to discuss. But I want to have this particular conversation with you naked. In the bedroom. You focused solely on me and me on you."

Her eyes widened and her cheeks remained pale and she stared intently up at him.

"Do you trust me enough to do what I'm asking, Bethany?"

It was a test. Not because he was being an asshole. But he needed to know he had her trust. He was about to take a huge step forward in what would be a very demanding relationship. He had to know she could handle that. He couldn't hold back much longer.

She licked her lips and dipped her chin, but he wouldn't allow her to look away. He wanted to see every thought that flickered through her eyes. Every reaction. Every doubt and every question.

"Are you still angry with me?" she asked softly.

Her eyes were troubled and she looked worried.

"I'm angry, yes. Not at you. I'm frustrated. Again, not at you. Our relationship is what's frustrating me at present. I'm holding so much back, Bethany, and it's killing me."

She cocked her head, her eyes narrowing in confusion. "Why are you holding back?"

He groaned. "Because I don't want to scare you away, baby. It's going to be intense. Overwhelming, even. I'm trying my damnedest to take things slow because I want to take care of you. Make sure you're with me every step of the way."

"I'm with you," she said quietly.

"No, baby, you aren't. Not yet."

"Then tell me. Show me. How can I know what it is you need from me if you don't show me? You've given, Jace, but you aren't taking. And I need to be able to give you something. I have nothing that you lack. There's nothing I can give you except me, and you don't want it yet."

"I want it," he said fiercely. "There's *nothing* I want more. But, baby, you have to be sure about this. We'll still take this in steps, but tonight we're going to take a big one if you're ready for that."

"How will I ever know unless we try?" she whispered.

His senses went on red alert. His entire body tightened and savage satisfaction gripped him by the throat.

"Get up and go into the bedroom," he said in a measured voice.

Calm descended and he took control. He had to do this right. Couldn't let himself fuck it all up. Not when Bethany was putting all her trust in him.

"Undress and kneel on the rug by my bed. Wait for me there."

chapter twenty-one

Bethany slipped the clothing from her body and folded it neatly, laying it on the dresser before going to the thick rug by the bed. She hesitated a long moment as she stared down at the floor.

She knew the significance of kneeling. Of waiting for Jace to come into the bedroom. It was a signal of her submission. He was asking her to submit to him, to trust him. Did she?

Her thoughts went back to the first night. The night she'd had sex with Jace and Ash. When Ash had very bluntly laid out the terms of being with them. They were dominant men, but Jace was perhaps more so. Ash seemed to be more laid back while Jace was . . . intense.

Had he been fighting his nature the entire time he'd been with her? Had he held back his true self for fear of frightening her away?

Her mood softened. He hadn't ramrodded her. Okay, so he'd definitely been forceful and demanding. No doubt there. But there was a controlled edge to it and she had the impression that if Jace wasn't holding himself back, things would be that much more intense.

Could she handle that? Him controlling every aspect of her life? Dictating her every movement in and out of bed? Would it be so bad?

In many ways, she relished the idea of relinquishing all control. Of having someone—a strong, dominant male like Jace—sweep in and take care of her. Make decisions. Pamper her shamelessly.

She'd never had that. She craved it.

She wasn't someone who longed for independence and to be self-sufficient. She'd been independent since she was a child. She'd been self-reliant her entire life. No one had ever taken care of her. Except Jack. And she'd done as much for him as he'd done for her.

Just once, she wanted someone to care about her. Just her. To take the burden from her. To make decisions. And she just wanted to *live*. To enjoy not having to worry about where her next meal came from, or whether she had a place to sleep. She wanted tenderness.

She wanted . . . love.

She sucked in her breath at that particular revelation because it was dangerous to want something she may never well have. Jace wanted her, yes. She didn't doubt that. But for how long? He couldn't love her. He didn't know her. He didn't even trust her.

What they had was physical and evidently she appealed to the protector in Jace. It was who he was. But she knew she wasn't his equal no matter what he said. They were an ocean apart. So different that she couldn't even relate to his life and she knew he certainly couldn't relate to hers.

She stared at the rug again, fists clenched at her sides.

And then before she was fully cognizant of doing so, she sank slowly to her knees.

Jace stood in the doorway, watching as a myriad of emotions crossed Bethany's face. It was obvious she was struggling with her decision. He could see confusion and sadness in her eyes. But he also saw need.

He wasn't even aware that he was holding his breath until his lungs protested and burned. He sucked in through his nose, his gaze never leaving Bethany. She didn't even know he was there watching. It would likely make her uncomfortable to know he could so clearly see her vulnerability.

And then she sank slowly to her knees and relief burned through his chest, robbing him of air.

She was submitting. And he knew well that she understood the significance of kneeling as he'd requested. He'd seen her entire thought process play out in those expressive, beautiful eyes.

He was weak with relief.

No, everything wasn't solved. He didn't have this in the bag. They still had a long way to go, but this was a huge step forward in the progression of their relationship.

It was a start.

He walked forward and her chin lifted, her gaze meeting his. He wanted nothing more than to wipe that fear and uncertainty from her eyes, but he knew only time would do that. Time and patience. He had to be willing to wait for as long as it took for her to fully come to terms with her place in his life.

He had a lifetime of her feeling second-rate to overcome and that wasn't going to happen in a day, a week or even a month. But damn if he wasn't going to do everything in his power to show her that he wasn't going anywhere.

He reached out to cup her cheek, allowing his fingers to glide over her silky skin.

"You're so beautiful," he said hoarsely. "I can't tell you the satisfaction it gives me to see you kneeling here, waiting for me. For the pleasure I'll give you."

Her eyes warmed, chasing some of the insecurity away. She smiled hesitantly, a sweet, shy smile that made his knees go weak.

God. What was it about this woman that inspired such an overwhelming response in him? Maybe he'd never know. Maybe this was what happened when you met your other half.

He nearly cringed at the cheesiness of such a thought, but he couldn't explain it any better than that. The women he'd been with before were filler. He'd been biding his time, waiting. For Bethany.

He'd seen Gabe through a marriage that had never been rooted in deep, abiding love. He'd seen his friend fuck his way through a multitude of women. And it was not until Jace had seen Gabe with Mia that he'd seen his friend come so alive.

Soul mates.

Gabe and Mia were soul mates. It was there to see in every look, every touch. Every time Gabe so much as glanced in Mia's direction.

And now all the things he'd found so baffling about Gabe's reaction to Mia were here in front of him.

"Do you trust me, Bethany?" Jace asked as his hand traveled into her hair, tugging slightly so that her head craned farther back.

Their gazes were locked and he saw hesitation in her brilliant blue eyes. His gut tightened. He hadn't realized how badly he wanted her trust. How important it was to him.

She was allowing him free rein. She was ceding power to him. She was submitting to him.

But without her trust, what did he really have?

"I don't know the rules," she said in a quiet voice. "I know you're asking me to . . . submit. To you. But I don't know the rules, Jace. Do I need permission to speak freely? To tell you what I'm thinking? To answer honestly the question you just asked me? I don't know how this works and I don't want to mess up before we even begin."

Jace dropped down to his knees, positioning himself so they were on eye level. No way in hell he'd have this kind of conversation in a position of dominance. This was too important.

He cupped her face in both hands and kissed her forehead. Just one gentle kiss and then he pulled away.

"You never have to seek permission to tell me what you're thinking."

Didn't she realize that her thoughts were the gateway to her? He had to know what she was thinking so he could work his way into her heart and soul.

She visibly swallowed and then inhaled sharply through her nose.

"I think the more important question is whether you trust *me*."

His eyes widened and for a moment he was at a loss as to how to respond.

Her lips trembled and she forged ahead, clearly afraid and yet determined to speak her mind.

"You thought . . . You thought some pretty terrible things about me, Jace. I know what I did didn't help, but you jumped to conclusions that tell me you think the worst of me. I know we don't know each other well. You don't know me. But that you thought I was playing you, that I was stealing from you . . ."

She broke off, inhaling deeply as if to compose herself.

Then she lifted her gaze and stared directly into his, her eyes earnest and awash with vulnerability.

"Why would you even want to sleep with me?" she whispered. "Why would you want . . . this . . . ?" She swept her hand down her body and around, clearly indicating her position. Her submissiveness.

"I know that this . . . arrangement . . . or relationship, whatever it is that we're doing, requires a lot of trust on my part. But it has to involve your trust as well. Besides the fact that I can't imagine why you'd want to have sex with a woman you think so poorly of, why would I want to give myself to a man who found me so . . . repugnant?"

His fingers tightened at her shoulders and then he forced himself to relax his grip. He'd bruise her, and he never wanted to hurt her. He took his hands away, not trusting himself not to squeeze her even tighter.

She looked hurt at his withdrawal and he let out a groan. He could do nothing right where she was concerned. Every touch, every word out of his mouth. It all came out wrong. He was fucking it up and this was too important. It was everything.

For the first time in his life, he was scared. Because he knew if he didn't handle this just right, he'd lose her. And that wasn't an option. No matter what it took, no matter what he had to do, she had to be part of his life.

Dear God, he was precariously close to begging, and he'd never begged for anything.

He cleared his throat and rocked back on his heels, his throat clogged with everything he needed to say.

Then he rose, extending his hand down to her. She glanced at him in puzzlement but slipped her hand into his. Yet another sign of her trust. Trust he hadn't been able to return or make her feel.

He sat on the edge of the bed and pulled her naked body into his hold, cradling her, positioning her on his lap so she'd be near him, touching him.

He rested his chin atop her slim shoulder and then turned his mouth down to kiss her skin. He inhaled deep, capturing her scent and savoring it.

"I'm sorry."

She went still, her gaze directed at the far wall. He reached up, slid his finger underneath her chin and gently redirected her gaze to him.

"You're right. I said and thought terrible things. It wasn't fair to you. I was afraid, Bethany. Terrified," he amended. "I reacted badly. This is new territory for me. I've never been so . . . I've never been so fucked up over a woman before. I'm used to control. You know this about me, or at least you've gotten hints. For the space of those few hours, I had *none*. I couldn't protect you. I had no control over what happened to you. It freaked me the hell out. And I took that out on you."

"I understand," she said softly.

He shook his head. "No. You don't. And you shouldn't have to. You explained what happened, and while I don't agree with what you did, I had no excuse for the things I accused you of. I have a temper, baby. You'll get to know that as well. I'm not used to things being beyond my control. But what you need to understand is that I'll never hurt you. Or at least I'll try very hard not to. Physically, it isn't ever going to happen. But I'll say shit because I'm pissed. I was afraid and I don't handle that well. I can't guarantee it's never going to happen again. But you need to know ahead of time that I'm not going to mean it. I know I'm asking a lot, but I need for you to be able to ignore me when I'm pissed and saying shit that hurts you. I'll try like hell not to do it, but I know me. My friends know me. I've been a dick to the people I care most about. You. Gabe. Ash. My own sister. But I know it hurts you. You aren't used to me. You can't see what's behind the anger and the things I say in the heat of the moment. But you *will* know me, Bethany. You'll know me because I'm not going anywhere, and what's between us is only going to grow stronger. I need you to believe that. I need you to want it as much as I want it because that'll tell me that you'll stick around and weather it with me."

Her eyes rounded in shock. Her expression was one of utter amazement. She gripped one of his arms, her fingers digging deep, and he doubted she even realized it.

Her lips parted and he waited as she collected her thoughts. He could see her processing all he'd said. Hell, he wasn't even sure *he'd* processed it yet. This spilling his guts was not something he indulged in on a regular basis. Or ever, for that matter. He'd never felt so goddamn vulnerable in his life and he didn't like it one bit.

He felt as though someone had opened him up and he was bleeding out in front of her.

"So what do you want from me?" she whispered. "I mean, really want? What am I to you, Jace? A fling? A temporary submissive? A charity case? You have to understand that I'm scared too. I don't know what you want from me. You've done so much for me but I'm afraid to embrace it because all I can think is that if you toss me out tomorrow, it's going to be that much harder to go back to my life. I'd rather never have known you and been able to savor our relationship than to suddenly be stripped bare and return to the existence I've led until now.

"I've lived it most of my life. Even the parts of my life when I wasn't on the streets weren't happy years. They were years of survival, of hoping for the best and usually not getting it. I'm okay with that life. It's all I've ever known. But you've shown me a *different* life."

Her voice cracked and the pain hit Jace in the chest, nearly suffocating him. He wanted to pull her into his arms and stop the bloodletting but he knew she needed to say this. They both needed it so they could forge ahead.

Tears filled her eyes and she looked so afraid that it gutted him all over again.

"You've shown me how things could be," she whispered. "And I want it, Jace. I shouldn't want it. I shouldn't even dare to dream that something so beautiful could happen to me. But I want it all the same. But if you're going to take it from me, if this is only temporary, some amusement for you, then I don't want it because it will kill me to go back to *my* life."

Tears slipped silently down her cheeks. To his shock, he found his own eyes burned, as if someone had thrown sand in his face.

"And I know it sounds crazy for me to be asking you this. We've known each other for such a short time. And it's not fair for me to demand this of you. But I have to know because I can't go back to where I came from after dreaming of how different things could be. Of dreaming how it would be to be with a man like you. Someone so far out of my league that I can't even wrap my brain around it. Don't lie to me. I need to know if that's all this is to you. Just something to pass the time with. A new challenge. Please give me that much respect at least and let me go if I'll never mean anything to you."

No longer able to listen to the aching pain in her voice, he crushed her to him, holding her so tightly he could feel her heart thudding against his chest.

"God, Bethany. Jesus, baby, I don't even know where to begin."

"With the truth," she said against his neck.

He pulled her away, his hands sliding almost frantically up and down her arms. He wanted to give her so much. Comfort. Reassurance. The words swirled in a cloud in his mind, but he had to get this sorted. He owed her the words. The truth she'd asked for, even if it stripped him utterly bare before her.

He sucked in a breath and leveled his gaze at her, hoping like hell she could see the sincerity in his eyes.

"The truth is I've never felt this way about another woman. The truth is I'm fucking obsessed with you. The truth is I want you in any way I can have you. The truth is if you told me right now that you could never submit to me, never give me what I want so badly from you, that it wouldn't matter. I'd take you any way I could have you. The truth is *I'm not letting you go.*"

Hope stirred in her eyes and it hurt him to see how quickly she made it go away. As if she was afraid to allow that emotion in.

"I'm never letting you go back to the life you've led up 'til now, Bethany. No matter what happens with us. And even if you ever decide I'm not what you want or need, I'm not letting you go back there. Even if you won't be with me, you'll always be taken care of and provided for. Do you understand that?"

She slowly nodded, her bottom lip pulled firmly between her teeth. Her grip was so tight on it that she'd break skin and bleed. He gently nudged her mouth open, freeing her lip.

"What do you want, Jace?" she asked again. "I need to know what you expect from me. I can't live with the uncertainty of not knowing if I'm doing it right or wrong or if I'm screwing up."

He sighed and ran his hands up her body and then back down again. She was cold. Chill bumps dotted her torso and her skin was cool to his touch. All thoughts of sex fled. His arousal had waned. Not because he didn't want her. Not because he wasn't desperate to possess her. But because some things were more important than sex and satisfaction. "Get dressed, baby," he said in a gentle voice.

Her gaze was immediately fearful.

He kissed her forehead. "You've done nothing wrong. You're cold and we need to talk." He hesitated another moment. "Would you come back to my apartment with me? I'll fix you some hot chocolate and we'll sit by the fire and we can talk. I'd like you to spend the night with me there."

To his surprise, she wrapped her arms around him, pressing her naked body to his. She hugged him tightly.

"I'd like that," she whispered.

chapter twenty-two

Bethany snuggled into Jace's couch and stared at the flames flickering in the fireplace. She'd taken her shoes off and curled her feet underneath her as she waited for Jace to return with the hot chocolate he'd promised.

A moment later, he approached the couch and handed her a steaming mug. He too was barefoot and she found the image of him in jeans, casual T-shirt and bare feet extremely sexy. But the man was just gorgeous. Head to toe.

His hair was delectably mussed, flipping up at his collar, and a dark lock fell over his forehead until her fingers itched to straighten it.

He settled onto the couch beside her and scooted in close so their bodies were touching. Then he simply wrapped his arms around her, holding her as she sipped the cocoa. In between the times she brought the cup to her lips, he pressed his mouth to her temple, kissing her skin and then sliding over her hair to retreat when she took the next sip.

It was a moment she'd long remember. The simplicity of them sitting in front of the fire, barefoot, comfortable. Relaxed. Just being. No place they had to be. No stress. Well, if she didn't count the impending conversation. But she'd gotten enough from Jace at her apartment to know that it would be all right. She was at peace, even though she still had hard questions to ask. Somehow she knew it would be okay, though. For the first time she could ever remember, she looked forward with anticipation and not dread. There was no resignation of her circumstances. Things were *good*.

They had things to discuss. She very much wanted to know what his expectations were. But he'd been completely sincere about wanting her. She believed him. Maybe that made her a fool, but she didn't doubt that he was committed to whatever this was between them.

And so was she.

She rested her head on his shoulder and sighed in contentment when he propped his chin on top of her head. She savored the last sips of the chocolate and when she would have leaned forward to go put the cup away, Jace wrested it from her grasp and set it on the coffee table.

For a moment they settled back into position, her in his arms, and quiet descended as she stared into the fireplace's glow. Then she shifted so she could look at him, saw the look on his face and knew he realized it was time as well.

"Can I ask you some questions?" she said before her courage deserted her.

He reached for her hand, squeezing reassuringly, and then he nodded. "You can ask me anything, Bethany."

"What was it like with the other women you had this kind of arrangement with?"

He blew out his breath in a long exhale, and his words were carefully said. "Bethany, you aren't like the other women."

She added her sigh to his. "Okay. I get that. I don't think you think I'm like your other women. This isn't about me comparing or me being jealous or anything. But I need to know what you expect. I get that you want me to be submissive and you like control. But that doesn't tell me anything specific. I need to know how it's going to be with . . . *us,* and me asking how it was with your other women is just me trying to figure out your expectations. I'm working blind here and that's what makes me nervous. Not you. I don't think you'll hurt me or freak me out. I just need to know what I'm supposed to *do.*"

He looked discomfited. He sighed again and then ran a hand through his hair, messing it up even more. It fell back over his forehead and this time she did reach up to smooth it. His gaze softened when she touched him, almost as if she'd given him much-needed reassurance.

"The first thing you have to understand is that Ash and I . . ." He broke off. "Jesus, there's no way to say this without it sounding all sorts of fucked up."

"Just *say* it," she urged. "I'm not going to be angry. How could I be? You don't hold my past against me. How could I hold yours against you?"

"You're so damn sweet," Jace murmured. "I don't how I got so lucky. When I think what would have happened if I hadn't seen you that night. If I hadn't found you at the shelter . . . It guts me, Bethany."

Her eyes widened and her heart pounded as his words washed over her, warm and so very sweet. She had to be dreaming. Never had she imagined meeting a man like Jace. He was so honest. So straightforward. He wasn't afraid to share his feelings. He wasn't afraid to be vulnerable.

He averted his gaze, took a deep breath and plunged ahead.

"Ash and I shared women. A *lot* of women. As in, it was a lot more normal for us to hook up with the same woman than it was for either of us to go solo. They weren't always one-night stands either."

"Like me," she said softly.

His eyes narrowed. "No. Not like you at *all*. You were different from the very first."

"Go on," she urged, not wanting to distract him from their conversation.

"The thing is, we had threesomes a lot. I'm no saint, Bethany, and I damn sure haven't lived as a monk. And like Ash told you that first night, we like control. In all aspects. It's a kink. It's a turn-on. But it goes deeper than that, at least for me. And maybe that's why I never really got into a serious one-on-one relationship with a woman. As long as it was confined to a kinky threesome, it seemed to fit better. It came off more as a game and no one took it very seriously. But for me, it *is* serious. It's what I like. It's what I *need*. And if you want or need an explanation as to why, I'm sorry, but I can't give that to you. It just *is*. I've never met a woman who made me consider suppressing that part of myself. Until . . . you."

Her body tensed in alarm, her protest immediate. "Jace, I don't want you to be someone else for me."

"But you don't know what you're getting into," he said in a low voice.

She shifted up on the couch, relieved they were finally getting somewhere. She pushed up, leaning closer to him, staring intently into his eyes.

"So *tell* me. Lay it out for me. How do you know what I can or can't accept if you won't tell me what your wants and needs *are*?"

"Because I'm afraid you won't want the same things I do," he admitted.

"I think I might surprise you, Jace," she said in a low voice. "You know about my . . . past. I told you how things were."

Jace's hand cupped her cheek, his eyes suddenly fierce. "Don't, baby. There's no need to rehash it all. I don't like how it hurts you, and it just reinforces in your mind that you somehow aren't good enough for me. That's *bullshit*."

She smiled, warmed by the intensity in his tone.

"What I was going to say is that not all of that sex was vanilla. The truth is, I think I tried it all. You aren't going to shock me. And I need to know what you expect so that I know if I *can* be that woman you need."

He leaned forward until their foreheads touched. His finger traced a line over the curve of her cheek and then down to feather over her lips.

"I like a woman to be *completely* under my control. There is something enticing about having a woman dependent solely on me for her care, for her pleasure, for *everything*. I like to pamper and spoil them but I'm also demanding. The thing is, I knew a long time ago that if I ever did enter a permanent relationship my control would extend out of the bedroom and into all aspects of our life together. There aren't a lot of women willing to sign on for that. At least, not a woman who's in it for the right reasons."

Her brow furrowed in confusion. "Right reasons?"

"Money," he said grimly. "When you have as much money as I do, there are many women willing to put up with anything for what it buys them. That's not the woman I want in my life or in my bed on a permanent basis. I want a woman who wants the same things that I do. Me in control. Me taking care of her. Me acting out my kinks with her. I want her to want *me*. Not my damn money, and I don't want her to suffer a relationship she finds abhorrent because the price is right."

"And those kinks are?"

He pulled back slightly but she caught his shoulders, forcing him to look at her.

"Tell me, Jace. You're not going to shock me."

"I like pain," he said quietly. "Inflicting pain."

He looked uneasy as he studied her for her reaction and she was careful not to give him one. Instead, she waited for what he'd say next.

When she didn't respond, he went on, his shoulders relaxing just a bit, almost as if he'd expected her to react strongly to his admission.

"I'm not saying I abuse women. God. It makes me sick to even imagine you thinking that about me. I sound like a hypocrite. I'm violently protective of the women in my care and yet I like to inflict pain."

"How so?"

She was still speaking calmly and he was studying her hard as if watching for her to get up and run screaming from the apartment at any time.

"Crops. Paddles. Belts. I like rough sex. I like role-playing. I like bondage. Sometimes I feel like a Dr. Jekyll and Mr. Hyde because there are times when I worship the woman I'm with. Savor. Touch, kiss, make love to. And other times? I want it my way. Any way I want. Tied up, helpless. Ass reddened by my spanking. Sometimes the sex is all about her and her orgasm. But sometimes it's all about mine."

"That doesn't sound so bad," she said calmly.

"Do you understand that I would be in absolute control over every aspect of our relationship, Bethany? Do you really get that? That every decision will be made by me. Where we eat, what we eat, where we go, where you go. When we have sex. When we don't have sex. What you wear. Who you talk to. Are you getting it yet? I'm a controlling bastard and that won't change. Are you really willing to sign on for something like that?"

"And if I'm not?" she asked, studying him every bit as intently as he studied her.

"Then I'll accept whatever you can give me," he said quietly.

She sucked in her breath until she was light-headed. *Oh my God.* After all he'd said. After all he'd explained. He'd push down all that made him who he was just to have *her.*

Tears stung and she sucked in a deeper breath than before as she blinked them away. It was no use. They burned until they finally spilled over onto her cheeks. Jace looked panicked, his expression dissolving into one of self-loathing.

"Don't cry, baby. Please don't cry," he whispered harshly. "We'll work it out. I swear, it'll be okay."

She shook her head. "No, you don't understand."

"Then make me understand. What's wrong? Why are you upset? It doesn't have to be that way. I was just trying to make you understand *me.*"

She surged forward, taking his mouth with hers. He seemed stunned but didn't push her away. Their mouths melted hot, tongues clashing wetly.

"Shut up. Just shut up and kiss me."

He groaned. "God, baby."

She ripped at her clothing, suddenly desperate to have nothing between them. She ripped at his until finally he helped her and their clothes went flying, this way and that, hitting the floor, the back of the couch and the coffee table.

She kissed him hungrily, her mouth moving hotly over his. She allowed all her desperation into her kiss, her hands as they roamed over his hard body. His cock was rigid between them, sandwiched tightly between their bellies. She reached down to grasp it even as she arched over him, wanting him inside her.

It registered that it was he who was supposed to be in control. He who was supposed to call the shots. But at this moment she didn't care. She only knew she wanted him, had to seal this special connection and make it something more permanent. She had to show him, with more than words, that she wanted what he could give her. Not just wanted but *needed*.

She fit him to her opening and didn't hesitate, sliding down and engulfing him in one motion. The shock of his entry made her gasp and his hands were suddenly at her hips, alleviating the pressure by lifting upward.

"Baby, *no*, don't hurt yourself."

His voice was strained and it was evident just how much he was holding back. Oh hell no. That wasn't what she wanted. She wanted it all. Everything he had to give her. And she'd settle for nothing less.

"You'll never hurt me," she whispered. "Not in a way I don't want, anyway."

He chuckled lightly and then slid his hands to her ass, cupping as she rose up to take him all over again. This time he didn't hold her back and she took all of him, to the balls, her ass coming to rest on his lap.

"Jesus, you feel so fucking amazing," he breathed.

"I just want you to sit back and enjoy it," she murmured.

His eyes glittered as he stared into hers. Then he loosened his hold and leaned back against the couch, his body going slack.

"I can do that."

His hands skated up her body to cup her breasts and she moaned as she rose and fell again, taking him deep. She leaned into him, following him back as she pressed her body to his, trapping his hands between them.

He was big inside her, large enough that it made movement difficult, but she reveled in the tightness. Each thrust was sweet agony as he pushed through her swollen pussy. Each time his balls pushed against her ass, she gasped and closed her eyes. She was so close and they'd only just begun.

"Don't hold back, baby. I want to watch you come. You're so fucking beautiful, I hurt just looking at you."

"Not without you," she gasped out.

"Oh, I'm there. I was there the minute that sweet pussy slid down my dick."

Needing no further encouragement, she quickened her pace, rising up and over him to give her better leverage. He palmed her breasts and then put his mouth to one nipple, sucking strongly. Then he dropped his hands back to her ass, squeezing as she shuddered against him.

"I want this ass next." The words rumbled gruffly from his chest. "Can't wait to get deep inside it. I didn't have your ass that first night. I was too focused on your pussy. Didn't want anyone else there but me. But now it's mine and I want to fuck it."

"Jace!"

His erotic words splintered over her, pushing her that last little bit toward her release. Her entire body bowed and then spasmed. She couldn't even hold herself up. She needn't have worried. Jace's arms came around her, holding her as he took over, pushing himself up and into her, faster, harder until she was sobbing his name.

He let out a low growl. His grip was punishing. She'd wear

bruises later and she didn't care. This was what she wanted. His possession.

She shattered. There, in his arms, him powering into her body, she went to pieces. It was nearly painful. So intense that the room fuzzed around her, her vision going dim.

She dropped her head to his shoulder, panting for breath as her body convulsed and seized. He powered into her, pushing rapidly, the smack of flesh meeting flesh loud in her ears. Her entire body shook and still he thrust as if he were trying to plant himself in the deepest recesses of her soul.

Then he cried out. Her name. *Bethany.* It was sweet in her ears, brushing over her skin like the finest silk. Her name. She belonged to him.

He went limp, gathering her even closer until she couldn't breathe. She didn't complain. Didn't say a single word as she lay sprawled across his body. He kissed her neck, her ear, and then nuzzled into her hair. It took her a moment to realize he was whispering endearments. Telling her how beautiful she was and how overcome he was that she was his, that she accepted what he wanted from her.

She curled her arms around his neck, holding on just as tightly as he held her.

"I want to stay," she whispered.

He went rigid against her and then he sagged as if relieved. He kissed her again, moving one of his hands to push the hair from her face. Then he pulled her back so she could meet his gaze. His eyes were intense. Nearly black as he stared at her.

"You're staying, Bethany. You're mine now. I still don't know if you fully know what you've agreed to but I'm not giving you the opportunity to back out now. You belong to me. I'm not giving you back."

She put her hand to his cheek as he'd done to her so many times. Offering comfort and reassurance. He leaned forward and brushed his mouth across hers. Once, twice, and a third time, as if he couldn't pull himself away.

"Why did you cry, baby?"

Just thinking back on all he'd said made her want to cry all over again. At his look of alarm, she realized she *had* teared up.

"Oh, Jace," she whispered. "You can't imagine how much it meant to me that you'd actually be willing to change who you are, what makes you who you are, because you think it's what I want. And that you showed me the heart of you. But you have to understand, I want *you*. All of you. I don't want a watered-down version of Jace. I want you. Controlling, dominant, arrogant, caring, loving, protective . . ." She trailed off, her voice husky with emotion and clouded with tears. "Do you understand?" she whispered.

He crushed her to him, still firmly embedded in her body. She could feel every heartbeat. He trembled against her as his hands tangled in her hair. Then he pulled away just enough to lean his forehead into hers, their mouths precariously close and their gazes hooded, connected.

"Don't know what I'd do if I hadn't found you," he said in a stark voice. "Kills me to even think about it. Don't know what I'd do without you. That makes me crazy too."

"Do you get it, Jace? Really get it? I want you. I want your dominance. I *need* it."

He stroked his hand down her hair, smoothing the strands, the motion comforting.

"You got me, baby. All of me. I hope to hell you're prepared for it. But you're getting it. All of me. One hundred percent. But you have to promise me something."

"What?" she whispered.

He kissed her first, a light smooching, warm and breathless. When he pulled his head back, his eyes were alight with satisfaction and contentment.

"Promise me that if it's ever too much, if you're ever overwhelmed, if I ever push too hard or too fast, that you'll tell me. You *have* to tell me. I couldn't live with myself if I knew what I was doing was scaring you or, God, *hurting* you. I never want to make you feel bad about what we do."

She kissed him this time, savoring the feel of him, of being in his arms. This was real. He was real. She was shaken to her very core by the magnitude of what was happening here. He wanted her. *Her.*

"I promise," she whispered against his lips.

chapter twenty-three

Bethany waited, breathless with anticipation. Nervousness. Her stomach was full of butterflies. Jace would be home any minute. He'd texted her to let her know he was leaving the office. Nothing else. No instructions. Nothing about their plans for the evening. And in light of their heart-to-heart discussion the night before, she had a very good idea of how she wanted to be waiting for him when he arrived.

A signal of her acceptance. Her obedience. Her willingness and desire to submit to him. To forge ahead in the kind of relationship they both wanted. Not just what Jace wanted. It meant the world to her—it undid her that he'd been willing to suppress his own wants and needs if she displayed any hesitation over the parameters of the relationship he'd outlined.

And maybe that was a huge reason why she was so willing to accept without reservations the things he asked of her. Because he hadn't demanded. He hadn't given her an ultimatum. He'd told her how he wanted things but just as quickly let her know that if she wasn't able or willing to commit to that lifestyle that *he'd* be the one to compromise and take whatever it was she felt comfortable offering.

Everything. She would give him everything. She wanted to make him happy because it's what would make *her* happy.

She slipped out of her clothing and arranged it in a neat pile in one of the drawers he'd allocated for her use. He'd made noises about buying furniture for her that would be solely hers. But for now, using his space was fine. They still maintained separate residences even though more and more of her belongings had crept into his apartment.

She checked the time and knew he could be coming up the elevator even now. She quickened her pace to the living room and carefully knelt on the plush carpet in a position that afforded her a view of the elevator doors. She'd see him as soon as he stepped out, but more importantly, the very first thing he'd see when he entered the apartment would be *her*. Waiting. Submissive. Giving him what he most wanted from her.

The minutes ticked by with agonizing slowness. Quiet descended in the apartment and only her soft breathing could be heard. And then the sound of the elevator arriving. Her pulse quickened as the doors slid open and she stared ahead, eager to see his face, his reaction when he saw her.

He stepped inside, briefcase in hand. He locked on to her immediately and the briefcase slid from his grasp, hitting the floor with a soft thump.

"Baby," he whispered.

Just one word but it conveyed a wealth of meaning. Surprise. Joy. Relief. Warmth flooded his eyes and they immediately went dark with desire. His entire face softened when before there'd been lines etched on his forehead and his jaw had been tense. He'd seemed distracted, as though he'd had a hectic day at work.

All of that melted away as he strode toward her, his focus solely on her, his gaze never once leaving her.

He stopped just in front of her, his hand delving into her hair, stroking through the strands before cupping her cheek and caressing the line of her jaw.

"How long have you waited like this?" he asked softly.

She smiled, leaning into his touch. She was starved for it. An entire day of waiting and wanting. Aching with need. Wanting to re-affirm what they'd already decided the night before. She wanted to reassure him, but perhaps she needed that reassurance even more.

"Not long. You texted when you left the office. I waited a bit and then came into the living room, here, so I could see you when you got off the elevator. So you could see me," she finished quietly.

"Never seen a more beautiful sight when coming home from work, baby. Never thought I'd come home to this. To you. Like this. So soft and sweet. You make me forget everything else but you and me and the world we've created."

"Good," she said huskily. "I want that for you. You do so much for me. I want to do as much for you."

He smiled down at her, his fingers rubbing lightly over her lips. "You do. You've made my entire day. Seeing you like this. I can't even remember my crappy day or what happened at work. Don't even give a damn. Because now I'm here with you and nothing else matters."

"I'm yours to command," she murmured. "Tell me what you want, Jace."

He hesitated, standing there, his eyes expressive, but he remained silent, almost as if he were afraid to voice his thoughts. Then finally he spoke. Careful with his words.

"I know we talked about this last night, baby. I know you agreed. I know I laid it out. But I don't want to rush into this. I want to give you time to adjust to my expectations. I want you to be sure that this is what you want. The very last thing I want is to overwhelm you. I want to take things slow. Work up and take it a step at a time. I don't doubt you. Don't want you to think that. I'm going to be careful with you because I care about you. I care about us. And I want us to last."

Her heart went soft, the ache intensifying. A knot formed in her throat and it was hard to speak around the growing emotion. "Don't you know, Jace? When you say things like that it only makes me want to please you even more. We don't have to pull out all the stops the first day of this new relationship. But I want to show you what I can be. What I want to be. For you. But not just for you. For me too. I want this. You want this. *We* want this. So tell me how to please you. Give me the words and let's begin something new and special."

"I want to fuck you," he said bluntly. "Right here in the living room. I want you to suck my dick with you on your knees looking so damn sweet and beautiful, your eyes glowing and soft. And then I want to bend you over the couch, tie your hands behind your back and fuck you long and hard. And then when I've come, I want to lay you out and make love to you like you've never been loved. I want to eat that pussy and I want to suck your tits until you're ready to come out of your skin."

"Is that all?" she teased.

He grinned, some of the worry easing from his expression. "It's all for now. There's a whole hell of a lot more I want to do to you—*will* do to you. But we've got all the time in the world and we don't have to do it all on the first day. We'll take it slow and when I'm sure you're with me all the way, we'll get there, baby. No doubt about that. I'm going to crop that ass, tie you up and fuck you in every conceivable manner a man can fuck a woman. But for now, I just want those sweet lips around my dick and then I'm going to dive into that warm, tight pussy."

She shivered, her clit throbbing until she squirmed to alleviate the ache.

He gave her a knowing smile and then reached for the fly of his pants. He unfastened the button and then lowered the zipper, the rasp sharp in her ears. He pulled his cock out, stroking it to hardness with firm pulls, and then he tilted her chin up with his other hand.

"Open your mouth, baby. Take me inside and suck me off. Take me to the edge, but I'm not going to come until I'm balls deep inside your pussy and you're bent over the arm of the couch, ass perched high in the air with your hands tied behind your back. That's when

I'm going to pump you so full of my cum that it'll run down your legs and I'm going to leave you that way just so I can stand back and look at you, knowing you're mine and that I just took what I own."

She closed her eyes as he slid inside her mouth, the erotic images he'd described bombarding her mind. His hands were gentle as he palmed her face, but his thrusts were not. It was an arresting contradiction, his touch versus the force with which he fucked her mouth.

"Now this is the way a man likes to come home," he whispered. "His woman waiting on her knees, wanting only to pleasure him. Waiting for his command. Accepting whatever it is he tells her to do. Fuck me, it doesn't get any goddamn better than this, baby."

She smiled around his cock, satisfaction gripping her, squeezing her heart until she was breathless. She loved that she affected him this way. That he was so wild for her and that she pleased him as no other woman had.

He thrust hard and then slowed, sliding more gently over her tongue, rubbing the tip over her lips before plunging back inside the wetness of her mouth.

"So beautiful," he murmured. "And mine. Fucking *mine*. You belong to me. Only me. No one else will ever have this, what I have, you on your knees, waiting for me to walk out of that elevator. If other men only knew what I had, they'd be jealous sons of bitches. You're a woman worth fighting for, Bethany. Men would kill to possess what I own, even for an hour."

His words sank deep and she soaked them up, holding them in the deepest part of her soul. Her chest tightened and her throat knotted, making it hard for her to take his length.

He frowned and then withdrew, leaving only the tip resting on her bottom lip. "You okay?"

She nodded, unable to formulate a coherent response. How could she when she was perilously close to tears? Happy tears. She was overwhelmed and not in a bad way. The very best way. Overcome. She had no idea what to say, how to respond. She could only show him what those words meant to her.

Leaning forward, she took the initiative and sucked him deep but then immediately glanced up, gauging his reaction, to see if her boldness had angered him. He feathered a hand over her cheek and smiled tenderly, almost as if he could read her every thought and knew just how affected she was by all he'd said.

Holding her head in place, he thrust one more time, deeper, pushing to the back of her throat until it convulsed around him. He let out a groan and then released her, pulling his cock from her mouth. Then he reached down with both hands and curled them around hers, lacing their fingers together. He pulled her carefully to her feet and remained in that one spot for a long moment while he waited to ensure she had her footing.

"To the couch," he said, his command stronger, holding more of an edge than before. "I want you to lean over the arm, belly down, forehead touching the cushion. Ass in the air and your feet don't touch the floor."

She swallowed and did as he'd dictated, positioning herself accordingly. He moved away, his footsteps retreating into the bedroom while she waited eagerly for him to return. When he came back, he carried a length of silken rope. Her arms were already twisted behind her, her hands resting at the small of her back.

He gathered her wrists in his hands and then, holding them firm with one hand, he began to coil the rope around them with the other. Though the rope was soft and nonabrasive, he tied it tight, binding her effectively so she couldn't move her hands.

"Seeing you this way . . . Baby, I don't even have words. It's a sight I'll dream about at night when you're in my arms, sleeping next to me."

His palm rubbed over her ass and then his other hand joined, caressing and then spreading her with both hands until her pussy was spread wide.

He positioned himself at her opening but paused, holding the tip barely inside.

"I'm not going to be easy," he warned. "Want you too much, baby. I'm having some pretty dark, caveman thoughts at the moment. This is going to be fucking. Crude, down-and-dirty hard fucking. When I'm done, then and only then, am I going to take care of you. But you don't come until then. This is for me. After is for you."

Before she could even process his statement, he drove deep, thrusting inside in one forceful lunge that took her breath away. Her entire pussy quivered and tingled. Arousal hummed through her veins. Need, craving, stronger than any need for a fix she'd ever experienced. How was she supposed to get through this without orgasming? She was ready to come *now*. Not whenever he finished slaking his own desires and tended to her afterward.

He gave her a warning smack on the ass when she shook uncontrollably.

"Get it under control, baby. You don't come yet. Disobey me and I'll forget all about taking things slow and I'll put a crop to your ass."

She groaned in frustration. Instead of dissuading her, his warning only fueled the fires of her lust and she edged ever closer to ultimate release.

She bit into her lip and closed her eyes, focusing intensely on not giving in to her orgasm. It was the hardest thing she'd ever attempted. She was unbelievably aroused and every thrust sent ripples of pleasure cascading through her body.

"Want that ass too," he growled. "But I'm too close. I'll fuck it another time."

Thank God. She wouldn't last even a minute longer and he was thrusting harder now, growing even larger as he swelled and tightened within her. She squeezed her eyes shut and tightened every muscle in her body to ward off her orgasm. Relief rushed through her veins when he leaned into her, his body covering hers, and his semen began to coat the walls of her pussy.

She sagged over the end of the couch feeling wrung out, and she hadn't even orgasmed. If he so much as touched her, it would be over. Every nerve ending was short-circuiting. Her skin was hyper-sensitive. Her clit ached and twitched. Just one touch. All he had to do was reach down and touch her and she'd find relief.

She sighed in frustration. She was so on edge that her skin felt alive. Like it was crawling and trying to turn itself inside out.

He pressed a kiss between her shoulder blades and then gently eased out of her body.

"Don't move," he commanded.

She heard his footsteps move away and become more distant. A moment later he returned with a warm washcloth and wiped the semen from between her legs. Then he carefully untied her wrists and rubbed the tender skin with his thumbs.

"Go in the bathroom and get cleaned up," he directed. "Not a fan of tasting myself when I'm eating you, baby. When you come out, I'll be waiting on the bed. I want you to sit on my face while I lick that sweet pussy."

He helped her to her feet and she wobbled on unsteady legs to the bathroom to do as he'd told her. She carefully cleaned herself, taking special care to remove all the stickiness. When she walked back into the bedroom, he was sprawled naked on the bed, his cock lying to one side over his thigh, only semi-erect now.

He was still beautiful and his cock was still damn impressive, even at rest.

He crooked his finger at her, motioning her over to the bed. He held out his hand to help her climb up and then he scooted down so his feet hung off the bed.

"Crawl up and put your knees on either side of my head," he said.

It was ridiculous for her to be shy, but she was a little mortified to be climbing up, bold as you please, in order to sit on his face so his mouth was pressed to her pussy.

She rocked up on her knees so she was still several inches from his mouth. When she started to lower herself, he put a hand to her waist to stop her.

"Use your hand and spread your pussy lips for me," he said huskily. "I want my tongue over every inch and I want you to come all over my face."

She sucked in a huge, steadying breath, but she was a wreck after all that had gone on in the living room and now his blunt, evocative words cut right to her core and sparked instant arousal.

She tentatively slid her hand down her belly and then into the curls between her legs, finding the plump folds. Her finger rubbed over her clit and she moaned.

"I can smell how turned on you are," Jace growled. "So fucking sexy. Spread for me, baby. Can't wait to taste you."

She parted her lips with her fingers and held herself open before lowering herself those last few inches. The instant she made contact with his tongue, she jerked and bucked upward. He grasped her hips with both hands, his grip hard, and slammed her back down onto his mouth.

He ate her like a man starving. Licking, feasting, sucking, sliding his tongue inside her and over all parts in-between her entrance and her clit. He worked her into a mindless frenzy, until she rode his face like she was taking his cock.

But then he slid his fingers between her ass cheeks and parted her just as she'd parted her pussy lips. His index finger inched closer to her anal opening, teasing and rimming the entrance. He pushed in the barest amount. Not even an inch. Just the tip of his finger, but it was enough to send her hurtling right over the edge.

She exploded into his mouth, drenching his lips and chin with a sudden flood of moisture. She bucked and writhed, wanting more of his mouth. Wanting those wicked fingers. Wanting everything he had to give her.

She sagged downward, her muscles going completely lax, and then she realized to her embarrassment that she was probably smothering him. She jerked upward, but he caught her hips and settled her down just below his chin so his mouth was pressed to her belly.

Her fluids glistened on his lips and his chin, and he licked his tongue over his lips, removing the traces of her release. It was insanely provocative and arousing to watch a man who greatly enjoyed going down on a woman. He looked satisfied and supremely smug, like the cat who got the cream. And, well, she supposed he had.

"Come here," he murmured, pulling her down so she was cradled in his arms, resting firmly against his chest. He rolled until they were side by side, her tucked into his neck, his hands possessively gripping her ass.

"Christmas is in a few days."

She propped her head up, because this was an abrupt change in topic and it made her wary. But he pulled her back down, holding her so her face was once again buried in his neck.

"Like you like this," he rumbled out. "Touching me. So close you're melted on my skin. Like a permanent tattoo. I like wearing you and nothing else."

She smiled against his neck.

"My baby likes that," he said smugly.

"Yeah, I like," she breathed.

"Anyway, as I was saying, Christmas is coming up shortly. We're spending it at Gabe and Mia's, and Gabe's parents will be there, as will Ash. You have a closet full of clothes but I want you to choose what you wear."

She stiffened in surprise. This wasn't one of their agreements. He made all the decisions. Even the insignificant ones like what she wore outside the apartment. Now for general errands, slumming around the house, running down to the market for something, she wore whatever. But when they went out for any reason together, he chose her clothing, and she had to admit he had impeccable taste.

"I want you to be comfortable and confident," he said in a low voice. "And if you don't have anything in your closet that's going to work for you and make you feel those two things then I want you to go out and buy something. No argument. You have credit cards. You have cash. It's about damn time you start using them."

"Thank you," she whispered. "Not for offering to buy me new stuff. I'm sure I have plenty to choose from in that huge closet. I have stuff that still has the tags on it! But thank you for making such an effort for me not to feel awkward."

He squeezed her to him. "Don't want you in any situation that you don't feel good in, baby. So get what you need. Pick out something that makes you feel good."

She raised her head despite his effort to keep holding her against his chest and she kissed him hard, wrapping her arms around his neck as she slid her tongue over his.

"You're so good to me, Jace," she said quietly. "But I thank God every single day for you."

chapter twenty-four

Bethany's anxiety was through the roof. She'd dressed with extreme care because she didn't want to disappoint Jace in front of his family. There had been plenty of outfits to choose from in her closet, many, as she'd told Jace that still had the tags, unworn as of yet. She'd chosen a sparkly silver cocktail dress because it seemed festive and appropriate for Christmas, and after debating and a huge amount of guilt, she'd bought matching sparkly silver heels to go with it.

Jace had sensed her anxiety and had gone to great lengths to reassure her. As she'd been in the bathroom putting her hair up in a silver clip that matched her dress, he'd come in and slipped a beautiful diamond necklace around her neck and fastened it while she stood gaping in the mirror.

"Jace!" she protested. "This is too much!"

He grinned and pressed a kiss to her neck just underneath her ear and then reached around her, holding a box with a matching pair of earrings.

"Then you'll definitely think this is too much, but deal with it, baby. Can't have my woman going to Christmas with my family and them thinking I don't spoil you ridiculously. I'll lose all credibility. So put them on. I like seeing my jewelry on you. And you look beautiful without it, but I want you to feel just as beautiful as I see you. There isn't a woman alive who doesn't love diamonds. You can't be the exception here."

Put that way, there wasn't a whole lot she could say.

He kissed her again and then patted her affectionately on the ass. "Need to leave in five minutes, so put a move on it."

She sighed as he left and then caught her reflection in the mirror as she fumbled with the box so she could slip the earrings in her ears. She was smiling. Happy. Her eyes warm with a contented glow. He always knew just how to make her feel more at ease. Not that she wasn't still a nervous wreck.

Christmas was a holiday she'd never really marked. In the beginning, particularly the first year she and Jack had been homeless, Jack had tried his best to infuse the occasion with holiday cheer. He'd gotten a shrub, which they'd decorated and set up in their tiny corner of a deserted park using discarded wrapping paper from a nearby shop.

They'd fashioned bows, little stars and a few other shapes that couldn't exactly be classified as recognizable symbols of Christmas, but Bethany had loved Jack for the effort he'd made. He'd also managed Christmas dinner, though he'd never told her how and she hadn't asked.

Where was he today? It was cold and snow had begun falling, covering the sidewalks in a white blanket. Did he have a place to stay? Was he warm? Did he have anything to eat?

She felt extremely guilty as Jace ushered her into his waiting car, warm and comfortable, on their way to Gabe's apartment, where they'd eat, enjoy time with Jace's loved ones and celebrate the holiday. She was well taken care of. Jace had seen to her every need. And Jack was out there alone for the first time in all the years he and Bethany had been together.

She put a hand to her hair for the sixth time since they'd left her apartment, worried that the careful arrangement would plummet down her neck at any moment.

Jace put his arm around her, pulling her to him so he could kiss her temple. "You look gorgeous," he murmured. "Stop worrying. You'll love them and they'll love you."

She smiled—or rather, she tried to. It was bad enough she was meeting his sister, her fiancé who also happened to be Jace's other best friend and business partner, and Gabe's parents, but Ash would also be there. This would be the first time she'd seen him since that night of their threesome and her stomach was in knots over it all.

How awkward would it be to exchange pleasantries with a man who'd fucked her with Jace? Jace couldn't be any more comfortable with it than she was. He'd made his feelings very clear on the matter. He didn't even like to discuss it, and so she'd avoided the issue, adopting firm denial that it had ever happened.

That would all change tonight.

And then another thought struck her. One that horrified her. What if the others knew that she'd slept with both Jace and Ash?

"Baby."

Jace's soft voice broke into her thoughts and she turned in his direction.

"You're tying yourself into knots over nothing."

He squeezed her hand and then brought it up to his mouth to kiss. He kissed every single one of her fingers, prying them loose from the fist she'd formed.

"It's Christmas. I want you to enjoy the holiday. Our first together," he added with a smile.

"I'm terrified," she blurted out.

Jace's gaze softened and he scooted closer to her. "There's no need to be. I swear it. These are the very best people. They're my family. I wouldn't subject you to any situation I thought would be harmful to you."

"Ash is going to be there."

Jace's eyes flickered, but he recovered quickly. But she'd seen his reaction and knew he didn't look forward to her and Ash being together any more than she did.

"Honey, listen to me. It's inevitable that you and Ash will cross paths. You're both very important to me. What happened happened.

We can't change it, no matter how much I wish differently. So the only thing we can do is face it and move forward. He's not a dick. He's not going to make things awkward. Ash is the best friend I have. He knows what you mean to me. Trust me when I say things are going to be fine."

She glanced down. "I'm sorry. I'm ruining Christmas for you before we even get there. I'm scared. I don't want to disappoint you. I don't want to let you down. And I don't want to embarrass you in front of the people you love. All I can think about is that they'll take one look at me and they'll know everything. They'll know I'm not good enough for you. They'll know you could have done better. And I can't stand seeing that look on their faces. How they'll look at you, wondering what on earth you're doing."

Jace's scowl was instant. "Now you're just pissing me off. That's a bunch of bullshit, and swear to God, Bethany, if it's the last thing I do, I'm going to get you beyond such asinine thinking."

She closed her eyes tightly, determined not to do something stupid. Like cry. It would ruin her carefully applied makeup anyway. Makeup that Jace had had to help her purchase because she hadn't had a clue what to buy or even how to apply it. A very patient makeup artist had gone through all the steps, showing her how and what to apply, and in what order. Then she'd sent Bethany home with an entire bag of cosmetics, half of which Bethany didn't even remember the purpose of.

"Baby, look at me."

It wasn't a request. It was a firmly worded command. One she instantly obeyed. While Jace was still holding back and easing her into their relationship, in the days since their emotional discussion about the course of their relationship, he'd become more comfortable demonstrating his dominance.

He'd gradually become more forceful, not only in bed, but in their everyday existence. And in the beginning, she'd truly wondered if she'd chafe at his authority over her, but in fact she'd embraced it. She reveled in her well-ordered existence. As soon as Jace had taken that step in exerting his dominance, a part of her had sighed in relief. It had been so freeing to hand over responsibility to someone who cared about her. Someone who took care of her and was insanely protective of her.

It gave her a measure of security she hadn't enjoyed until now. It made her feel . . . safe.

"You do Gabe and Mia and Ash a huge disservice by thinking they'd feel any such way about you. They aren't judgmental. They aren't snobs. They're not going to care about your past or where you came from. All they're going to care about is that you make me happy because they care about me. And by extension, because they care about me, they're going to love you. All I'm asking is that you give them a chance."

She was suddenly ashamed because Jace was right. She wasn't giving them a chance. She'd already passed judgment on them. The very thing she feared they'd do to her.

"I'm being a reverse snob," she said quietly. "You're right. I'm not being fair."

He squeezed her to him again and kissed the side of her head. "You're understandably nervous. I don't fault you for that. What I'm saying, though, is that it's going to be okay. Trust me?"

She nodded and he looked relieved.

They arrived a few minutes later and Jace helped her from the car. He wrapped his arm around her and cautioned her not to slip as they hurried toward the entrance to Gabe's apartment building.

Butterflies took over, swarming her stomach as they rode the elevator to the top floor. When it opened, she was immediately assailed by delicious smells. A mixture of cooking food, and what smelled like scented holiday candles. Peppermint and pine?

The interior of the apartment was aglow with candles and in the corner of the living room was a huge tree, twinkling with hundreds of lights. The entire living room was decorated festively and the fireplace was on.

"Jace!"

A petite, dark-haired woman hurried over and immediately engulfed Jace in a huge hug. Jace's smile was instant as he hugged her back. Then she pulled away and turned her warm smile on Bethany.

"You must be Bethany. I'm Mia, Jace's sister. I've heard so much about you. I'm so happy you're here!"

Bethany started to stick out her hand but Mia enfolded her in a hug similar to the one she'd given Jace. Bethany awkwardly returned it.

"Thank you for having me," Bethany murmured.

"Hey, there you guys are."

Bethany glanced up to see a gorgeous, tall man walk up behind Mia and slip his arm around her waist. She remembered him from the party. Actually, she remembered both of them. She's stared wistfully at them as they'd danced and had thought they looked so much in love. She wasn't about to draw attention to the fact that she'd been part of the waitstaff at their engagement party, though, and so she pasted a bright smile and pretended this was the first time she'd ever seen either one.

Gabe slapped Jace on the back and then turned to Bethany.

"Hi, Bethany. I'm Gabe, Jace's friend and business partner. About to become his brother-in-law, if my bride to be will put me out of my misery and set a wedding date."

"Hi, Gabe," she managed to choke out.

Jace's arm came around her, steadying her and offering silent support. In that moment she loved him for that.

"Come on in the kitchen," Mia said. "That's where everyone is congregated, drinking wine and snacking on the fruit and cheese tray."

She tucked Bethany's arm underneath hers so that Bethany was flanked by both Mia and Jace and then pulled them both toward the kitchen.

Bethany's stomach dropped when they met Ash in the doorway. She nearly ran into him as he scooted to the side to get out of the way.

"Hey, man," Ash said. "Glad you two made it."

Then he leaned forward and kissed Bethany on the cheek.

"Hello, Bethany. You look beautiful."

She was positive she blushed. Try as she might, she couldn't control her instant mortification as she stared at Ash. Ash was playing it cool. Jace was playing it cool. She was the only one acting like an idiot.

"Thank you," she said, forcing a smile to her lips.

Ash smiled warmly at her and then reached down to squeeze her hand. He leaned forward as if to kiss her other cheek in greeting and whispered so only she could hear.

"It'll be fine, Bethany. Don't be nervous."

With that simple gesture, Bethany relaxed and allowed herself to fully breathe for the first time since leaving Jace's apartment. This time her smile was genuine and she squeezed Ash's hand back in thanks.

Jace shot Ash a look of gratitude and the tension that perhaps she'd imagined to begin with dissipated. Jace curled his arm around Ash's shoulders and the two engaged in mock wrestling.

"Not much changes around here," an older woman said as she pushed forward. Her smile was indulgent and it was obvious that she regarded Ash and Jace with affection. "You boys still act like you did as teenagers."

Jace smiled and pulled her into his arms. "Hello, Mama H." He kissed her temple and then turned to Bethany. "Bethany, I'd like you to meet Gabe's mom. Mrs. H., this is Bethany Willis."

Enfolded in another warm hug, Bethany felt her reserve slowly melting around the infectious charm of Jace's family.

"It's wonderful to meet you, dear."

"Oh hey, here's Mr. H. now," Jace said.

Bethany looked beyond Mrs. Hamilton to see an older man push forward.

"Nice to meet you, young lady," he said in a gruff voice. "Jace is very fortunate."

Bethany blushed and extended her hand. Ignoring it, Mr. Hamilton hugged her. Bethany had never been around such a spontaneous, huggy bunch of people. It was weird and yet . . . nice.

"So did you cook, Mia? Or did you cheat and have it catered?" Jace said in a teasing voice.

Mia shot him a dirty look. "Gabe's mom and I cooked. I'll have you know it's pretty awesome, if I have to say so myself."

"It smells wonderful," Bethany said quickly.

Mia smiled. "Thanks. It's good. Promise."

Then Mia turned and made shooing motions with her hands. "Okay, guys, out of the kitchen. You're in the way. Go in the living room and do whatever it is guys do. I need half an hour and then we can eat." She glanced at Bethany. "Want to hang out with us in the kitchen? You can always go with Jace but we don't bite."

Bethany found herself smiling in response to the other girl's open warmth. "I'll stay."

Jace embarrassed her when he leaned down to brush his lips across her mouth. "I won't be far," he murmured.

She blushed because everyone had seen him kiss her. How could they have missed it?

Mia grinned and exchanged conspiratorial glances with Mrs. Hamilton. They both looked delighted.

The men sauntered out of the kitchen, leaving the women.

"Okay, sit, Bethany," Mia ordered. "You too, Mrs. H. This won't take me long. I just need to make the gravy. Rest is all done."

"You sure you don't need help?" Bethany asked hesitantly.

Mia shook her head. "Sit, sit. We'll have girl time. Which, speaking of, I've already told Jace this, but knowing him he didn't pass the info along. You have to go out to the club with me and my girlfriends. You'd love them. They're all really terrific. We go out every once in a while, have a blast and then let Gabe get us home afterward. I only made the mistake of taking a cab home alone once. Let's just say Gabe wasn't very pleased with me."

Bethany's eyes widened both by the invitation and the fact that Gabe had been angry with Mia.

Mia laughed. "He pitched a fit but he got over it. To keep the peace, I let him have his way and now we take a car home. Gabe's happy so it works out."

"I don't drink, but I'd love to go."

Mia's expression became sympathetic and she reached over to squeeze Bethany's hand. "You and I can drink water. I don't tolerate alcohol very well. I had the hangover last time to prove it."

There was something in Mia's expression that bothered Bethany. Almost as if Mia knew . . . Of course. Jace would have told her. Bethany's face went warm as a flush crept up her neck. Shame followed closely behind. She dropped her gaze and folded her shoulders inward in an instinctive, protective gesture.

"Bethany?"

Mia's soft voice filled the silence.

"I'm sorry. Was it something I said?" Mia asked.

Bethany lifted her gaze, meeting the concern in Mia's eyes. "It was your expression. It said it all."

"Jace told you about me," Bethany said bluntly. She was amazed she was being so bold and putting it out there. It wasn't typical of her. She avoided conflict at all costs. She certainly never instigated one.

It was then Bethany noticed that Mrs. Hamilton had quietly left the kitchen. Mia walked around the bar and climbed onto the stool next to Bethany.

"Yes, he told me," Mia said in a calm voice. "I don't think he would have but when I suggested you going to the club with us, he warned me. He's obviously protective of you and he knows how my girls and I are when we go out. He didn't want us to push you into anything. But Bethany, you have to understand, what he told me doesn't make me think badly of you. It doesn't make me think anything at all other than my brother has found a woman he cares deeply about and that makes me happy. You make him happy. So I'm going to like you no matter what's in your past."

Bethany swallowed against the knot forming in her throat. "I hope I do make him happy," she whispered. "I don't have anything to give him."

Mia smiled. "And you think I have anything to give a man like Gabe? Like he doesn't have everything he could possibly want or need? He seems to just want me and is happy with just that. I have a feeling Jace is the same way."

Bethany smiled back. It was hard not to like Mia. She was genuine. There wasn't an ounce of fakeness to her.

"Okay, let me get this gravy done," Mia said, sliding from the barstool. "The menfolk will start to get restless and cranky."

Twenty minutes later, everyone was seated at the formal dining table. The centerpiece was beautiful. Gorgeous, vibrant red poinsettias with elegant tapered candles on either side. Elaborate candelabras were positioned on the sideboard and the lights were dimmed to cast an intimate glow over the table.

Gabe and his father occupied the two ends of the table with Mrs. Hamilton on her husband's left and Mia to the left of Gabe. Bethany had been positioned across the table from Mia and Gabe and Jace were on either side of her, with Ash next to Mia and across the table from Jace.

The food was delicious but Bethany found herself lost in the flow of conversation. The problem with being homeless and penniless was that she had nothing in common with these people. No common interests. She hadn't kept up with recent events. She was clueless about sports, the world of finance, and even more clueless about business.

The longer the meal went on, the more conspicuous Bethany felt because of her prolonged silence. The others were starting to glance at her with concerned looks and Bethany pasted on a bright smile, nodding and acting as though she were concentrating on her food. And she was. Even being with Jace for as long as she'd been now, it was still ingrained in her not to waste food. She still lived with the idea that she never knew when her next good meal would be and so she had to make the most of the one she was enjoying.

As if finally sensing just how ill at ease she was, Jace reached underneath the table, rubbed his hand down her thigh and then lightly squeezed just above her knee.

He leaned over her to get a roll and murmured, "Relax, baby."

She was mortified when it appeared that Gabe heard Jace. Gabe glanced in her direction, his eyes softening.

She just wanted the floor to open up and swallow her whole. Better yet, she really just wanted to go back to her apartment. She was in sensory overload. Too many people. Too much conversation. She wasn't used to having to perform social niceties.

It wasn't that they were horrible or that she didn't like them. It was just awkward and out of her scope. She felt completely inadequate despite Jace's repeated attempts to make her feel as though she belonged.

That was on her. Jace, his family, no one had made her feel that way. It was strictly her own doing. Her own insecurity.

"I love your tree," Bethany said quietly in Mia's direction.

Mia beamed. "I do too. I adore Christmas trees. Jace used to always take me to Rockefeller Center for the lighting of the tree. It was a tradition I looked forward to. It was where Gabe proposed to me."

Bethany's heart twisted at the instant warmth that spread over Gabe's features. His gaze was riveted on Mia.

"I love Christmas trees too," Bethany said wistfully. "I never had one. A real one, I mean. In an actual home."

As soon as the words popped out of her mouth, she wanted to die.

Her look of horror couldn't be contained. She couldn't believe she'd just blurted that out. She couldn't bear to gauge the others' reactions to what she'd said.

Before she said anything else to humiliate herself, she shot up from her seat. Jace reached for her, but she was just beyond his grasp. She left the table, heading blindly for the kitchen.

"Jesus," Ash muttered. "She's never had a Christmas tree?"

Jace was standing, torn between going after her and giving her a moment to compose herself. He glanced at his friend and then at the grim expressions on Gabe's and Mia's faces, the soft sympathy in Mrs. Hamilton's eyes.

"This has been torture for her," Jace said quietly. "This whole day. Damn it, I shouldn't have made her come."

"Did we say anything wrong?" Mia asked anxiously.

"No, baby girl, you did everything fine. I appreciate it. This is just hard for her. She's not used to any of the things we take for granted. She's not used to being around people, much less people who care. She was a nervous wreck about meeting you all. She doesn't want to embarrass me." He broke off with brittle laughter. "She doesn't think she's good enough for me."

"Shit," Gabe murmured. "I hope you put an end to that crap."

"I think maybe we should go," Jace said, casting a look of apology to the table.

Mia nodded and Gabe rose, putting his hand on Jace's shoulder. "If you need anything, let us know."

"Will do. Thanks for the great food, Mia. You outdid yourself."

"Give Bethany our love," Mia said softly.

Jace smiled at her. "I will."

chapter twenty-five

Jace hugged Bethany to his side as they hurried into the cold and toward his waiting car. She hadn't met his gaze once after he'd told her they were leaving. Mia and Gabe, hell, even Ash—*especially* Ash—had been extremely gentle with her, hugging and kissing her good-bye and acting as though nothing had gone wrong.

But Bethany had been mortified. It was evident in the tight lines of her body and the anguish in her eyes.

He ushered her into the car and kept her close to him as they pulled into traffic. He'd already given his driver their destination when he'd called to tell him they were ready to leave Gabe's apartment. She didn't even notice when they didn't head in the direction of either of their apartments. She likely thought he planned to take her to her apartment. Maybe even thought he'd stay over with her.

As if she was staying anywhere but his place on Christmas night.

He was growing more and more impatient with the distance between them. He wanted her in his apartment, in his space. In his bed every night. No, there hadn't been a single night since he'd moved her into her apartment that they'd spent apart, but many of those nights had been spent at her place.

His mind told him not to move too fast, not to push too hard, that the end result could be disastrous. His heart just wanted . . . her. In his arms, his bed, his life. Any way he could make it happen.

When they pulled up in front of Saks Fifth Avenue, Bethany finally became aware that they hadn't gone back to her apartment. She lifted her head and gazed around in consternation.

"Where are we?"

He leaned over to silence her by kissing her. Then he opened his door and gently pulled her from the car.

"Jace, what are we . . ."

She broke off when her gaze lighted on the Christmas tree that towered above the ice skating rink. Tears immediately filled her eyes and it made his chest squeeze painfully.

"Oh, Jace."

She went silent, her eyes rapt and alight with joy. She stared, motionless, her breath puffing out in a cloud.

"I came here once," she whispered. "It was my first Christmas in the city. Mine and Jack's. We walked forty blocks in the rain because I just wanted to see this one time."

Jace struggled to breathe at the ache in her voice. His hands tightened and curled into fists. "How long ago was that, Bethany?"

She was twenty-three. So young and yet she seemed years older. Hardened by time. With the cynicism of someone much older than her tender years. He wasn't sure he wanted to know just how long she'd been on the streets.

"Four years," she murmured.

He stifled the curse that blistered his lips. She'd been living on the streets of New York City for four fucking years. She'd been nineteen. An age when most girls were looking forward to the start of their lives. Fresh out of high school. In college. Having fun. Taking on the world.

He was more determined than ever to shield her from every bad thing in her life. He wouldn't allow anything else to touch her. He only wanted to surround her with good things. Happy memories. He wanted to give her that.

"Let's go closer," she said, her voice trembling with excitement.

She took hold of his hand, tugging him forward. He couldn't help a smile at her excitement. Her eyes danced and her entire face lit up just like the Christmas tree.

She was so beautiful when she smiled she made his gut ache. And every time she smiled, he was always struck by the fact that she did it so rarely. It was another thing he was determined to coax from her. He wanted to give her a reason to smile every damn day.

She weaved her way through the small crowd and then stopped in a spot where they wouldn't be elbow to elbow with anyone else. She stared at the tree in silence, her hand leaving his to clasp with her other in front of her.

Damn it but he should have made sure she brought her gloves with her. Her hands were cold. For that matter, she wasn't dressed appropriately to be standing outside. She had a coat, but it was the lighter of the two he'd bought her. He'd thought they'd only be going from the car to the apartment and back.

But she didn't seem to notice the cold. Her focus had drifted to the ice skaters and she wore a soft smile of pleasure.

Suddenly her face lifted and her lips parted in delight.

"Jace, it's snowing again!"

She held her hands up, capturing the slowly drifting flakes on her palms. They melted instantly but she chased after more.

She spun around, laughing as they landed on her nose and cheeks and caught in her hair. He was transfixed by the picture she presented. So lovely she took his breath away.

"Do you know, this is the first time I've ever been excited about snow?" she said in a wistful voice. "Before, I knew if it snowed I'd be cold and wet and I'd never get warm. But now? I can enjoy the beauty and elegance of snowfall because I know I'll be warm and dry afterward."

The simple words cut him to the quick. It physically hurt him that she'd led such a spartan, lonely existence. He didn't know how she'd survived. If he thought too long about what could have happened to her, he came undone. He tried to focus on the fact that the past no longer mattered. That she was here with him and he wasn't letting her go. That she never had to go back to that life.

But it wasn't so simple, because that life had shaped her, made her into what she was today. She had wounds that hadn't healed. Scars that ran soul deep. Insecurities that only time would appease.

He pulled her roughly into his arms, wanting her against him, more to comfort him than her. She was a lot more accepting of her past circumstances than he was.

"Thank you for this," she whispered. "I'll never forget tonight. The tree is beautiful. And that I got to see it with someone who cares about me . . ."

Care? He didn't goddamn care. He *loved* her. With every part of himself. It was crazy. Insane. Lunatic, even. Shit like this didn't happen in real life. You didn't meet a woman and fall instantly and completely in love with her after only knowing her a little over a week.

But it did and he had.

Jesus.

"Jace?"

Her worried voice cut through his thoughts.

"Is something wrong?"

He slid his hand over her cheek and then bent his neck to kiss her. "Nothing's wrong, baby. Things couldn't be more right."

She smiled, her eyes brightening and reflecting the glowing lights. Then she leaned up on tiptoes and kissed him. It was rare that she initiated any affection with him. Not because she didn't want to. But she was reticent. Always conscious of doing the wrong thing at the wrong time.

He lived for times just like this, when she forgot to worry about doing the wrong thing and she just let herself go.

Her lips moved warm over his, a contrast to the cold. So damn sweet. He wrapped his arms around her, lifting her so their mouths were on the same level. She laughed in delight as her feet dangled down his legs. Resting her arms on his shoulders, she looped her hands around his nape and then kissed him again.

"This was the best Christmas ever."

He smiled. "I'm glad."

Her expression sobered and the light died in her eyes. "I'm sorry I ruined things at your sister's."

"You didn't ruin things, baby," he said gently. "It was a lot to ask of you. I should have introduced you to them separately and before I threw you to the wolves at Christmas. I wasn't thinking. I was too caught up in wanting you to meet them and spend time with them."

She pressed her forehead to his and sighed softly over his lips. "I'm working on it, Jace. I swear I am. I'm trying not to overthink things and freak out. I want to be someone you can be proud of."

At that his frown was fierce and quick. "I am proud of you, damn it," he growled. "There isn't a single goddamn thing about you that I'm ashamed of."

"Okay, so maybe I want to be someone *I* can be proud of," she whispered.

He squeezed her and then slowly put her back on the ground again. "One day you'll see you like I see you, baby. If it's the last thing I do, I'm going to make it happen."

She turned up her face and then stuck out her tongue to catch a drifting snowflake. Her laughter rang out when one melted in her mouth.

He suddenly wanted nothing more than to have his dick where that snowflake had been. Him melting on her tongue. Him coming all over her mouth.

Despite the cold and the snow, heat flushed through his body. Sweat bathed him.

"We're going now," he ground out.

"Okay," she whispered.

"My place."

"Okay."

"I'm going to fuck you senseless, Bethany."

"O-kay."

Her response was shaky and drawn out but her eyes told the real story. She was excited. It was all the encouragement he needed.

Grabbing her hand, he tugged her back in the direction of the car. It would take a lot of doing not to fuck her in the backseat of the car. Tonight he would take her his way. Not that the last week hadn't been his way. He'd definitely dictated the pace, the how and where, but he'd still been . . . conservative.

Even after she'd been clear in that she would be a willing participant to whatever he wanted to do to her, he'd still held back, because he was deathly afraid of screwing up.

But enough of that. Maybe if he'd been more forceful she wouldn't still be so insecure. She was a woman who needed stability and security above all else. She needed structure. Routine. All the things she'd been denied.

She needed love.

His love.

They got into the car and for the entire drive to his apartment, it was silent and tense. Sexual awareness was taut and crackling, a tangible aura that surrounded them. Bethany's eyes glowed in the dim light cast by passing streetlights. Her hair was delectably mussed and her lips were swollen from his kisses. Just the way he liked them.

Hell, he had to stop looking at her lips. His dick was already about to bust out of his pants. He had to focus on something else because all he could imagine were those swollen lips wrapped around his cock.

She ran her tongue over her top lip, a nervous gesture that made him groan out loud. She jumped when the sound exploded from his mouth and he reached automatically to reassure her.

"Christ, baby, if you only knew what I was imagining about those lips and then you run your tongue over them. There's only so much I can take."

A gleam entered her eyes. "How long do we have?"

His brows furrowed. "How long do you need?"

She slid her hand between his legs. "I think that depends on you."

He fumbled for the intercom. "Take the long route."

"Yes, sir."

Bethany's hand had already slipped into his pants, past his boxer briefs. His breath escaped in a long hiss when her fingers curled around his rigid length. Then she leaned in, her mouth hovering precariously close to his.

"Do I have permission to suck your cock?"

He nearly came on the spot. Her breath blew warm over his mouth and it took every ounce of his control not to roll her over on the seat and fuck her until they both passed out.

"Hell yeah," he breathed.

"Help me out," she murmured as she tugged at his fly.

"Happy to oblige."

He yanked his pants down and heard the ripping of material. He shoved them down his thighs, allowing his swollen, aching dick to surge upward.

"Tell me how you want it," she whispered.

Her gaze found his and he saw uncertainty shining. His heart softened. She was trying but she was also scared and unsure. She wanted his dominance. She needed it. Just like he needed her.

His hand tangled in her hair and he brought her forward, pulling her head down to the tip of his dick.

"Take it deep," he said.

Her tongue tentatively found the slit where precum already beaded and he groaned when she traced a path around the head of his cock. He curled his hands around her nape, stroking and massaging, offering silent encouragement.

She slid her lips down his length, covering him inch by inch with her warm, wet mouth. The pleasure was intense. Almost unbearable. So fucking exquisite.

"When I tell you to stop, you stop immediately, okay?" he said.

She glanced up, his dick sliding from her lips. She nodded.

"You feel fucking amazing, baby. But if I come now, it's going to shoot my plans for the evening all to hell. I'll let you work me up until we get to my place. But then I'm taking you up to my bed and I'm going to tie you up, hold you down, and fuck you until you scream my name."

A shiver worked up her body. Her pupils flared and her lips parted in a quick gasp. Her pulse accelerated against his fingers where he circled her wrists. He smiled at her reaction. It was definitely time to take the gloves off. She was ready. He sure as hell was ready.

But still, he'd give her one last chance to opt out. To tell him if she wasn't ready. He'd never do anything to push her too hard, too fast.

"If you're not ready for this, you need to tell me now, baby. You need to understand what's going to happen tonight. I've held back because I didn't want to rush you. I didn't want to overwhelm or frighten you. Tonight, though, it's going to be a different story. I'm going to use a crop on your pretty ass. I'm going to mark you. I'm going to own you. I'm going to fuck you like you've never been fucked. Do you understand? Can you accept that? Tonight you step into my world."

She nodded slowly, her eyes wide.

"Be sure, Bethany. Be very sure of this. And at any point, if it's no longer what you want, then you tell me no. It's that simple. You say no and it stops. Instantly."

"Okay," she whispered.

"Are you afraid?"

She shook her head.

"Is this what you want?"

She nodded.

"Baby, talk to me. You're starting to worry me."

She smiled then and his relief was crushing. She wasn't afraid. She truly wanted this.

"I want you, Jace. The real you. I don't want you to hold back. What you want excites me. I just hope I won't disappoint *you*."

He groaned. "Jesus, baby, you have to stop with that shit. You aren't going to disappoint me. The fact that you're giving yourself so sweetly to me. That you trust me. That you'll allow me to do any damn thing I want to. That's a fucking dream. Hell no, you won't disappoint me. It's not possible."

She leaned forward to kiss him, her hands curling around his erection once more.

"How much more time do we have now?" she murmured against his mouth.

chapter twenty-six

Bethany knelt on the rug in Jace's bedroom, her entire body taut with anticipation. Jace stalked around her, circling her like a predator would his prey. She felt deliciously hunted. She tingled from head to toe over all the things Jace had said he would do to her tonight.

She had told Jace the truth when she'd said that she'd just about tried it all during her sex-as-oblivion phase. Kink, no kink, she'd been open to anything. The overwhelming difference, however, was that she'd never done any of those things with a person who truly cared about her and whose priority was her well-being and pleasure.

She was positively itching to experience all of that at Jace's hand. She loved his dominance, his strength and his authority over her. Loved his firm hand. But she'd known he was holding back, not giving her all of him. Finally, that would come to an end. Or at least she hoped it would.

Adrenaline buzzed through her veins, soaking her in a high like she'd never experienced. No pill or drug had ever given her anything close to this. If only she could bottle it.

She jumped when the tip of a leather crop skimmed over her shoulder and down between her breasts. She hadn't even seen him get it out. Had been too lost in her excitement.

He was still dressed, and she was completely naked. His sleeves were rolled up. She reacted to that image. He looked as though he were about to go to work. On her. She licked her lips, suddenly nervous, terrified, excited as hell and unbelievably turned on.

He trailed the edge over the tips of her breasts in turn. Her nipples hardened as he stroked the leather over them, coaxing them to further rigidity. Then he let the crop drift lower, to her belly, and then lower still until it glided over her mound and then around the curve of her body to between her legs.

She gasped when it slid between her folds, over her clit and into her wetness. And she was wet. Very wet. He rubbed it lightly, going lower until it touched the mouth of her pussy and then he shifted it higher to stroke her clit once more.

Her breathing sped up and she closed her eyes, helplessly arching upward, unable to control her reaction to the featherlike brushes. The crop could be used for pleasure. Just as it could be used for pain. The contrast fascinated her. Made her want to experience the opposite sensation. The snap of the leather against her skin, marking her as he'd promised.

His marks. His stamp of possession. Proof that he owned her.

God, it sounded so barbaric. So unbelievably delicious and decadent. Owned.

Protected.

Cherished.

She moaned softly as he lifted the crop through her curls and back over her mound. Then he lifted the tip to her mouth, her eyes widening when she guessed his intent.

"Lick it clean," he said huskily. "Lick your juices from the leather, Bethany. Taste yourself. Taste your desire."

Hesitantly, she stuck the tip of her tongue out to the leather, her eyes glued to him, seeking his approval. There was satisfaction in his eyes. No sign of disappointment.

Growing bolder, she pulled the crop farther into her mouth, never letting her gaze drop from his, and she sucked lightly at it and then laved her tongue over the surface, catching the slight musk of her moisture.

Without warning, he pulled the crop away and snapped it over the side of her breast, catching her nipple and areola with the flat edge.

Fire—and surprise—caught her unaware and she gasped, rocking back on her heels. It was the most perplexing sensation. Pain. Instant sharpness. But then a throbbing ache that slowly faded to a warm hum. Strangely addictive because she wanted more. Wanted that burn because she knew what would follow.

Her nipples were on fire. So very hard, puckered and rigid, straining outward as if begging for the crop. Was she insane? She was practically begging him to hit her again.

He popped the other breast and fire exploded over that nipple. She closed her eyes and swayed, drunk on the instant buzz that settled into her blood.

"You'd look fucking hot with nipple piercings," Jace said in a silky voice.

Her eyes popped open in surprise. Jace did not look like a guy who appreciated body piercings in the woman he was involved with.

"No one would ever see them but me," he murmured. "Our little secret. And it would drive me crazy knowing what was underneath your bra."

It made her want to run out and find the nearest place to pierce them. Only, ouch. It sounded painful and not in a good way.

"Get up on the bed," he commanded. "On your hands and knees, ass out to the edge. Keep position, no matter what I do. You aren't to move. You do, however, have permission to make whatever sound you like. I want to hear them. Want to hear each gasp, each cry, every moan when the crop strikes your flesh."

She reached down with her hands to push herself upward, knowing she didn't have a prayer of remaining steady. She was already so drunk on desire. She weaved unsteadily and he immediately reached out to grasp her arm, ensuring she didn't fall. When he was certain she was steady, he let her go and she crawled onto the bed, positioning herself exactly as he'd commanded her.

"Now, lay your cheek on the mattress, ass up, head down. Put your arms above your head and lay your palms flat on the bed. And keep them there."

Slowly she lowered her head, her stomach clenching at the vulnerability of the position. She was utterly helpless this way. No defense.

To her surprise, he stepped away but he returned just as quickly. He grasped one ankle, tugging firmly, forcing her thighs wider apart so that her pussy was completely bared. Then to her shock, he began to coil rope around her ankle. She felt it pull tight so she couldn't even move it and she realized he was tying the other end to the bedpost at the foot of the bed.

Holy shit. She really was going to be completely helpless!

When he was finished with that ankle, he moved to her other and secured it in an identical fashion to the headboard. She was stretched wide, both ankles spread and tied securely.

She thought he was finished but then he walked around to the other side of the bed and from the corner of her eye, she saw he held more rope.

Silently, he tugged at both her hands, drawing them above her head so her arms formed a *V*. Then he coiled the rope around her wrists, securing them together. He pulled the rope down toward the floor and tied it to the bed frame so she was stretched forward, her body pulled in several different directions.

She was rendered immobile. She had no choice but to take whatever he chose to do. Her only defense was the word *no*, and she was determined not to use it. "No" hadn't even entered her mind.

She wanted this too much. Wanted the full power of Jace's desire. No more holding back. No more carefully orchestrated restraint.

She turned her head to the side, seeking him out, but she couldn't find him with her gaze. But he was there. Close. She could feel him. All that coiled tension seething for an outlet.

She flinched when the tip of the crop touched between her shoulder blades and then trailed a seductive line down her spine to the cleft of her ass. It left her and she held her breath, but he didn't strike her right away. He waited until she was forced to exhale and then fire cracked over her buttocks.

She gasped and tensed and then closed her eyes when the burn turned into euphoria, warm and sinfully pleasurable. A heady buzz entered her bloodstream, invaded her mind, her very soul.

"Talk to me, Bethany. I want to know what you're feeling. Every step of the way."

Jace's husky voice made her eyes open. She blinked, struggling to even find the words. How could she?

Another blow, harder, more forceful this time. Her cry caught in her throat and before it could be transmitted to one of pain, it morphed into a moan of pleasure, humming from the deepest part of herself.

"Tell me," he ordered again.

"It's pain," she said, a catch in her voice.

The crop left her ass where it rasped over sensitive, marked skin.

"Too much?"

There was worry in his voice. A promise that if she said the word, he'd stop.

"No!"

Her protest was immediate. A denial. She didn't want him to stop.

"It's pain and then it's pleasure," she whispered. "Beautiful, exquisite pleasure. Like nothing I've ever felt. The pain is just pain. But the pleasure is indescribable. It makes me crave the pain because I know what will follow."

"And you want me to give you that? You want me to give you more?"

"Yes," she breathed. "Please. *Please.*"

He leaned down to kiss the burning flesh over her ass. His lips pressed against the soft skin, sending a shiver quaking through her body. Then he pulled away and the crop descended, giving her what she wanted. Pain. Heat. Burning fire that reached underneath her skin and spread to every muscle and joint.

She went weak as the heady rush of pleasure pulsed like wild fire. Unpredictable. Sudden. Overwhelming.

"You like the pain," he whispered. "I like giving you pain. But giving you pleasure, seeing you arch for the kiss of the crop, is magical. I ache to give you more."

She sighed, closing her eyes as she waited for the next wave of pleasure. He rewarded her with another lash of the crop. Harder this time. Punishing and yet so very pleasurable.

"Let's see how much you can take."

His voice was unimaginably sexy, stoking the fires inside her higher. Until it was an inferno, blowing wilder, brushing across her skin. She couldn't move. Couldn't escape. She was his captive. His willing captive. And she gloried in every demonstration of his dominance.

He peppered her ass with varying lashes. Some harder, some softer. Never in the same place twice. He brought her to a frenzy until she was panting, begging, pleading over and over, and she wasn't even sure what she begged for.

Pain had long since fled. There was only the sweetest of pleasure. Ecstasy like she'd never imagined. No one had ever taken her on such an amazing journey.

Then strong hands cupped her ass, kneading over super-sensitized flesh. Parting, spreading. His cock touched the opening of her pussy and nudged inward, pausing as he stretched her around his width.

She sucked in her breath and reveled in the sensation. Stretching. Burning. So deliciously full.

He pushed inward, his hands sliding to her waist, holding her, not that he needed to hold her down. She was prevented from moving by the ropes. Her legs were stretched wide, her arms pinned over her head.

But his fingers dug into her waist and then slipped down to her hips, gripping as he thrust deeply into her body.

He wasn't all the way in. He stopped, breathing raggedly, his fingers pressing into her skin, marking her just as the crop had marked her ass.

"Okay, baby?" he whispered.

She didn't answer. Couldn't. But she didn't say no and so he powered the rest of the way into her, sealing their bodies together as his balls pressed against her mound.

At first he fucked her gently, withdrawing only to ease his way back in. But as she went wetter around him and his entry grew easier, he picked up his pace. His movements became more powerful. Her entire body jostled with the force of his thrusts.

His hips smacked against her ass. He pushed deep. Touching a part of her that hadn't been touched before. Every time he stroked over that one spot, her entire body jumped and pleasure rocketed through her system, flinging her perilously close to release.

It was as if she had no control whatsoever over her own body. He commanded it. He owned it.

He pressed into her with a deep groan, straining upward and inward, his body mashed so hard against hers that her legs were pulled taut by the rope.

"Are you close, Bethany? I want you with me, baby. Not coming without you."

Her heart melted. So much of this scene was about him. His wants and desires. And yet he was absolutely focused on her pleasure. He'd checked constantly to make sure he wasn't pushing her too far, that she was okay with everything he was doing.

The flutters of her orgasm had begun long ago. She'd likely have come already if she'd given in to the urge. But she gritted her teeth and warded it off, wanting to come when he came. Together.

"I'm close," she said faintly.

"Tell me what to do, baby. Tell me how to help you."

"Just touch me," she whispered. "And take me hard, Jace. Don't be easy. I need it hard and fast. I want you deep."

His growl echoed through the room as though her blunt words made him lose the last vestiges of control. He was like a crazy person. Frantic. He began pumping into her as hard and as fast as she'd asked for.

The room went blurry around her and her orgasm built and built and, impossibly, built some more until her entire body was one giant rubber band at full stretch. Oh God, she couldn't take much more. She needed release and yet the explosion hadn't occurred. It was still climbing, higher and higher until she couldn't breathe, couldn't think, couldn't process anything but the excruciating tension that coiled in her belly.

She squeezed her eyes shut. Her fingers curled into tight fists above her head. Her knees locked and her back bowed as she raised her head up, trying desperately to achieve relief from the vicious ache assailing her.

He thrust again. Hard. Almost savage. Hell, it *was* savage. Each powerful push took her breath until her lungs screamed for mercy.

She ground her teeth together, tensing from head to toe. It had to come now. She couldn't take any more without breaking.

And then in a tumultuous flash, it roared over her like a tidal wave. Fierce. Powerful. All-consuming. Her body went flying in a dozen different directions. Something inside her snapped loose. Relief from the incredible tension.

She sagged into the bed, her cheek pressing to the mattress. Eyes closed, body limp, she lay there as Jace continued to pump into her body. Each thrust sent a delicate shiver, almost unbearable, through her pussy. She was hypersensitive. So much so that every movement was a delicious sort of agony.

She whimpered and Jace went still deep inside her and then she felt him pulsing wetly. She was slick with his semen, but still, he held himself there, his cock twitching until the very last of his release was wrung from it.

He leaned forward, his body pressing warmly to hers. He kissed the center of her back just between her shoulder blades as his hands skated hotly up her sides and then back down again to cup her hips.

"So beautiful," he murmured. "I've never seen a more beautiful sight than you tied to my bed, pussy open, waiting for me, your ass red from my crop."

She shivered underneath him and then he pushed upward, withdrawing wetly from inside her. He left her, his footsteps disappearing in the distance.

She lay there, sated, exhausted, her body humming in the aftermath. She drifted off, existing in a haze between awareness and unconsciousness. Unsure of how much time had actually passed, she was roused when Jace's hands slid back over her ass. When he leaned in, his cock was rigid again, surprising her. More time than she'd realized had to have passed.

He wanted her again.

Her arms and legs ached from being pulled so tight with the ropes, but she didn't complain. He would take care of her afterward. He'd never push her too far. He seemed very in tune with her limits and he'd exhibited extreme patience while working up to this point. She trusted him.

"Going to fuck that sweet ass," he murmured close to her ear. "Been dreaming about it. You're in a perfect position. Legs spread. On your belly. Helpless. Not a damn thing you can do. Going to come all over your ass. Inside, outside. I'll be in you so deep you'll feel me in your belly."

A full-body shiver worked its way from her shoulders to her feet. Chill bumps broke out and raced across her skin until every part of her tingled with awareness.

He lifted himself off her again and left her only to return a few seconds later. Something warm dribbled over the crack of her ass. Then he spread her cheeks and squeezed more over her opening. His fingers glided over the area, spreading the lubricant, pausing over her entrance before pressing inward.

One finger slipped easily past the barrier, coating the opening and just inside. Then he added more lubricant and gently pushed another finger, stretching her to accommodate both digits.

She moaned softly, the burn in her ass edgy and sharp. Not unlike the crop. Both pleasurable. Just in different ways.

"I should spend more time preparing you," he said in a strained voice. "But I can't. Want you too badly. I need you to relax and work with me, baby. I'll try to go slow."

His fingers withdrew and then he added more lubricant, smoothing it around the opening. Then the blunt head of his cock pressed against the entrance. Pressure built as her body resisted, refusing him entrance.

A low growl sounded in his throat. She shivered again, aroused, on fire, burning. Just for him.

"Let me in, baby. Relax. Don't fight it."

She sucked in her breath and let it out in a long exhale as she tried to force herself to do as he'd commanded. She let out a whimper as he pushed relentlessly forward, opening her body to his advance. She clamped her mouth shut, worried he'd stop. But he didn't. He seemed too far gone to heed any sign of distress from her.

He continued to exert steady pressure, pushing, pushing, until finally her body gave way and he sank halfway in. His hands tightened at her waist, his fingers flexing spasmodically.

"God, baby," he groaned.

He pulled back, his cock dragging over super-sensitized, distended flesh. Withdrawal was potent, extremely pleasurable, the relief enormous. But then he pushed forward again and her body's natural resistance to the invasion kicked in, making it difficult and painful as he pressed in all the way to his balls.

"Fuck me," he said in a strangled voice. "Take me whole. Goddamn, Bethany. What you do to me."

He dragged himself back, slowly retreating, her opening quivering around him. He nearly left her, only leaving the head of his penis tucked inside her opening. He waited for the opening to close, fitting snugly around his cock head, and then he ruthlessly opened her again, thrusting forward, his strength overcoming her resistance.

Her mouth opened in a silent scream. Her breaths rushed from her nostrils and then, not able to suck in enough air through her nose, she gave up and gulped in mouthfuls, her chest heaving against the mattress as she fought the bombardment of divergent sensations.

Pain. Pleasure. Fear. Arousal. Powerlessness. Strength. Unrelenting pleasure.

Safety.

Comfort.

His possession.

"I'll take care of you afterward," he murmured as he leaned forward, his cock stroking through her distended opening. "This is for me."

And then he began to pound against her ass, his thighs slapping against her cheeks, each thrust sending a shockwave through her body. He palmed her cheeks, pushing upward to make her ass more accessible. The movement stretched the opening around his cock tighter and he let out a low moan.

He levered himself up and over her, positioning all his weight so he was atop her fully. Blanketing her. Covering every inch of her back as his hips worked in and out, driving deeply into her ass.

His teeth grazed her shoulder. His hands reached over her head to find hers, cupped his palms over the wrists that were bound and he gripped her tight as he continued to hump himself over her body.

Hot spurts of semen exploded into her ass. He continued thrusting, each forward motion depositing more of his release deep into her body. On and on, in a seemingly never-ending stream, he pumped more into her until finally he collapsed against her, his body heaving with exertion.

His cock was wedged inside her ass and twitched with the last vestiges of his release. Some of the semen had worked its way out of her ass with the forceful thrusts and was sliding warmly between her legs.

He lay there a long while, still inside her, as his breaths calmed and he quieted above her. He kissed her shoulder and then smoothed his hands down her arms and then down her sides.

"So beautiful," he whispered. "And mine. You're mine, Bethany. You belong to me. Only to me."

She wasn't going to argue. She was perfectly content to be his for as long as he wanted her. And she tried not to dwell on how short a time that might be.

chapter twenty-seven

Jace rose quietly from bed, careful not to wake Bethany. She was sleeping soundly. She hadn't stirred since he'd untied her and carried her into the bathroom to bathe and pamper her before putting her to bed. The moment her head had hit the pillow, she'd fallen asleep. Which was good because in order for him to pull off his Christmas morning surprise, he'd definitely needed her oblivious.

It had gutted him to hear she'd never had a Christmas tree, but what hurt him the most was that he hadn't put up a tree in their apartment. Their home. He hadn't even put one up for her in the other apartment she spent time in. Trees had been something he'd always done without fail for Mia when she was growing up. He'd taken her to see the lighting of the tree at Rockefeller Center. But when she'd gotten older and they had separate residences, he'd never bothered putting up a tree. It hadn't made any sense when it was just him, and so he hadn't even thought about putting up a tree for Bethany.

After they'd gotten home, and Bethany had fallen asleep after they'd made love, he'd made a few emergency calls and Gabe, Mia and Ash had come over with an artificial tree and ornaments and they'd quietly decorated it in the living room. Jace had left the lights twinkling so that Bethany would see them when she went into the living room the next morning. He couldn't wait to see her face. Moreover, he'd make damn sure she never went without a tree again.

He went to his dresser and opened the top drawer, pulling out the small wrapped gift for Bethany. Then he returned to bed, glancing at the window as first light softly illuminated the room.

She was beautiful in the pale light of dawn. Her hair spread out on his pillow, her fingers clutching his sheets. In his bed. Which was where she belonged.

He crawled back into bed, putting the present between them as he propped himself on his elbow, content to watch her while she slept. He could wait. He loved to watch her wake up, her eyes all dreamy and content. Fogged with sleep, a soft smile on her face. It was the way she awakened every morning. As if she were grateful for every moment away from her old life.

It hurt him that she'd ever lived that life. He'd give anything to be able to erase it. But he couldn't change the past. He could sure as hell change the future though.

After a few moments, no longer able to withstand the temptation, he reached his finger out to trace the soft lines of her face. He followed the curve of her cheekbone, enjoying the satiny skin.

Her eyelashes fluttered and her eyes opened, immediately finding his gaze. Her eyes were soft and oh so sweet, cloudy but welcoming as if she were the most content woman in the world. What man wouldn't love his woman waking up with that kind of look on her face? Like there was no place on earth she'd rather be.

"Merry Christmas," he murmured as he leaned down to kiss her.

"Merry Christmas," she returned.

He pushed the box across the bed so it was right in front of her. "I got you a present. Well, it's only one of the presents I got you."

Her eyes widened. "Jace, we agreed no presents."

She sounded genuinely distressed and Jace's chest clenched. He put his finger over her lips to hush her.

"No, *you* agreed no presents. I never made any such agreement," he said gently.

"But I have nothing to give you," she said in agitation.

He smiled, his entire heart softening. "After what you gave me last night, you can honestly say that this morning?"

She flushed and dropped her gaze. He wouldn't allow it, though. He tipped her chin up with his finger, forcing her to look at him again.

"Bethany, you gave me something more precious than I will ever give to you. You gave me your trust. You gave me yourself."

Her cheeks went pink but pleasure sparked in her eyes.

"Now open this present. I wanted to give this one to you separately."

She pushed herself upward so she could sit cross-legged in front of the box. She stared down at it as if it would bite her. Then she hesitantly pulled the bow from the top and tore the paper off.

It took two attempts before she managed to open the box and then she pulled out an intricate leather choker with a huge diamond teardrop in the very middle, designed to rest in the hollow of her throat.

He'd spent a lot of time searching for just the right piece of jewelry. It wasn't just a necklace. Far from it. It was a stamp of his possession. A signal of his ownership. It was a . . . collar. Not that he would tell her that. Later. When she was more comfortable in their relationship. For now, he was content with the knowledge that he knew what it was and that she would wear it.

He'd looked at diamond chokers. He'd looked at beautifully rendered precious stones in an array of decorative patterns. But nothing had stood out as being something that suited Bethany. Until he'd seen the rustic leather design. He'd had the diamond teardrop added because it elevated the leather choker from simple to elegant and expensive. Something more worthy of the woman he considered his.

"Jace, it's beautiful," she whispered. "Will you put it on me?"

Even as she spoke, she held out the choker to him and when he took it, she turned, presenting her back to him. She reached back to lift her hair and he arranged it around her neck, securing it in back. It fit perfectly, snug against her slim neck.

When she turned back around, he was able to see the full effect, and it was magnificent. His cock swelled and his body surged to life at seeing his collar around her neck. She was his and now the world would know it.

The leather bands flowed in a delicate pattern, crisscrossing as they made their way around her neck. The diamond dangled in the middle, making the necklace look dainty and delicate. Just like Bethany. It was bloody perfect. *She* was perfect.

"I want you to always wear it," he said in a low voice. "Never take it off. Promise me."

Her eyes widened, but her face was flushed with happiness. "I promise."

He leaned forward, taking her mouth, plundering it with his tongue until they were both gasping for breath.

"Put on one of my robes so you don't get cold. I'll go turn on the fireplace and you can open the rest of your presents."

Her lips twisted into an unhappy frown. "I wish you hadn't gotten me presents."

He grinned. "Tough, baby. You need to get used to the fact that I'm going to spoil you at every opportunity. Getting you Christmas presents is my present. Seeing you happy is the best gift I could ever ask for. Watching you opening the stuff I bought for you will make this the best Christmas I've ever had."

She surprised him by launching herself into his arms. She tackled him and knocked him flat on his back on the bed. She hugged him fiercely, peppering his face with kisses.

"Thank you. You can't know what this means to me," she whispered.

He smiled tenderly up at her as he smoothed the hair from her face. "Not as much as you mean to me. That I can guarantee."

He patted her on the ass and then said, "Now, let's get up. You have a surprise in the living room."

She heaved an exaggerated sigh. "Jaaace." His name came out as a plaintive wail but he only grinned and rolled her off him.

"Come on. It's Christmas morning. Time to get your ass out of bed so we can celebrate."

She grinned, her eyes lighting with excitement. Regardless of the fact that she'd been adamant that he not get her presents, there was no way in hell he wasn't going to make the most of their first Christmas together.

He handed her a robe so she wouldn't be cold. He didn't want her dressed because he planned for them to spend the day in bed right after she saw her tree and opened her presents.

Pausing only to pull on pajama bottoms, he tugged at her hand and guided her into the living room.

She came to a full stop when she saw the tree with hundreds of white lights and the presents piled underneath. Tears immediately filled her eyes and her mouth fell open.

She turned to him, her expression one of joy and surprise. "How did you do this? Oh, Jace, it's beautiful! I love it!"

He tugged her into his arms and kissed her forehead. "Merry Christmas, baby. Now go open your presents."

She all but ran to the tree like an eager child on Christmas morning. His heart ached to think of her never having this experience, but he was damn glad he could be the one to give it to her.

"They're so beautiful I don't want to open them," she said in a hushed, reverent tone.

He laughed. "The fun is ripping the paper off as fast as you can."

Needing no further encouragement, she ripped into the packages, exclaiming in delight as she uncovered each one. Her favorite were the shoes. He'd bought her an array of sexy, high-heeled, sparkly shoes. Of all the things she'd loved when he'd first taken her shopping, the shoes had gotten her attention the most. She'd looked at several pairs wistfully and then flinched at the price tags.

Second on her favorites list was the huge basket of gourmet hot chocolate in a variety of flavors, from milk to dark chocolate.

After she'd opened all the gifts, she launched herself into his arms and they ended up on the floor, him flat on his back laughing as she peppered his entire face with kisses again.

He gazed up at her, taking in her beautiful smile and the joy burning bright in her eyes.

"Have to say, this is the best Christmas ever," he said softly.

"Wait, that's my line," she protested. "And how can you say that? I didn't get you anything!"

He shook his head solemnly. "All I wanted is right here in my arms. You smiling and looking at me like I just handed you the world. There'll never be a better present than that, baby."

chapter twenty-eight

Bethany stirred as Jace slipped from underneath the sheets. He leaned down to kiss her forehead and he murmured, "Sleep, baby. I have to go into work today. You can stay here."

She sat up, pulling the sheets to cover her breasts. It was an absurd notion that she should try to hide herself. She'd spent most of Christmas naked. In Jace's arms. He'd made love to her until they'd both fallen into an exhausted sleep.

But now she felt self-conscious and a little nervous. Her hand fluttered to the choker he'd given her and she traced the lines of the leather design with her fingertip.

She didn't feel comfortable staying in Jace's apartment all day when he wasn't there. None of her things were here. It was Jace's place. Definitely a bachelor pad. It looked and smelled all male. And while she didn't have much, at least the apartment she was staying in looked feminine. She was comfortable there. It was starting to feel like something of her own.

"Actually, I thought I'd go back to my apartment if you're going in to work," she said quietly.

He frowned but recovered quickly. "If that's what you want. I'll swing by after I finish at the office. We can spend the evening there if you want."

She nodded. Despite her having her own place, they hadn't spent a night away from each other since they'd met. In fact, other than the time Jace spent at work, they'd been inseparable.

"If you want, I'll drop you off on my way to work."

"I won't make you late?"

He smiled. "I'm the boss, remember? I can go in whenever the hell I want."

"Okay. I'd like that."

"Give me five minutes in the shower and then it's all yours."

She watched him walk naked toward the bathroom, all his masculine beauty and rough edges on display. His hair, which was tousled from their endless lovemaking, only made him look all the more delicious.

He paused at the doorway of the bathroom and glanced back, his eyes glittering with fire, almost as if he'd known the direction of her thoughts. Then he grinned, his face transforming. She caught her breath because his smile was extraordinary. He didn't smile often. He had a darker look about him. Almost always serious. Brooding. But when he smiled, she couldn't breathe.

She sat up when he disappeared inside the bathroom. He'd left the door open, though. An invitation? She licked her lips, her mouth suddenly dry.

If they showered together, they'd get done in half the time. Or maybe not. Because if she got in with him, they wouldn't just shower.

Which wasn't necessarily a bad thing.

No, it would be a very, very *good* thing.

Throwing aside the sheets, she crawled out of bed, shivering lightly as she left the warmth. Heat that was still present from when he'd been lying in bed with her.

She hesitated a moment, eyeing the bathroom, waiting for the telltale sign of steam from the shower. After a few minutes, she heard the water turn on and she quietly made her way to the door.

His shower was huge. Easily big enough for two. Or even three. Completely glassed in with multiple showerheads, one overhead and two jets mounted on the wall. His outline was visible through the fogged glass and she could see him washing himself, his hands drifting lower and lower . . .

She opened the stall door and stepped inside before she lost her nerve. His eyes came open, his hand circled around his cock. He blinked in surprise, but the surprise quickly turned to molten desire. His eyes went liquid and his hand stroked over the length of his cock.

He went from a semi-flaccid stage to erect and straining in two seconds flat. If there was any doubt in her mind that he'd welcome her into his shower, it fled as his body came to life in front of her eyes.

"That's my job," she murmured as she slid her hand over his erection, removing his in the process.

"By all means," he said.

Water streamed down his back and rolled down his gorgeous body. His hair was soaked and she could see it was longer than she thought it was. With the weight of the water, there was no body to it, no slight unruly curl. It hung past his neck to the tops of his shoulders.

"You're so beautiful," she whispered as she moved closer so their bodies touched.

The water hit her, pulling her in, the heat an exquisite temptation.

His body tensed and his eyes grew rougher, darker. His arms came around her, molding their bodies together as she continued to caress him with her hand.

"You're the beautiful one, Bethany. I never get tired of just looking at you."

She smiled and rolled up on the balls of her feet so she could kiss him.

"I've never had shower sex before," she said huskily against his mouth.

"Then we most assuredly need to remedy that right away."

She slid down his body to her knees, water raining down over them. She glanced up to see his gaze locked with hers, and then it drifted to his groin, where she caressed him to further hardness.

As light as a hush, her mouth feathered over the mushroomed head, her tongue flicking out to tease the sensitive underside. Drops of water hit her tongue, filling her mouth as she sucked him deeper.

A tortured groan sounded above the spray of the water. His hands went to her hair, now drenched and plastered to the side of her head. He framed her face with his palms and held her tightly as he pushed inside her mouth.

His features were harsh, lines forming at his mouth and at his temples. She could see his chest work up and down, his breath coming in ragged bursts as she worked him deeper, to the back of her throat.

Applying light suction, she took him even deeper, boldly making love to him. He hit the back of her throat and she swallowed. This time he emitted a hiss, the violent expulsion of air loud over the sound of rushing water.

He stroked over her head, then to her cheeks, lightly caressing the lines of her face as her throat worked around him. His touch was infinitely gentle, so tender that her heart squeezed in response.

He was her addiction. Replacing everything else. With him, there was no need for the coping mechanisms of the past. He was her anchor. He was what sex and pills used to be for her. A safe place in a world of uncertainty.

Had she merely traded one addiction for another?

The thought took root in her mind, a shadow that gave her pause. But she shook it off, determined not to let her past ruin what she had with Jace. Right here and now. She was finished living in the past, wasn't she? Jace had given her new life. He'd made her believe that they were starting new and fresh, that what had been no longer mattered. That it was what was to come that was important.

With everything else he'd given her for Christmas, this was the most precious gift she could ever hope to receive.

She sucked deeply again, pouring every bit of her heart, her feelings for him into her movements. She hoped he could see, could *feel* what she was giving him. It was the only thing she had to give him. She just hoped it was enough.

Jace's grip tightened on her face. Then he roughly slid his hands down and underneath her arms. He lifted, hauling her up his body. His mouth met hers in a heated clash that left her gasping for breath.

Then he hoisted her and, in one swift movement, he turned and pressed her against the wall of the shower.

"Wrap your legs around me," he growled.

The fierce command sent shivers down her spine. Her belly clenched and butterflies took flight in her chest. Already his cock had found her opening and as she hooked her ankles at the small of his back, he plunged, finding his depth in one forceful thrust.

His fingers dug into her buttocks, massaging and molding, holding her open as he pounded into her again. His mouth brushed teasingly against her neck and then he sunk his teeth into the sensitive column, eliciting another gasp from her.

He sucked as he plunged over and over, driving her body against the shower wall. His hands seemed to be everywhere, his mouth driving her insane with lust. She'd have a mark on her neck later, evidence of his possession and the bruising force in which he took her. And yet she wanted more. More strength. More ferocity. It would never be enough.

"Not going to last long, baby," he said roughly, his voice strained and garbled. "How close are you? Want you there."

She took one arm from around his neck where she was gripping him tightly and slid her hand between their bodies, down to her clit. As soon as she touched herself, her body coiled into a tight knot.

"Close," she gasped.

"Good. Get there."

He leaned into her, trapping her hand between them. She barely had room to caress the taut bundle of nerves between her legs. He pounded into her, driving her against the wall, driving himself deeper into her. She felt bruised and shaken, the force with which he took her overwhelming.

She was his. She truly belonged. To him.

Her thighs shook, her entire body quaked. Desire rose, sharp and edgy. Overpowering. Her climax built into a crescendo that was nearly deafening. The roar in her ears. The pounding of her heart. She screamed hoarsely and then his shout of triumph joined her cries.

He leaned into her, buried deeply, his chest heaving with exertion. He kissed her neck. Her jaw. Then her lips, his breaths mingling with hers.

Dimly, she became aware of the water still rushing over them. The steam was choking, the air so moist it was hard to breathe in.

"Christ," Jace muttered. "You undo me, Bethany. How the hell am I supposed to even move now, much less finish showering and get to work?"

She smiled against his neck and then let her body slide down the wall until she stood on shaking legs.

"Guess I'll just have to finish washing you," she murmured.

"Oh hell no," he grumbled. "I'm going to wash your hair and then kick you out of my shower. If you put your hands on me again, we'll never leave the bathroom."

Her grin broadened and she leaned up to kiss his firm jaw. "I'm not going to argue with a man who wants to wash my hair for me."

chapter twenty-nine

When Jace's car pulled up to her apartment building, he acted as though he were reluctant to let Bethany get out. He held on to her hand for a long moment before leaning over to kiss her. Fierce. Possessive. She struggled to pull in a breath when he finally released her and his gaze glittered, his eyes going dark and sultry.

"I'll be over when I finish at work."

She nodded and then opened her door.

"Be careful. The rain is picking up. I don't want you to get wet."

She smiled. "A little rain never hurt anyone, Jace."

"Still, it's cold. I want you inside quickly so you don't come down with something."

She leaned back in to kiss him and then she got out and as he'd requested, she made a dash for the entrance, dodging raindrops as she went. A burst of laughter escaped and she marveled at how happy and light she sounded. She turned just inside the door to see Jace's car pull away into traffic and she stood staring until it disappeared from sight.

She was about to push in and go up to her apartment when she heard her name.

Frowning, she turned and to her shock, Jack stood a few feet away. He was wet and bedraggled, carrying only his tattered backpack.

"Jack!"

His name came out as a whisper and then she hurried forward, stepping once more into the cold drizzle.

"Jack, what are you doing here?" she asked. "How long have you stood out here?"

He gave her a half smile. "Wasn't sure when you'd be back. I had the doorman ring up to your apartment yesterday but you weren't here. So I hung around, hoping to catch you."

"Oh, Jack, I'm so sorry." Her voice was stricken. And guilt flooded her. While she'd been happy and warm, celebrating the holiday with Jace and his family, Jack had been here, waiting for her in the cold. No place to sleep or be out of the elements.

"Nothing to be sorry for, Bethy. If it's not a good time, I can come back . . ."

"No!" she said fiercely. "Come inside. You need to get out of the cold. I had no idea you'd come. I'd hoped you would. If I'd known, I would have been here."

She took his arm, dragging him toward the entrance. When they met the doorman, she thrust her chin up, daring him to pass judgment.

"This is Jack. He's my brother. I'm giving him a key. If I'm not here and he needs in, you're to let him pass."

The doorman respectfully nodded. "Of course, Miss Willis."

She hurried Jack toward the elevator and winced as he dripped all over the inside. He was shivering and he looked even thinner than the last time she'd seen him. Had he been eating anything at all?

She should have looked after him better. Should have made more of an effort to make sure he was taken care of. She had so much now and it killed her to think of Jack still on the streets. Not when she could provide a place to stay and food to eat.

"Nice place," Jack muttered when she shoved him inside her apartment.

"Yeah, it is. Go into the bathroom and take a hot shower. I'll lay out some of Jace's clothes. They'll be big on you, but they'll at least be warm and dry."

Again that crooked grin as she bustled him into her bedroom.

"Jace the guy who hooked you up with all of this?"

Bethany softened, a smile curving her lips. "Yeah. He's a good man, Jack. The best. I'm . . . happy."

Jack reached out to touch her cheek. "I'm glad, Bethy. You deserve to be happy."

"So do you," she said fiercely.

His smile was sadder this time. "I'm sorry about what happened. I never meant for you to be involved."

"I know," she said in a soft voice. "Now go. Get a shower. I'll fix you something to eat, okay?"

As Jack disappeared into the bathroom, Bethany pulled out a pair of Jace's jeans and one of the T-shirts he'd left in her apartment. She found a pair of socks that would fit Jack, wanting his feet to be warm. Shoes. She needed to buy him new shoes. The ones he wore now were threadbare, the soles coming off and there were holes. They were no barrier to the cold.

After leaving the clothing where he could find it, she went back into the kitchen.

She pulled out bacon, a carton of eggs and some ham and cheese. An omelet would be quick and it had lots of protein. She busied herself with the preparation and by the time Jack reappeared, dressed in Jace's clothes, she had his plate ready.

"You want juice or milk?" she asked when he took a seat at the bar.

He shrugged. "Doesn't matter. I'll drink whatever."

After pondering a moment, she pulled two glasses down and poured a glass of each. The extra nutrition certainly wouldn't hurt.

"I can't stay long," Jack said. He was already digging into the omelet with gusto. Bethany cringed to imagine when his last good meal had been. "I have shit to see to. I just wanted to see you and leave my pack here, if that's all right."

"Of course it's all right," she said. "But why can't you stay?"

"I'll be back. Just some things I need to take care of and I didn't want to have my pack. Could get stolen out there. You know how it is. Always someone wanting what someone else has."

He was vague and it bothered her.

"What's in the backpack?"

He ignored her question and then reached into his pocket. He pulled out a pill bottle and her stomach clenched.

"I got these for you, Bethy. I know you need them sometimes."

Her heart began to pound when he slid the bottle across the counter.

"No, Jack." She shook her head adamantly. "I don't do that anymore. You *know* that. I can't go back to that. *Ever.*"

"Still, they'll be here if you need them."

"How did you get them?" she asked, dread crowding her chest. "How could you afford that? Tell me you didn't borrow more money."

He glanced up, swallowing the last bite of his omelet. "I didn't borrow money. Someone owed me a favor. He hooked me up."

She closed her eyes. "Jack, you can't keep doing this. You know it's no good. It's no way to live. I don't want you taking drugs either. You can beat this. It doesn't have to be this way. Not now."

His gaze hardened. "The way we've been living is no way to live. We survive, Bethy, we don't live. You know that. And sometimes the pills make the surviving a little easier. Besides, you may have moved up in the world, but I haven't."

"That's not true!" she protested. "What's mine is yours. You know that."

Jack shook his head. "Do you really think your new boyfriend is going to want me hanging around here? Think about it, Bethy. What man would want his girlfriend's homeless *brother* as excess baggage? You can't be that naïve."

She sucked in her breath as pain exploded in her chest. "You know I won't choose between you two. You know I'd never do that. I love you, Jack. I owe everything to you. I'm not going to forget that. If Jace can't accept that, then he and I don't have a future."

Jack reached across the bar to put his hand over hers. "Don't be stupid, babe. Don't throw your chance away on me. You've got a chance to make something good. Don't ruin it."

Tears filled her eyes. "I won't just forget about you. I'm not like that. Do you honestly think I could live here, make a new life, while you're out there on the streets? If you do think that then you don't know me."

His gaze softened. "You're the only person in this world I love and who loves me. And that's why I want the best for you. Do this for me, okay? I just need to leave my stuff here for a few hours. I'll come back. Maybe we can have dinner together. I always thought it would be cool if we had a place where you could cook and we could pretend we were normal people just like everyone else."

She nodded, her pulse still hammering in her veins. She'd call Jace. He'd understand if she called off their evening. "I can cook something. Tell me what you'd like. I'll make sure I have the stuff for it."

"Whatever you want to cook. I'll eat whatever. Surprise me."

She turned her hand so she could squeeze Jack's. "I'm just glad you're here. Really. I've been so worried about you."

"You shouldn't worry about me, babe. You know I can take care of myself."

He pulled his hand back and then drained both glasses before setting them back down. "I need to roll. Got shit to do. I'll try to make it back by dark."

"Please be careful," she begged.

He gave her that cocky grin again. "Always do. Thanks for the food and the clothes. I left my pack in your bedroom. I'll get it later, okay?"

262 · Maya Banks

She nodded and watched as he walked out of her apartment as fast as he'd come in. Then her gaze lighted on the bottle he'd left and she snatched it up to put it away in one of the cabinets.

Worry and anxiety ate at her until her stomach tossed and turned. What was Jack into?

She checked her watch and then went to the drawer where Jace had left money for her to use. She wasn't sure where the nearest market was, but she could ask the doorman. Hopefully it wasn't a long walk. The weather sucked and she didn't want to waste money on a cab.

Already she was running possibilities through her head. She would cook a fabulous meal. All of Jack's favorites. And she'd make him sandwiches to take with him because she knew he wouldn't agree to stay. She could buy nonperishable items he could stow in his bag so he'd have something to eat for more than a few days.

She peeled off several of the bills and stuffed them into her jeans pocket and then headed down to ask the doorman for the nearest place she could buy groceries.

Bethany ducked out of the cab after paying the fare and hurried, bags in hand, to her building's entrance. The doorman had advised her to take a cab and she'd relented when she'd seen the increase in rain. It had morphed from a light drizzle to more of a steady downpour. Not what she wanted to be caught out in on her way back from the market carrying groceries.

When she unlocked her apartment and walked in, she was stunned to see Jace in the living room, his expression dark and forbidding. He advanced on her before she even had time to deposit the bags on the kitchen bar.

"Where the fuck have you been?" he demanded.

Her eyes widened and she glanced down at the grocery sacks. "I—I went shopping."

"Anything else you want to tell me?"

The accusation in his voice stung. What on earth did he think? Did he believe she was cheating on him? Sneaking out to see a lover? How had he even known she was gone to begin with?

He wrested the bags from her grip and dropped them with a *thud* on the bar before turning his furious gaze back to her.

Her mind blanked. She took an instinctive step back and Jace swore.

"I'm not going to hurt you, damn it."

"Why are you so angry?" she asked. "I just went down to the market. I was only gone an hour."

"You think this is about you going out for groceries?"

His tone was incredulous.

"What else am I supposed to think? You're acting ridiculous, Jace. I went to get groceries, for God's sake."

"Let's try this instead. I'm at work in an important meeting and I get a call from Kaden, who informs me you have a visitor."

Her mouth dropped open in shock. "How does Kaden know anything about who's at my apartment? He's not even supposed to be protecting me anymore." Her eyes narrowed as understanding slowly dawned. "You *still* don't trust me." It nearly killed her to say those words, the truth. And it was the truth. He was bristling with rage and he'd hired those men to watch her. "He wasn't here to protect me. He was here to spy on me."

"It would appear I have good reason," Jace snapped.

Hope died inside Bethany. She turned her painful gaze on him, hurt beyond words. "Jack was here. But then you already know that."

"Yes. *Jack*," he spat out. "What the fuck was he doing here?"

Her brow furrowed and this time she took a step forward, anger tightening her features. "He came to see me. He was here at Christmas, only I wasn't here because I was with you. He had to spend the holiday alone. No food. No warm place to be. Alone, Jace. On the streets. I don't need to tell you what a wonderful holiday that makes for."

"How did he even know to show up here?" Jace demanded.

She blinked. "I gave him the address."

"And when did you do this?"

She flushed. "The day I went to see him."

Jace's lips tightened into a nearly indistinguishable line. "You invited him here."

She nodded. "Of course."

He swore again. "There is no 'of course' to it, Bethany. What the fuck were you thinking?"

"What is wrong with you?" she demanded. "Am I not allowed to invite people to this apartment? Did I get it wrong and it's not really for my use? Or is it only uses I have your approval for?"

"You invited a man who damn near got you killed. He got you attacked. He's the last person you need to have anything to do with."

The blood drained from her face. "He never intended for me to be hurt. He'd never do anything to hurt me."

Disgust flooded Jace's face. His eyes were swamped with it.

"Really, Bethany? And why do you suppose he's here now?"

She didn't like his tone. His expression. She liked nothing about this confrontation. He was so angry. Sickness pitted deep in her stomach, curling and knotting into a painful ball.

"He came to see me," she said in a low voice. "He's cold and hungry. I fixed him something to eat. I went out for groceries so I could cook dinner for him."

Jace reached over the back of the couch and pulled up Jack's backpack. He dangled it from his finger, his eyes going cold with rage.

"Is that the only reason he came? Where is he now?"

"I don't know what you're trying to imply. He said he had things to do. He wanted to leave the backpack here because he didn't want it stolen from him. You don't understand how it works out there. If someone sees you have anything, they take it. They'll stab you, hurt you, kill you to get it. You can get murdered for five dollars."

"Oh I have no doubt someone would kill him for what's in here," Jace bit out.

He yanked it and gaped open the top so she could see inside. What little blood was left in her cheeks fled and she wavered, teetering unsteadily until she had to reach out to the bar to gain her balance.

Drugs. Lots of drugs. Prescription pills. What looked like marijuana and other stuff she had no idea of but it looked . . . bad. Really bad.

"I found this in your bedroom," Jace bit out. "With this shit in it. I hope to fuck you didn't know what was in it when you agreed to let him leave it here."

"I didn't know," she whispered.

"Jesus, Bethany. How long are you going to allow him to manipulate you? Until someone kills you? What's it going to take for you to wake up and see the truth staring you in the face?"

"He won't hurt me!" she shouted. "Just stop it!"

Jace tossed the bag back onto the couch, his entire body shaking with anger.

"I won't have it. Not here. Not where you are. As long as you wear *my* collar, you're under my protection. He's not allowed here, Bethany. Either you tell him that or I will and next time I won't come alone. I'll bring the police and I'll have him arrested. I don't give a fuck if that pisses you off or not. My one and *only* concern here is you. I don't give a fuck about a man who holds you in so little regard that he'd expose you to this."

"I won't choose between the two of you!" she yelled. "I won't! You don't understand. I can't turn my back on him. I won't!"

"So that's it then," Jace said grimly.

"It doesn't have to be! Why can't you just leave so I can work this out with Jack? Why can't you trust me that much?"

"It's not you I don't trust," he said just as loud. "Damn it, Bethany, use your head! Do you know what would happen if you were found with this shit? It would be *you* going to jail, not your precious Jack. You'd take the rap for him, and do you think it would make any difference?"

She shook her head. "No. No! Just go, Jace. I'll take care of this. Just go."

"You forget this is *my* apartment," he ground out.

She went even whiter, feeling sensation leach from her face. She went numb to her toes. Then she turned around and walked stiffly to the door.

"Bethany, stop."

It was a command. One that, for the first time, she ignored. When she heard him start after her, she started running. Out the door toward the elevator. She got inside, hearing Jace as he ran down the hall shouting her name. She punched the button repeatedly, praying it would close.

It slammed shut when he was two feet from the door, his curses ringing in her ears as the elevator began its descent.

When she got to the lobby, the doorman tried to stop her. Jace had probably called him. But she darted around him, ignoring his pleas for her to stop. She ran outside, and into the street, nearly getting hit by a cab that came to a screeching halt mere inches from her legs.

Before he could get out, she ran to the passenger side and threw open the door.

"Are you crazy?" the cabbie bellowed. "I could have killed you!"

"Just drive," she choked out. "I don't care where, just get me out of here, please."

She must have looked deranged. Tears she hadn't even realized she was shedding now formed wet trails down her cheeks. The taxi driver's face softened before he turned around and then accelerated, waving at angry drivers behind him who'd been forced to stop when he'd braked so hard. Horns blared but faded in the distance as they sped down the street.

chapter thirty

Bethany walked the last block to her apartment, numb. Numb from cold. Numb from the relentless rain soaking through her clothing. She hadn't gone far in the cab. She hadn't had much cash left on her from her shopping trip. And so she'd walked. Endlessly, her thoughts in turmoil, hurt crashing through her heart.

Jace had a right to be angry. She didn't refute that. But he hadn't even given her a chance to explain. He'd been so furious. And then he'd reminded her that he owned the apartment. That she was there due to his generosity. He'd reminded her that she had nothing. Nothing but the hopelessness of their situation.

He didn't trust her. He'd hammered that point home to her over and over. And she couldn't exist in a relationship where he suspected the worst at every turn. She'd never be able to overcome that. No matter how hard she tried, how much she gave to him, she'd never get to a place where she had his trust.

She wasn't even sure why she was back. But she needed her things. She'd take some of the clothing. Certainly not all of it, but she knew she needed the coat. And the jeans and the shirts. She could take the food she'd bought for Jack and then maybe wait for him to come back. Had he already been back? Had she missed him?

At least they'd have something to eat for the next while. She could check with the shelters she frequented and maybe, just maybe, one would have a bed.

Or maybe she should just call Jace. Try to explain. He deserved that much at least. He needed to know *why* she could never turn her back on Jack. She'd never fully explained. Never shared that part of herself.

Would he understand? Could he possibly understand?

But what good would it do if he was never going to trust her?

When she trudged into the entrance of her apartment building, the doorman looked alarmed. She waved off his concern and headed for the elevator, only wanting to be somewhere warm and dry, even if it was temporary.

There had to be a way to fix this. Jace was the best thing in her life. The only thing that was good and untarnished. She didn't want Jack's problems to touch Jace. Jace didn't deserve that. He deserved someone without the stains she carried on her soul. Somebody he could trust fully. And maybe she didn't even blame him for the seeds of mistrust that had been planted. She wanted his trust, wanted him to have faith in her, but in reality, with all he knew of her, was it even reasonable that he'd trust her so readily?

A wave of sadness overwhelmed her. She didn't want to be the person she'd been for so long. She wanted to be someone worthy of love and trust. She wanted someone to believe in her. She'd thought Jace could be that person. She'd been wrong.

She let herself into her apartment and went into the kitchen, intent on making some hot cocoa. When she opened the cabinet where the mugs were kept, her gaze lighted on the bottle of pills Jack had left. For the longest moment she simply stared. And then as if she were in a daze, her hand slowly reached out, her fingers curling around the plastic bottle.

She brought it down and set it on the counter in front of her. One pill. Just one. It would make things more manageable. It would transport her to a warmer, happier place. It would give her a sense of well-being. It would give her confidence and a much-needed boost so she could make decisions.

It would take her away from the awful reality she was facing. And it would get her through her impending confrontation with Jace.

Before she could think better of it, she opened the bottle with shaking hands and shook out a pill. Or should she take two? It had been a while. Forever, it seemed, since she'd taken any. One would probably knock her on her ass. Two might just knock her out. Period.

She put the second back in the pill bottle and then threw the other one into her mouth. She grabbed a glass and filled it with water, brought it to her lips and filled her mouth with enough liquid to swallow the pill. And froze.

Oh God, oh God. What was she *doing*?

She spit the water and the pill forcefully into the sink, gripping the edges as sobs welled from her chest. What had she almost done?

Angrily, she grabbed the bottle and dumped all the pills down the drain, running water to wash them down. Then she flung the now empty bottle across the kitchen, listening as it clattered on the floor. Then she buried her face in her hands and wept.

Oh God, she couldn't do this. Not again. *Never again.*

She had to end it now. This wasn't good for her. If this was what her relationship with Jace drove her to, she had to end it now. She couldn't do this to herself. Not after having worked so hard for so long to clean her life up and to break her addiction.

She might not have much, but at least her life *meant* something now.

Without changing, she bolted for the door, knowing she had to see Jace now before she lost her courage. She had to end it, tell him she was moving from the apartment. She had to confront him and end it face-to-face.

She wouldn't leave him to wonder her fate or what she was doing. She would go to his apartment and she'd tell him she was gone. And then she'd go back to her life. It may not be the best life, but it was one she could live with her pride and sanity intact.

Remembering she had no cash left, she went back to the drawer and pulled it all out. What was left after the cab fare she'd give back to Jace. She wouldn't take more from him than she had to. Then, remembering Jack's backpack still on the couch, she yanked it over her shoulder before exiting the apartment.

When she hit the lobby, the doorman looked alarmed.

"Miss Willis, where are you going? I think it would be better if you waited here."

She ignored him and plunged back into the cold to hail a cab.

"Where is she?" Jace demanded as soon as he entered Bethany's apartment building.

The doorman sighed. "I tried to call you again, sir. She came back. That's when I called you the first time. But she came back down just a few minutes later. I tried to stop her. She was soaked through and she hadn't changed from when she'd been out before. She looked upset."

Jace closed his eyes and swore long and hard. "You have no idea where she was going?"

He glanced outside at the sheets of rain mixed with ice that pelted the sidewalks. His stomach dropped as he imagined Bethany out there. Cold. Upset. Alone.

She was probably going back to Jack. Precious fucking Jack.

God, but he'd fucked up badly. He'd been pissed. He'd unleashed all his fear and fury on Bethany and she'd bolted. Just as he'd been afraid she'd do from the start.

"No, sir. I'm sorry, but she didn't say anything when she left. She was carrying only a backpack."

Jace's blood went cold. He'd kill Jack if Bethany was hurt over this. She was probably going back to Jack, but there was no guarantee Jace would even be able to find her now. It had taken him weeks before. But now? She wouldn't *want* him to find her. Before, she hadn't known he was looking for her. Now she'd be aware that he would be. If she even thought that he cared enough to go after her. He hadn't given her any reason to believe he would care enough to go after her. That gutted him the most.

Now she was out there on the goddamn streets, carrying a fortune in illegal drugs. People had been killed for a hell of a lot less.

He pinned the doorman with a tired stare. "If she comes back, you sit on her if you have to. You do *not* let her leave again. Understand?"

The doorman nodded. "Yes, sir. I'll do my best."

His shoulders sagging, Jace turned toward the door, wondering where the hell to look for Bethany next. His cell rang as he was about to step into the rain and he pulled back, lifting his phone. He didn't recognize the number.

"Jace Crestwell," he said impatiently.

"Mr. Crestwell, sir, she's here at your apartment building."

Jace recognized the voice of Roger, his doorman. His pulse sped up and he ducked into the rain, motioning for his car that was parked a short distance away.

"I'll be right there," Jace said. "Do not let her go anywhere."

"You need to hurry, sir," Roger said in a quieter tone. "She refused when I tried to get her to wait in your apartment. She wouldn't even wait inside the lobby. She's outside in the rain and she's soaked through and shivering."

"What?"

Jace couldn't control the fury in his voice.

"Sir, I tried. She's not right. She's upset about something. It's not good. You need to get here fast. I'll keep an eye on her until you arrive."

Jace swore and rang off and then directed his driver to get back to his apartment as fast as possible. The entire way, Jace's chest tightened with dread. He mentally went over what he wanted to say, repeating it in his mind. But somehow it didn't seem like enough. It seemed lame. What the hell was he supposed to say to the woman he loved, the woman he'd completely and utterly fucked up with?

He sat tense and waiting, dying a little more every time traffic dragged them to a stop. What if he didn't make it in time? What if he got there and, as was the case when he got to her apartment, she was already gone? Was he doomed to forever chase an elusive dream? He wouldn't allow himself to think it. Bethany was his. He wouldn't let her go without fighting for her. Maybe she'd never had someone willing to fight for her, but that was going to change.

Finally the car pulled to a stop. Jace jumped out, in the rain, and strode toward the entrance, his gaze scanning rapidly for Bethany. His heart thumped when he didn't see her. Maybe the doorman had been able to persuade her to go in. Or maybe she'd left.

He was almost to the entrance when he saw her. His heart damn near stopped when he saw her huddled against the building. She was hunched down, her knees drawn to her chest, water dripping from her hair and clothes, puddling around her on the concrete.

"Bethany."

Her name came out in a long exhalation, a whispery sound he wasn't sure she'd even heard. It was all he could get out around the tightness in his chest.

He squatted down and touched her arm. She started, her gaze swinging up to meet his. Her eyes were wide and fearful but most of all they were swamped with grief. Overwhelming emotion welled in their depths. It was like seeing into the darkest recesses of her soul.

He urged her to her feet, wincing at the icy coldness of her hands, her skin. She was chalk white and shivering violently.

"Baby, let's get you inside."

His voice was purposely gentle, as soothing as he could make it when his pulse was about to explode out of his temples.

He tried to pull her toward the door but she jerked back, taking a step away from him. Her wounded eyes stared at him, a sheen of tears making them shiny in the glare of streetlights.

"Don't," she said in a low voice. "Jace, I can't. I came here because I owe it to you to say this to your face and not just walk away."

He held up his hand to stop her because he couldn't bear for her to complete what he knew was coming. He *never* wanted to hear those words from her. His heart was about to beat out of his chest and his eyes burned as he stared at the hollowness in hers.

"Baby, please, I need you to listen to me. But I have to get you out of this rain and cold. You're freezing. You're going to make yourself ill."

She shook her head, her arms clutching herself protectively. God, was she scared of him? Had he really made her think he would harm her in any way? He wanted to puke at the thought that she feared violence from him. If only he could have those few minutes in her apartment back.

"No, just listen, Jace. Please. Don't make this any more difficult. I have to do this before I lose myself. Before I lose what self-respect I've managed to gain the last couple of years."

Her voice ended in a sob and she gulped in breaths of air. She was shivering so hard that it took everything Jace had not to forcibly haul her into his apartment. Only the knowledge that this moment, whatever it was she had to say to him, was the single most important moment in his life. He couldn't afford to blow it. Not like he'd already done at her apartment.

"Tell me," he urged.

Tears now ran unchecked down her cheeks, mixing with the rain pelting her face. Her hair was plastered to the sides of her face and clung wetly to her body. Raindrops glistened on her eyelashes, outlining beautiful, haunted eyes.

She was the most beautiful thing in his world and he was perilously close to losing her.

"Jack brought a bottle of pills this morning when he came. He brought them for me."

Jace's breath hissed out as rage consumed him. He wanted to track the son of a bitch down and beat the ever-loving hell out of him. How could he be so careless when it came to Bethany? A woman he was supposed to care about. And Bethany couldn't see that Jack was bad news. Very bad news. Her vision of him was locked in the past.

"I told him I didn't want them. I *never* want them. He was trying to help me. In the past, I would have taken them. I would have done anything for them. But not now. I'm *better* than that. But then you came and we had that terrible argument and you reminded me that I have nothing."

"Oh God, baby, that's not what I meant," he choked out. "That's not what I meant at *all*."

She went on as if she hadn't even heard him. She seemed so lost in her thoughts that she was rambling, trying to get it all out, like ridding poison.

"And I left because it hurt too bad to stay. But then I came back, because I knew the way I left wasn't cool. I needed to stop running. Face you. Do this logically. But there I was in the kitchen, feeling like my world had come to an end. I was cold and wanted a cup of hot chocolate and when I opened the cabinet, there was the bottle of pills staring me in the face and I knew if I just took one that I'd feel better, that I'd be better able to cope with the mess that is my life."

"Oh God," Jace breathed. *"Baby."*

"I was *this* close," she said, holding up her trembling fingers an inch apart. "I was this close to doing it. I had the pill in my mouth. I took a drink of water, fully intending to swallow it. It was right there. At the back of my throat. And then I realized what I was doing. What I almost allowed to happen."

She choked on a sob and then bowed her head, her fingers balled into tight fists at her sides.

"But you didn't," Jace whispered, guessing.

"But I almost did," she said in a voice filled with desolation. "I wanted it. I needed it. And I spit it out and washed all the pills down the sink. I can't go back there, Jace. We have to end it now before we destroy each other. If this is what being with you does to me, I can't do it anymore. I'm not good for you. I'm not good for *me*," she finished on a whisper.

Fear seized him by the balls. He shook his head, unable to wrench the words from his closed throat. He was devastated by what she'd almost done—not because he judged her, but because she'd hurt so badly that she'd nearly done the unthinkable. What if she hadn't stopped at one?

What little restraint she was holding to seemed to dissolve with the rain. A gut-wrenching sob tore from her throat and then she clutched herself around the middle, sinking to her knees as she rocked back and forth.

Jace followed her immediately, his arms going around her, hugging her tight against him. He kissed her soaked hair and rocked with her as the rain pelted them.

"I hate myself for that," she sobbed. "For my weakness. For even being tempted. I hate myself for hurting you, for disappointing you. But I can't just turn away from Jack. I don't expect you to understand it. I've never explained."

His rage at Jack, at the situation, burned through him, hot and fierce.

"Why do you risk so much to protect him? He's an utter fuck-up, Bethany. Why do you *continue* to allow him to rule your entire existence?"

She pushed away from him and shot to her feet. "Because he took so much for me!" she screamed out, rain sliding down her face, mixing with her tears. "He did so much for me. Things I can *never* repay! You don't understand. You could *never* understand all he suffered for me."

Grief was so thick in her voice that she choked on every word. She was distraught, barely clinging to her composure, and she shivered violently in the cold.

There was something in her voice, in those yelled words, that made him go cold from the inside out. Whatever was in her past, what connected her to Jack, haunted her on a day-to-day basis. And whatever it was he had to know. It was pivotal to understanding her and why she clung so fiercely to Jack.

"Then make me understand," he said quietly. "But we're going to talk inside where it's warm, after you've gotten into dry clothes. Then I'll listen and you'll explain. We'll figure this out. Together, Bethany."

She started to shake her head but he stood, scooping her up with him.

"I'm not taking no for an answer," he bit out. "The *hell* I'm letting you walk out of my life. We're going to sort this out and you're going to tell me why you have such blind loyalty for fucking Jack. And by God, when it's all done with, you're not walking out of my life. You're not going anywhere but to bed with me."

chapter thirty-one

Jace breathed a discernible sigh of relief as soon as the elevator doors shut behind him in his apartment. He'd make damn sure she didn't get anywhere near the elevator. Not for a damn long time.

He carried her into the bathroom and after setting her down on the closed toilet, he reached in to turn on the shower. Then he immediately began to peel off the soggy clothing. His hands were shaking—not from cold—and he was powerless to make them stop. He was utterly wrecked by the magnitude of what he'd almost done. *Had* done.

"Jace, please, just let me go," she said in a soft voice choked with emotion. "There's no need to prolong this. Just let me go back to my life and you go back to yours."

He grasped her face in his palms and stared fiercely into her eyes. "I'm not letting you go. Ever. It's not happening. How the fuck am I supposed to get back to my life when you *are* my life? As if my life would mean a goddamn thing if you weren't in it. Now we're getting into the shower and warming up. We're both freezing our asses off. You more than me. You've been out in the fucking weather for hours. I'll be lucky if you don't have hypothermia."

Her eyes widened, and then he released her face and pulled her to her feet, shedding his own clothes as he shoved her toward the shower.

He couldn't control the shaking that had invaded his limbs. He could barely manage to hold on to her in the shower, but he anchored her firmly against his body, using the heat of the water as well as the heat from his own body to warm her.

She was like a block of ice, the cold so deeply ingrained that it had chilled her blood. It killed him that she'd been so long out in the rain, desolate, distraught, all because he'd handled things completely wrong. He'd made her believe she was nothing. That she had nothing. When she was goddamn *everything* to him.

He loved her. If there'd been any doubt before this, it was gone now. And you didn't treat someone you loved like he'd treated her. He hadn't shown any understanding. He hadn't listened to her, hadn't waited for her to explain. All this time, he'd been patient, waiting for her to discuss her past, to share that part of her with him. And when he'd had the opportunity, he'd blown it.

That would never happen again. And he'd be damned if he let her walk out of his life when he'd waited thirty-eight years for her to walk into it.

Heat swelled and surrounded them and he felt her shivering finally ease as she sagged into his arms, warm and pliant and so very precious. All he'd ever wanted, he held right now in his arms. He wasn't letting go. He never lost a battle he was truly invested in and this was the most important one of his life.

He kissed her temple and let his mouth slide down her soft cheek to her chin. His. His woman. His lover. His *wife*, if he had any damn thing to say about it. He was going to tie her so tightly to him that she'd breathe the same air as he did.

"Are you warm now?" he murmured against her ear.

She nodded and he reluctantly pulled her from his embrace and turned the water off. He hurried her out of the shower and rubbed her briskly with a towel so she wouldn't grow chilled again. When he got to her hair, he pulled it from her neck, his gaze settling on the choker he'd given her for Christmas. She hadn't taken it off. Even when she'd been so hurt. He traced the lines with his finger and then leaned in to kiss the space between her ear and the choker where her pulse fluttered under his lips.

She took a step away, her eyes still haunted and guarded. "Jace . . ."

"Shhh, Bethany. Just give me some time here. You need to be warm and dry and then we're going to talk. About everything. And you aren't leaving. Don't even think about it. I'll tie you to my bed and not suffer an ounce of remorse, if that's what I have to do to keep you here."

She bit her lip but went silent, allowing him to wrap her hair in the towel. Then he grabbed his robe from the hook on the back of the door and helped her into it, tying it securely around her waist.

He took only a few moments to towel off and pull dry clothing on before he urged her into the living room.

He turned on the fire and settled her on the couch.

"Give me just a few more minutes to make you a cup of hot chocolate and I'll be back."

He waited, hesitant to leave her for even that amount of time, but the fact that she was only in his robe—something he'd done purposely—reassured him that she wouldn't be bolting out of his apartment.

But still, he waited for her agreement and when she finally nodded, his chest lightened in relief.

It seemed to take an eternity for the milk to heat in the microwave. He hastily stirred in the mix and sweetened it just how she liked it and then he went back into the living room where she was cuddled on the couch.

Her feet were tucked underneath her as if she were seeking more warmth and she'd taken the throw from the end and positioned it over her lap. He wasn't sure if she needed the extra warmth or if she was adding layers as a protective measure . . . from him.

He'd allow no barriers between them. Not anymore. But first they had to get everything out in the open.

He handed her the mug and she clasped it in both hands, absorbing the warmth into her palms. He settled onto the couch next to her, turning so they faced one another. He pulled his knee up and toward the back so that it was touching hers. She didn't move away, something he took as a positive sign, but he knew he had a lot of ground to make up.

"I owe you an apology," he said in a low voice. "I'm sorry, Bethany. I just lost it. When I thought of all the things that could have happened to you, I went a little crazy and I said things I didn't mean. I never meant to make you feel like you were nothing or had nothing. If you believe nothing else, believe that."

The mug shook in her hands as she lowered it from her mouth. "I understand. I do. But, Jace, I told you what I almost did."

Her face was a wreath of pain and shame. It was nearly his undoing. No longer able to keep any distance at all between them, he took the mug from her hands and placed it on the coffee table before returning and moving closer. He looped one arm along the back of the couch so his fingers touched her shoulder and he pulled her other hand into his, caressing her palm with his thumb.

"'Almost' is the key word, baby. You almost took a pill. But you didn't. You stopped. You didn't do it."

She closed her eyes and his heart clenched when a tear slipped down one cheek.

"I had come such a long way," she whispered. "Until today. Until I saw those pills. I don't think about them. I mean, I hadn't. I haven't wanted them. Not since I got clean. And then today I wanted it more than *anything*. It was a compulsion."

She shuddered and bowed her head. He slid his fingers underneath her chin and gently lifted until she was forced to meet his gaze once more.

"Baby, *you didn't do it*," he said quietly, with emphasis. "It doesn't matter what you wanted, what you thought. You didn't take it. That took strength. You beat it and it doesn't have you in its grasp any longer. Didn't today prove that to you?"

Hope was so poignant in her eyes that it cut him in two.

"Do you think so?"

"Yeah, I do. I don't want you beating yourself up over this. And from now on, I'm going to be here to help you. You don't have to be alone. You won't be alone. You're moving in with me. I've waited. I didn't want to push you too soon. That's why I moved you into my sister's old apartment. But I'm done with that. You're going to be here with me."

Her eyes widened. Her mouth opened to protest and he silenced her with a kiss.

"You're mine, Bethany. You belong to me. I belong to you. You belong here. That's not negotiable."

"But Jack . . ."

He drew away, some of his mood deteriorating. "We do have to talk about Jack. He's dangerous to you, Bethany. I won't tolerate that. I won't tolerate any threat to you."

Her breath stuttered out and it was obvious she worked to control the tears that threatened.

"I can't just turn my back on him, Jace. I don't expect you to understand."

"Make me understand. Tell me why. Tell me what hold he has on you."

She closed her eyes and the tears she'd battled slipped in silent, silver streams down her cheeks.

"He took so much for me. He protected me. You can't *imagine* what he took for me, Jace."

His chest burned and a knot formed in his throat. He knew with certainty that he wouldn't like what she was about to tell him, but he would sit and listen if it killed him. This was her past and she was finally giving everything to him. Trusting him with the secrets she'd kept and the dark pain in her eyes.

"We were in and out of foster homes. We aren't related by blood. You know that. But we'd bonded and social services tried to place us together when possible. It wasn't always. But they knew if we went together that we were less likely to cause trouble and so when they could they accommodated our need to be together. We were the only family each other had."

She paused and sucked in deep, steadying breaths.

"Go on, baby," he said gently. "I'm listening. Nothing can hurt you now."

"When I was twelve, Jack was fifteen. He was big for his age. I know he doesn't look it now. He's too thin, but when he's healthy and well fed, he's a big guy. Tall and broad shouldered. Anyway, we were in a home together and the father . . ."

Jace tensed, his entire body bristling with rage. He didn't like where she was going with this.

"The father used to look at me and it worried Jack. Jack would never let me out of his sight or leave me alone with our foster dad. It turned out the father didn't much care if it was girls or boys."

She shuddered in revulsion, her face going pale. Distress radiated from her in waves. He pulled her into his arms and held her tightly, turning her face so she could continue speaking. He stroked her hair, trying to offer her comfort in any way he could.

"He took that for me," she whispered. "He put himself in the way every single time the father came after me. Jack allowed that man to abuse him so that I wouldn't be abused and, oh God, I can never forget that, Jace. I can't forget it. He took that for me for *months* until we were finally able to get away."

"Oh baby. I'm so sorry."

"Jack's always taken care of me. When I was in the car accident. Before that. After that. It's always been him who made sure we had food to eat, clothes to wear. When I wasn't able to get more pain medication prescribed—and at that time I was still having so much pain—Jack got the pills for me. And then, when I became addicted, he risked arrest and God knows what else to make sure I had what I needed."

Jace sighed. It was a sticky situation, no doubt. He saw Jack in a new light, but it didn't mean he was okay with the man fucking things up for Bethany now. Jack was into more than just a habit for prescription drugs. He was buying, if not dealing, the hard shit. The kind of stuff that could get a person killed or sent to prison for a very long time. There was no way in *hell* he was going to let Bethany be exposed to that.

"I understand why you feel the way you do, baby, but listen to me. Jack has gone beyond that now. He's in deep and he's putting you in serious danger. I can't allow that. I *won't* allow it. I'll never agree to anything that can harm you. Do you understand that?"

She shifted and raised her head so she could look him in the eye. "I do understand, Jace. I do. I'm not making excuses for him. I don't like what he's doing, but the idea of him being cold and hungry and in danger himself . . . it breaks my heart. I can't help but wonder if he'd be like he is if it weren't for me."

Jace shook his head, making sure she saw his vehemence. "You can't take the blame for this. I won't let you. He protected you. I'll always be grateful he did that. But baby, even he wouldn't blame you for what he is now. We all make choices. He made some bad ones, but that doesn't mean *you* have to pay the price."

"But what am I supposed to do? I can't just walk away from him. I can't just leave him alone and with nothing. Not when I have all the things he doesn't."

Jace stared into her tear-drenched eyes and realized that she wouldn't be the woman he loved if she could just walk away from her family. He stroked her cheek, wiping away the dampness, and then he sighed.

"I'll figure something out for Jack. But you have to understand if I step in, that means you step away."

Her eyes became troubled and she dropped her gaze again.

"Could he . . ."

She bit into her lip and went silent.

"Could he what, baby? You don't have to be afraid to ask me anything."

"But I have no right to ask this," she said in a low voice. "You've given me so much and I've given you nothing in return."

"You *are* everything to me. *Everything*, Bethany. I don't say that lightly. I've damn sure never said that to another woman. Hell, I've never said it to another human being."

She stared at him with such confusion and amazement that he couldn't control himself any longer. He hauled her into his arms and against his chest, anchoring her so tight that it was doubtful she could breathe.

"Ask, Bethany."

"I was going to ask you if Jack could stay in the apartment," she whispered. "Just for a little while. Until he gets on his feet and can afford a place of his own."

Jace carefully extricated Bethany from his hold and set her far enough away so that she could see him and he could see her. His expression was utterly serious as he stared down at her.

"If you move in with me, I'll see what I can do about letting Jack move into your apartment."

She didn't react to the subtle blackmail. Not that it was even subtle. But he wasn't above using whatever means necessary to get her into his space, in his bed and more firmly entrenched in his life.

"You'd do that?" she whispered.

Hell yes, he'd do it. And not suffer one iota of guilt in the process.

"Yes, I would do that."

She threw her arms around him, nearly toppling him backward

on the couch. "Thank you," she said fiercely. "I don't deserve you, Jace. I thank God every day for you, though."

He frowned at her assertion but since she hadn't balked at the idea of moving in with him he didn't push the matter.

"I can't wait to tell Jack," she said. "He won't believe it."

Jace held up his hands. "There are a few conditions, Bethany."

She went silent and looked questioningly at him.

"I won't have drugs in that apartment. I won't have them anywhere *near* you. If Kaden or Trevor finds them at any time, he's out. And if you see Jack, you'll do it with either Kaden or Trevor or myself. *That* I won't bend on."

Bethany was quiet. He could see the wheels turning in her mind. He found himself holding his breath, wondering if he'd been too forceful. But it was who he was. He couldn't change that, wouldn't change it for something as important as her safety.

"All right," she said quietly. "I'll explain to Jack."

"No."

She lifted her brows and they furrowed in confusion.

"*I'll* explain to Jack," Jace said grimly. "I won't put you in an uncomfortable situation. Let me be the asshole. I have no problem with that role when it comes to you."

"You're not an asshole," she said in a fierce voice that made him smile.

"Does that mean you'll be happy to stay with me and not think me a huge asshole for manipulating you into moving in with me?"

Her eyes went soft and then she leaned into his embrace, her body melting like liquid satin over his skin. So smooth and warm. So fucking perfect. His hands glided down her back, wishing like hell his robe wasn't covering her.

"I never wanted to leave," she said faintly. "I thought it was what you wanted."

"Shhh, baby, no. Don't say that. Never that."

"And I worry, Jace. I do. I worry where this is going to go and how long you're going to be happy with . . . me."

The unspoken fear was as evident as if she'd voiced it. She was worried that this was temporary for him and she worried what would happen to her when, in her mind, he got tired of her and moved on.

"And I still worry that I'm not good enough for you," she said in a starkly vulnerable voice.

"Oh, baby."

She shook her head and continued on. "I don't fit into your world. How could I? I'm afraid that one day you're going to realize that."

He stroked her face with his palm, allowing her to keep her head nestled against his shoulder. "You *are* my world, baby. We've been over this."

He could feel her squeezing her eyes shut and she trembled. He hugged her tighter and kissed her silky hair.

"I want to believe that," she whispered. "Because you're mine, Jace. And that scares me. You're my entire world. Everything that's wonderful. The best thing that's ever happened to me. I've lost a lot in my life, and I survived. But if I lost you, it would devastate me as nothing else has or ever could. You have so much power over me and that's frightening."

He closed his eyes, inhaling deep as her words washed over him. She hadn't said she loved him, but he was convinced that it was only because for her that was the final bridge to gap. A sign of her ultimate submission. And maybe she wasn't ready for that yet. He could wait. Forever, if it took that long. He was more than happy to spend the next forty years convincing her that he wasn't going anywhere. Eventually he'd hear those words from her lips and that day, when it came, would be forever engraved in his memory.

"Baby, listen to me."

She shifted back again, her gaze meeting his. He touched her mouth, tracing the bow.

"The kind of power you're talking about isn't about control. It isn't about your submission. It isn't about my dominance. It's about emotional power. But baby, you have exactly that same power over me. When it comes to our relationship, you have far more power than I do."

Her eyes widened in surprise.

"It's true," he said before she could put her protest to words. "You have more power, more control than you could possibly imagine. My heart is in your hands. That's not bullshit. I'm not saying stuff I think you want to hear in order to manipulate you. I can't be any more honest than this. I'm yours, baby. I'm putting it out there. My heart, my soul, it all belongs to you."

"Jace."

His name exploded in a rush of air as she stared stricken into his eyes. Her mouth rounded in shock and her hands trembled as she raised them to his face. When she touched him, he nuzzled into her palm and then pressed a kiss to the soft skin.

"Really?" she whispered.

He smiled. "You can't think I have a habit of saying this shit to every woman I sleep with."

She shook her head. "No. I can't imagine that at all."

"Then believe it, baby. See me. Believe in yourself. In *us*. This is real. As real as it gets. Nothing has ever been more real in my life."

"Okay," she said in a quiet, breathy voice that sent a sweet rush over his skin.

"You'll move in?"

She nodded.

"You'll let me handle things with Jack?"

She nodded again.

"Are you prepared to fully submit to me? And not just in the bedroom, baby. In all aspects of our relationship."

There was only a brief hesitation before she nodded a third time.

"Never run out on me again, Bethany. No matter what happens, you stay and fight. Yell at me, argue, throw something at me, whatever you want to do, but never walk away from me. You stay and fight for what we have. You know I have a temper. And you know I'll say stupid shit I don't mean. But you can't tuck tail and run when things get rough. Promise me that."

She wrapped her arms around his neck and leaned into him, warm and sweet. "I promise."

chapter thirty-two

"Jace," Bethany whispered close to his ear.

"Yes, baby?"

Bethany was cuddled into his side, her body limp and sated from their lovemaking. And if Jace had any doubt as to whether it was lovemaking before, that doubt had disappeared. They'd spent endless hours kissing, touching, discovering each other's bodies, and he'd been especially delighted by Bethany's boldness in bed.

She was still adorably shy and sometimes hesitant, but she was growing in confidence and Jace delighted in every initiative she took. There'd been no place for dominance and kink in last night's rediscovery of one another. He'd simply poured every ounce of his emotion into their lovemaking until they were both spent.

She levered up on her elbow, her head leaving its place on his shoulder. He wanted to pull her back, not liking the sudden absence of her in his arms, but she was looking at him with furrowed eyebrows. Something was on her mind and he didn't want to shut her down.

She lifted her hand to touch the choker around her neck, her fingers tracing the lines as she seemed to collect her thoughts.

"What is this to you?" she asked quietly. "What is it really? You told me in the apartment that as long as I wore your *collar* that I was under your protection. What does that mean?"

He sighed, hating his inability to control his tongue when he was pissed off. This wasn't the way he wanted to explain the significance of her wearing his jewelry.

"It's a symbol of my ownership," he said in a careful tone. "It's a gift a man gives to his submissive. To a woman he cherishes who is in his care. It means that you belong to me. That you're submissive to me."

Her brows furrowed harder and she was silent for a long moment.

"Why didn't you tell me when you gave it to me?"

He pushed up to one elbow so they were more eye to eye. He reached out to touch her cheek, caressing the smooth skin. Then he let his fingers drift down to the choker, to the diamond that rested against her throat.

"I was afraid that it was too soon. That you wouldn't fully understand. I didn't want to pressure you. I was afraid you wouldn't want it if you knew what it truly meant."

She bit her lip pensively. "But Jace, why would you want me to wear it if I didn't understand the significance? It's not real until I know what it means. Any satisfaction you felt at having me wear it had to have been hollow because I didn't know what it was I wore."

His lips twisted ruefully. "You have me there. And you're right. For me it was enough to see it around your neck and for *me* to know what it meant. But you're correct. It could never mean what it should until *you* recognized and accepted its true meaning."

"It's important to you," she said, not as a question but as a statement of fact.

He nodded. "It is. But perhaps not for the reasons you think. It's not that I'm this asshole who has to mark you as a possession. The simple truth is I like seeing it around your neck because I gave it to you and it's a symbol of your gift to *me*."

Her eyes widened. "I hadn't considered it from that perspective."

He smiled. "No, you're still convinced that you give me nothing, that you have nothing to give. But that's not true, baby. You've given me the most precious gift I'll ever receive. Yourself."

Tears glittered brightly in her fierce blue eyes. Then to his surprise, she reached back to unfasten the choker. She let it slide from her neck and then held it out to him.

Panic took hold and he stared wordlessly back at her. Was she rejecting it?

"I didn't know what it meant before," she said, still holding the choker out to him. "I want you to put it on when we *both* know what it means."

His chest nearly exploded as it tightened and swelled. His hand shook when he took it from her fingers. He pushed himself upright to his knees and then he said, "Get on your knees, baby. Kneel for me here on the bed."

She positioned herself in front of him, so achingly beautiful with her tousled hair and sleepy eyes. Eyes that were full of something he didn't dare hope for. Love.

He held the choker so she could see it spread in his hands. Then he met her gaze.

"Will you wear my collar, Bethany? It's not only a symbol of my possession. It's a symbol of your gift to me but also my gift to you. I will absolutely cherish and protect you. See that your every need is met. Your body will be mine, but mine will also be yours. I will love and adore you with everything that is me."

"Yes. Oh, Jace, yes," she breathed.

He slipped the choker once more around her neck. It was all the more sweet this time because as she'd said, now she knew its significance. She accepted it and *him*. Could he possibly ask for more than this?

He fastened it and then ran his fingers around to the front, touching the diamond teardrop so it dangled just so. Then he leaned down and claimed her mouth, his tongue finding hers in a heated rush that made him dizzy.

"I love you, Bethany."

"Jace!"

But he wouldn't allow her to cry. Not in his bed and not while he held her. He wanted only her happiness and as long as he had the power to keep those tears at bay, he'd do so.

"Make love with me, baby. Again and again. This time with us both knowing that you belong to me heart and soul."

Her arms wrapped around his neck and she pulled him toward her until she folded beneath him, falling back on the mattress. He went with her, pushing her firmly into the bed, his mouth devouring hers, his body covering hers.

"Never felt like this for a woman," he murmured against her skin. "Never before. Never will again."

"Jace," she whispered, a husky catch in her voice. "Love me. Please."

"I do. I will. Love you. You never have to ask for that, baby. It's yours. I'm yours. That's never going to change."

He kissed his way down to her breasts, tonguing one nipple into a rigid peak before turning his attention to the other. He licked and then sucked, loving the excited hum that emanated from her. Her entire body went taut beneath him and she arched into his mouth.

Her hands tangled in his hair, pulling and then holding him firmly against her breast.

He smiled. "My baby likes that?"

She groaned. "The only thing I love more is when you have your mouth down . . . there."

Still adorably shy. He loved that about her. How hesitant she was when it came to telling him her wants and needs.

"Never let it be said I didn't make every effort to satisfy my woman," he purred as he moved down her body.

He spread her thighs, opening her sweet pussy to his gaze. He traced a finger down the delicate folds, opening her wider so he had access to the swollen, pink flesh. It glistened with her moisture and his dick went even harder as he imagined her taste on his tongue.

He licked roughly, swiping the entire pad of his tongue over her entrance and up to her clit. He swirled delicately around the velvety nub and then carefully pulled it between his lips with a light sucking motion.

She bucked beneath him, arching, her fingers diving into his hair to hold him in place. He feasted on her. Eating, licking, sucking, sliding his tongue inside her, fucking her with liquid strokes.

He couldn't get enough. He'd never have enough of her taste, the sensation of her, silky and sweet against his lips. He loved how she trembled beneath his touch, her little gasps and breathy sighs. Never had he imagined being so gutted over a woman. He hadn't lied when he'd told Bethany that she held immense power over him. Far greater power than he'd ever wield over her. Because without her, he had nothing.

Without her, his money, wealth, prestige, none of it meant a damn thing. She didn't believe herself worthy of him because he had material things she didn't. But what she gave him was sweeter, was without price or measure.

"Jace," she said on a soft moan. "Baby, please."

It was the first time she'd ever used an endearment and he liked it. He liked it a hell of a lot. He'd never considered himself a man who wanted his woman to call him cutesy names. He himself had never used them with another woman. But with Bethany, the words came so easily. Affectionate terms that slipped from his lips before he even knew they were coming.

"Say it again," he said huskily.

She lifted her head, her eyes soft with love and warmth. "Say what?"

"You called me *baby*."

A smile curved her lips and her eyes shone as her smile broadened. "You liked it?"

"Yeah," he said gruffly. "I did."

"Baby," she whispered.

He closed his eyes and licked over her sweet pussy again, enjoying the intense shiver his mouth forced from her.

"Tell me how you want it," he said. "Do you want to come in my mouth or do you want me inside you?"

"I get a choice?"

There was amusement in her voice and he lifted his head to see the teasing glint in her eyes. God, he loved this. The comfortable, easy rapport that had built between them. He could well imagine them laughing and loving this way for the next several decades.

"Yeah, baby, you get a choice. Either way, you come, so I figure it's a win-win for you. And it's a win-win for me as well. Either you come all over my tongue—definitely no downside to that choice—or you come with my dick so deep inside your pussy that my balls are straining to get inside you too. *Definitely* not a downside."

She laughed softly and her head fell back against the pillow, a contented sigh escaping her chest. "Well. It is a hard decision because you have such a wicked, wicked tongue. But I really love it when you're inside me."

"Say no more," he growled as he shifted up her body until their mouths lined up.

He kissed her, stroking his tongue deeply over hers, allowing her to taste her essence, the sweet musk he carried on his tongue.

"Help me inside you, baby. Guide me in."

He nearly lost it when her fingers curled around his rigid cock and then with her other hand she spread the folds of her pussy and positioned the head of his dick at her opening.

She paused a moment, stroking lightly with her fingertips, sliding them up to cup his balls. She massaged and rolled gently until he was damn near panting with need. He was so close to spending himself all over her pussy before he ever got inside her.

She did that to him. Made him crazy with need. Made him forget his control, his patience. He closed his eyes and held his weight up off her with his forearms.

"You ready?" she whispered.

"Little tease," he whispered back.

She grinned and then arched up, sheathing him an inch. Then her hand left him and she wrapped her arms around his shoulders, pulling him down so he was flush against her body.

"Take me. Make love to me, Jace."

He slid inside, slow and gentle, pushing until his hips met the backs of her thighs. She hooked her ankles around his back, moving with him, countering his thrusts.

He kissed her lips, moved to the corner of her mouth and then kissed a line down her jaw to her ear. He nibbled playfully at the lobe and then sucked it between his lips, mimicking the attention he'd given her breasts.

She went wet around his cock, bathing him in instant heat.

"My baby likes that too," he murmured.

"Mmmm," she moaned. "My ears are so sensitive."

He licked the lobe and then traced the shell of her ear until she shivered violently beneath him. Her pussy contracted and then clenched tightly, sucking him deeper.

"She really, really likes that," he said with chuckle.

Her teeth sank into his shoulder and it was his turn to shudder and tighten over her.

"Hmmm, *my* baby likes that," she said smugly.

"Hell yeah, I do. I like your teeth, your mouth, your tongue. Any part of you I can get, baby. I like it all."

"In that case . . ."

She nipped her way up his neck to his ear and then back down again. His nerve endings sizzled and went haywire. His cock surged forward, hammering into her until he feared hurting her. But he was beyond control, his body taking over his need and instinct to find release.

"Get there," he gritted out. "Get there, baby. I'm close. Won't last much longer."

She circled his neck, hugging him against her as she lifted her body to his as if seeking more.

"I love you," she whispered, the words fluttering over his ear.

Those words. God, those words. It was the only thing left he'd wanted from her. The one thing she hadn't given until now. It was the most beautiful sound he'd ever heard in his life.

Euphoria filled him, spreading to the darkest recesses of his soul and shining light on every shadow.

"Bethany," he choked out. "God, baby, I love you too. So damn much. Come with me now."

"I'm already there."

The sweet words, her sweetly whispered *I love you* still echoing in his mind, sent him into free fall. His semen erupted from his cock, jetting deep into her pussy, the heat and friction nearly painful in its intensity. And still he kept coming and coming, his orgasm an unstoppable force. He bathed her pussy in his release and then he pushed deep and held himself locked against her, wedged as deeply as he could manage. He remained there, wanting to plant himself into her womb.

In that moment, he cursed birth control. He had a savage need to give her his baby, to make her pregnant with his child. Their child. A son or a daughter. The image of her swollen with his baby kept him hard when he should have been losing his rigid erection.

He slumped over her, falling into her delicate softness. God he loved the feel of her underneath him. She sighed in contentment and kissed the side of his neck as her hands rubbed up and down his back and down to his ass.

"If I had my way, I'd stay inside you forever."

He felt her smile against his skin.

"Tell me again," he urged. "I want to hear the words again, Bethany."

She didn't hesitate. Didn't misunderstand what it was he asked for.

"I love you."

He closed his eyes and breathed in deeply. He would never ask for more than this. For what he had right here and now in his arms.

"I love you too, baby."

chapter thirty-three

Jace woke to the sound of a ringing phone. He roused and glanced at his watch and then swore. He never overslept. Not even in college had he ever been late to a class. It was past nine and he hadn't even stirred until now. It was the second time he could ever remember waking late and unaware. And both times had been after a soul-stirring night with Bethany.

He glanced down to where Bethany's dark head lay on his shoulder. She hadn't stirred either. They'd made love countless times until they'd both fallen into an exhausted sleep.

He reached for his cell phone lying on the nightstand and saw that Kaden was calling.

"Jace Crestwell," he answered.

"Mr. Crestwell, I thought you'd like to know that Kingston returned to the apartment."

"He's there now?" Jace asked in a low voice.

"Yes, sir. Came in a few minutes ago. Let himself in and he hasn't left yet."

"Make sure he doesn't," Jace said curtly. "I'll be right over."

"Yes, sir."

Jace disconnected the call as Bethany stirred beside him. She lifted her head and gazed at him with sleepy eyes.

"Everything okay?"

He kissed her forehead. "I have to go out for a while." He hesitated a moment. "Jack came back to the apartment."

Her eyes became more alert, shaking off the veil of sleep. "I'll go with you."

He shook his head. "No. I'll handle this, Bethany."

She became agitated and before she could work herself up and become more upset, he said firmly, "I don't want you involved in this. We had an agreement on this. I need you to trust me. I'll handle it."

"Okay," she said quietly.

He kissed her again. "It'll be fine, baby. Trust me."

"I do," she whispered.

"While I'm there, I'll arrange for your stuff to be moved here."

She bit her lip.

"Are you having second thoughts?" he asked warily.

She shook her head. "No. I want this. I want you. And I do trust you, Jace. Please don't think I don't. This is hard for me. Jack is important to me. You both are. I know he's not perfect. I know he's done things that aren't . . . good. But I just want him to be safe and have things most other people take for granted."

"I know you do, baby. Don't worry. I'll call you when I finish up with Jack, okay? Is your cell charged?"

She shrugged and he rolled his eyes.

"I'll plug it in before I leave. It'll be on the kitchen counter."

He pushed aside the sheets and slid out of bed but then he leaned over, wanting to kiss her again, to savor the feel of her under his lips one last time before he handled the issue of Jack.

This wasn't a situation he wanted to be in. But for Bethany he'd do it, even if his preference was to tell Jack to fuck off and stay the hell out of Bethany's life from now on. But Bethany would never forgive him that, and he wasn't going to risk losing her when helping Jack would make little difference in his life other than the inconvenience of confronting the other man.

A part of him relished it. He wanted to see for himself what Jack's position was regarding Bethany. While Bethany considered him a brother, Jace wasn't convinced that Jack's feelings toward her were very brotherly.

That he'd keep to himself because Bethany was naïve when it came to a lot of things, Jack included, and she'd never see the situation the way someone with perspective might. But then, Jace had little perspective when it came to her.

"I don't want you to worry about this, baby. It'll be all right. Jack can call you and you can call him. I don't even mind if you see him as long as Kaden or Trevor is with you when I can't be."

"Thank you, Jace." Her eyes were bright and earnest. "This means so much to me."

"Love you," he said huskily.

Her entire face softened and the worry fled her eyes. He realized then what reassurance those words gave her and he vowed on the spot not to let a day go by without giving them to her.

"I love you too."

He walked into the bathroom before he said to hell with Jack and pressed Bethany back onto the bed to make love to her for the rest of the day. He was already going to be very late getting into work, which was unlike him. He'd call Eleanor on his way out to give her a heads-up. Despite it being just after the holidays, things were business as usual, and they had multiple projects in the works. Projects that needed his, Gabe's and Ash's constant attention.

And if he were honest—and he was—he knew that it had been weeks since he'd been able to give work his undivided attention. Maybe he'd never make work his number one priority again. He had Bethany now and she was the most important thing in his life. Not work, not business, not even his partnership with his two best friends.

· · ·

Forty-five minutes later, he strode into the apartment complex and was met by Kaden in the lobby.

"He's still here?" Jace asked shortly.

Kaden nodded. "Yes, sir. He hasn't come down since he arrived."

"Very good. I'll want you and Trevor to constantly monitor his presence. Even when he leaves. I want to know where he goes, who he sees and what he does. And I especially want to know if and when he contacts Bethany, if he sees her or arranges to see her. Under no circumstances do I want him seeing her alone. I've let her know she isn't to see Jack without you or Trevor or myself, but if Jack attempts to seek her out, she may not know about it until he's there in her face. And I want you in between them. She is to be protected at all costs."

"Understood," Kaden said grimly.

Jace walked to the elevator and Kaden fell into step beside him. Jace cast an inquisitive glance in his direction and Kaden's jaw went firm.

"Sir, it stands to reason that if he's a potential risk to Bethany's safety and you're going to confront him that he's a risk to you as well. I'd feel better if I was present for this discussion. I will, of course, maintain a discreet distance and keep in confidence anything I chance to overhear."

Jace cracked a grin as they stepped into the elevator. "You make good points."

They rode up in silence and when they arrived at the door of the apartment, Jace didn't knock or announce himself. He inserted his key and went in.

"Bethy, it's about time," Jack called from where he was sprawled on the couch in the living room. "I was beginning to think I was never going to get that dinner you promised."

Then Jack looked up and his gaze became hooded and wary when he saw Jace and Kaden.

"Where's Bethany?" Jack demanded.

"She's safe," Jace said curtly. "And she's going to stay safe. You and I need to have a discussion, *Jack*."

"You have me at a disadvantage," Jack drawled. "Who the hell are you?"

"I'm the man who intends to make sure you stay the hell away from Bethany, you arrogant prick."

Jack's eyebrows went up. "So you're the boyfriend. Nice place you gave Bethy. Very generous of you."

Jace's eyes narrowed at the sarcasm in Jack's voice.

"She's not going to be living here anymore," Jace said.

Jack rose from the couch, his eyes flashing anger. "What did you do, you bastard? Did you kick her out? If you hurt her, I'll kill you."

Kaden stepped forward, his features menacing. Jace held up his hand and Kaden stepped back once more.

"Bethany is moving in with me, and she stays with me from here on."

Something flickered in Jack's eyes. Sadness? Jealousy? It was hard to say because the man instantly looked away.

"That's good," he said in a low voice. "I told her not to worry about me. She deserves a better life."

"On that point we agree," Jace clipped out.

"You here to kick me out then?" Jack asked, the arrogant drawl back in place.

Jace took a deep breath. It was on the tip of his tongue to say yes. To tell him to get the hell out and stay out and never to go near Bethany again. It would be so easy. But if Bethany ever knew, she'd never forgive Jace and he wasn't willing to risk it. He wanted her happy, and she'd never be fully happy unless she no longer had to worry about fucking Jack.

"No," he finally said. "You're welcome to stay in the apartment. I'm going to have Bethany's things moved to my apartment but the rest is yours to use."

Jack's eyes narrowed suspiciously. "What's the catch? No way a guy like you just hands something like this to me. You have Bethany. Why would you do this for me?"

Jace advanced, anger tightening his chest. "Let's get something straight, Jack. I'm not doing this for you. I'm doing it for Bethany. She loves you and she worries about you. As for the catch? There's no catch, but there are conditions."

Jack smirked and then flopped back on the couch. "Do tell."

"You won't bring drugs into this apartment," Jace snarled.

Jack's face whitened and for the first time he looked distinctly uneasy.

"Yeah, I know about the bag. I have it, and you aren't getting it back. I should kick your fucking ass for bringing that shit into Bethany's apartment. And what the fuck were you thinking, bringing her painkillers when you know damn well she was addicted to them once? What kind of a fuck-up does that to someone he's supposed to care about?"

Jack swallowed visibly and went whiter. "I have to have that bag back. You don't understand. I'm a dead man if I don't get that back. I left it here because it was safer that way."

"Safer for you, maybe, asshole. But not safer for Bethany. She could have taken the fall for you."

Jack shot to his feet again. "Look, I have to have that bag. I have to deliver it. After that, you won't ever see that shit again. I swear it. I won't bring it here. I won't take it near Bethany. I'll be done. But if I don't deliver that bag tomorrow, my life won't be worth a shit."

"Give me one goddamn reason I should give a shit," Jace bit out.

Jack flinched and then looked away. "Because they know about Bethany."

Jace flew at him in a rage, grabbing Jack's tattered shirt and doubling it in his fists. He slammed him back against the couch until Jace was hunched over him, his face mere inches from Jack's.

"What the fuck have you done?"

Jack closed his eyes. "I had to give them something they could use against me as insurance and Bethany is all I have. She's all that's important to me."

A low growl echoed through the room and it took a moment for Jace to realize it had come from Kaden, who stood just a foot away, bristling with rage.

"You stupid son of a bitch," Jace swore.

"Look, just give me the bag and I'll be out of her life," Jack said. "You'll never see or hear from me again."

Jace shoved him back with enough force that Jack's neck snapped against the couch and his head bobbed.

"While I'd love nothing more than for you to disappear and stay the fuck out of Bethany's life, it would hurt her, and she's all I'm concerned about. For once, think about someone other than yourself," Jace said in disgust.

"I *am* thinking of her," Jack said quietly. "She has you now. She doesn't need me. She's never needed me. She likes to think that I took care of her, but that wasn't the case. It was always her taking care of me. She deserves better than a life on the streets with a fuck-up like me."

Jace glanced in Kaden's direction. "Can you go to my apartment and get the bag? I only want you to bring it back here to him. After that, he's on his own. I don't want you involved. And I don't want that shit staying here. If he doesn't leave with it as soon as you deliver it, then I want it turned over to the police."

Kaden nodded, and Jack paled again.

"Consider it done," Kaden said tersely. He glared at Jack the entire time, never once lifting his gaze to Jace during the exchange.

"You can stay here," Jace said to Jack. "You can contact Bethany. You can see her. But only if Kaden, Trevor or I am present. If you bring drugs into this apartment or if you bring them anywhere near Bethany, I'll have you arrested so fast you won't know what hit you. We clear?"

Jack nodded.

"Furthermore, if you ever fucking offer Bethany drugs again, I'll kick your goddamn ass. That clear too?"

"Yeah," Jack muttered.

"I have to go into the office," Jace said to Kaden. "I'll give you a key to my apartment and I'll let Bethany know you're coming by. I don't want her to know anything of this. Just get the bag. It's sitting inside the door on the floor."

Kaden nodded and caught the elevator key card Jace tossed to him.

Then Jace fixed Jack with his stare, putting emphasis into his words.

"You can stay here, but this isn't a free ride. Get your shit together and get a job. I don't give a fuck what it is. The utilities will be paid and groceries will be delivered twice a week. Anything else will be on you."

"Be good to her," Jack said quietly.

There again in his eyes was that flicker that told Jace that Bethany meant more to Jack than a sibling.

"You need to understand this isn't a temporary thing with me and Bethany," Jace said, not caring that he was being merciless. Jack needed to understand where Jace stood and that Bethany was *never* going to be a possibility for Jack.

"Yeah, I get it," Jack muttered. "I knew I never had a chance with her, but she's always belonged to me."

"Not anymore," Jace said. "She's mine and I protect what's mine. You ever try to hurt her and I'll crush you."

"Just make her happy. That's all I ask."

"*You* can make her happy by cleaning up your act," Jace pointed out.

Resignation was dark and churning in Jack's eyes. For the first time, Jace got a glimpse of the demons driving the other man. Demons that had once held Bethany in their grip too.

"I'll try," Jack said flatly.

chapter thirty-four

Jace and Bethany spent New Year's Eve with Gabe, Mia and Ash. Things were less awkward for Bethany this time, but Jace still kept close watch on her. Jack was a constant worry for her and Jace cursed the selfish bastard for putting her through this.

The day after Jace had given the pack back to Jack, Jack had disappeared, and he hadn't returned to the apartment since. Nor had he phoned Bethany or attempted to contact her in any fashion. Jace knew this because while Trevor kept close watch on the apartment, Kaden watched over Bethany from a discreet distance.

Even though Jace had made it clear that Kaden was to shadow Jack's movements, Jack must have been aware that he was being watched because he made certain he disappeared and that his steps weren't traceable.

So while Jack was off doing whatever the fuck Jack did, Bethany had made herself sick with worry.

Jace had enlisted the aid of Gabe, Mia and Ash in an attempt to give Bethany a New Year's Eve where she would relax and enjoy. They'd gathered at Jace's apartment—he'd thought if they entertained in a place Bethany felt at home that perhaps she would feel more at ease—and Jace had ordered in all of Bethany's favorite finger foods. He also made certain he had plenty of black cherry soda—Mia's favorite—on hand, and he'd quickly discovered that Bethany loved it at first taste. He immediately made a mental note to stock more on a regular basis.

"I wanted you all to be the first to know this," Gabe said when conversation had quieted down.

Jace turned his attention to his future brother-in-law. He and Mia were sitting on the love seat, while Jace and Bethany were cuddled on the couch. Ash occupied the armchair on the other side of Jace and Bethany.

They'd eaten themselves silly and then relaxed in the living room with drinks, the television on in preparation to watch the ball drop in Times Square. Mia had suggested they all venture down to the square for the event, but Gabe and Jace had vetoed the suggestion, not wanting to brave the crowds. There was also the fact that since Jace had no idea where Jack was or if he'd cleared up the matter of the drugs, he wasn't taking any chances with Bethany's safety.

Gabe gazed tenderly down at Mia, who returned his smile, her eyes sparkling with excitement.

"We've finally set a date," Gabe said after a long pause. "Or rather, Mia has set the date," he added dryly.

Mia thumped him on the arm in reprimand and he chuckled, holding his arm in mock pain.

Bethany smiled and leaned forward eagerly. "Oh, that's wonderful, Mia! When?"

"She's making me wait until April," Gabe said with a groan. "She wants a spring wedding. I tried to convince her to elope tomorrow so we could marry in Vegas on New Year's Day. I can't think of a better way to start the year than making the woman I love officially mine."

Mia's face went absolutely soft as she stared up at Gabe. Jace felt a tightening in his own chest and he squeezed Bethany back against him, enfolding her more firmly in his embrace.

This was nice. Hanging out with his family. The people who

meant the most to him in this world. The woman he loved in his arms. Him watching his sister with the man who loved and adored her beyond measure.

The only thing missing was . . . Ash. Not that Ash wasn't here. But Ash was conspicuously single. The only loner in the group.

"You make a very romantic argument for that elopement," Mia murmured.

Gabe's eyes gleamed mischievously. "Does that mean you'd consider it? I could have the jet fueled and ready to go in an hour."

She whopped him again and rolled her eyes. "Nope. I want a wedding. My brother giving me away. The whole shebang." Her expression grew wistful. "A gorgeous dress, a beautiful cake and for everyone to see me become Mrs. Gabe Hamilton."

"And I want you to have whatever you want," Gabe said in a serious tone that dropped all pretense of teasing. "All I want from the deal is you as my wife. Anything else is just icing on that beautiful cake you want."

She leaned up and kissed him and Jace rolled his eyes in Ash's direction. Ash shook his head in response.

"This means we'll be subjected to this shit for the next four months," Ash groaned.

Gabe laughed and Mia glowered in both Jace's and Ash's directions. Then she turned her attention to Bethany.

"I'd like you to be an attendant in my wedding, Bethany," she said softly.

Bethany went tense against Jace, her mouth opening in surprise. She seemed genuinely befuddled and at a loss for words. Jace squeezed her reassuringly.

"But you hardly know me," Bethany said. "I don't want you to feel obligated to include me because of me and Jace . . ."

Mia smiled. "I don't. I want you there. It's my big day, according to Gabe, and every girl should have things exactly her way on her big day. And I want you with me."

Bethany's cheeks went pink but her eyes glowed with pleasure at Mia's request. Jace wanted to hug his little sister for making Bethany feel important and included.

"Then I'd love to," Bethany said quietly.

Mia beamed at her. "And while I'm in command mode, my girls and I are going out this week to Vibe."

Before she could go any further, Gabe broke into a groan and Jace added his own.

"Shush, you two!" Mia admonished. Then she looked apologetically at Bethany. "As I was saying. My girls and I are going to the club and we'd love for you to come."

Bethany glanced quickly up at Jace as if seeking his approval and he frowned.

"Of course you can go," he whispered so the others couldn't hear. "You don't need my permission."

She sent him a look that suggested she was adhering to the rules of their relationship. Something agreed upon by both of them. And he loved her for that, that she was so willing to cede power and control to him. But he wasn't going to be a bastard about it either. He'd damn near give her the moon if she wanted it.

Besides, he already knew Mia had planned to invite Bethany for a night out with the girls. When he'd explained the situation with Jack and how down and worried Bethany had been the last several days, Mia had seized the opportunity and declared that what Bethany needed was a girls' night out.

"I'd love to," Bethany said to Mia.

Mia's face lit up in delight. "Good! It's settled then. Night after next, we'll hit the club. I'll run by and get you from Jace's apartment and then we'll swing by to get the other girls on the way. Gabe's providing a driver for the evening."

"Damn right," Gabe muttered. "Last thing I need is a bunch of drunken girls wobbling all over fucking Manhattan."

Ash chuckled. "No shit."

"*Our* apartment, Mia," Jace corrected gently. "It's mine and Bethany's apartment. Not mine."

Mia flushed, her eyes growing worried. "Of course! I'm so sorry. I'm so used to calling it your apartment. I'm sorry, Bethany. I wasn't thinking."

Bethany looked embarrassed and sent Jace a frown of reprimand that had him grinning. He wasn't the least bit repentant for reminding the others of Bethany's place in his life.

"It's okay, Mia. I knew what you meant," Bethany said.

"Oh look!" Mia exclaimed. "It's almost midnight. The countdown is on!"

Their gazes jerked to the television just in time to see the clock wind down to midnight.

"Happy New Year!" Mia cried.

"Happy New Year," Ash said, raising his glass in toast.

"Happy New Year," Gabe echoed.

Jace leaned down, touching his lips to Bethany's. "Happy New Year, baby."

"You too," she whispered as she kissed him back.

"Know what I plan to be doing New Year's Day?" he whispered.

"What?" she whispered back.

"Making love to you. They say whatever you do on New Year's Day you'll be doing the entire rest of the year."

She grinned. "For real?"

"So the saying goes."

"In that case, I vote we do exactly that," she said before kissing him again.

"No arguments from me."

"And they say we're bad," Mia grumbled, jerking Jace back before he completely lost himself in Bethany's kiss and forgot where they were.

He shot his sister a glare. "Oh please. Like anyone is worse than you and Gabe."

Gabe looked amused but kept his mouth shut.

"Try being me," Ash muttered. "Jesus, it's like a couples' retreat around here."

"So find you a woman," Mia said lightly.

Ash rolled his eyes and then drained his wineglass. "No hurry there, sweetheart. Besides, who in their right mind would ever marry into my crazy-ass family?"

Mia gasped. "Did he just insult us?"

Jace smiled, loving her even more in that moment. Ash looked dumbstruck for a moment and then a warm smile lit up his entire face and his eyes gleamed with affection.

Mia had effectively reminded him that *they* were Ash's family. Not his father or mother or batshit crazy siblings. Here in this room was Ash's real family. The ones who supported him unconditionally.

"Never that," Ash said. "And thanks for the reminder, sweetness."

Bethany was looking at the others with something akin to wonder. Her smile was achingly filled with longing. For what the others shared. That unbreakable bond. One that extended to her now, even if she hadn't fully grasped it.

"They're your family too," he murmured into her ear.

She turned to him, her eyes bright with happiness for the first time in days. They were clear and not clouded with sadness and worry.

"Yeah," she breathed. "I guess they are, aren't they?"

He kissed her lingeringly, hugging her tightly to his chest. "Feels good, doesn't it?"

"It's the best," she said fiercely. "It's something I never imagined having. I still can't believe it. I still wake up and have to tell myself this is really happening and not some crazy dream I've hatched."

He smiled gently, his chest aching with the love he felt for her. "Believe it, baby. It's real and it's yours."

chapter thirty-five

"I feel so guilty," Bethany said.

Mia glanced over from where she sat beside Bethany in the limo, her brow furrowed in question.

Bethany sighed. "I have no idea where Jack is. If he's dead or alive, hungry or cold. Nothing. And yet I'm going on about my life, going out with girlfriends clubbing. It seems so . . . cold and heartless."

Mia reached over and squeezed Bethany's hand. "Oh honey, you're anything but cold and heartless. Give yourself a break here. Jack is a grown man. He's made his decisions, whether they're good or bad, and you have to accept that. You can't live his life for him. You can't make him do the right thing. But what you *can* do is live *your* life, be happy and make your own choices free of guilt."

Bethany blinked at the other woman, astonished by how much sense Mia made.

"I'm an idiot."

Mia laughed. "First you're cold and heartless and now you're an idiot?"

Bethany breathed a deep sigh. "You're right. I know you're right. Jace has been telling me the same thing, only I haven't been listening. And then you say it and suddenly it makes so much more sense."

"That's because I'm smarter than Jace," Mia said smugly.

Bethany grinned, feeling lighter than she had in an entire week.

"Thank you for inviting me tonight," she said, reaching over impulsively to hug Mia.

Mia hugged her back fiercely. "Thank you for making my brother happy."

Bethany drew away, her lips curving ruefully. "I only hope I continue to make him happy. I love him."

"And he loves you," Mia said matter-of-factly. "It's so plain to see. I've never seen him so gaga over a woman. I have to tell you, it's astonishing to witness!"

The car pulled to a stop in front of another apartment complex, where four women stood waiting. Mia jumped out, pulling Bethany with her.

"I'll make this quick. It's freezing!" Mia said. "Bethany, I want you to meet my best friends on earth, Caroline, Chessy, Gina and Trish. Guys, this is Jace's girlfriend, Bethany."

"Ah damn it, Mia, break my heart, why don't you," Chessy said dramatically.

Bethany looked at the pretty woman in confusion.

Mia laughed. "She's had the hots for Jace forever. It's slaying her that he's off the market now."

Bethany burst into laughter. "Sorry. Well, not really."

The others laughed with her.

"I wouldn't be sorry either," Trish said. "Jace is one fine specimen of a man. You're a lucky woman, Bethany."

"What about Ash?" Gina asked hopefully. "Is he off the market too then?"

Mia's eyes widened. "Oh shit. No, no! Bethany is only with *Jace*."

Bethany's cheeks warmed as she blushed furiously. Obviously they all knew of Jace and Ash's propensity for having threesomes. Now they thought she was involved with both of them. There was no way in hell she'd ever admit that she'd had sex with both men.

The other girls' eyes widened. "Damn," Caroline breathed. "Jace is going solo now. Wow, Bethany. You must have really rocked his world."

"Okay, okay, enough of tormenting Bethany with my brother's sexual exploits," Mia groaned. "Let's get in the car and go have fun!"

"I'm down with that," Chessy said. "Caro, is Brandon working tonight?"

Caroline's entire face lit up. "Yeah, he said he'd totally take care of us."

The others snorted as they piled into the limo.

"Caroline's boyfriend works as a bouncer at Vibe," Mia explained. "They live together now and he's hugely protective of her and, well, us when we go out. We don't have to worry about anyone messing with us. Brandon spread the word with the other guys who work there and we're totally VIP all the way. Whatever we want, we get, and they all look out for us. Gabe had to discuss it with Brandon and sign off before he'd let us all go back."

She said the last with a roll of her eyes and the others dissolved into giggles.

"I want one of those insanely overprotective men," Chessy drawled. "They're kind of nice to have in a caveman, knuckles-dragging-the-ground sort of way. And they're the bomb in bed, so Mia and Caroline tell us."

She reached forward, all but pouncing on Bethany. "And now we have you to regale us with how awesome Jace is in the sack. You don't know the amount of time we've spent fantasizing about that particular unknown."

"Just please don't tell us he's all vanilla and boring," Gina said with a shudder. "If he's that, lie to us and let us live in our dream land a little longer."

Bethany burst into laughter again.

"You guys!" Mia hissed. "Give her a break. You're going to scare her off before we ever get to the club and if she goes home and tells Jace all this shit, he'll never let her go out with us again!"

"Throw us a bone at least, girl," Trish said to Bethany.

Bethany grinned. "He's not vanilla or boring."

They all groaned.

"That's bad. Teasing us with what we'll never have," Gina grumbled.

Bethany relaxed, enjoying something she'd never experienced before. Girlfriends. Friendships. It had always been just her and Jack. She'd never gotten close to anyone and now she wanted this. Camaraderie. A night out with the girls. It was *fun*.

When they pulled to a stop in front of the nightclub, the door opened and a gorgeous, Latino-looking man with a goatee and one earring held out his hand to Caroline to help her. He immediately enfolded her in his muscled arms and laid one on her that had the others sighing and whistling.

"Damn," Chessy muttered. "I'm one jealous bitch right now."

"That must be her boyfriend," Bethany murmured to Mia.

Mia smiled. "Yes, that's Brandon. He's head over heels for Caro and she's the same for him."

"Ladies," Brandon said, offering his hand when he'd released Caroline. "Let's get you inside where it's warm. You have a table waiting and your own waitress for the night. The boys will be looking out for you and if you have any trouble at all, you see me. I'll take care of it."

"Holy crap," Bethany whispered. "He gives me the shivers!"

"Like you don't get that at home," Gina grumbled as she took Brandon's hand.

They all piled out and Brandon escorted them inside.

Music vibrated the walls and a cascade of neon and flashing lights nearly hurt Bethany's eyes. It wasn't her first time inside a club. She'd met up with a lot of men in her days of meaningless sex. For a moment, the memory robbed her of breath as hurt and shame crowded into her chest.

The clubs she'd visited hadn't been as classy as this one. More like seedy bars and places that women like her went to hook up for the night.

"Hey, what's wrong?" Mia yelled close to her ear.

Bethany smiled. "Nothing. Nothing at all."

She shook the past from her mind, determined not to let it interfere with tonight's fun. She was a different person now. She had Jace. Jace, who knew about her past and accepted her anyway. She didn't have to be that person anymore. She could be who she'd always wanted to be.

When they got to the table, a smiling waitress immediately appeared and Bethany noticed that two bouncers took position near their table. Brandon hadn't lied when he said they'd be well taken care of.

When the waitress got to Mia and Bethany, Bethany put out her hand to Mia.

"Let's have a drink. I know you planned to drink water with me but why not have fun?"

Mia's expression became troubled. "Are you sure? I don't mind having sparkling water with you."

"I never had problems with alcohol addiction," Bethany said gently. "I know Jace worries, but he doesn't have to. I'm not that person anymore. I'm so glad you invited me here with your girls. Let's have a good time. You said someone will get us home afterward, right?"

Mia grinned. "Oh absolutely. Look for Gabe to make an appearance in a few hours. The man is still pissed about the one time I went out with the girls and took a cab home alone, drunk off my ass. He's cool with me drinking. He just makes sure he's around to get me home afterward."

"Then let's do it!" Bethany said.

Mia turned to the waitress. "I want a Cosmo. What do you want, Bethany?"

"Amaretto sour, please."

A few minutes later, the waitress returned with a tray of drinks and Mia held up her glass in a toast. "Drink up, girls. Tonight we're going to have fun!"

"And get plastered!" Chessy interjected.

"I'll drink to that," Gina said, holding up her glass.

Bethany joined in the fun, holding her glass to clink with the others. They all laughed and chugged down their first drink.

The sweet drink hit Bethany's tongue and blazed a warm trail into her belly. She put the empty down, surprised when the waitress immediately passed out another round.

Mia laughed. "She always gets our table when we're here and she knows we always toast and down the first one immediately, so she double orders for us. She knows us now."

"Works for me," Bethany said, reaching for the next drink.

"Let's dance!" Chessy yelled. "The night is young and there are men waiting."

"You can be my dance partner," Mia yelled to Bethany over the music. "Well, you, me and Caro will split off. Brandon would have a kitten if she danced with another guy. The others are on their own."

"Sounds good!" Bethany returned.

They hit the dance floor and Bethany allowed the music to take over. For the space of a few hours, she could forget Jack and her worries. She embraced the newness of having girlfriends and fun and having a wonderful, loving man to go home to at the end of the night.

She, Mia and Caroline danced in a tight circle, laughing and letting loose. They shimmied up close, teasing the crowd as they bumped and grinded, gyrating in time with the frenetic beat of the music.

After dancing four songs, they returned to their table, where new drinks were waiting. Brandon was standing there, amusement twinkling in his dark eyes.

He put his arm around Caroline, pulling her in close to his side. "Babe, I gotta tell you, if you and your girls don't stop that sexy shit, me and the boys are going to have a hard time pulling the guys off you."

Caroline laughed and turned her face up for his kiss.

"I have rounds to make. I'll be back later to check in on you."

After that, he kissed her and it wasn't just a simple peck. It was a sexy as sin, tongue-kissing mark of possession. Bethany wasn't fooled. He'd done it to let anyone watching know that Caroline was his and to keep their hands off. It also helped that the man was built. No one in their right mind would take him on in a bar fight.

Caroline sighed and her eyes were slightly glazed—the alcohol having nothing to do with the slighty drunk look.

"He's amazing," she yelled to Mia and Bethany.

"We see that," Mia teased.

"Drink up!" Caroline said. "Tina is coming back with more. No alcohol goes to waste here!"

Mia and Bethany laughed and quickly downed their drinks.

By the time two hours passed, Bethany was buzzing on alcohol and laughing ridiculously at everything the girls said. They danced more, getting bolder in their shenanigans and occasionally returning to the table to down more drinks.

The third time they went onto the dance floor, Bethany was definitely drunk. Mia wasn't in any better shape from what Bethany could ascertain and they were giggling madly as they bumped and swayed, getting more provocative in their movements.

"I'm so glad Jace isn't here to see this," Bethany hollered over the music. "I think he'd kill me!"

Mia giggled and then her eyes rounded. "Oh shit."

"What?"

"I was about to say that I was glad Gabe hadn't made it yet either, but, uhm, he's here."

Bethany whirled around and nearly toppled over when the room kept moving after she'd stopped. The heels she'd worn, which at the time seemed a good idea because they were totally sexy with enough lift to make her legs look damn good, suddenly didn't seem like such a good idea because she damn near tripped and broke her ankle.

It had felt good to dress up even though she wasn't going any-where with Jace. She'd chosen a really kickass sparkly cocktail dress that fit her like a dream and actually gave her the appearance of curves. She was still slim—too slim from too many missed meals and the life she'd led—but ever since she'd met Jace, she'd put on at least ten pounds, five of which had to have been on her boobs. Not that Jace was complaining about the new plumpness to her chest.

She'd carefully done her makeup, pulled her hair into a loose knot so tendrils floated down her neck and worn huge dangly earrings that she thought looked pretty damn hot.

It was a far cry from the tattered jeans and threadbare shirts she'd worn for so long. She felt pretty. Actually, she felt . . . gorgeous. Like someone worthy of attention from a man like Jace.

"Ah, whoops!" Mia said, catching her arm so she didn't face-plant on the floor. Then they both dissolved into giggles when Gabe's eyes narrowed as he took in just how tipsy they were.

"I vote we don't go over there just yet," Bethany said. "He, uhm, well . . . he looks kind of intense."

"Hell no," Mia said belligerently. "Let's give him a show instead."

Bethany's eyes widened as they turned away from Gabe. "Do you think that's a good idea?"

Mia laughed. "Oh yeah. Because after? When he drags us home? He'll be so hot for me that we won't even make it inside the door of his apartment and he'll be tearing off my dress. Although he'll leave the heels on because my man loves me in these heels."

Bethany's mouth fell open as she stared back at Mia's mischie-vous smile.

Mia winked. "Drunk sex is the absolute best. I bet Jace will be the same with you. A tipsy, sexy woman in the heels you're wearing and in that dress? He'll be all over you the minute you step back into his apartment."

A shiver worked over Bethany's shoulders. "I'd planned to sober up before we went back home. I didn't want Jace to know I got drunk.

He'd worry and probably disapprove. But if what you're saying is true . . ."

Mia bumped into Bethany's side and threw her arms up in the air. "Oh it's true," Mia shouted. "He won't be able to resist!"

"In that case, let's get our drink on some more!" Bethany shouted back.

"After we give Gabe a show he won't soon forget," Mia said with a wink.

Bethany laughed and the two got into the beat of the music. Caroline joined them a moment later, her face flushed and her eyes sparkling with happiness. The three put on a show that later would mortify Bethany when she thought back on it, but it was so much fun, and she couldn't remember the last time she'd really let loose and had such a fabulous time.

When the song ended, Mia grabbed Bethany's arm and the two fell all over each other getting back to the table where, predictably, the waitress was waiting with another round of drinks.

Gabe's lips were twitching in amusement when they teetered up to the table. His eyebrow lifted when both Bethany and Mia reached for their drinks and downed them in two seconds flat.

"You girls are tying one on tonight," he observed. His gaze drifted lovingly to Mia. "You going to pass out on me, darling?"

Mia grinned cheekily and then lifted up on tiptoe to plant a scorching kiss on Gabe's mouth. Then her mouth slid over his cheek and she murmured something in his ear that had Gabe's entire body tightening. His jaw clenched and his eyes darkened.

Bethany's stomach churned just witnessing his reaction to whatever it was Mia said, and Bethany was convinced it was extremely naughty. Apparently she was absolutely right about this drunk sex thing.

She waved to the waitress and held up her glass for another.

Gabe put his arm loosely around Bethany and pulled her close so she could hear him.

"You okay, sweetheart? How much have you had to drink?"

She flashed him a bright smile. "I'm fine! And Mia said you were getting us home tonight so I didn't have to worry about how drunk we got."

His arm tightened at her waist. "Damn straight. I'll be taking you home to Jace, so do what you want. I just want to make sure you can handle it."

She smiled again. "You're sweet."

He rolled his eyes. "Sweet isn't a word I'd use to describe me."

No, she supposed it wasn't. Power emanated from him just the way it did with Jace. There was a glint in his eyes, particularly when he looked at Mia, that just made her shiver from head to toe. Even now when he'd put his arm around Bethany to steady her, he had a lock on Mia's wrist and he made certain there was little space between them.

"Just don't make yourself sick," he said. "I want you girls to have fun and not to worry about anything else. When you're ready to go, I'll get you all home."

"Thanks!"

"Let's dance again, Bethany!" Mia yelled.

Gabe groaned. "Got to tell you, baby, that dancing you're doing? Should be illegal. I'm going to have to beat every man's ass who's staring at yours."

Mia grinned and then snagged Bethany's hand, dragging her toward the dance floor again.

For the next hour, they danced, drank and then danced some more. And then drank again.

The last time they left the dance floor and got to the table, Bethany knew she couldn't tolerate another drink. She was fuzzy and completely enveloped in a warm haze. She laughed at everything, whether it was funny or not. Gabe wore a perpetually amused look and Brandon grinned when he checked in on them again.

"I think I'm done," Bethany said breathlessly. "But I don't want to ruin the night for the rest of you." She stared up at Gabe, who was holding Mia upright. She had her own tight grip on the table, worried that if she let go, she'd hit the floor with a resounding *thud*.

"No, I'm ready too," Mia said. "You ready, baby?" she asked Gabe.

"Been ready," he growled.

She giggled. "We have to get Bethany home first. I imagine Jace is fit to be tied by now."

"I texted him," Gabe said dryly. "He knows what to expect."

"Let me go grab the others," Mia said. "Caro is hanging out until Brandon gets off work."

"I'll call for the car," Gabe said. "You're not walking out of here without me. You'll fall on your faces."

Bethany grinned and waited, still holding on to the table, while Mia rounded up the rest of the group.

"Tonight was fun," she hollered at Gabe. "Thanks for getting me home. Mia is great."

Gabe smiled, his eyes warm and affectionate. "Glad you had fun, Bethany. And yeah, Mia is the best. No problem on getting you home. No way I'd let you go home by yourself. Jace wouldn't allow it either. If I hadn't come to get you, he would have."

Mia returned a moment later with Chessy, Trish and Gina. They were all as drunk as Mia and Bethany were and giggling like lunatics. Gabe rolled his eyes and then motioned for Brandon.

Brandon appeared with one of the other bouncers and they guided Chessy, Trish and Gina toward the exit while Gabe put an arm around both Mia and Bethany.

Bethany teetered and then giggled when Gabe's arm tightened around her.

"Jesus, how much did you two drink anyway?"

Mia looked innocent and then held up her hand, trying to count. After three attempts of staring at her fingers in confusion, she threw up her hand and said, "A lot."

"I'm getting that," Gabe said with a chuckle.

He guided them out to the waiting car and stood patiently while Brandon and another bouncer got the other three girls inside. Then Brandon flashed Gabe a sympathetic grin.

"Good luck, man. Looks like you have your hands full."

"No shit," Gabe muttered.

He got Bethany and Mia seated and then slid in to sit beside Mia.

"You're aces," Chessy said, flashing a grin in Gabe's direction.

"Absolutely," Trish and Gina both chimed in.

"We told Mia if she ever lets you get away, she's an idiot," Trish said solemnly.

Chessy nodded just as solemnly. "But just so you know, if she ever is that idiot, I'm more than willing to step up."

The girls dissolved into laughter while Gabe sent his eyes heavenward in a seeming plea for help.

They stopped off at each of the girls' apartments and Gabe patiently escorted them in and made sure each was safe before returning to the car.

"He really is terrific," Bethany whispered to Mia as they watched Gabe return from escorting Chessy up.

"Yeah," Mia whispered. "I'm so lucky to have him."

"We're just lucky bitches," Bethany said. "Gabe and Jace rock."

"Yeah," Mia said again. "But then, so do we."

"We do, don't we?"

"Absolutely."

Then they both broke into laughter again, still giggling like fiends when Gabe slid back into the car.

He shook his head. "Don't know what I'm going to do with you two, I swear."

A devilish gleam entered Mia's eyes. "Well, if you don't know what you're going to do with me . . ."

"Didn't say that, baby," he said gruffly. "Got plans for you."

Mia sent a knowing grin in Bethany's direction that clearly said, "I told you so."

"Jace is meeting us in the lobby," Gabe said when they neared Bethany and Jace's apartment building.

Bethany's heart fluttered with anticipation. She hoped like hell that Mia hadn't been wrong. Now she was suddenly nervous and her mouth went dry.

Mia reached over to squeeze her hand. "Trust me."

Bethany squeezed back and Gabe sent them both a suspicious glare.

When the car pulled up, Gabe got out and then helped Bethany extricate herself from the backseat. She wobbled unsteadily on her heels as they started toward the entrance to the building.

"You're going to kill yourself in those damn heels," Gabe muttered.

"But they're sexy," Bethany defended. "At least, I thought so."

"No doubt there, sweetheart. You look killer in them. Jace is going to swallow his damn tongue. But if you kill yourself before you get to him, they won't have done much good."

"Mia said Jace would want to fuck me in these shoes," she said and then was mortified by what she'd blurted out.

Gabe chuckled, his eyes gleaming with amusement. "Did she now? Well, Mia is an authority on being fucked in killer heels, so if she said that it's probably true."

Bethany grinned cheekily as they entered the building. Jace was standing a short distance away, and his gaze narrowed as he took in the unsteady gait in which she walked.

"Gabe thinks I look sexy," she announced when Jace stopped in front of them. "And he totally said you'd fuck me in these shoes." She stopped and frowned, her thoughts suddenly muddled. "Or maybe it was Mia who said you'd fuck me. Either way, I wanna be fucked in these shoes."

Gabe shook with laughter next to her.

A slow grin curved Jace's lips. "I think that can be arranged."

She nodded. Then she turned and leaned up on tiptoe to kiss Gabe's cheek.

"Thank you again for taking such good care of us tonight."

Gabe chuckled. "Anytime, sweetheart." Then he turned to Jace. "Better get a hold on her. Once I let her go, she'll likely take a header."

Jace chuckled but took firm grip on her arm as Gabe turned to walk away.

"Thanks, man. Next time it'll be my turn."

"Thank fuck," Gabe muttered. "You have no idea what I was subjected to tonight. Let's just say there isn't a damn man in that club who wasn't drooling on the floor at their antics."

Jace's eyebrows went up and then he glanced down at Bethany, his gaze inquisitive.

She sent him a dazzling smile and he grinned at her in return.

"Gotta say, the shoes are definitely sexy on you," he murmured.

"Mia was right," she said smugly.

He turned her toward the elevator and half carried her into it.

"What was she right about, baby?"

"She said you'd take one look at me, drunk, in these sexy heels and you'd want to instantly fuck me. While I'm still wearing the shoes."

He laughed as the elevator opened into his apartment. "Can't say I'm going to argue with that assessment, although can't say hearing that about me from my sister is at the top of my list of priorities."

"She said Gabe wouldn't make it to the bedroom and that he'd fuck her in her heels just inside the doorway," she said solemnly.

Jace winced. "Baby, you gotta stop. Definitely don't want to be hearing about some man fucking my baby sister and definitely don't want the details."

She laughed and then weaved when he let her arm go.

"Whoops!" she said as he caught her again.

"Just how much did you have to drink tonight?"

"Lots," she said smugly. "I wanted to have drunk sex with you and I wanted you to tear my dress off me and fuck me in my heels like Gabe's going to fuck Mia."

Jace groaned. "Baby, you have to stop. I'm more than happy to fuck you any way you want but can we please leave Gabe and Mia out of this?"

She nodded. "Or maybe I'll fuck you." She brightened at that idea and then her eyes narrowed fuzzily on Jace. "Can I do that?"

He laughed and then tugged her toward the bedroom. "Oh, hell yeah. Baby, you can do whatever your sweet little drunk ass wants to. I'm more than willing to let you take advantage of me in your drunken state."

She wobbled after him into the bedroom and shivered at the sultry look he sent her way as soon as the door closed behind them. His eyes were dark with lust and amusement, the good kind that told her everything Mia had predicted was absolutely true.

Her hands went to unfasten her dress but she couldn't quite get the hang of the zipper and she nearly fell over when she angled her arms higher.

"Oh, let me," Jace murmured. "You don't have to do a single thing, baby. I'm going to take full advantage of your inebriated state and since you've planned this the entire evening, I'm not going to spare an ounce of guilt for all the things I'm going to do to you. But you better damn well remember it in the morning."

She shivered again when his hands slid up her back and then eased the zipper down, loosening the dress.

"I'm not *that* drunk," she said, defending herself.

He chuckled, his breath sizzling over her bare neck just before he pressed his mouth to her nape, sending chill bumps racing down her spine. "Oh, you're drunk. And you're cute as hell. I'm going to fuck your mouth, your pussy *and* that sweet ass. If you pass out on me, I'm not going to be pleased."

She closed her eyes, weaving unsteadily until he caught her shoulders and pulled her back against his chest as he let her dress fall to the floor. No way in hell she was going to miss this.

"Love the lingerie," he whispered as he nuzzled just behind her ear. "Love those heels even more. And yeah, I'm absolutely going to fuck you in them."

A low whimper of need welled in her throat.

"Don't see any reason to tie you up tonight," he said in amusement. "You're as helpless as a kitten. I'm liking it. I'm thinking a regular girls' night out would be a *very* good thing."

He unfastened her bra and lowered the straps down her arms before tossing it aside. Then he turned her around to face him and backed her slowly to the bed until she bumped into the mattress. He eased her down and with a firm hand pushed her until she was lying on her back, her legs hanging over the edge.

Leaning over, he kissed just below her navel, above the thin band of her panties, and then he hooked his thumbs into the lace and yanked, rending the material in two, baring her pussy to his glittering gaze. He reached down, curling his fingers around her ankles, and pulled upward, bending her knees. Then his fingers glided over the spikes of her heels, gripping them as he spread her farther.

"I've been bad," she said in a pouty voice.

His eyebrows rose and his eyes twinkled in amusement. "Oh really," he drawled.

She nodded solemnly. "Very bad," she whispered as though it were a secret.

Then her brow crinkled and she pursed her lips.

"I probably need to be punished."

Jace looked down, his lips twitching as he watched a wide range of expressions cross her face. She was adorably cute and very drunk. And he was turned on as hell.

"What pray tell have you done that warrants punishment?"

"I flirted," she said in a hushed tone. Then she frowned. "No, wait. I didn't flirt." She shook her head adamantly, her breasts jiggling in a supremely tempting fashion. She leaned up, her expression turning serious. "Guys flirted with me, though. But Brandon and Gabe wouldn't let anyone get close. But me and Mia were naughty. We danced and it was *hot*."

He pressed his lips more firmly together to keep the laughter back.

"That deserves punishment, right?"

She sounded so damn hopeful that he lost the battle and laughed.

Her eyes narrowed and she glared up at him. "It's not funny," she huffed. "I was a very bad girl, and bad girls are supposed to be punished."

He nodded. "Can't argue that, baby."

She immediately brightened and he shook his head, more laughter threatening to bubble out of his chest.

"You should probably spank me," she said, adopting a look of utter seriousness.

He slid his hands down the insides of her legs, and she shivered, chill bumps racing over her skin.

"I'm a little conflicted," he said, adopting a mock serious tone to match hers. "You've indeed been a very bad girl, but you've also been very, *very* good."

Her lips twisted into another pout and he leaned down, kissing those delectable lips.

"I think the solution is to punish you first and then reward you."

"Oh, that's a perfect idea," she said in a breathy voice that hitched with excitement.

"Up on your knees, baby," he ordered in a tone he knew she'd respond to.

Her pupils flared and heat flushed her cheeks. Her eyes darkened immediately and her nipples puckered. Hell, he hadn't even begun yet and just his promise of what was to come had her entire body reacting. She was fucking perfect. Perfect for him. Made for him. He'd never have another woman that could come as close to matching him as she did.

She struggled upward and then a wide, goofy grin split her lips, making him want to take her mouth and ravage it. He grasped her wrists and helped her to a sitting position and then she clumsily turned to get on her hands and knees. She fell flat on her face and a giggle erupted, her entire body shaking. Her ass quivered and his dick hardened to the point of bursting. Oh yeah, he was going to have her mouth, her pussy and that sweet ass, and he was going to fuck her until they both passed out.

When he got her into position, she fidgeted impatiently, turning to look at him over her shoulder. And those eyes glowed with lust and excitement. His hands shook and he clung to his control with a frayed thread.

"So what's it going to be, baby?" he asked in a silky, teasing tone he knew would drive her crazy. "My hand? The crop? Or . . . we could try something new."

She went utterly still. "New?" It came out in a breathy sigh filled with anticipation.

"I haven't used a belt and I haven't used wood. I have a pliable wood paddle. It has just the right amount of snap and it'll redden that beautiful ass until it glows."

"Oh," she whispered, the word coming out as a soft moan.

"Your choice, baby," he murmured. "I'll give that to you. Let you decide tonight. I'm in a particularly generous mood. Because, honey? When I'm done reddening that ass, I'm going to eat that delicious pussy and you're going to come all over my tongue. But I won't be done then. Not by a long shot. Because after I make you come, I'm going to fuck your mouth. Then I'm going to fuck that pussy and then I'm going to fuck your ass until you come screaming my name."

"Oh my God."

He smiled and stroked lovingly over her ass, anticipation building with every second he waited for her response.

"The w-wood," she husked out. "I want the wood."

"Excellent," he purred. "Very good choice. So good that your reward will be extra nice. You please me very much, Bethany."

She went soft under his touch, her entire body going lax as her sigh of contentment filled his ears. She turned and looked at him again, her gaze so sweet and loving that his heart clenched.

He leaned down and kissed the dimple just above the crease of her ass. "Be right back, love."

He fetched the thin paddle from his closet and took his time walking back across the room to the bed, savoring the sight of her on hands and knees, ass perched enticingly in the air as she waited for him. He caressed one ass cheek and then stroked over the other until she arched into his touch and quivered beneath his fingers.

"Give me your pain. Give me your pleasure," he growled. "I want it all, Bethany. Every sound. Every reaction. I want all of you."

He snapped the paddle across her ass and she flinched, emitting a gasp of surprise. He smiled. It wasn't a sound of pain. It was a sound of discovery. Experiencing something new.

He popped again, a little harder this time, and then inflicted one on the other cheek. A red, rosy glow shimmered, turning the skin pink. The contrast between the pale areas he hadn't yet touched and the spots he'd struck was enticing. He couldn't wait to redden her entire ass.

But he paced himself, wanting them both to experience ultimate pleasure from the moment.

"Ten," he whispered. "I'm giving you ten. This is new for you, baby. I don't want to overwhelm you. Just give you a taste. Count them out for me. Start at one now."

He cracked the wood over the fleshiest part of her ass, satisfaction gripping him when the red immediately popped.

"One."

It came out as a moan that made his balls ache.

"Two," she whispered.

He made himself slow when he realized how quickly he'd administered the third, fourth, fifth and sixth blows. She tensed in anticipation, waiting for the seventh, but he smoothed his hand over her reddened ass, petting and soothing.

"Please," she begged.

He gave her what she asked for. Seven. Eight. Nine and then ten, featherlight, much softer than the others. She sagged downward and then she turned her face, gazing at him with drunk, drowsy eyes that were now intoxicated with far more than alcohol. She was high on lust and the haze brought on by that edgy line between pain and pleasure. She'd slipped beyond the here and now and he wanted to bring her back down just so he could work her up in an entirely different manner this time.

"Turn over, baby."

He held his hands out to guide her as she unsteadily turned, falling onto her back, a dreamy smile curving her luscious mouth.

"Gonna have to be bad more often," she purred. "Had fun and then got to come home to you. Best night ever."

His heart went soft and he leaned down to gather her in his arms, wanting to hold her before he did anything else.

"You'll always come home to me."

"Yeah," she said in contentment.

"Love hearing you say that, baby."

She smiled and reached up to brush his hair from his forehead. Then she tipped her mouth up for his kiss and he took the silent invitation, feasting greedily on her lips. Tasting her. Making love to her mouth just like he was going to feast on her pussy.

"You sobering up yet?"

She shook her head, opening her eyes so he could see they were still fuzzy with the remnants of alcohol and the haze of pleasure. There wasn't a better look on a woman. Drunk on pleasure. Dreamy. Looking at him like he was the only man in her world. Like there'd never been another.

"Going to eat that pussy now," he growled against her mouth.

"Oh."

Her excited gasp escaped into his mouth and he swallowed it up, inhaling her deep into his lungs, savoring her there at the very heart of him.

"Prop those sexy heels up on the bed and grab your knees and hold on. Spread yourself and don't move your hands. Open yourself for me, baby. I'm feeling greedy tonight and I want you to come all over my tongue."

She arched her body and awkwardly propped her feet on the bed, digging the spiked heels into the mattress. Hell, she'd probably put holes in it but he didn't give a fuck. He'd buy a new bed tomorrow. The fantasy of fucking her in those heels like she'd wanted so badly was worth the cost of a new mattress. Later he wanted to have her hold the heels of the shoes all spread out while he fucked her ass. Oh yeah, definitely worth whatever damage they did to the bed.

Her hands cupped her knees and she shyly spread her thighs, pushing her legs outward until her pussy lips opened, baring her glistening flesh. The contrast of the dark curls and the puffy pink flesh, moist with her juices, made his mouth water. He knelt on the floor so his head was at a perfect angle and he moved in, dying to fuck her with his tongue.

The moment he licked her, she bucked upward and cried out his name.

"Hands, baby," he commanded. "Keep your hands on your knees and keep yourself spread for me."

She opened farther for him and he took a long, leisurely swipe with his tongue from her entrance up to her clit, where he toyed and teased, running a lazy circle around the taut nub before flicking it over and over with the tip of his tongue.

She squirmed and fidgeted, but she kept her hands on her knees and she kept her thighs splayed wide.

She got wetter as he ate her, grazing his teeth ever so lightly back down to her opening. He tongue-fucked her, pushing in, licking from the inside out, sucking in her taste and the sweetness of her arousal.

"This is the sweet, baby. You took the pain, now take the sweet."

"Jace," she whispered. "Don't you know? Everything you give me is the sweetest pleasure I've ever known. The pain is pleasure. The pleasure is pleasure. Your love is more than I could have ever dreamed of."

Her words were earnest and so damn sweet that they took his breath away. He tasted her. Ate her. Drank from her and still he wanted more. He wanted to give this to her. Wanted to make it last. Wanted her crazy with lust and high on more than just alcohol.

"I want your cock," she said, the words thick and clumsy. He didn't know if it was the alcohol slowing her or if it was her intense arousal and need.

He glanced up and then grinned when he took in her unfocused gaze. She was staring hard at him but she looked to be having difficulty directing her stare where she wanted. So damn cute.

"You'll get my cock, baby, just as soon as I get you off. You're going to get a damn lot of my dick before we're done tonight."

"Oh yum," she said with a cheeky grin. "I want to taste you like you're tasting me."

He groaned. Alcohol definitely made her less inhibited. She was adorably shy, but tonight the alcohol had given her liquid courage and he may not survive it. He was already about to come in his pants, and he was nowhere near inside her yet.

He had to pace himself. It was something he constantly had to remind himself or else he'd toss those killer heels over his shoulders and fuck her brains out right here and now. And if she knew what he was thinking, she'd be encouraging him to do just that. Tonight she was an impatient, greedy wench and he loved it.

Lowering his head back down he began to lick and eat more boldly, applying more pressure, touching her in the places he knew she was particularly sensitive. He knew every inch of her body.

Knew she loved when he slid his finger into her pussy and pressed just so against her G-spot. She loved when he rolled his tongue around her clit, but she didn't like when he sucked it too hard. And she loved to have the rim of her pussy opening toyed and teased with his tongue, his fingers and his cock. The quickest way to drive her insane was to fuck her with very short, shallow strokes with barely the head of his dick inside her.

"You are a genius with your mouth," she said dreamily. "I gotta tell Mia about this. All she said was that Gabe fucked her just inside the door, but I bet she doesn't get *this*."

He raised his head, leveling a baleful stare in her direction. "Not cool, baby. Not cool at all."

Her eyes danced merrily and she giggled, momentarily releasing one knee to cover her mouth to stifle her laughter.

"Hands," Jace growled.

"Oops!"

"And while I'm giving my beautiful submissive her orders, do not mention my sister while we're having sex. Ever."

"Yes, sir," she said primly. "Or maybe I should say 'yes, master.'"

"Cheeky wench," he said with no heat.

He loved the lighthearted exchange. Loved the fun, flirty mood they were enjoying. Bethany had enjoyed herself tonight and it showed. He was seeing another side of her. He was seeing her *happy*. It made him ache because here and now he was getting a glimpse of the future. Of how things would be between them. And he loved every goddamn minute. It made him hungry for more and he was a greedy bastard where Bethany was concerned.

He licked her roughly from her opening up to her clit, rolled the nub with his tongue and then flicked repeatedly until she squirmed and went rigid beneath him. He worked a finger gently through her swollen, damp flesh and as he teased her clit, he pushed in to the knuckle, flexing the tip of his finger into the wall of her pussy.

"Jace!"

"Want you to come," he said roughly. "Going to work you right up to that point and then I'm going to suck you dry while you come all over my tongue."

"Oh God," she said weakly.

She convulsed around his finger and bathed him in a flood of quick moisture. He caressed the slick, velvety tissues while he worked her clit with his tongue. When her breaths grew desperate, like she was starved for oxygen, he pulled his finger out and quickly put his mouth over her entrance, shoving his tongue deep and sucking.

She went off like a rocket, hips bucking, her hands flying off her knees to tangle in his hair. She gripped the strands so hard that it was nearly painful, but she held him tightly against her pussy as if she were afraid he'd let her go right in the middle of her orgasm.

She arched and rose, pushing herself more firmly against his mouth, her movements frantic. He sucked and licked, eating like a man starved. When she began to relax and her pussy quivered against his tongue, he nuzzled more gently, working her down from her explosive release.

Lapping slowly and leisurely, he alternated swipes of his tongue with tender kisses to the still-trembling flesh.

"Can I pass out now?" she moaned.

He chuckled against her pussy and then lifted his head so he could meet her gaze. She looked even drunker than before, her eyes glazed over, cheeks flushed and her words slurring past stiff lips.

"I'm still going to fuck you, baby. Whether you're conscious or not. I'd prefer you be awake for the event."

"Mmmm, me too. Jace?"

"Yeah, baby."

"I'm drunk."

He laughed. "I would have never guessed."

"But it was worth it to have you fuck me in these shoes."

"Haven't fucked you yet, baby. I'm getting to that part."

She let out another dreamy sigh. "I like these shoes."

He grinned. "I like them on you while I'm fucking you."

"You gonna fuck me now?"

He laughed at the pouty impatience in her tone. Then he moved up and over her, her breath quickening as she stared up at him, the flirty lightness gone, replaced by lust.

"I'm going to fuck that pretty mouth of yours just as soon as I get rid of my clothes."

She licked over her lips and his dick screamed for him to get out of his fucking pants.

"Hurry," she whispered.

"That I can do," he murmured. "While I'm undressing, I want you to lie on your back, head toward me, and slide over the edge so the back of your neck is on that edge. Wait for me like that. Going to fuck your mouth just like it was your ass on the edge of the bed, your pussy all spread out for me to fuck."

Though he'd told her to do it while he undressed, he stood next to the bed until he was certain she wasn't going to fall on the floor. He helped her position her head and made sure she was comfortable before stripping out of his clothing in record time.

His dick sprang free, painful as hell after spending so much time stuffed into his damn pants. His balls ached and he was ready to dive deep. Knowing he planned to fuck her three ways before he came in her ass made him temper his movements. They were both going to enjoy this even if it killed him.

He palmed her face, holding her steady as his dick bobbed just above her lips.

"Open your mouth, baby," he ordered. "I want you to relax and let me do all the work. Just lie there while I fuck you."

Her lips parted on his command and he pushed inside her liquid warmth. The tip slid over her tongue and his eyes nearly rolled back in his head. Jesus, he was going to come all undone in two seconds flat.

He arched over her, pushing up in a position of dominance. He flexed and slid deep, gliding over her velvety tongue. To the back of her throat, resting a moment before retreating in slow, sensual thrusts. She lifted her hands, reaching back tentatively to curl around his thighs until her fingers teased over his ass, almost as if she were asking permission to touch him. He liked it too damn much to tell her to put her hands forward, and she was gloriously uninhibited, determined to explore and delight in her inebriated state.

Low, sexy sounds hummed from her throat, vibrating around his dick every time he sank deeper. As his movements became more forceful, wet sucking sounds filled the room. It was hot. Everything about tonight pushed every one of his buttons. He'd never fucked a drunk woman before. It was a definite no in his book because he never wanted it to be construed that he'd taken advantage of a woman who wasn't fully cognizant of her actions.

But Bethany was with him. She wanted this. Hell, she'd all but demanded to be fucked in her shoes, adorably tipsy, eyes glowing and cheeks flushed. And he was going to give her what she wanted, absolutely.

He closed his eyes, rocking up on his toes, his palms tightening on her face and then sliding to tangle in her hair as he pulled her to meet his thrusts. Long, slow and deep, he drew out his pleasure, feeling every lick, every suck, every time her cheeks hollowed and then puffed out.

Then he stopped, his breaths tearing raggedly from his chest. She made a low murmur of protest when his hands left her face and he smiled down before leaning in to drop a kiss on her upturned lips.

"Want to fuck that pussy, baby."

She sent him a goofy grin, her eyes lighting up. "I want that too. How do you want me?"

The simple request sent a dark thrill through him. So submissive. So willing to please.

"Turn around and give me those gorgeous legs. I'm going to wrap them around me and then I'm going to hold those heels, spread you wide and fuck you hard."

She shivered uncontrollably, her nipples puckering so delectably that he couldn't control the urge to lean over her body and suck each one in turn into his mouth. She moaned and arched into him as he licked and teased.

"Like that, huh," he said with a low chuckle.

"Mmm hmmm."

He helped turn her around, smiling at the drowsy, drugged droop to her eyes. She fell back onto the bed, her legs sprawling apart. One of her shoes was hanging precariously from her toes and he slid it back over her heel before gripping her ankles and hauling her roughly to the edge of the bed.

Bending her knees back, he wrapped her legs around his waist and entered her in one hard thrust. She gasped. He gasped. So tight, but she was wet around him, easily taking him to the balls. He stayed that way for a long moment, collecting himself so he didn't come.

Then as he'd promised, he reached back to unhook her legs, pushed her knees toward her body, spreading her wide. His hands glided over the expensive, glittering heels and he grasped the thin four-inch spikes.

"Ready?" he ground out, his voice cracking every bit as much as his control threatened to shatter.

She nodded solemnly, her eyes glittering and heavy with the effects of the alcohol.

He began to fuck her. Hard, forceful thrusts. He lunged into her, his body slapping into hers as his grip tightened around her heels. Her pussy tightened and then fluttered around him, signaling her impending orgasm. But he didn't want her to come yet. Not yet. Not until he was deep in her ass. If she came again so quickly, she wouldn't be ready to take him in her ass. It would only cause her discomfort and he wanted this to be perfect for them both.

"Try to hold off, baby," he whispered. "Going to fuck you a little while longer. Love this pussy. But then I'm going to have that sweet ass and that's when you get to come."

"I want on top," she said, her lips pouty and cute.

He raised an eyebrow. "Think you can take me in your ass that way?"

Her bottom lip pushed out more until all he wanted to do was kiss her senseless and suck on that luscious, full mouth.

"I wanna be on top and fuck you with my heels on. Know I said I wanted you to fuck me in these heels, but I'm thinking I could fuck you."

He chuckled and pushed in, taking her breath in a gasp. "You have to know I can't ever tell you no, especially when you're so damn cute when you pout."

Her eyes brightened with excitement. He leaned over her, blanketing her body as he let her heels fall down his legs. He nuzzled and sucked at her nipples, tasting and rolling the puckered tips with his tongue.

"I love that," she sighed. "You have such an amazing mouth. Even when I'm not drunk."

He laughed and shook against her body. "Thank fuck for that, baby. I'd hate to know I was only good in the sack when you were three sheets to the wind."

She pushed impatiently at him and he bit back another grin. He was supposed to be in control here but she was determined to have her way and she wanted it now. Far be it from him to ever hold back a lusty, gorgeous, drunk woman who wanted to have her evil way with him.

He lifted himself off her and then reached for the lubricant in the nightstand. He crawled onto the bed and reclined on his back, reaching his hand to help her climb up over him.

He handed her the tube, his expression going serious for a moment. "Know you're having fun, baby, but I don't want you to hurt yourself. Make damn sure you use enough lubricant and take it slow and easy until I'm inside you."

She sent him a dazzling smile that made his gut tighten.

"Love you," she said, slurring the *L* and drawing out the *you* until it became two words.

He went soft all over. "Love you too, baby. Now have your fun and take your man. I'm just going to lie here and let you do your thing."

"Oh, I like the sound of that," she purred.

She concentrated intensely on applying the lubricant to his dick. She covered every inch until he was about to lose his mind. If she didn't hurry, he'd never make it inside her.

When she seemed satisfied with her effort, she tossed the tube aside and then planted her palms on his chest, her unfocused stare finding him, gravely serious.

"I'm not at all sure what I'm doing," she said as if imparting something of great importance. "I might need your help."

He suppressed a chuckle and then reached down to grasp his slippery cock.

"Just hold on to me like you're doing. When I tell you, start to ease down and take it slow. I'll take care of you."

She sighed and sent another dazzling, heart-stopping smile his way. "I know you will. You take such good care of me."

He guided her hips down with his free hand and then held his cock firmly in position. He reached down to part her ass and tucked the head at her puckered entrance. Her eyes widened when the tip pressed into her tiny entrance.

"It's all up to you now," he said.

Her lips tightened in concentration and her palms dug into his shoulders as she began to push downward. Thankfully, with the amount of lubricant she'd applied and the fact that he was hard as a fucking stone, he penetrated her easily. She paused when he was halfway in, her expression almost comical.

"You're huge," she whispered.

He laughed. "I haven't gained size in my dick, baby. It's the same size it's always been."

"Okay, but it feels a lot bigger," she grumbled.

And then she pushed down, taking him to the balls. He groaned at the instant pressure surrounding him. She gripped him like a fist, squeezing and milking his dick like she wanted every drop of his cum.

"Oh hell," he muttered. "Need you to move, baby. This is going to be fast."

She shook her head and frowned. "Not until I say."

He lifted an eyebrow in question.

"You can't come until I say," she said with a fierce glare.

He laughed again and gripped her hips, holding her down in place. "Then you better say soon or you're going to have an ass full of my cum and there won't be a damn thing you can do about it."

She looked disgruntled but then she sat back, her hands sliding down his chest to his abdomen. She rotated experimentally, twitching her body this way and that until he was to the point of begging her to stop. She was going to be the death of him.

Then she found her rhythm and began to move up and down, his dick coming halfway out before she'd slide back down, taking him fully. He helped keep her steady so she didn't pitch over sideways and he lifted his hips to aid her movements.

"This is nice," she breathed.

"Nice?" He had to laugh again. "Wouldn't call it nice, baby. It's fucking torture."

She gave him a wicked, crooked smile, her eyelids half closed and sexy as hell as she studied him.

"Do I get to come now?" she pouted.

"Hell yes, as long as I get to come with you."

"I need some help in that department," she said. "If I pick up my hands, I'm gonna fall off and I don't want to do that."

His body shook with amusement. "No, I don't want you falling off either. You just keep holding on. I'll take care of you, baby."

He moved one of his hands from her hip to slide between them so his finger caressed her clit. She immediately tensed over him and her eyes closed dreamily.

"'Kay, you can come now," she declared.

If his dick wasn't about to explode, he'd chuckle again, but he was too far gone to laugh at how damn cute she was being. Instead he increased the pressure on her clit and began to surge upward, burying his cock as far into her ass as he could manage.

She came first, her head thrown back, his name a cry on her lips. He had to catch her as she fell forward, her entire body going limp as a dishrag. He wrapped both arms around her, holding her tight as he continued to arch into her. He closed his eyes and clenched his jaw and then he let out a roar that vibrated the walls as he exploded inside her.

Jet after jet pumped into her body. He came violently, an endless stream, his balls tight, his dick straining until it neared the point of pain. He lifted his hips one last time, holding himself as his back bowed.

"Jesus," he muttered as he collapsed back onto the bed, her body blanketing his.

She was warm and sated, limp and completely his. His cock twitched inside her and she nuzzled her face against his chest.

"Gonna have to do this again," she slurred, her words barely audible. "I like when you fuck me in my sexy shoes."

His body shook and his grip tightened around her, holding her close, hugging her to him, never wanting to let her go.

"Baby, I like fucking you any way I can, but the shoes are definitely a plus. I'll buy you a different pair for every day of the week if this is what I have to look forward to."

chapter thirty-six

"Still no sign of Kingston?" Jace asked grimly.

"No, sir," came Kaden's brisk reply. "I've had Trevor poking around down where he and Bethany used to hang when she was on the streets. Haven't seen any sign of him and he hasn't been back to the apartment."

Jace sighed. "Okay, keep me posted."

He disconnected the call and leaned back in his chair. As he lifted his gaze, he saw that Ash stood in the doorway, a frown marring his face.

"Trouble?" Ash asked as he sauntered in to take a seat.

Jace shook his head. "Well, yes and no."

He studied Ash closely, looking for the usual anger in his eyes he wore around the holidays. Though Ash's family typically only bugged him through New Year's, this year they'd been persistent even after the holidays and it had only made Ash's mood blacker.

"Anything you want to talk about?" Ash asked.

"Not much to discuss," Jace muttered. "Kingston is still a no-show. Which is good, don't get me wrong. I'd be happy if he disappeared from Bethany's life permanently. But Bethany is sick with worry and it's starting to wear on her."

"Didn't she go out and hang with Mia and her gaggle of girls?"

Jace couldn't help the smile that attacked his lips at the memory of Bethany drunk and cute as hell and thoroughly bent on seduction.

His body still came to life remembering the lusty way she'd made love to him that night.

"Yeah, she went out with them a week ago. Had a good time. Got drunk as hell and wanted me to fuck her in her heels," Jace said with a grin.

Ash shook his head. "Not cool, man. I get that I'm not even allowed to think about her anymore, but you giving me images of her drunk off her ass and teetering around on fuck-me shoes? Not cool."

Jace held his hands up, grateful they could now joke about the fact Ash had slept with her.

"Problem is, after she slept off the hangover—and we fucked again," he added, just to needle Ash. He was rewarded with another glare and he chuckled. "Anyway, problem is, while she was out with Mia and her girls, she wasn't thinking about Jack. When she was fucking me, she wasn't thinking about Jack. And when she realized she hadn't been thinking about him, she felt guilty. And now she's more worried than ever because he's disappeared."

"That sucks," Ash muttered. "What an asshole."

"Maybe he's trying to do the right thing. Between you and me, his feelings for her were not brotherly. She doesn't know that, but then, she's so naïve about shit like that. She saw him as a brother. I know that absolutely. She didn't have feelings for him beyond that. But he, on the other hand, saw her as a woman. A woman he wanted, and he didn't like it too much that she hooked up with me because that took her away from him. So I figure he's either sulking and doesn't want to see her knowing he can't have her, or he's actually trying to do the right thing and bow out of her life so she can move forward and be happy. Problem with that is, she's worried and she misses him."

"Sucks for you, man," Ash said.

"Yeah. I want her happy, and in order for that to happen, she needs to know that Jack is safe and taken care of."

"So what are you going to do?"

Jace shrugged. "Hell if I know. I have Kaden and Trevor keeping an eye on things. What I don't want is him showing up to see Bethany when none of us are around. I don't trust him. Not after that shit he pulled."

Ash's brows furrowed. "What shit? Are you talking something specific or just his normal bullshit of popping in and out?"

"I didn't tell you," Jace murmured. "I'd forgotten you didn't know all the crap that went down that day it all went to shit and I thought I'd lost her for good. Jesus. Talk about a total cluster fuck."

"What the hell?"

Jace sighed and leaned back in his chair. "Jack showed up at her apartment when I'd taken her back by there on my way to work. I got a call from Kaden that Jack was there. So I go over there, only she's no longer there and I find his backpack in her apartment and it's full of drugs. We're talking several Gs worth of shit."

"What the fuck?"

"Yeah. That was my reaction too. So then Bethany comes home and I was an asshole. Lost my shit. Said a bunch of crap I didn't mean. Made her feel like she had nothing. She took off before I could stop her. So I spent the rest of the afternoon losing my mind because I couldn't find her. Then I got a call that she was back at the apartment, only when I get there, she'd already bolted again. Then the doorman at my building calls to say that she's at my place but she wouldn't come in and she was standing in the fucking rain freezing her ass off."

"Holy shit," Ash murmured.

"Oh, it gets worse."

Ash lifted an eyebrow.

"Yeah, apparently when I decide to be an asshole, I go all the way."

"Uh-oh."

"Yeah, I get to my place, relieved as shit that she's still there. Only she's standing in the rain, crying her eyes out and she tells me it's over and that I'm bad for her."

Jace had to break off and collect himself because the memory of that day still burned too bright in his mind. Of what he'd almost driven her to. It still had the power to knock him to his knees. He could have so easily lost her. All because he was so fucking obsessed with her that he lost all reason around her. His instinct was to hold too tight, to lay down the law and to completely take over.

"She was so upset by our earlier argument—and this I didn't know at the time, but our good friend Jack, a man who's supposed to care about her, had brought the shit she used to be hooked on to her apartment. A little gift for her, apparently."

"Oh hell no," Ash growled.

"She told him she didn't want his shit but he left it there and so when she got back to her apartment after walking around in the rain crying her eyes out over the shit I'd said to her, she almost took a pill. Had it in her mouth, about to swallow, when she realized what she was doing and so she dumped the entire bottle down the sink."

"Good for her," Ash murmured.

"Yeah. She's strong. She thinks she's weak but she's fucking fierce."

"So what happened then?" Ash asked.

"She was so devastated by what she'd almost done that she went straight to my apartment to break things off. She was prepared to go back to her old life because at least then she knew who she was and what she was. She didn't think she was good enough for me. And she couldn't take the emotional strain of our relationship any longer."

"Christ, man, that sounds heavy. I'm sorry."

"Looking back, it was probably the best thing for us. It forced me to listen to her and I also learned about her past and the shit she went through and why she's so fucking loyal to Kingston. But it was as hard as hell at the time and it still scares the shit out of me when I think of how close I came to losing her."

"You're in love with her," Ash said quietly.

"Hell yes, I'm in love with her. Isn't it obvious?"

"No, I mean she's really it for you. I admit I had my doubts, but she's the one, man. I'm happy for both of you. And I'm sorry I gave you such grief in the beginning. I owe Bethany one hell of an apology."

Jace gave him a crooked grin. "Yeah, she's it for me. I would have never thought it possible to fall in love with a woman as fast as I fell for her, but Jesus. It was like being hit by lightning. The best and worst feeling in the world. It's no fun being this gone over a woman and feeling the uncertainty of knowing if I don't play it just right I'll lose her."

"Yeah, no thanks," Ash said sourly. "Guess I'll be the only one remaining who adheres to the 'play hard and live free' motto."

"Asshole. Just wait until it happens to you, man. Gabe and I will be laughing our asses off."

Ash snorted. "Don't hold your breath."

"So what's up with the family from hell? Why they still giving you shit?"

Ash sighed. "Don't really want to talk about them. Ruins my day."

Jace continued to stare at him expectantly.

"Just same old shit. Apparently the dear grandfather isn't feeling well. He's convinced he's going to kick the bucket any day. Never mind he's been saying this shit for years. And his wish is to have his dear, loving family with him on his deathbed. Mom and Dad are just worried that if I don't come to heel they'll be cut out of his will and so they're on my back wanting me to come to family dinners and play nice with the rest of the clan. Self-serving leeches, all of them."

Jace winced. "Sorry, man. That sucks balls."

"You're telling me."

"You tell them to go fuck themselves?"

Ash went silent and dropped his gaze.

Jace immediately sat forward. "You did tell them to go fuck themselves, right?"

Ash sighed. "I like the old man. He's the only one who ever gave a fuck about me. If it was just Mom and Dad and my siblings, yeah, I'd tell them to fuck off."

"Jesus, you're going to do it, aren't you? You're actually going to play nice with them for him?"

"I don't know what I'm going to do yet," he muttered. "Haven't decided. I've been invited to dinner next week. Granddad is going to be there. The whole fucking family will be there."

"I'll go with you," Jace said quickly. "Gabe will too. And Mia."

Ash looked back up at him, fierce love reflected in his green eyes. "You know I love you guys. You've always had my back. I'll never forget that. But you and Gabe have Mia and Bethany now. I don't want either of them—or you and Gabe—exposed to my nest of vipers."

"That's bullshit," Jace cut in impatiently. "We're your family. You're *real* family. And family doesn't leave family to deal with this shit alone."

"I'm a big boy now. I can deal with their bullshit. I'd rather Mia and Bethany not be exposed to their manipulations. They're malicious on a good day. Can you imagine what they'd do to Bethany if they knew about her past? They'd rip her to shreds without a thought. Do you honestly want that for her when things are still so new between you?"

Jace slowly shook his head. "No, I don't. We don't have to bring her. I can go with you and leave her at the apartment. Or I'll have Mia spend the evening with her. I just don't want you going without someone at your back."

Ash stood. "I appreciate that, man. More than you'll ever know. But some things I have to do on my own. This is one of them. I'll go. Make it clear they can't fuck with me like they used to. I'll make an appearance for Granddad, but the rest of them can kiss my ass."

"Okay, but if you change your mind you know Gabe and I will be there with you, no questions asked."

"Yeah, I do know. And thanks."

Ash started to walk to the door and then he turned. "Want me to check with my people and see if Kingston has borrowed any more money or gotten into shit over his head? I can put out some feelers and see if anything comes back. Might even figure out where the fuck he's hiding."

Jace hesitated and then finally shook his head. "No. Sometimes ignorance is bliss. I don't want to ever be in a position where I lie to Bethany, and if I knew Jack was in trouble, I'd definitely lie to her. I wouldn't want her involved in any way. It's better if neither of us knows."

Ash nodded. "Okay. Let me know if you change your mind."

"Will do, and Ash? Let me know how things go, okay? We'll get together after your dinner with the family from hell. You, me, Gabe, Mia and Bethany. We'll have dinner."

"Sounds good. See you around."

Jace watched as Ash walked out, his chest heavy. He didn't miss any part of the threesomes they used to indulge in, but he did miss that connection with Ash. It was twisted, but they'd been friends who shared damn near everything for a lot of years and now suddenly things were very different.

Hell, he hadn't even seen much of Ash since meeting Bethany. He and Gabe both had been focused on the women they loved, which meant Ash had solidly been pushed from the tight circle he used to occupy a huge part of.

His office line rang and he picked it up. A few minutes later, he was swearing and striding into Gabe's office.

"What the fuck is up with the Paris deal?" he demanded. "I just got a call that two of our biggest investors have pulled out."

chapter thirty-seven

Bethany picked up the phone when it rang and uttered a hesitant hello.

"Miss Willis, Mr. McIntyre is here. Shall I send him up?"

Her pulse sped up. Jace wasn't home yet and it was past his usual time. Maybe Ash thought he'd be here already?

"Uhm, sure," she replied.

She wiped her hands nervously down her jeans and then castigated herself. Ash had been the epitome of polite and nice ever since the night she'd had sex with him and Jace. There was no reason for her to work herself into knots every time she had to face him.

A few moments later, the elevator opened and Ash stepped out.

"Hello, Bethany," he said, offering her a warm smile.

"Hi, Ash. Jace isn't home yet."

Ash frowned. "Damn. Thought he'd be here. I needed to give him a folder. Deal's going south on us. He may have been tied up at the office longer than I thought, trying to straighten this shit out."

Her brow crinkled. "It sounds bad. Is it?"

He smiled. "Nothing we can't handle. Shit like this happens all the time. Just another day at the office."

"Come in. Don't just stand there. My manners are horrible. Why don't you sit in the living room? I'm sure he'll be here shortly. Would you like some hot chocolate? I was just making some."

"Sure," he said, walking farther in. "Going to have a cup with me?"

She smiled, relaxing under his easy charm. "Yeah, go sit and I'll grab us both a cup."

She puttered around the kitchen, heating two cups and mixing in the chocolate. She sweetened hers and paused, not sure how Ash liked his. Oh well. She shrugged and made his like she preferred hers.

Then she carried the cup into the living room and handed him his.

"Thanks, sweetheart."

He stared at her over his mug as she took a seat in the armchair a good distance from where he sat.

"So how you doing?" he asked quietly.

"I'm fine," she said brightly.

He gave her a look that clearly said bullshit.

She sighed. "I'm good, really. Worried about Jack. Which is stupid, but I can't exactly control it. I guess I just feel guilty because I have so much now and he still has nothing."

"I wouldn't exactly call a free place to live nothing," Ash said dryly.

Her shoulders heaved. "You're right. And I think that's what pisses me off. Jace really went out on a limb for him. And he did it for me. I know Jace hates it. He has every right to. But he did that for me and he did it for Jack because he knew it would make me happy. And it pisses me off that Jack is being so stupid about it."

She scowled, realizing she really *was* angry. She'd been so buried in worry and anxiety that she hadn't really delved into the fact that she was mad at Jack for being so dismissive of all Jace was doing for him.

"He could at least let me know how he's doing, you know?" she continued, becoming more pissed by the minute.

"Yeah, he could," Ash agreed. "But, honey, listen to me. You have to stop wasting so much emotional energy on this guy. He's a big boy. You can't make his decisions for him and, furthermore, you damn sure shouldn't feel guilty because you straightened out your life and he refuses to do the same."

"You're right," she murmured. "I know you're right. But it's hard. Really hard to just do a complete one-eighty when for the last several years he's all I've known. It's natural for me to worry about Jack because I've always worried about him."

Ash cleared his throat. "There's actually something else I wanted to talk to you about. Now is as good a time as any since we're alone. You and I have only seen each other a couple of times since that first night, and it's not exactly a topic I wanted to get into around other people."

Heat suffused her cheeks. Oh God. He was going to bring up the night of the threesome. Mortification seized her and she couldn't meet his gaze.

"Honey, look at me," Ash said gently.

She shot to her feet, leaving her mug on the coffee table and turned away to stare out the window over the city. Outside, lights twinkled as day faded to night.

"Bethany."

She jumped when she heard his voice directly behind her. He'd followed her to the window and now she had no choice but to face him.

He touched her shoulder and she slowly turned to meet his gaze. There was warmth and understanding in his eyes.

"I know you probably don't think I'm good enough for him either," she said in a low voice. "Especially with how we met. That night . . ."

He put his fingers to her lips. "That's bullshit," he said bluntly. "I owe you a huge apology and I'm going to say it now."

Her eyes widened. "Why would you have anything to be sorry for?"

"Because in the beginning, I didn't think you were a good idea for Jace. I'm his friend and I was worried."

She nodded, her heart sinking. Logically, she'd known his friends wouldn't have embraced her in his life, but somehow hearing it made it hurt more than thinking it on her own.

"I was wrong."

She blinked. "You were?"

"I was one hundred percent wrong, honey. You're the best thing that's ever happened to Jace. And I brought up that night, not to make you uncomfortable, although that's exactly what I've done, but because I don't want this awkwardness between us to go on. Jace is like a brother to me. We've been friends for years. I don't want that to change. You're important to him. He's important to me. Which makes you important to me as well."

"Really?" she whispered.

He smiled. "Yeah, really. I won't say I didn't enjoy that night. That's a fact. You're a beautiful, desirable woman. Can't change it. Don't really want to. You're special, Bethany. But I also know Jace loves you a hell of a lot and I can see that you love him too. What I'd like is for us to be able to put that night behind us and move forward. I'd like us to be friends."

She smiled, her entire face widening with joy. "I'd like that too."

He reached out and touched her cheek, caressing a line down her cheekbone with his thumb. "There you have it then."

"What the fuck is going on here?"

Jace's voice exploded into the living room and Bethany jumped, Ash's hand sliding from her face as both she and Ash whirled in the direction of Jace's voice.

Bethany's eyes widened in alarm while Ash's darkened with anger. Jace looked . . . furious.

Jace punched the button for the elevator and seethed with impatience as he rode up to his apartment. The day had gone to hell fast with the departure of two investors for their Paris hotel project.

Damn it, he'd worked long and hard on getting them committed and now they'd waffled at the eleventh hour.

He and Gabe had spent most of the afternoon on the phone trying to find out what the fuck was up and he'd left far later than he'd planned. All he wanted to do was see Bethany, take her for a nice dinner and then make love the rest of the night. Tomorrow morning would suck because with the withdrawal of the two largest investors, it was entirely possible others would follow suit. They had to repair the problem and fast. Even if it meant sinking more of their own capital into the venture.

The doors opened and he was greeted by the sight of Bethany and Ash standing across the living room in front of the window. And she was smiling. Her entire face was lit up like a goddamn Christmas tree. It was the first time he'd seen her really smile with that much enthusiasm in a week. She was looking at Ash like he'd just hung the fucking moon.

And then Ash touched her face. It wasn't a casual gesture at all and it sent alarm bells clanging in his head. There was an intimacy to that touch. And the look on Ash's face. Tender. Affectionate.

What the fuck was going on?

His temper exploded, a result of a shitty day gone even shittier by finding Ash in his apartment, touching his woman and her smiling at fucking Ash in a way she hadn't smiled for him in days. All he could think about was that night. Ash's mouth on her skin, his dick inside her mouth, her ass. The gasps of pleasure that Ash had wrung from her. It made him crazy.

"What the fuck is going on here?" he asked icily.

Ash and Bethany both whirled around to look at him, Ash's hand sliding from Bethany's face. Bethany's eyes widened in alarm while Ash immediately looked pissed off. Fuck that.

"Ash came by to see you," Bethany said in a low voice.

"Yeah, I can see that," Jace growled.

"You know what? Fuck you, man," Ash snapped. "Can't believe

you'd come in here like this, especially after all we had to say in the office today. Moreover, can't believe you'd disrespect Bethany this way."

"The way I see it, I'm the one being disrespected in my own apartment," Jace bit back.

"I'm out of here," Ash snarled.

He paused and sent Bethany a look of apology.

"I'm sorry, honey. Really sorry. If you need anything, call me, okay?"

And that just set Jace off even more. That Ash was actually suggesting that Bethany would need him as a result of whatever the fuck was going on here and now.

"I'm sorry too," Bethany whispered.

Her face was a wreath of mortification, red suffusing her cheeks. As Ash stalked by Jace, he muttered, "What a dick," and then got into the elevator.

When Jace glanced back up at Bethany, prepared to demand an explanation, tears glittered in her eyes and her shoulders were slumped in defeat. She wouldn't even look at him.

His stomach knotted and he immediately regretted the conclusions he'd jumped to. He couldn't even call them conclusions. He'd lashed out because he was already pissed, frustrated and tired. All he'd wanted was a quiet evening alone with Bethany and he'd arrived here to see Ash up close and personal with Bethany.

Fuck, but he'd done it again. Spoke without thinking. And now Bethany was next to tears. He'd embarrassed her and he'd pissed off his best friend. He was beginning to make a regular practice out of being a first-class asshole.

"Bethany," he said in a quiet voice as he closed the distance between them.

She flinched away the moment he tried to touch her. She turned her head, clearly trying to hide her tears from him. And that pissed him off even more. Not at her. At himself. Because he'd fucked up.

"You still don't trust me," she whispered brokenly. "I don't know why we're doing this. I can't do this, Jace. I won't be with a man who continues to think the worst of me when I've done nothing to deserve it. I've given you everything. My trust, my heart. You may have given me material things, but you've given me nothing that truly matters."

"My love doesn't matter?" he demanded.

This time she met his gaze with her liquid eyes. They were fiercely determined, her mouth drawn into a tight line.

"You cannot stand there and tell me you love me when you think so poorly of me. You may be in lust with me, you may be infatuated. But you do *not* love me."

"Don't tell me I don't love you!"

His pulse was roaring in his ears and panic clawed at his throat. He damn well did love her, and the hell of it was, he did trust her. After he'd calmed down, he knew damn well she and Ash weren't doing shit behind his back. He trusted her and he damn sure trusted his best friend. Neither of them would ever do anything to betray him.

But he'd reacted emotionally and lashed out at the two people he cared most about. Because he was a hotheaded dick with a shitty temper and a propensity for biting the people closest to him.

Jesus, he had to get his shit together. Starting right now.

"You say you love me, but your actions say otherwise."

Her voice was quiet and resigned.

"Words are just words. The evidence is in how you act, how you react. What is wrong with you? You never even asked what Ash was doing here. Didn't ask why. Other than asking us what the fuck was going on in that accusatory, shitty voice. And it wasn't really a question you wanted an answer to anyway. It was more of an 'Aha! I caught you in the act!'"

Jace closed his eyes. "I'm sorry, baby. I know damn well you weren't doing anything behind my back. I knew it then too. I'm in a shitty mood, had a shitty day and I took it out on you and Ash."

"Apologize to *him*," she choked out. "You hurled a horrible insult at him. He's your best friend. You've been best friends for twenty years. You've only known me a few weeks, so I guess I can't ask for more in the trust department. But what you thought of him was just shitty."

"I know. I know, baby. And yeah, I'll absolutely apologize to him, but first I have to make it right with you."

"You can't make this right," she said sadly. "No amount of saying *I love you* and *I trust you* makes it true when it isn't."

"What are you saying?" he whispered, fear paralyzing him.

"I'm going to pack my stuff and go. And no, I'm not running off or being irrational. But I can't stay here. Not anymore. I'll go back to the other apartment. It's not like Jack is there anyway. I'll figure out what to do next."

As she started toward the bedroom, Jace caught her arm and pulled her roughly against his chest.

"No. You aren't going," he said with fierce determination. "The hell you're going anywhere. We've been over this, baby. You stay and fight. Throw something at me. Yell at me. Do whatever you have to do. But you stay and fight for what we have."

Her gaze was heavy and dull when she looked directly in his eyes.

"What good does it do for me to fight when you won't?"

He sucked in his breath. Then he tightened his grips on her shoulders, curling his fingers inward to keep him from shaking.

"You aren't going anywhere tonight," he growled. "It's cold and it's snowing. You stay here where it's safe."

She closed her eyes, averting her face with a sigh. "Fine. I'll sleep on the couch."

"The hell you will."

He fingered her collar, flicking at the diamond.

"You sleep in my bed. That's not negotiable. No fucking way you're going to sleep on the couch."

Her shoulders slumped even further and she wrenched away

from his grasp. Without a word, she walked toward the bedroom, leaving Jace kicking himself with every breath.

Christ. He had to catch Ash before this went too far. He had been a complete dick. He'd let Bethany cool off. He'd catch Ash, apologize and then he'd come back to Bethany when emotions weren't running so high. And then he was going to grovel like hell and swear on all that was holy that he'd hold his fucking tongue in the future.

He pulled out his cell and punched Ash's number in.

"What the fuck do you want?" Ash demanded.

Jace winced at the fury in his friend's voice.

"You very far?"

"I'm getting into the car now."

"Don't. Have him circle. I'll be right down. Meet me in front."

"Fuck you."

"Just do it, Ash," Jace said softly. "You and I both know I was an asshole. I'm not letting you leave pissed off."

"Too late for that," Ash snapped.

"I'll be down in two minutes."

He disconnected the call and hoped like hell Ash wasn't so pissed off that he wouldn't come back inside. He already felt like the biggest jackass on the planet.

Jace hurried into the elevator and rode down. When he got off, he made certain he positioned himself where he'd see if Bethany tried to bolt. When he glanced toward the entrance, he was hugely relieved to see Ash stalking back through the doors.

When Ash saw Jace, his features twisted into a glower and he strode to where Jace stood.

"What the fuck is your problem, man?" Ash demanded. "I cannot believe the shit you just pulled. Apart from the fact that you insulted the hell out of me, you shit all over Bethany. A woman who has done nothing but love you and put up with your bullshit from the start. You want to talk about being an asshole the other day? What the fuck was that shit you pulled just now?"

Jace held up his hands. "I'm sorry, man. I know there wasn't anything going on. I do. I don't even question it. Don't need to know what was up because I know whatever it was is cool. I've had a shitty day and all I wanted was to get home to be with Bethany and when I walked in and saw you touching her and saw her fucking smile . . . God, she hasn't smiled like that for me in days. She was lit up like a fucking Christmas tree. It was so bright and breathtaking that it goddamn hurt to look at her. And I just snapped. It was stupid. Neither of you deserved it. But I took out my anger and frustration on you both."

Ash just stared at him for a long moment. "This shit's got to stop. This is twice you've bit at me. I'm not taking it a third time."

"I get it," Jace said quietly.

"What the fuck, man? Did you honestly think she would cheat on you? Or is this some fucked-up response to me sleeping with her that first time we were all together? Because she doesn't deserve that from you. She accepted something we offered and you've been punishing her for that ever since. If you want to blame someone, take a look at yourself. If you'd been honest from the start, that night would have never happened and you would never have to look at her and remember me fucking her."

Jace flinched at the blunt assessment. But Ash was right. One hundred percent right. It was twisted, but he realized Ash had hit on something Jace hadn't even realized. He was, in a small way, punishing Bethany for something she hadn't even orchestrated. He couldn't stand to see her and Ash together because he was reminded of that night. And even though he'd been able to joke with Ash about it in the office earlier, it was because Bethany hadn't been there.

"No, I don't think she'd cheat on me," Jace said quietly. "And you're right. She doesn't deserve this. *You* don't deserve this. I couldn't let you walk away without apologizing. I don't want this between us anymore."

"If you don't want it between us, then you need to deal, Jace.

Because Bethany and I are cool. We're okay with what happened and we're okay moving forward. She's still embarrassed as hell over it, which makes what you just did even worse. We'd worked it out. That's what we were discussing when you barged in acting like an asshole."

Jace's brows drew together. "What do you mean, 'worked it out'?"

"It means I told her I didn't want her to be uncomfortable around me and that I wanted us to be friends. I see the way she looks at me when we're together and how awkward things are. If you and she are going to be together, I thought it was important that we bury the hatchet and that I try to make things as comfortable and as easy between us as possible. That's what you saw, Jace. Certainly not me making moves on your woman."

Jace rubbed his temples. "I'm sorry. I fucked up again. Swear to God, it's all I do."

"And why are you down here apologizing to me when it's Bethany you need to be begging forgiveness from?" Ash demanded.

Jace blew out his breath. "She's upset."

"Understandably so."

"Yeah. Absolutely."

"So, then why aren't you up there with her?" Ash persisted. "Tell me you aren't giving her up. Because I'm telling you right now, you do that and I'll move in and I won't be the asshole you're being."

Jace's nostrils flared. "What the fuck? So you *do* have feelings for her."

Ash shook his head. "All I know is that she's a beautiful, desirable, sweet-as-hell woman. That already places her miles above the women we typically fuck. I'd be perfectly happy to see where a relationship would take us. I already know we're compatible in bed."

"Fuck you," Jace snarled.

Ash smirked. "Then maybe you should get your ass up the elevator and make sure she's not going to leave your ass."

Jace averted his gaze. "There was something different this time. She wasn't so much pissed as she was . . . defeated. It was scary as fuck. She got teary-eyed, but she tried to hide that from me so it wasn't like she was manipulating me with tears. And she was just so resigned and matter-of-fact. I went too far this time, Ash. Trust has been an issue with us before. My mouth has gotten ahead of my brain more than once and I've bit at her, said shit I didn't mean, and it hurt her. Just like I hurt her a while ago. Not sure she's going to be so quick to forgive this time."

"Well, you won't know until you get your ass up there," Ash said calmly.

"Are we good?" Jace asked in a quiet voice.

Ash's shoulders went up and down as he blew out a deep breath. "Yeah, man, we're good. But swear to God, you won't get a third time to pull that shit with me."

Jace nodded and then held up his fist. Ash bumped it. Hard. Jace nearly winced as Ash's knuckles cracked over his.

"Go make this right with your girl," Ash said. "Because if you don't, I will."

Jace scowled and Ash laughed.

"Knew that would motivate you," Ash said, amusement heavy in his voice.

Jace punched him in the arm and then turned back to the elevator. "Later, man."

"Let me know how it goes with Bethany," Ash said quietly.

"Will do."

When Jace entered the bedroom, he saw that Bethany was already in bed. She was curled into a tight ball, her back turned to the center of the bed so she'd face away from him.

She was also wearing pajamas when she always wore nothing to bed. It was one of his rules—the first she'd blatantly broken.

He sighed, knowing damn well he wasn't going to take her to task for not obeying the no-clothing-to-bed dictate.

He undressed and then slid into bed next to her. He edged closer to her until her back was pressed to his chest and he curled an arm around her body, pulling her even tighter to his body.

She went rigid, tension boiling off her body.

"We need to talk, baby."

She shook her head. "No. Not tonight. I have nothing to say. I'm too upset and we'll end up saying things we regret. Isn't that what you've basically said happens with you? That you say shit you don't mean? For once, I want you to say something you *do* mean. I'm tired of guessing. I'm tired of having to tiptoe around, never knowing how you're going to take things or how you'll react or what fucked-up way you'll interpret something that is absolutely meaningless."

He sighed and kissed her shoulder, leaving his lips pressed against her skin.

"You haven't even eaten anything. It's early yet."

"I'm not hungry," she said in a low voice. "Please, Jace, just leave me alone. I'm not going anywhere. I'm not running. Go eat or do whatever it is you want to do and let me work this out on my own."

He rolled away from her onto his back and stared up at the ceiling.

"Not crazy about you lying here hurting because of me, baby."

She didn't respond, but he saw the slight wobble of her shoulders and he cursed silently. She was fucking crying. And she wanted to be left alone. Didn't want to be comforted. Didn't want his arms around her. Didn't want him holding her.

He squeezed his eyes shut. Yeah, he'd fucked up royally. Even worse than the last time. When would he stop doing this shit?

How could he even go into work tomorrow when he'd be paralyzed with the fear of her leaving the minute he was out of sight?

He couldn't live like this. And he knew she couldn't either. He was destroying her with his mistrust. And the hell of it was, he *did* trust her.

Maybe this was a product of their relationship only being a few weeks old. These were issues all couples had to work out, weren't they? He'd moved fast. He knew that. Most normal people drew out the dating and get-to-know-you stage a little longer than he had. But then, he'd always gone after what he wanted with single-minded determination. Bethany had been no different in that regard.

Knowing he'd never go to sleep this early, he eased out of bed. Her back was still to him but he also knew she was still awake. Her body was too rigidly set for her to have fallen into sleep.

"I'm going into the kitchen to get something to eat," he said softly. "I'd love it if you joined me. Or I can bring you something to eat in bed."

She sniffed ever so lightly and his heart clenched all over again. Fuck it all. She was still crying.

He turned and strode out of the bedroom, fear and remorse vying for equal airtime. He'd said he trusted her. Part of that was giving her space to work things out her own way. As long as she did it here in his apartment, in his space, in his bed, he could deal. He'd said he trusted her. It was time to show her he meant that.

He made a sandwich, more to have something to do than because he was hungry. He remembered when Gabe had fucked up so badly with Mia, she'd told him that if he ever had a hope of getting her back that he'd have to crawl. And Gabe had crawled. He'd humbled himself in front of half of New York City in order to get Mia back.

Jace hadn't really gotten it at the time. He'd thought Gabe was being a bit too dramatic, but now he realized the desperation Gabe must have been feeling. Jace would crawl. He'd do whatever it took to get Bethany to stay.

After hours of churning over every word he wanted to say, he went back into the bedroom only to find the lights out. She'd gotten up long enough to darken the room. When he climbed into bed, he could hear her soft breathing, but what pained him more was the fact that even in sleep, she softly hiccupped, a sign that she'd cried for quite some time.

He turned into her, inhaling her sweet scent. He buried his face in her hair and curled his arm around her middle, anchoring her against his body.

Sleep was a long time coming, and when it finally did, it was filled with haunting dreams of a world without Bethany.

chapter thirty-eight

Bethany came awake to soft lips brushing over her shoulder. She winced when her eyes opened and pain instantly stabbed through her head. Her eyes were puffy and swollen. Her throat was scratchy and achy from the tears she'd shed the night before.

"Baby, wake up for me, please."

Jace's soft voice drifted over her ears and she closed her eyes again as a flood of pain rocketed through her all over again.

"Bethany, I need you to look at me."

Grudgingly she turned halfway to her back so she could meet Jace's gaze. He winced when he saw her face. She must really look bad based on his reaction.

He stroked his fingers over her face and then he leaned in to kiss her.

"Baby, I know what I did was wrong. It wasn't fair to you or to Ash. I've made things right with Ash but I have to make them right with you."

He went silent a moment as if allowing her to digest his words. Then he continued on.

"I have to go into the office this morning. Unless you want me to stay and talk now. Nothing is more important than you. But if you need more time, I'm going to go into the office, make a few calls, get caught up with Gabe and Ash, and then I'm coming home so we can work this out."

She nodded, her throat too raw to speak.

"I want you to rest, take it easy today," he said gently. "When I get home, we'll talk. Then we'll go get something to eat. Spend the evening together, just you and I."

"Okay," she said hoarsely.

She rolled back to her side as he moved away from the bed. And she closed her eyes again, drifting back into the dark void.

Her thoughts were chaotic. She'd thought about the situation all night. Only in the hour before dawn had she been able to drift off fully.

The problem was that there was nothing she could do to fix the issue between her and Jace. He either trusted her or he didn't. There was no magic solution. Nothing she could do to change it. It was on him and if he didn't trust her, nothing she did or said would ever change that fact.

She had no doubt that he was truly regretful for the way things had gone down the prior evening. But that didn't mean he trusted her, and it didn't mean that it wouldn't happen again.

She listened as he quietly readied himself for work. When it was time for him to go, he came back over to the bed and leaned down to kiss her forehead. He lingered there a moment longer, as if he was reluctant to leave.

A part of her didn't want him to go. Wanted him to stay and hold her so she could pretend this issue didn't exist between them. The other part wanted him to leave so she could have time to herself to sort through her mixed feelings.

Finally he drew away after smoothing the hair from her face and forehead. Then his footsteps sounded and retreated from the bedroom until she could no longer hear him.

Her eyes burned with more tears and she closed them tighter, determined not to give way to them again. She'd spent the entire night alternating between anger and deep sadness. She still wasn't sure which was the clear winner. Her emotions were a mess lately. Between Jack and Jace she was on a roller coaster from hell.

She dozed fitfully, checking the clock each time she awoke. She finally realized she was willing time to pass knowing that Jace would be home much earlier than usual.

Even after all of that, she was eager to see him.

She sighed, knowing full well that she'd forgive him and they'd move on. The question was whether Jace would truly make the effort to control his temper and hold his tongue in the future. Some might say she needed to develop a tougher skin, but to hell with that. No one deserved to be flayed alive because someone else was in a crappy mood. Shit happened to everyone. It was no excuse to take it out on others.

Anger felt much better than the pathetic weariness she'd displayed the evening before. She could deal with anger. It made her feel stronger, less vulnerable. Despair and damn tears were for the birds.

But there was also the fact that trust took *time*. Was she really being fair to Jace? He'd only known her such a short time and trust was earned. What had she really done to earn it yet?

Calm settled over her. They could work this out. Trust wasn't automatic. Sometimes it took months, even years to fully achieve. Nothing about her life or her past was exactly conducive to gaining instant faith. And Jace was trying. She knew that without a doubt.

Her cell phone rang and she automatically reached for it. She glanced at the LCD screen, holding her breath as she realized she hoped it was Jace. She frowned when she saw Kaden's name as the identifying contact.

"Hello?"

"Miss Willis, this is Kaden. I tried to call Mr. Crestwell but he's currently unavailable. So I wanted to let you know that Mr. Kingston is back at the apartment."

She sat up fully in bed. "Jack's there?"

"Yes, ma'am. He returned a half hour ago."

She threw off the covers and swung her legs over the side. "Where are you right now? Are you still there?"

"Yes, ma'am."

"I'm coming over. Stay there, please. Jace wouldn't like if I was there alone. Just don't let Jack leave before I arrive, okay?"

Kaden hesitated a brief moment. "Okay. I'll be here and I'll go up with you. Those are the conditions."

"Of course," she said hastily. "I'll leave right away."

She disconnected the call and hurried out of bed to dress. She looked like crap but she wasn't going to take the time to shower and make herself look any better. Jack might not be there that long. Who knew what he was thinking?

A few minutes later, she went down to the lobby and asked the doorman to get her a cab. Twenty minutes later, she arrived at the apartment building. Kaden was waiting for her just outside the main entrance.

"He's still here?" she asked breathlessly as she ran up to the door.

"Yes. I'll go up with you now. I left a message with Mr. Crestwell's receptionist, but I was told he's in closed-door meetings for the next while."

"Yes," Bethany murmured as they got into the elevator. "He's really busy this morning."

She used her key to get inside the apartment and Kaden came in with her, sticking close to her side.

"Jack," she whispered when she saw him standing by the bar in the kitchen.

Jack's head came up and his eyes sparked with surprise when he saw her.

She flew around the bar and hugged him fiercely.

"Jack, I've been so worried. Where have you been? Why haven't you called? Why did you let me think the worst?"

Jack pulled her away and grinned crookedly at her. He looked awful. Paler and thinner, more gaunt. And he had shadows under his eyes that told her he hadn't slept in forever.

"Had shit to do, babe. Told you that."

Anger whipped up her spine. "That's bullshit! You had a nice place to stay. Jace did this for you. All of it. And you didn't even stop to think that I was worried sick about you."

Jack's eyes grew hooded. "He didn't do it for me, babe. He did it for you and we both know it."

"Does it matter who he did it for?" she all but shouted.

"Yeah, it does."

She turned in agitation and glanced over to where Kaden stood, his expression indecipherable. "Can you give us some privacy?"

Kaden didn't look thrilled at that prospect.

"He's not going to hurt me," she said in exasperation. "You can stand just outside. No way for either of us to go anywhere as long as you're guarding the door."

Kaden's shoulders heaved and then he reluctantly went to the door, walked out and then closed it behind him. Then she turned back to Jack.

"What the hell is going on with you, Jack? What about the drugs? What are you into?"

A bleak expression entered Jack's eyes. "Let me make you a cup of hot chocolate. Already made me one. We can talk then. You're cold and hate to say this, babe, but you look like shit. Crestwell not taking care of you like he promised?"

The accusation in Jack's voice just pissed her off even more. He busied himself making another cup of cocoa and set it next to his to stir in the mix while she stood there and continued to stew.

"Jace is taking care of me just fine. This isn't about me. This is about you. You have the chance to do something better with your life. Why are you so determined not to take it? He's willing to let you stay here as long as you need to. You could get a real job. Get out of the life you're in now."

Jack finished stirring and then turned back to the sink to drop in the spoon and put away the milk. She grabbed one of the mugs from the counter and walked into the living room to sit on the couch. She was angry and she needed to get it under control. But it ate at her. This wasn't the Jack she knew. He seemed like he didn't give a shit about himself one way or another. It infuriated her that he had a chance to be better now and he was just pissing it away.

She sipped at the chocolate, allowing it to burn a warm trail into her belly.

Jack came in and sat across from her in the armchair, his own mug in his hands. But he didn't drink. He just watched her with sad eyes.

"You can't worry about me now, Bethy. You have a life. You have a man who cares about you. You need to focus on that and quit worrying about me."

She made a sound of exasperation and downed half of the chocolate.

"I can't just stop worrying about you, Jack. I've been worrying about you for too many years. That just doesn't go away because my circumstances have changed. Why don't you care more about yourself?"

"I came back because I'd planned to call you from the phone here," he said quietly. "Wanted to say good-bye."

Alarm raced down her spine. "Good-bye? Where are you going?"

"Away," he said simply, not elaborating.

She finished off the cocoa and set the cup back down on the coffee table with a *thud*.

"Where?" she persisted. "What are your plans? Don't do this, Jack. Please, I'm begging you. Stay here. I'll help you find a job. You can have a good life. You can turn this around. Please, I love you."

He gave her a tender look. "You don't love me, Bethy. Not like you love him. I see the way he is about you. You deserve that. You deserve more than I could ever give you. You being happy is enough for me. That's all I ever wanted."

"Just because I love him doesn't mean that what I feel for you is any less," she said emphatically. "It's a different kind of love. You're my brother, Jack. Family."

"I'm not your brother," he said quietly.

It was then she realized. It hit her and she wondered how she could have been so blind. She sucked in a deep breath and the room went swimmy around her. She blinked to ward off the sudden dizziness but the room continued to sway around her. She frowned and shook her head to clear it.

"You have feelings for me," she whispered. "You don't see me as a sister."

"Now you see it," he said, an edge of bitterness to his voice.

She bowed her head and closed her eyes but then struggled to open them again. God, what was wrong with her? She suddenly couldn't think clearly, couldn't even summon the words she wanted to say.

"I'm so sorry, Jack." Her words slurred and her tongue felt too thick in her mouth. "I never knew. Never realized . . . I love Jace. Completely and utterly love him. I love you absolutely, but not in that way. I'm so sorry. I never meant to hurt you."

The room was starting to blank around her. She tried to stand but her legs wouldn't cooperate. She staggered upward, pushing herself. She saw Jack's look of alarm and then utter panic entered his eyes. He glanced down at his cup of hot chocolate and then reached over to grab hers, swearing when he found it empty.

"Jack?"

It came out as a whimper. Something was wrong. Terribly wrong with her.

"I don't feel so well," she whispered.

The last thing she saw was Jack lunging for her, but he wasn't in time. She hit the floor and the world blanked around her.

chapter thirty-nine

"Mr. Crestwell, I'm sorry to interrupt, but you have an urgent phone call from a Kaden Ginsberg. I told him you were in meetings but he insisted on speaking to you at once."

Jace rocketed up from his seat and strode from the office where he, Gabe and Ash were on a conference call with the group of investors for their Paris hotel. Gabe and Ash both rose in concern, but Jace left to go into his office without another word.

"Crestwell here," Jace barked when he picked up the phone.

"Mr. Crestwell, you need to get to Roosevelt Hospital as fast as possible," Kaden bit out with no preamble.

Jace's blood froze and he had to sit down before his legs gave out. "What the fuck is going on?"

"It's Miss Willis. I called her this morning to tell her that Kingston had come back to the apartment. I escorted her up myself and stayed with her. I stepped just outside the apartment so the two could speak privately. When I came back in, she was unconscious on the floor of the living room."

"What the fuck?" Jace exploded.

"Sir, it's not good. She's not good. Looks like an overdose," Kaden said quietly.

Jace's heart fell and panic seared through his brain, rendering him incapable of thought or speech. Overdose? Oh God. Had she tried to kill herself? Had he driven her to this?

"Overdose?" he croaked. "Are you certain?"

"I'm not certain of anything. I called for an ambulance but her respirations were so light I could barely detect them. Scared the shit out of me. I did mouth-to-mouth. She still had a very faint pulse. When the medics got there, they intubated her and loaded her up as fast as they could. We're en route to the hospital now. Should be there in a couple of minutes."

"I'll meet you there," Jace said shortly.

He hung up the phone and lunged from his chair. He ran headlong into Gabe and Ash, who'd both been standing at the door listening.

"What the fuck is going on?" Ash demanded.

"Bethany's on her way to the hospital. It's not good," Jace choked out. "Overdose."

"*Jesus,*" Gabe breathed.

"I've got to get to her," Jace said, trying to push past his friends.

"Fuck no. You aren't in shape to be driving anywhere," Ash said, holding his arm. "Gabe and I will drive you."

"I don't give a fuck who drives. I just have to get there *now,*" Jace roared.

"Cool it, man," Gabe said. "Get your head on. Last thing you need is to lose your shit. Take a deep breath. Be strong for Bethany. We'll get you there. Ash, call for the driver. Mine is on standby. I'd planned to take Mia to lunch after our meetings so he's waiting. Have him pull to the front immediately."

"How can I cool it when I fucking did this to her?" Jace asked in a haunted voice.

"Jesus," Gabe cursed again.

"Come on, we're wasting time," Ash clipped out.

They ran out to the car that had just pulled up when they exited the building. Gabe climbed in front and directed the driver while Jace and Ash got in back.

His mind was numb. His heart flayed open. The only thing he

could feel was paralyzing fear. It choked him until he couldn't breathe. He was absolutely gutted. All he could think of was last night, the look on her face, the devastation in her eyes and her accusation that he didn't trust her, that he'd never trust her. Her saying she wanted out, to leave. Her saying she didn't want to sleep next to him.

Memories flooded him. Bethany the first night he'd seen her. Her beautiful eyes. Her breathtaking smile. How she'd responded to his touch. And now that could all be taken away in one cruel moment because he'd been the worst sort of ass. He could have prevented this. If only he'd stayed with her this morning. He should have worked it out. He should have made certain she *knew* that she was the single most important thing in his life. But he hadn't and now she was on a stretcher in an ambulance fighting for her fucking life.

"Jace, man, you have to breathe," Ash murmured. "Keep it together. You need to be strong for her."

He lifted his gaze to meet Ash's. Cold and numbness crawled through his body until it blocked everything else. "I did this to her. Jesus Christ, I drove her to this. You were there. You know what I did. What I did to you both."

"You don't know that," Ash snapped. "Keep your shit together until we know what happened."

"Kaden said she was barely breathing. He had to do mouth-to-mouth on her. The medics had to intubate her. Kaden said it looked like an overdose. Now you tell me. After what you saw last night when I lit into you both, how upset and devastated she was because I was a complete asshole. You tell me I had nothing to do with this. This is on me, man. I left her this morning when I damn well should have stayed with her to make things right. But I left because I wanted to give her some space. I put a business deal before her and what she needed from me. I left her to think that I still didn't trust her. You didn't see her. Eyes swollen and puffy from crying her fucking heart out last night. We went to bed and she had her back to me all goddamn night. Fuck, she wanted to leave last night and I wouldn't let her. She wanted to sleep apart from me and I wouldn't allow that either. So she laid in that bed next to me last night and she cried because I'm an arrogant dickhead who lost his shit over *nothing*."

"Man, you have to chill," Gabe said grimly. He turned in the front seat so he could look at Jace, and his eyes were hard. "You don't know what happened. None of us do. Until you get there and she explains it, you can't jump to conclusions. You can't do that to her."

"She was barely breathing," Jace bit out. "She may not even be alive when I get there. God, I can't lose her. Not like this. Hell, I'm not even good for her. She tried to tell me. I knew what our relationship was doing to her. It almost happened before. She almost took a pill when I upset her last time. But I hung on because I was too selfish to do anything else. I was only looking at my wants and needs and I need her more than I need to breathe."

"Pump the brakes," Ash ordered. "Until we get the story, you can't be making stupid, rash decisions. She needs you, man. She needs you more than ever right now. Whatever happened, it's not good and she's going to need you to be her rock. Whatever happened, you can fix it. But not if you're already checking out and being all noble and shit by saying she's better off without you. Do you honestly think she's better off on the streets with fucking Kingston, who obviously doesn't give a shit about the kind of life she has? Hell, he was pushing drugs at her. Does that sound like the kind of man she needs to be with?"

"I can give her a better life. I just don't have to necessarily be in it," Jace said bleakly. "I hurt her. I've hurt her time and time again. No one should have to put up with that shit. I can give her a better life and step away. Let her make her own choices. I'll make damn sure she always has whatever she needs, but maybe the biggest thing she doesn't need is . . . *me*."

"Swear to God, I'm going to beat your ass if you don't shut the fuck up," Gabe growled. "Now isn't the time for you to wimp out.

Man up and be there for her. Find out what happened and then work it out. Bethany is fragile, but now? She's going to be even more so. We don't know what drove her to this. There's a lot of questions we don't have the answers to. And until we get those answers, the thing she needs most is you. There by her side. Supporting and loving her."

Jace went quiet. He closed his eyes, torturing himself with images of Bethany's lifeless body. Face pale in death, shadows from the night before still hanging permanently on her cheeks. Of her dying thinking he didn't love her or trust her. Or her thinking she wasn't the single most important thing in his life. Of her dying without him ever telling her how sorry he was and how much he fucking loved her.

She was *everything* to him and he was goddamn well going to make sure she knew it.

Gabe was right. No matter what had happened or why Bethany had done this, she needed him. He wasn't going to let her go unless she convinced him she truly didn't want him or his love. And even then he'd make damn sure she was always provided for. Even if it ripped his heart and soul right out of him not to be a part of her life.

"Going to marry her as soon as possible," Jace said hoarsely. "Swear to God, if she survives this, I'm going to marry her and spend every goddamn day making sure she knows where my heart is at."

"Now that's more like it," Ash said.

Jace lifted his haunted gaze to Ash. "I'm sorry, man. More sorry than you'll ever know. I didn't even think you did anything. Was just a shitty day and I went off without thinking. Just wanted to bite at someone and you and Bethany happened to be there at the wrong fucking time."

Ash made a sound of impatience. "We already went over this shit. You said what you needed to say last night. It's done. Won't say I'll ever tolerate that bullshit again, but it's done. You just have to make it up to Bethany now."

"Yeah," Jace whispered. "If I only get the chance. God, don't let her die. She has to live. We have to get through this. Please don't let her die."

Grief was choking, cutting off his air. It was a weight pressing down on every part of his chest until it was unbearable. He couldn't lose her. Not like this. Never like this. He'd never survive this if she died.

"She'll need help," Gabe said in a low voice. "Counseling. If she tried to kill herself, she's going to need professional help."

"She'll have whatever it is she needs," Jace said. "However long it takes. But I'll be there with her every step of the way. She's never going to be alone again."

The driver roared to a stop outside the emergency room entrance and Jace jumped out, running inside, where he was immediately met by Kaden. Jace grabbed the much larger man by his shirt, pulling their faces close together.

"Where is she?"

"They're working on her now," Kaden said grimly. "Doc came out briefly to ask about family. I told him you were on your way. Said it was definitely an overdose but they can't rouse her enough to ask what she took or how much."

"Fuck!" Jace exploded.

He dropped his hold on Kaden and then stalked toward the desk and the wary-eyed receptionist.

"Bethany Willis," he bit out. "I want to see her now."

She rose and walked around the desk as Gabe and Ash came up behind Jace.

"Sir, they're working with her now. You'll have to wait out here."

"The hell I will! Take me back to her now. I have to see her. She's not going to die alone. I have to see her."

She looked helplessly at Gabe and Ash as if asking for their help in calming him. Thankfully neither did or said a word and stared the woman down to show her that Jace had their full support.

"Belinda, let him come back," an older doctor said from a few feet away.

Jace immediately turned to the physician. "Is she okay?" His heart hammered and he staggered, struggling to remain upright. Icy fear gripped him. What if the doctor had come out to tell him she was gone?

"Come with me," the doctor said in a quiet voice.

Jace followed behind, every step filled with overwhelming dread. He was led into a room where Bethany lay pale and quiet on a bed. Surrounding her was a bevy of doctors and nurses. There was a tube down her throat, and one down her nose. They were injecting some nasty-looking shit into the tube in her nose.

"Is she . . . is she still alive?" Jace choked out.

"We've managed to stabilize her but she still hasn't regained consciousness," the doctor said. "We don't know what she ingested or how much so we're treating her blind. We've tried to get her to rouse so she can tell us what happened, but so far we've had no luck. Maybe you can try to get a response from her."

Jace surged toward the bed and one of the nurses stepped out of his way so he could get to Bethany's side.

He picked up her limp hand and curled both of his hands around it. He brought it to his lips, pressing his mouth against it. Tears burned his eyes and he swallowed, sucking in deep breaths so he didn't lose his composure.

"Bethany, baby, you need to wake up," he said in a low voice.

"You need to speak louder," the doctor advised. "I know you're instinct is to be gentle, but she needs to regain consciousness."

Jace leaned over and kissed her forehead as he swept one hand through her bedraggled hair. "Bethany, baby, can you hear me? You need to wake up and talk to us. We're worried sick, honey. Come back to me. Please just come back to me."

He broke off as a sob welled in his throat. She lay unmoving, all those damn tubes running everywhere.

"What about the tube in her throat?" Jace demanded. "If she wakes up, she's going to panic. She can't talk around that damn thing."

"Right now it's the only way she's breathing," the nurse said gently. "If she starts to come around, we can remove it. But we need to find out what she took and how much."

Jace closed his eyes as tears ran freely down his cheeks.

"Baby, please," he choked out. "Wake up and talk to me. You have to come back to me, Bethany. I'm lost without you."

He pressed his forehead to hers and his tears seeped onto her skin.

"Please come back to me. I love you. We can work this out, baby. Just please open your eyes for me. I'm begging you. Don't leave me. For God's sake, don't leave me."

As he pulled back, her eyelids fluttered sluggishly. He could tell how hard it was for her to even open her eyes. And then he saw the brilliant blue and the constricted, pinpoint pupils. She was clearly disoriented and then panic surged into her eyes.

Joy flooded into Jace and he turned excitedly to tell the nurse, but they were already moving in, monitoring her vitals before taking the tube out. Bethany struggled, panicking and gagging. Jace gripped her hand and squeezed until he was sure he was hurting her.

"Don't fight it, baby. Just give them a few minutes. It'll be over soon, I swear it. They had to put a tube in to help you breathe."

Tears filled her eyes and they widened and then focused on him.

"That's it, baby. Just focus on me. Look at me and breathe. Just breathe for me," he said brokenly.

A few minutes later when the tube was gone, Jace had to step back long enough for them to ensure Bethany could breathe on her own. They placed an oxygen cannula in her nostrils to replace the rebreather bag that had accompanied the tube in her chest. And then finally they stepped back to allow Jace access once more.

Bethany struggled to keep her eyes open. He could see the strain it caused her. Several times she blinked sluggishly as if she'd slip back into unconsciousness but he surged forward, demanding that she stay awake and stay with him.

"Jace?" she whispered, her voice nearly gone.

"Yes, baby, I'm here."

He took her hand and put his face close to her so she could see him and feel him.

She weakly raised one hand, touching his damp cheek where his tears had been and she frowned.

"I don't understand. What happened?" she whispered.

Confusion was heavy in her eyes and she glanced rapidly around, taking in the hospital environment and all the medical staff in her room.

"Baby, you overdosed," Jace said gently. "We need to know what you took and how much so they can help you. You have to fight, Bethany. I can't—won't—give up on you or us. Whatever happened, we can fix it. I love you. We can get past this, I swear it. It doesn't matter to me. Whatever happened, why you did it, it doesn't matter. You're the only thing that matters."

Her eyes widened and she struggled against the sluggishness of her lids. Her mouth opened and she tried to speak. She closed her lips and then reached for him, urgent, frantic.

"Jace . . ."

"What, baby? Talk to me. Fight this. Please, for me. For us."

"I didn't do it," she said fiercely. "I didn't take anything. I wouldn't. You have to believe me."

He stared back at her in shock. "Baby, you passed out. You almost died. You have to tell us what happened."

"I don't know what happened!"

Her voice rose, hysterical. She became agitated and an alarm went off, causing one of the nurses to rush forward.

"Sir, you need to leave now," the nurse said briskly. "She's not getting enough oxygen and her vitals are dropping."

He was shoved aside as the medical team crowded in. They put a mask over her face, but she fought it and them.

"Jace!"

"I'm here, baby. I'm here!"

"I didn't do this! Please, you have to believe me," she sobbed.

Then he was shoved more firmly from the room. Gabe and Ash were there to pull him back the minute he was forced out.

The door was shut firmly in his face and he turned, putting his fist into the wall.

Gabe and Ash grabbed him, subduing him before he could punch the wall again. They forced his back against the wall he'd just punched and Gabe got into his face.

"Cool it, man. You have to keep calm."

Jace shrugged them off and stalked back to the waiting room, where Kaden still stood.

"Where is Kingston?" Jace snarled.

Kaden's eyes darkened. "I don't know. I didn't give a fuck about him when I saw Bethany on the floor. My sole concern was her. We loaded her into the ambulance and left. He was still at the apartment."

"You go find him and you bring him here," Jace roared. "I don't give a fuck what you have to do. You get him here *now*."

"I'm on it. I'll call Trevor. He was on his way over after I called. I'll make sure he sits on Kingston until I get there."

"You do that," Jace said tersely.

Kaden walked briskly away and Jace turned to see Gabe and Ash standing there, confusion in their eyes.

"What the fuck was that about, man?" Ash queried.

Jace was seething with fury. His fingers curled and uncurled as he tried to gain control of his rage.

"Bethany says she didn't do it. She didn't take anything."

Gabe's brows furrowed. "You believe her?"

"Hell yes, I believe her!" Jace exploded. "You didn't see her. When she came to, she was scared and confused as hell. You should have seen her face when I told her she'd overdosed. She got hysterical. Vitals tanked. They shoved me out. But she said she didn't take anything. Didn't know what the fuck I was talking about. She asked *me* what the hell happened."

"Then what the fuck?" Ash demanded.

Jace's nostrils flared and he sucked in deep, steadying breaths. He had to get control. He had to be strong for Bethany.

"What it means is that if she didn't take that shit, then someone gave it to her. And Kingston was the only other person in that apartment."

chapter forty

Jace paced the floor of the waiting room in agony, not knowing how Bethany was doing. They'd kept him from her room as they worked to rid her system of the drugs she'd ingested. He didn't know how or why Jack had forced them on her, and he wouldn't know until the bastard showed up. It would be a miracle if Jace didn't kill him before he could wrest an explanation from him.

And then the gloves were off. No more would he allow this to go on. He didn't give a fuck how upset it made Bethany, Jack was gone. Out of her life. If Jack had given her the drugs, Jace would file charges and have him arrested. He could rot in jail for all Jace cared.

Mia had rushed to the hospital the moment Gabe had called her and she kept vigil with the others. She worried incessantly over Jace's state of mind, but she'd backed off when Gabe had murmured to her to leave her brother alone. He'd sent Gabe a grateful look. The last thing he wanted was to lash out at his sister when she was only trying to help. And he appreciated them all being here. Appreciated their unwavering support, though God only knew he didn't deserve it after the way he'd treated them all. Especially Ash. But Ash hadn't moved from the waiting room the entire time. He sat just as worried as the rest, fretting endlessly over Bethany's condition.

And then Kaden came through the door, shoving Jack in front of him. Kaden held up his hand when Jace would have launched himself forward, and hustled Jack into one of the private family waiting rooms. Jace followed behind, with Ash and Gabe on his heels. They likely wanted to make sure he wasn't going to commit murder in a public facility.

As soon as the door closed behind them, Jace slammed Jack into the wall and got into his face.

"What the fuck did you do to her, you bastard?"

Jack's face was twisted with grief. He looked haggard. Completely wrung out. His eyes were bloodshot and he didn't even attempt to defend himself.

"What did you give her?" Jace snarled. "She's in there fighting for her life and we need to know what the fuck she ingested so they can help her."

"Narcos," Jack said in a shaky voice. "An entire bottle. I think there were forty or so. I don't know exactly."

"I'll go let them know," Gabe said in a low voice.

"Why did you give them to her? How the fuck did you give them to her without her knowing? She would have never taken that shit."

"It wasn't supposed to be her," Jack choked out. "Never supposed to be her. She took the wrong cup. It was hot chocolate. She drank the wrong one."

"What the fuck?" Jace snarled.

"It was supposed to be me," Jack said in a resigned voice. "I didn't expect her to show up. She wasn't supposed to. Had no idea you were having the place watched."

"What the fuck are you saying? That you were going to commit suicide?"

"Yeah, that's what I'm saying. I put the pills in the hot chocolate. I was going to leave her a note and then I was going to do it quietly."

"You stupid fuck. You claim to care about her and you'd put her through that shit? Do you think it wouldn't have destroyed her if you took the coward's way out and killed yourself? That is so unbelievably selfish. Did you even stop to think what it would do to her for you to go down like that?"

"Look, I was doing you a favor," Jack said angrily. "You should be glad that I'm out of the picture."

"You disgust me," Jace seethed. "Unbelievable. This isn't about me. I don't have to like you, but Bethany loves you and I love her. I want her happy. That's all I care about. And you dead would not make her happy."

Pain and regret filled Jack's eyes. "I didn't mean for it to happen. You have to know I'd never do anything to hurt her."

"You fucking offered her drugs before!"

"That was different. She wouldn't overdose on them. She never did. She only took them when she needed them. I just wanted to make sure she had what she needed."

"She doesn't need that shit. Ever," Jace snapped.

"Is she going to make it?" Jack asked fearfully.

"Jace, man, you need to come," Gabe said from the door. "She coded, man. They're trying to get her back now."

Jace fell to his knees, grief crushing through his heart. "No!" he roared. "No! I can't lose her! Goddamn it, *no!*"

Ash looked stricken and pale. Mia was suddenly there, her arms around Jace, but he was numb. Couldn't feel anything but overwhelming devastation. Jack stumbled back, Kaden shoving him into a nearby chair with a harsh command not to move. Gabe moved forward, his face a mask of regret and sympathy.

"No," Jace whispered, his voice choking off in a sob.

Then he lurched to his feet, only knowing that he had to get to her. He wouldn't let her go this way. She had to fight! For her. For him. For the both of them.

He pushed away from Mia's restraining hold. When he got to the door, both Ash and Gabe tried to hold him back. He threw them forcibly out of his way, desperate to get to Bethany. She couldn't die. Wouldn't die alone surrounded by medical staff. Around people who didn't love her the way he loved her.

He ran toward her room and pushed inside the door, ignoring the urgent commands of the nurses for him to leave.

"Bethany!" he cried, the blood leaving his face when he saw them trying to resuscitate her. "Don't you give up!" he said fiercely. "Don't you dare give up, baby. You fight, damn it! You fight!"

His gaze was locked on the tube they'd reinserted into her lungs. The doctor doing chest compressions. The oxygen being pumped into her body. The medication being inserted into her IV line.

But the one thing he focused on to the exclusion of all else was the flat line running across the heart monitor, only jumping with the compressions being performed.

"Don't leave me," he said brokenly. "Baby, please don't leave me."

"Sir, you have to leave," one of the nurses said in a low voice filled with sympathy and understanding. "I know you want to be with her, but you have to let us get her back. You're in the way here."

"I'm not leaving her alone," Jace said fiercely. "I need to be with her so she understands. So she knows how much I love her. I won't let her die alone. I won't let her die, period!"

"If you want her to live, then get the hell out so we can get her back," one of the doctors snapped. "That's what you can do for her. Let us do our jobs."

"Man, come on, let them work," Ash said quietly. "They'll get her back. You have to believe that. Best thing you can do is to get out of their way."

Both Ash and Gabe grabbed Jace and forcibly pushed him out of the room.

"Bethany!" Jace roared just as the door was closing. "Don't you fucking give up! I love you, goddamn it. Fight!"

The tension in the small waiting area was through the roof. Jace sat, head in his hands, his shoulders slumped. He'd replayed every single memory of Bethany in his mind. From the time he'd seen her across the room at Mia's engagement party. Every smile. Every laugh. Every time they'd made love. When he'd put the choker around her neck the second time. The night she'd been drunk and so damn cute and the way she'd lustily made love to him. And the pain and sorrow in her eyes the night before when he'd hurt her unforgivably.

"Jace."

He glanced up to see Mia sitting beside him. She wrapped her arms around him and hugged tightly.

"She'll be okay. She's strong. She's defeated insurmountable odds. No way she'll go down over this."

Jace crushed her to him, holding on just as tightly. He buried his face in her hair and just held on. He was losing his grip on his sanity. He was slowly breaking. With every minute that passed with no word, he died a little more himself.

"I can't lose her, Mia. I can't lose her."

"You won't," Mia said fiercely. "She's stronger than that, Jace. She'll make it."

Jace lifted his head and over Mia's shoulder, his gaze locked on to Jack, who sat in the corner, face buried in his hands. Anger crushed through him all over again. It took all his restraint not to go over and take him apart with his bare hands. He was furious that Jack could have been so careless with Bethany. It didn't matter that Jack hadn't intended to hurt her. It had happened and now he could lose her. If that happened, Jace wouldn't rest until Jack paid for what he'd done.

"Love you, baby girl," Jace whispered against Mia's hair. "Thank you for being here and for believing in Bethany."

"I love you too, Jace." Her voice was filled with sorrow. "I love Bethany. She's perfect for you and you're perfect for her."

"Not perfect for her," he said in a muffled voice. "I've done so much wrong, Mia. I'm gutted by all I've done wrong with her. If she pulls through this, I just pray she'll forgive me."

"Honey, listen to me," Mia said, pulling away. She put her hand to his face and cupped his jaw. Her eyes were so full of love and understanding. "We all make mistakes. Look at the mistakes Gabe made. I was so furious with him. I was devastated when he pushed me away. I've never hurt like that in my life. You know that. You saw me. You and Ash took me away at Thanksgiving and you saw how I was that whole time. But you know what? He made it right. And no matter what he did, it didn't change the fact that I loved him. I may have been hurt and angry, but it didn't mean that I didn't love him. She loves you," Mia said softly. "And that didn't change because you hurt her. You'll get the chance to make it right, Jace. You have to believe that. It's what she needs right now more than anything. Faith. We have to believe that she's going to pull through this, and you need to believe in your love."

"Thank you," Jace breathed. "You're right. I know you're right. She's going to make it. She's a fighter. She's damn sure not a quitter or she would have quit long before now. And I'm going to be right there with her every step of the way. I'm not giving up, just like she won't give up."

Mia smiled and then leaned forward to kiss his cheek. "I like you in love, Jace. She's good for you. I'm glad you've found that special someone. You deserve it for all the years you sacrificed to take care of me."

Jace caught her hand and held it between them, anchoring himself in family and the unconditional love surrounding him. "It was never a sacrifice, Mia. I don't have any regrets. I was waiting my entire life for her and now I've found her. I'm just glad we're both happy now and have a very bright future to look forward to. Can't wait for you to give me nieces and nephews to spoil shamelessly. I can't wait for my own children to do the same with."

Mia's smile was breathtaking, lighting up her entire face. "That's a wonderful thought, isn't it? Us building families together. One big family."

"Yeah, it is," Jace returned softly.

"Mr. Crestwell?"

Jace whirled to see a doctor standing in the doorway.

"You can come back and stay with her now if you like."

Jace surged to his feet, fearing the answer to his next question. "Is she okay? Did she . . . make it?"

The doctor's expression was relieved but grim. "We got her back and we managed to get most of the drugs from her system. She's resting comfortably now. She probably won't come around for a while, but you can sit with her if you like."

There was no question. He would stay with her until she woke again and he'd never leave her side.

Before he left, he turned his hard gaze on Kaden and then nodded in Jack's direction. "You make sure he doesn't go anywhere. I haven't yet decided what's to be done about him."

"Yes, sir."

Jace hurried back to Bethany's room. It was much quieter than before. His breath caught in his throat when he walked through the door and saw her on the bed, lying so pale and still.

He took a seat by her bedside, pulling the chair so he was right next to her head. She looked extremely fragile, like a porcelain doll, so still and quiet. He reached up to tuck a strand of hair away from her cheek and let his fingers trail down her skin.

The only sound was the heart monitor and the steady rhythm of her heart. She still wore a cannula, which fed oxygen into her nostrils. Other than that, she didn't stir. Her breaths were so light that he leaned forward to reassure himself she was still breathing.

He pressed his lips to her forehead, closing his eyes as he savored the reassuring sound of the heart monitor. She was alive. She was breathing. Her heart beat. It was enough. No matter what happened from here on out, it would always be enough that she was alive and in his life.

"Come back to me, Bethany," he whispered. "I love you so much."

chapter forty-one

Bethany's dreams were tormented. Or maybe she was awake, but she couldn't seem to make her eyes open. But she'd had the most horrible dream that she'd been in a hospital and Jace had been standing over her, fear blazing in his eyes. And then he'd told her that she'd overdosed. That she'd taken drugs and tried to kill herself!

Her heart hurt. Did he really think she could do something like that? And why couldn't she seem to wake up so the horrible dream would go away?

She wanted Jace. Wanted him to hold her and to soothe the horrible ache in her chest. To tell her he'd never believe something so terrible of her. But then, he didn't trust her yet. The other night had taught her as much.

She tried to open her eyes again and shake away the heavy veil that weighed her down. It hurt. God, it felt as though someone had driven a stake through her head. But she struggled on, determined to break free of the fog surrounding her.

Her eyelids slowly fluttered, each blink beating like a hammer. She dragged her lids upward and for a moment, utter panic swamped her. It was dark and unfamiliar and the smell—it was so sterile. Like a . . . hospital.

She glanced frantically around, trying to make sense of her surroundings. She was in a strange bed. Not very comfortable either. A rhythmic *beep-beep* sounded loudly in her ear, making her wince.

"Jace?"

It came out more panicked sounding than she'd like, but she was scared and alone and she wanted Jace.

Then movement beside her, making her startle, and then Jace was suddenly looming over her, his eyes filled with anguish and relief.

"Bethany, baby, you're awake. Thank God, you're awake."

His voice was clogged with emotion. It sounded as though he'd been crying. There was so much relief and worry all packed into those simple words that she was stunned and more befuddled than ever. What had happened? What was wrong?

She licked dry lips and swallowed. Her tongue was thick and like sawdust in her mouth.

"I had the most horrible dream," she whispered. "What's wrong with me, Jace? Where am I?"

He pressed a kiss to her brow and she could feel him trembling against her skin. Almost like he was desperately trying to maintain his composure. Then he took her hand, squeezing it in his. It was then she realized there was an IV in her arm.

"You were very sick, baby. I almost lost you. Thank God you came back to me."

Maybe it hadn't been a dream. Oh God, did that mean he thought she'd tried to kill herself? Hysteria rose in her throat and she made a strangled sound. She began to shake violently and Jace enfolded her in his arms, holding her tightly against him.

"Shhh, baby, it's going to be all right now."

"I didn't do it, Jace," she said vehemently. "Please, you have to believe me. I didn't take anything! I wouldn't!"

He stroked his hand down her hair and rocked her back and forth in his arms. "I know you didn't, baby. I *know*."

She went still and then pulled back so she could see his face. "You do?"

"Of course. You told me you didn't so I knew you hadn't."

She sagged, going limp against the pillow. Relief, sweet and heady, rushed through her veins. He believed her.

"You believe me," she whispered, relief making her light-headed. Then she frowned, her lips pursing in confusion. "But how then? I don't understand."

"How much do you remember?" Jace asked gently.

Her brow furrowed and she tried to concentrate but her head hurt too badly. "I don't know. I went to Jack's. Kaden called me. Said he was back. I went over, but I made sure Kaden was with me," she rushed to say.

Jace's hand tightened around hers. "I know, baby. You did fine. You did everything right."

"I was so angry with Jack. I was yelling at him. Asking him why he was so determined to fuck things up. He said he wanted to say good-bye and when I asked him where he was going he just said 'away.'"

A scowl darkened Jace's face.

"He made me hot chocolate. That's all I remember," she said faintly.

"It's all right, baby. You're going to be okay. That's all that matters."

She looked up at him, grief coiling in her chest. Tears clogged her throat and she could barely breathe.

"Jack," she whispered. "He did it, didn't he?"

Tears slid down her cheeks and a sob welled in her throat.

Jace looked tormented, his eyes tortured as he stared back at her. "I'm afraid so, baby. I'm sorry."

She closed her eyes. *"Why?"*

Jace sucked in a deep breath and he caressed her cheek, wiping away the tears. "He didn't mean to hurt you, honey. He's an idiot, but he didn't mean to hurt you." He hesitated a long moment, his face a mask of regret. "He meant to kill himself."

"What?"

Pain exploded in her chest. No. He wouldn't. But then memories filtered through her mind. Jack so quiet and resigned. Him telling her he was leaving and when she asked where he was going he'd simply said "away."

"Why would he do something like that?"

Jace shook his head. "I don't have an answer to that, baby. Sorry. I don't know what he was thinking. I busted his balls over it. I wanted to kill him myself for what he did to you. You almost died. You *did* die. Thank God they got you back. I can *never* forgive him for that."

She went silent, sadness overwhelming her. This time Jack had gone too far. He'd done something he could never make amends for. Jace would never forgive him and she wasn't sure she could either. He'd crossed a line he could never go back from.

"Where is he now?" she asked quietly.

"He's here. In the waiting room. Kaden is keeping an eye on him."

"Don't let him do it," she whispered. "Don't let him try it again."

Jace slid onto the bed next to her, his hip resting against her side. "Right now I'm more focused on you and you getting better. How do you feel? Is there anything I can get you?"

"Just groggy," she replied. "Muggy. Like my head is all swimmy. Having a hard time concentrating."

"That's to be expected," he said gently. "Can you forgive me, Bethany? Are you willing to give me a chance to make things right between us?"

She looked up in surprise. "What do you mean?"

He closed his eyes and when he reopened them there was a swarm of emotions. Relief. Sadness. Worry. Fear.

"Do you have any idea how much it slays me that you'd even ask me that? Or the relief I feel at the same time? You act as though

I did nothing wrong. Like I didn't cut you so deep that you cried yourself to sleep while I was next to you, unable to do a damn thing about it."

He sucked in a deep breath and she could see how truly shaken he was. He looked haggard, completely strung out. Like he hadn't slept in days.

"Baby, you have no idea how bad you scared me. I thought I'd lost you. I'll never be more fucking grateful than I am to that team of doctors and nurses who refused to let you go and brought you back to me."

To her astonishment, a tear slid down his cheek and he hastily wiped it away as he inhaled deeply through his nose.

"How long have I been out?" she whispered.

He smiled shakily, relief still simmering in those dark eyes. "Over twenty-four hours, baby. They brought you in yesterday morning."

Her mouth dropped open. "That long?"

"That long," he whispered. "The longest twenty-four hours of my life."

"I'm sorry," she said hoarsely, still stunned that she'd been unconscious for that long.

"Sorry?" He broke off in a garble laugh. "Baby, you have nothing to apologize for."

"I'm sorry you were so worried though," she said anxiously.

"It was worth it because I have you back. Never leave me, Bethany. Stay with me. Be with me. Love me."

"I do love you, Jace. I'm sorry . . ."

He held up his fingers to her mouth, silencing her gently with his touch. "Don't apologize for another damn thing. You're going to lie there and listen to *my* apology."

He turned, positioning himself on the narrow bed so he could lie next to her. It was crowded and cramped, the two of them barely fitting, but he made it work by sliding his arms around her and anchoring her firmly to his body. He put one arm underneath her head so it was pillowed against his shoulder. Then he let out a long breath, his body relaxing. For a moment he was silent but he still trembled against her. He touched her, his hand sliding up and down her body, stopping over her heart, his fingers splayed wide as if reassuring himself of her steady heartbeat.

Then he slipped his fingers higher, to her neck, feeling the thud of her pulse.

"Never felt a sweeter thing, baby," he whispered. "Your heart beating. You breathing. I'll never take that for granted. Going to wake up every day knowing it'll be the best damn ever because you're still here, in my life, loving me, waking up next to me."

Tears gathered in her eyes and spilled down her cheeks. Her chest rose with a quiet sob and she turned her face into his neck, her breaths hiccupping over his skin.

"I'm sorry, baby. So damn sorry for that night. I had no right to say those things. You didn't deserve it. Ash didn't deserve it. I lashed out at you both when you're the last people on earth I'd ever want to hurt."

"It's okay," she said, her words muffled against his neck.

"No, it's not okay, baby. It's not. But I can guarantee you it'll never happen again. Not that. I'm sure I'll say shit that hurts you. I won't even swear that it'll never happen. But I'll never make you feel like you did that night again. You'll never go another day without my trust. I trust you absolutely."

"I know," she said quietly. "I know, Jace."

He went still. "How could you possibly know that? I've certainly given you no proof."

"You believed me when I said I didn't take those pills."

His grip tightened around her. "No, baby. At first I did because that was what I was told. But you told me before. When you were so out of it. The one time you briefly regained consciousness. You told me then and I knew you hadn't."

A fresh surge of tears welled in her eyes and spilled onto his neck. "Thank you for that. You don't know what that means to me."

"I do," he said quietly. "And I'm sorry it took me so long to give you that. I'll never hold that back from you again."

He turned so he could press a kiss to her forehead and he left his lips there, warm and sweet against her skin. She closed her eyes and savored the rightness of being in his arms. She was alive. He was here. She couldn't ask for anything more.

"Can you forgive me?" he asked again.

"Oh, Jace, I already forgave you. The morning you left for work. I know that trust takes time. We're so new. We fell into each other so hard and fast and things were so intense. And trust takes time to build. We've only known each other such a short time and we're still learning one another."

"You're so sweet and forgiving," he said in an aching voice. "I don't deserve you but I want you more than I want to breathe. And I'm never letting you go, baby."

"Don't, then," she whispered into his neck. "Don't let me go, Jace. I'm lost without you."

"You'll never be lost, baby. Never again. I'll always find you. No matter where you go, I'll always be there to bring you home."

"I'm hungry," she murmured. "Will they let me eat anything yet? When will I be able to go home? Is there anything . . . wrong . . . with me? Will I be okay from this?"

She couldn't keep the anxiety from creeping into her voice.

"Not sure when you'll be able to go home. The doctor said you'll make a full recovery. They'll be running tests to make sure there isn't any liver damage but he didn't expect there'd be any permanent ramifications. As for food, I'll go check with the nurse right now. If they say you can eat, I'll order in the most fantastic meal ever. No hospital food for you."

She smiled, relief swelling in her chest.

"I need to let the others know you're awake and okay," he said. "Mia, Gabe and Ash have camped out in the waiting room the entire time you've been here. They've been worried sick about you."

"Jace?"

He sat up, picking up on the worry in her voice. He glanced down at her, concern burning brightly in his eyes.

"What is it, baby?"

"What's going to happen to Jack?"

Jace's expression went grim. "That I'm not sure of. This had to be reported to the police. At first it was reported as a suicide attempt."

She blanched at that, mortified that anyone would think she'd done this to herself. Embarrassment crowded in, heavy and suffocating. She'd moved beyond her past. And now she was right back where she'd come from.

"Don't look like that, baby," Jace said in a gentle voice. "I spoke to the officer who investigated. He knows about Jack and his involvement. He also knows it wasn't intentional. Not sure what this will mean for him, but it's serious. He'll have to face the consequences of what he did."

Sadness crept into her heart, squeezing until it was a painful ache.

"I'll see what can be done, baby. Let me worry about Jack, okay? All I want you to do is focus on feeling better so you can come home with me. Do you trust me to take care of this?"

She slowly nodded. She knew it was beyond her reach now. She could no longer protect Jack. He'd gone too far this time and she was powerless to protect him from the consequences. But it still saddened her that he'd opted to end his life rather than embrace the things that Jace had done for him. Life was sweet. Even when it was bad, there was always the hope of better. The future. And Jack could have made a better future for himself. That was his choice and Bethany couldn't make that choice for him.

She couldn't live her life for Jack. She had her own life to lead. With Jace. She wanted a better future.

It was time to let Jack make his own way.

"I know this hurts you, baby," Jace said in a soft voice. "And I'm sorry. I'll do my best for Jack, but you have to know I'm pissed as hell at him. He could have killed you. He could have taken you from me. He almost did."

"I know," she said quietly.

He leaned down to kiss her and then moved back from the bed. "Will you be okay for a few minutes while I go tell the others you're awake and see about getting you some food?"

"Yeah, I'll be fine."

He walked to the door and then stopped and looked back at her a long moment as if memorizing her every feature. His eyes glowed warm with love and relief. So much love that she couldn't possibly mistake it for anything else.

She smiled, infusing as much love as she could into her own gaze. He got it. Recognized it. Then he smiled back before turning and walking out the door.

chapter forty-two

Jace stepped into the waiting room in time to see a police officer cuff Jack's hands behind his back. He walked over, forgetting for the time being that he was there to inform Mia, Gabe and Ash that Bethany was awake.

"Can I have just a moment?" Jace asked the police officer.

The officer hesitated and then said, "Two minutes. I have to take him in."

Jace nodded and the officer took one step back but remained close as he eyed Jack.

"Wanted you to know Bethany is awake and she's doing well," Jace said in a low voice. "She also knows what happened and how."

Jack's face grew grim and regret haunted his eyes. Then he stared directly into Jace's eyes.

"Take care of her for me."

"I will," Jace said shortly.

"And tell her I'm sorry," he added quietly. "Tell her I love her. I'll always love her."

"If you love her, you'll take this opportunity to straighten your life out," Jace said. "If you'll stick it out, I'll hire a lawyer for you. Try to work out a deal where you go to rehab and get probation as opposed to a jail sentence. Can't guarantee anything. I don't want you anywhere near Bethany. She's been hurt enough. If things work out, I wouldn't be opposed to you keeping in touch with her."

Jack stared at Jace for a long moment. "You'd do that for me?"

"I'm doing it for Bethany," Jace said stiffly. "Only for her."

Jack nodded. "Thanks, then. I'll do it. It's time to do something . . . different. Better. I almost killed the person who means the most to me. Can't even say what that does to a man. I won't touch that shit again. Ever."

"I hope you're telling the truth. I hope you straighten up and get clean."

"Time's up," the officer said, moving forward to guide Jack out.

"I'll have a lawyer come see you," Jace said.

It went against every instinct not to let them make Jack rot in jail. Not that he'd probably do any time anyway. But he was doing this for Bethany, because it would be her who'd be hurt knowing Jack had gone to jail for his foolish actions. And he'd do anything at all to spare her more pain. Even if it meant helping the man who'd nearly ended her life.

It was twisted and fucked up in every way. His gut screamed to take revenge. To make Jack suffer for what he'd done. But Bethany would suffer the most and Jace couldn't bear that.

"You're a good man," Jack said. "You'll be good for my Bethy. I want her to be happy."

"She's mine," Jace corrected.

"But she was mine first," Jack said softly.

And then the officer led him away and Jace stood staring after him as he shuffled like a man much older than his twentysomething years.

"Jace?"

He turned to see Mia standing a short distance away, flanked by Gabe and Ash.

"Is it true? She's awake? I heard you talking to Jack."

Jace relaxed and then smiled at his family. "Yeah, she woke up a while ago. We talked. She was disoriented. Had no idea what happened." His smile faded. "Had to tell her about Jack."

Sympathy brimmed in Mia's eyes.

"How'd she take it?" Gabe asked gruffly.

"Not very well. She's upset," Jace said with a sigh. "But she's tough and she realizes she's done all she can do for him."

"Can we see her?" Mia asked.

"Yeah, baby girl. But first I need to see if they'll let her eat something. She's hungry and I promised her a good meal if they'll let her have it. None of this hospital shit."

"I'll run out and get us all something," Ash offered.

"That would be great. Thanks. I'm sure you're all starving. You've been here all damn night. You should probably all go home and get some rest."

"We'll go home after we see Bethany. I want her to know she has people here who love her," Mia said.

Jace pulled her into a hug. "Thanks, baby girl."

She squeezed him back, then pushed away. "Go see if they'll let her eat. I for one am starving and would love part of this fantastic meal you've promised her."

Bethany glanced up when her door opened and Gabe, Mia and Ash walked in, relieved smiles on their faces when they saw her sitting up in bed. Jace squeezed her hand and smiled.

"Looks like dinner is here."

Ash walked forward, several takeout bags and carry-out boxes in his hands. He spread them over the end of the bed and then walked up the other side of her bed and leaned over to give her a kiss.

"Scared the shit out of us, sweetheart."

She smiled up at him and then he enfolded her in a fierce hug.

As soon as Ash let her go, Gabe pressed in with a ferocious hug of his own and then Mia latched on to her, hugging and babbling a nonstop stream that had Bethany's head spinning.

"Brought you supper. Well, brought it for all of us. Haven't had much to eat during our vigil," Ash said.

"Thank you all for being here," she said softly. "It means a lot to have people who care. I've never had that before."

Jace tightened his hold on her hand, giving her a fierce squeeze. Ash's gaze softened while Mia looked as though she was going to cry. Gabe gave her another quick hug and then kissed the top of her head.

"You're family," Gabe declared. "Maybe not the most normal family in the world, but you're stuck with us now."

She grinned. "Can't think of a better family to belong to."

Ash brought her a foam container filled with wonderful-smelling food. She peeked inside to see he'd loaded it down with finger foods. Fried cheese, crab wontons, barbecue riblets, French fries, Asian noodles and an eggroll. It was so unbelievably perfect that she could only stare as her stomach protested the fact she hadn't dug in yet.

When he produced a bottle of orange juice, however, she lost the battle and burst into tears.

Ash looked horrified. Mia and Gabe exchanged panicked glances and Jace leaned in, concern flaring in his eyes.

"Baby, what's the matter? Is that not what you wanted? I'll get you whatever you want to eat."

"It's perfect," she said with a sniffle. "It's all my favorites and he remembered orange juice."

Ash cracked a grin and Jace sat back, relief soaring in his eyes. Then Mia and Gabe burst into laughter and Ash joined them. Soon Jace was chuckling and Bethany giggled, wiping the tears from her cheeks.

"God, I'm such a dork," she said. "I get the best food ever and I start crying like a moron."

"I'm with you," Mia said, settling down with her own plate of yummy goodness. "Best food evah!"

Ash took a seat at the end of her bed, his thigh resting against her feet. "Did you find out when she can go home?"

Jace sighed. "In a case like this—well, I should say, when suicide is actually attempted, they put the patient under psychiatric evaluation, have the shrink come, wait for him to sign off, et cetera, et cetera. But in this case, given the circumstances, if all her tests come back okay, she can go home as early as tomorrow. The police have already taken a statement from Kaden, and they'll likely be around to see Bethany later on this afternoon, but she doesn't remember much so she can only provide information on the events just prior to her blacking out."

Bethany sighed, chewing on a cheese stick as sadness settled into her chest. Jace squeezed her knee and continued talking to the others about all the doctor had to say.

"Is he in jail now?" She spoke up when Jace had finished.

Jace gave her a look of sympathy. "Yeah, baby. They took him away right after I left your room to see about getting you something to eat. He agreed to go to rehab. I offered him a lawyer if he'd go into rehab and straighten out his shit. If the lawyer can work it out with the D.A., he'll get probation under the condition that he checks into rehab."

"Thank you," she said. "You didn't have to do that. I know you're angry and you have every right to be. But thank you for doing that for him."

"I did it for you, baby."

"I know," she whispered. "And I love you for that."

His eyes went soft, like melting chocolate. "Love you too, baby."

She stifled a yawn and stuffed a crab wonton in her mouth, savoring the yummy flavor. She followed it with a forkful of noodles and then got barbecue sauce all over her fingers when she devoured a riblet. By the time she'd put a sizeable dent in the food Ash had brought her, the yawns were coming faster than she could eat.

"We're going to head out now," Gabe said. "Bethany's tired and we're all exhausted as well. Going to head home and get some sleep."

"Thank you for being here," Bethany said again. "It means a lot to me. Thank you for caring."

Gabe smiled and ruffled her hair before bending down to kiss her cheek. Mia gave her a huge hug and then Ash kissed her brow and gave her a big hug as well.

"Catch you later, sweetheart. Rest up so you can go home tomorrow."

"That I can do," she said with a smile.

They all left the room and Bethany sagged back on her bed, her food container still resting on her lap. Jace cleared it away, setting it aside, and then he began lowering her bed so it was fully reclined.

"Time for you to get some rest, baby."

"Are you staying?" she asked, worried he would leave and she'd be alone.

He frowned. "I'm not going anywhere. I'm going to crawl onto this bed with you and you're going to sleep in my arms."

She sighed with contentment. "Good. I really didn't want to be alone tonight. Hospitals give me the creeps."

"You'll never be alone again," he said tenderly, his eyes full of love and promise.

He climbed into bed with her, fully dressed, and positioned himself on his side, instantly pulling her tight against his body just as he'd done before. He kissed her brow and then rested his cheek against her forehead.

"Love you," she whispered.

"Love you too, baby. Almost lost you. Not ever going to do that again."

She smiled and snuggled further into his embrace, feeling the security and comfort of his strong body. She was absolutely where she belonged.

chapter forty-three

"Jace, where on earth are you taking me?"

He chuckled and led Bethany by the arm as they walked farther into the unknown.

"You'll find out soon enough. Is that blindfold on right? I don't want to ruin the surprise."

"Yes, it's on," she said in exasperation. "I can't see a thing! I'm going to kill myself in these shoes!"

"Not going to happen, baby. I'm not going to let you fall. Besides, you look killer in those heels. Later, I'm going to fuck you in those shoes and nothing else."

A hot flush traveled from head to toe. Her nipples hardened and her clit tingled in anticipation. Jace had bought her the most awesome shoes ever. Full of sparkle with a heel so high she hadn't been sure she could walk in them. But she'd known instantly that these were shoes she'd get fucked in later, which meant she was walking in them no matter what.

"Like that idea, do you?" Jace murmured.

"So not fair," she complained. "You're torturing me!"

He laughed again and then halted. She listened for any clue of where they were, but there was only silence. He'd blindfolded her before they left the apartment and had led her down to the waiting car, bundled her inside and made her wear it the entire way to wherever he was taking her.

The last few weeks had been so sigh-worthy. Ever since she'd been released from the hospital, he'd treated her like the most precious thing in the world. He'd taken a solid week off from work, leaving Gabe and Ash to clean up the Paris deal, which fortunately they'd salvaged thanks to an investor Gabe had located. And he'd spent every minute of every single day pampering her endlessly. Feeding her. Making love to her. Spoiling her absolutely rotten. She wasn't complaining a bit. The weeks had been a slice of heaven.

The only downer to the entire time had been Jack. But even that had its positives. True to his word, Jace had secured a lawyer for Jack and he'd worked out a plea agreement with the D.A. Ninety-day rehab program and then probation. Jace had secured a job for Jack when he got out and it would be up to Jack to turn his life around.

Bethany had no idea if Jack would follow through, but he was the only one who could change his life. No one else could do it for him.

"Ready to see your surprise?" Jace asked.

"Yes!"

He reached up to remove her blindfold and the minute it was gone, she was greeted by the sight of Mia, Chessy, Trish, Gina, Caroline, Brandon, Gabe and Ash all standing around a table that held a ginormous four-tiered cake.

"Surprise!" they all shouted. "Happy Birthday, Bethany!"

Her mouth fell open and she stared at them in absolute shock. Then she turned to Jace as they all started to sing an off-key rendition of "Happy Birthday."

"How did you know?" she whispered. "I didn't even remember it was my birthday."

"I have my ways," he said smugly. "Couldn't let your birthday go uncelebrated, baby."

Then he leaned down and pulled her into a scorching, toe-curling kiss. Complete with tongue and hoots and hollers from the others.

When he finally released her, she was dazed and wore a stupid grin. She turned to the others with that goofy smile, joy filling every part of her heart.

"You guys! I can't believe this!" she exclaimed.

"Happy birthday, sweetheart," Ash said, coming forward to hug her.

One by one, all the others came to wish her a happy birthday, hugging and kissing her until she was aglow with happiness.

Jace caught her hand and tugged her toward the table.

"There's another reason to celebrate at this party, but first you have to open your present from me so we can get to that part," Jace said with a huge grin.

There was a mischievous glint in his eyes and he looked excited and . . . happy. Then he handed her a square wrapped present with a gorgeous ribbon and bow arrangement.

"Open it!" Chessy squealed. "Oh my God, I can't wait to see what you got!"

The others chimed in with their encouragement, and Bethany tore into the pretty wrapping, more excited than a kid at Christmas. When she opened the box and found a small jeweler's box inside, her heart started pounding. With shaking fingers, she opened the smaller box and then gasped when she saw the glittering ring inside.

When she looked to the side for Jace, he had gone down to one knee, his hand already reaching for hers. He took the box from her, plucking the ring from its clasp.

"I love you, Bethany. More than I could have ever imagined loving a woman. You're my heart and soul and I want to spend the rest of my life with you. Will you marry me?"

She stared openmouthed down at him, her heart about to beat right out of her chest. Tears filled her eyes, happy tears this time when for so long they'd signaled sadness. She wanted this moment to last forever. It would forever be burned into her memories.

"Oh, Jace," she breathed. "I love you too. So much. And yes, I'll marry you. Absolutely!"

The room erupted in cheers as he slid the ring on her finger. His hands shook. Her hand shook. It was a wonder they were even able to get the ring on without dropping it. Then he stood and pulled her to him, wrapping his arms around her. He lifted and whirled her around and around before finally stopping and allowing her to slide down his body until their lips met in a heated rush.

"Love you so much," he whispered. "I'll always love you, Bethany."

"I love you too," she whispered back. Then she wrapped her arms tightly around his neck and squeezed for all she was worth.

He laughed and spun her around again.

"Let's cut the cake!" someone yelled.

There, surrounded by her friends and newfound family, Bethany celebrated her twenty-fourth birthday. The very best birthday she'd ever had.

As soon as the cake was cut and devoured, the bar in the ball-room of the Bentley Hotel opened up and a hired band began to play music.

Two hours into the festivities, Bethany was buzzing on amaretto sours and was smiling so much her cheeks ached. She danced with everyone. Gabe, Ash, Mia, Chessy, Brandon, Gina, Trish and Caroline. Even Kaden and Trevor arrived to wish her a happy birthday and to claim their dances as well.

But then Jace claimed his dance and swept her into his arms as the music slowed and became sultry.

They swayed in the middle, uncaring of the others around them as they stared into each others' eyes.

"Can I ask for one more birthday present?" she asked hesitantly.

Jace looked curiously at her. "Baby, you can ask for anything you want. If it's within my power to give it to you, consider it yours."

She ducked her head shyly but he coaxed her chin back up with his fingers.

"Baby, what is it?" he asked softly.

She took a deep breath and put it out there. "I want to go to school.

College. Get a degree. I've always wanted to but could never dream of affording it. I want to make something of my life. I know you'll always have my back, always protect me and give me my heart's desire. But I want to do more than just stay at home and be Mrs. Jace Crestwell. I want to do something. I want to make a difference."

Jace's eyes warmed and he gave her a look so filled with love that she instantly melted.

"I think that's absolutely a wonderful idea," he whispered. "You can be anything you want to be, baby. Just promise me that you'll always be mine no matter what else you become."

"Always," she whispered.

Their mouths met and he kissed her so tenderly that those happy tears glittered on her eyelashes once more.

Fairy tales *did* exist for girls like her. And she'd found her very own Prince Charming. She glanced down at the sexy, sparkly stilettos as Jace whirled her around the dance floor. She even had the shoes to prove it.